Penguin Crime Fiction
Editor: Julian Symons
The Moving Toyshop

Edmund Crispin writes that he 'was born in 1921, and
educated at Merchant Taylors' School and St John's,
Oxford, at which College his friends and contemporaries
included Philip Larkin, Kingsley Amis, John Wain, Alan
Ross and Edward du Cann, and where for two years he was
organist and choirmaster. After a brief spell of teaching,
he became a full-time writer and composer (especially of
film music). Among other variegated activities in the same
departments, he has produced concert music, edited many
science-fiction anthologies, and written for most
periodicals and newspapers.

Since 1967 he has been the regular crime-fiction reviewer for
the London *Sunday Times*. He is of a sedentary habit – his chief
recreations being music, reading, church-going and bridge.
Like Rex Stout's Nero Wolfe he leaves his house as seldom
as possible, in particular minimizing his visits to London,
a rapidly decaying metropolis which since the war he has
come to detest.

He is married and lives in Devon, in a quiet corner
whose exploitation and development he does his
utmost to oppose.'

For Philip Larkin

in friendship and esteem

Note

None but the most blindly credulous will imagine the characters and events in this story to be anything but fictitious. It is true that the ancient and noble city of Oxford is, of all the towns of England, the likeliest progenitor of unlikely events and persons. But there are limits.

E. C.

Contents

Sketch Plan of OXFORD (Simplified)

Key

A Toyshop (second position)
B St Christopher's
C St John's
D Balliol
E Trinity
F Lennox's
G The 'Mace and Sceptre'
H Sheldonian
I Rosseter's office
J Market
K Police Station
L Toyshop (first position)

1. The Episode of the Prowling Poet

Richard Cadogan raised his revolver, took careful aim and pulled the trigger. The explosion rent the small garden and, like the widening circles which surrounded a pebble dropped into the water, created alarms and disturbances of diminishing intensity throughout the suburb of St John's Wood. From the sooty trees, their leaves brown and gold in the autumn sunlight, rose flights of startled birds. In the distance a dog began to howl. Richard Cadogan went up to the target and inspected it in a dispirited sort of way. It bore no mark of any kind.

'I missed it,' he said thoughtfully. 'Extraordinary.'

Mr Spode, of Spode, Nutling, and Orlick, publishers of high-class literature, jingled the money in his trousers pocket – presumably to gain attention. 'Five per cent on the first thousand,' he remarked. 'Seven and a half on the second thousand. We shan't sell more than that. No advance.' He coughed uncertainly.

Cadogan returned to his former position, inspecting the revolver with a slight frown. 'One shouldn't aim them, of course,' he said. 'One should fire them from the hip.' He was lean, with sharp features, supercilious eyebrows, and hard dark eyes. This Calvinistic appearance belied him, for he was a matter of fact a friendly, unexacting, romantic person.

'That will suit you, I suppose?' Mr Spode continued. 'It's the usual thing.' Again he gave his nervous little cough. Mr Spode hated talking about money.

Bent double, Cadogan was reading from a book which lay on the dry, scrubby grass at his feet. ' *"In all pistol shooting,"* ' he enunciated, ' *"the shooter looks at the object aimed at and not at the pistol.*" No. I want an advance. Fifty pounds at least.'

'Why have you developed this mania for pistols?'

Cadogan straightened up with a faint sigh. He felt every month of his thirty-seven years. 'Look,' he said. 'It will be better if we both talk about the same subject at the same time. This isn't a Cheknov play. Besides, you're being evasive. I asked for an advance on the book – fifty pounds.'

'Nutling . . . Orlick . . . ' Mr Spode gestured uncomfortably.

'Both Nutling and Orlick are quite legendary and fabulous.' Richard Cadogan was firm. 'They're scapegoats you've invented to take the blame for your own meanness and philistinism. Here am I, by common consent one of the three most eminent of living poets, with three books written about me (all terrible, but never mind that), lengthily eulogized in all accounts of twentieth-century literature . . . '

'Yes, yes.' Mr Spode held up his hand, like one trying to stop a bus. 'Of course, you're very well known indeed. Yes.' He coughed nervously. 'But unhappily that doesn't mean that many people buy your books. The public is quite uncultured, and the firm isn't so rich that we can afford – '

'I'm going on a holiday, and *I need money*.' Cadogan waved away a mosquito which was circling round his head.

'Yes, of course. But surely . . . some more dance lyrics?'

'Let me inform you, my dear Erwin' – here Cadogan tapped his publisher monitorily on the chest – 'that I've been held up for *two months* over a dance lyric because I can't think of a rhyme for "British" . . . '

' "Skittish," ' suggested Mr Spode feebly.

Cadogan gazed at him contemptuously. 'Besides which,' he pursued. 'I am sick and tired of earning my living from dance lyrics. I may have an aged publisher to support' – he tapped Mr Spode again on the chest – 'but there are limits.'

Mr Spode wiped his face with a handkerchief. His profile was almost a pure semicircle – the brow high, and receding towards his bald head, the nose curving inward in a hook, and the chin nestling back, weak and pitiful, into his neck.

'Perhaps,' he ventured, 'twenty-five pounds . . . ? '

'Twenty-five pounds! Twenty-five pounds!' Cadogan waggled his revolver menacingly. 'How can I have a holiday on twenty-five pounds? I'm getting stale, my good Erwin. I'm sick to death of St John's Wood. I have no fresh ideas. I need a change of scene – new people, excitement, adventures. Like the later Wordsworth. I'm living on my spiritual capital.'

'The later Wordsworth.' Mr Spode giggled, and then, suspecting he had committed an impropriety, fell abruptly silent.

But Cadogan pursued his homiletic regardless. 'I crave, in fact, for romance. *That* is why I'm learning to shoot with a revolver. That is also why I shall probably shoot you with it, if you don't give me fifty pounds.' Mr Spode stepped back alarmedly. 'I'm becoming a vegetable. I'm growing old before my time. The gods themselves grew old, when Freia was snatched from tending the golden apples. You, my dear Erwin, should be financing a luxurious holiday for me, instead of quibbling in this paltry fashion over fifty pounds.'

'Perhaps you'd like to stay with me for a few days at Caxton's Folly?'

'Can you give me adventure, excitement, lovely women?'

'These picaresque fancies,' said Mr Spode. 'Of course, there's my wife . . . ' He would not have been wholly unwilling to sacrifice his wife to the regeneration of an eminent poet, or, for the matter of that, to anyone for any reason. Elsie could be very trying at times. 'Then,' he proceeded hopefully, 'there's this American lecture tour . . . '

'I've told you, Erwin, that that must not be mentioned again. I can't lecture, in any case.' Cadogan began to stride up and down the lawn. Mr Spode noticed sadly that a small bald patch was beginning to show in his close-cropped, dark hair. 'I have no wish to lecture. I decline to lecture. It's not America I want; it's Poictesme or Logres. I repeat – I am getting old and stale. I act with calculation. I take heed for the morrow. This morning I caught myself paying a bill as soon as it came in. This must all be stopped. In another age

11

I should have devoured the living hearts of children to bring back my lost youth. As it is' – he stopped by Mr Spode and slapped him on the back with such enthusiasm that the unfortunate man nearly fell over 'I shall go to Oxford.'

'Oxford. Ah.' Mr Spode recovered himself. He was glad of this temporary reprieve from the embarrassing claims of business. 'A very good idea. I sometimes regret moving my business into Town, even after a year. One can't have lived there as long as I did without feeling occasionally homesick.' Complacently he patted the rather doggy petunia waistcoat which corseted his plump little form, as though this sentiment somehow redounded to his own credit.

'And well you may be.' Cadogan wrinkled his patrician features into a grimace of great severity. 'Oxford, flower of cities all. Or was that London? It doesn't matter, anyway.'

Mr Spode scratched the tip of his nose dubiously.

'Oxford,' Cadogan went on rhapsodically, 'city of dreamspires, cuckoo-echoing, bell-swarmed (to the point of distraction), charmed with larks, racked with rooks, and rounded with rivers. Have you ever thought how much of Hopkins's genius consisted of putting things in the wrong order? Oxford – nursery of blooming youth. No, that was Cambridge, but it makes no odds. Of course' – Cadogan waved his revolver didactically beneath Mr Spode's horrified eyes – 'I hated it when I was up there as an undergraduate: I found it mean, childish, petty, and immature. But I shall forget all that. I shall return with an eyeful of retrospective dampness and a mouth sentimentally agape. For all of which' – his tone became accusing – 'I shall need money.' Mr Spode's heart sank. 'Fifty pounds.'

Mr Spode coughed. 'I really don't think . . . '

'Nag Nutling. Oust Orlick,' said Cadogan with enthusiasm. He seized Mr Spode by the arm. 'We'll go inside and talk it over with a drink to steady our nerves. God, I will pack, and take a train, and get me to Oxford once again . . . '

They talked it over. Mr Spode was rather susceptible to

alcohol, and he loathed arguing about money. When at last he went away, the counterfoil of his cheque-book showed the sum of fifty pounds, payee Richard Cadogan Esquire. So the poet got the better of that affair, as anyone not wholly blinded by prejudice would have expected.

When his publisher had departed, Cadogan piled some things into a case, issued peremptory instructions to his servant, and set out for Oxford without delay, despite the fact that it was already half past eight in the evening. Since he could not afford to keep a car, he travelled on the Tube to Paddington, and there, after consuming several pints of beer in the bar, boarded an Oxford-bound train.

It was not a fast train, but he did not mind. He was happy in the fact that for a while he was escaping the worrying and loathsome incursion of middle-age, the dullness of his life in St John's Wood, the boredom of literary parties, the inane chatter of acquaintances. Despite his literary fame, he had led a lonely and, it sometimes seemed to him, inhuman existence. Of course, he was not sanguine enough to believe, in his heart of hearts, that this holiday, its pleasures and vexations, would be unlike any other he had ever had. But he was pleased to find that he was not so far gone in wisdom and disillusion as to be wholly immune to the sweet lures of change and novelty. Fand still beckoned to him from the white combs of the ocean; beyond the distant mountains there still lay the rose-beds of the Hesperides, and the flower-maidens singing in Klingor's enchanted garden. So he laughed cheerfully to himself, at which his travelling companions regarded him warily, and, when the compartment emptied, sang and conducted imaginary orchestras.

At Didcot a porter walked down beside the train, shouting, 'All change!' So he got out. It was now nearly midnight, but there was a pale moon with a few ragged clouds drifting over it. After some inquiry he learned that there would be a connection for Oxford shortly. A few other passengers were held up in the same way as himself. They tramped up and down the platform, talking in low voices, as though they

13

were in a church, or huddled in the wooden seats. Cadogan sat on a pile of mail-bags until a porter came and turned him off. The night was warm and very quiet.

After rather a long time a train drew in at the platform and they all got into it, but the porters called out 'All change!' again, so they climbed out and watched the lights being extinguished, carriage by carriage. Cadogan asked a porter what time the Oxford train was expected, and the porter referred him to another porter. This authority, discovered drinking tea in the buffet, said without any apparent sense of outrage that there were no more trains to Oxford that night. The statement provoked some opposition from a third porter, who maintained that the 11.53 had not come in yet, but the porter drinking tea pointed out that as from yesterday the 11.53 was not going to come in any more, ever again. He banged his fist on the table with frequency and force to emphasize this point. The third porter remained unconvinced. A small, sleepy-eyed boy was, however, dispatched to consult with the driver of the train that had just arrived, and he confirmed that there were no more trains to Oxford that night. Moreover, the boy added unhelpfully, all the buses had stopped running two hours ago.

Faced with these unpalatable facts, something of Cadogan's enthusiasm for his holiday began to wane; but he quickly shook off this feeling as being shamefully indicative of a middle-aged desire for comfort and convenience. The other passengers, grumbling bitterly, had departed in search of hotel accommodation, but he decided to leave his bag and make for the Oxford road in the hope of getting a lift from a belated car or lorry. As he walked he admired the effect of the weak, colourless moonlight on the ugly brick houses, with their diminutive asphalt paths, their iron railings, and their lace curtains, and on the staring windows of Methodist chapels. He felt, too, something of that oddly dispassionate lifting of the heart which he knew meant poetry, but he was aware that such emotions are shy beasts, and for the moment he turned a blind eye to them for fear of frightening them away.

Cars and lorries, it seemed, were reluctant to stop – this was 1938, and British motorists were having one of their periodical scares about car-thieves – but eventually a big eight-wheeler pulled up at his hail, and he climbed in. The driver was a large, taciturn man, his eyes red and strained with much night driving.

'The Ancient Mariner did this better than me,' said Cadogan cheerfully as they started off. 'He at least managed to stop one of three.'

'I read abaht 'im at school,' the driver replied after a considerable pause for thought. ' *"A thahsand, thahsand slimy things lived on and so did I."* And they call that poetry.' He spat deprecatingly out of the window.

Somewhat taken aback, Cadogan made no reply. They sat in silence while the lorry bucketed through the outskirts of Didcot and into open country. After about ten minutes:

'*Books,*' the driver resumed. 'I'm a great reader, I am. Not poetry. Love stories and murder books. I joined one o' them' – he heaved a long sigh; with vast effort his mind laboured and brought forth – 'circulatin' libraries.' He brooded darkly. 'But I'm sick of it now. I've read all that's any good in it.'

'Getting too big for your Boots?'

'I 'ad a good un the other day, though. *Lady Somebody's Lover.* That was the old firm, if you like.' He slapped his thigh and snorted lecherously.

Being mildly astonished by these evidences of culture, Cadogan again failed to answer. They drove on, the headlights picking out mathematical segments of the flying hedges on either side. Once a rabbit, dazed by the glare, sat up and stared at them for so long that it only just escaped the wheels.

At the end of a further interval – perhaps a quarter of an hour – Cadogan said with something of an effort:

'I had a pretty bloody journey from London. Very slow train. Stopped at every telegraph pole – like a dog.'

At this the driver, after a pause of earnest concentration, began to laugh. He laughed so immoderately and long that

Cadogan feared he was going to lose control of the vehicle. Before this could happen, however, they fortunately arrived at Headington roundabout, and pulled up with a violent screeching of brakes.

'I'll 'ave to drop yer 'ere,' said the driver, still shaking with silent mirth. 'I don't go into the tahn. You walk down that there 'ill, and you'll be in Oxford quickern' no time.'

'Thanks,' said Cadogan. He clambered down into the road. 'Thanks very much. And good night to you.'

'Good night,' said the driver. 'Like a dawg, eh? That's rich, that is.' He put the engine into gear with a noise like an elephant treading down a tree and drove off, laughing loudly.

The roundabout, with its scattered lights, seemed very lonely after the sound of the lorry had passed out of earshot. It occurred to Cadogan for the first time that he did not know where he was going to sleep that night. The hotels would be tenanted only by night porters and the colleges would be shut. Then suddenly he smiled. Such things didn't matter in Oxford. He had only to climb over the wall of his college (he'd done it often enough in the old days, God knows) and sleep on a couch in somebody's sitting-room. Nobody would care; the owner of the sitting-room would be neither surprised nor annoyed. Oxford is the one place in Europe where a man may do anything, however eccentric, and arouse no interest or emotion at all. In what other city, Cadogan asked himself, remembering his undergraduate days, could one address to a policeman a discourse on epistemology in the witching hours of the night, and be received with neither indignation nor suspicion?

He set out to walk, past the shops, past the cinema by the traffic lights, and so down the long, winding hill. Through a rift in the trees he caught his first real glimpse of Oxford – in that ineffectual moonlight an underwater city, its towers and spires standing ghostly, like the memorials of lost Atlantis, fathoms deep. A tiny pinpoint of yellow light glowed for a few seconds, flickered, and went out. On the quiet air he heard faintly a single bell beating one o'clock, the precursor of others which joined in brief phantom chime, like the bells of the sunken cathedral in Breton myth, rocked momentarily by the green deep-water currents, and then silent.

Obscurely pleased, he walked on at a quicker pace, singing softly to himself – his mind drained of thought: only looking about him and liking what he saw. On the outskirts of Oxford he became a little lost, and wasted some minutes in finding the right road again. Which was it – the Iffley road or the Cowley road? He had never been able to get them clear in his mind, even as an undergraduate. No matter; at the end of it was Magdalen Bridge, and the High, and beyond that again the College of St Christopher, patron saint of travellers. He felt a little disappointed that his journey should end thus uneventfully.

There had been neither pedestrian nor vehicle to be seen during his walk from Headington; and in this respectable, rather tawdry quarter of Oxford the inhabitants were long since in bed. Shoplined on either side, the road stretched long and deserted before him. A small wind had risen, creeping in little gusts round the corners of buildings, and it caught and gently stirred a white awning which some negligent tradesman had left down in front of his shop. Cadogan fixed his eye idly on it as he walked, since it was the only one showing, and when he came up to it looked for the name of the owner; but it was hidden under the shadow of the awning. Then he glanced at the shop itself. There were blinds drawn against the windows, so he could not see what kind of shop it was. Moved by an idle curiosity, he strolled to the door and tried it. It opened.

And now he stopped and considered. It was not usual, certainly, for tradesmen to leave their shops unlocked at night. On the other hand, it was very late, and if burglars had got in it was unfortunate, but certainly none of his business. Probably the owner lived over the shop. In that case, he might be pleased at being woken and informed, or he might not. Cadogan had a horror of meddling in other people's business; but at the same time he was curious.

Stepping back into the street, he regarded the blank, unpleasing windows above the awning for a moment; and then, coming suddenly to a decision, returned to the door. After all, he had embarked on his holiday with a desire for excitement, and the door of the shop, if not exactly the portal of romance, presented a problem sufficiently unusual to be worth investigating. He pushed it wide, and felt a windy vacuum in the pit of his stomach when it creaked noisily. It was possible that he might catch a burglar, but more likely, on the whole, that he would be arrested as one himself. He closed the door again, as softly as he could, and then stood quite still, listening.

Nothing.

The beam of his torch showed the small, conventional interior of a toyshop, with a counter, a cash-register, and toys ranged about it – Meccano sets, engines, dolls and dolls'-houses, painted bricks, and lead soldiers. He moved farther in, cursing his own lunacy, and succeeded in knocking over a box of large balloons (deflated), with a considerable clatter. It sounded in his ears like some vast detonation.

Again he stood stock-still, hardly daring to breathe.

Again, nothing.

Beyond the counter were three wooden steps leading up to a door. He crept through this door and found himself at the bottom of a short flight of bare, steep stairs leading up to the floor above. These he climbed with further inward malediction, kicking the treads, creaking, banging, and stumbling. He arrived, exhausted, and with his nerve practically gone, in a short passage, linoleum-covered, with two doors on either side of it, and one at the end. He now was quite resigned to the appearance of an infuriated householder with a shot-gun, and was engaged in inventing explanations which might pacify him. After all, it was reasonable that anyone finding a shop door open should come in to make sure nothing was amiss . . . though not, perhaps, with such elaborate and futile attempts at silence.

But yet again, there was no sound.

This is ridiculous, Cadogan told himself severely. The

front rooms are probably the living-rooms. You will enter one of these and make certain nothing is wrong. After that, honour will be satisfied, and you can beat a retreat as quickly as may be.

Nerving himself, he crept forward and turned the knob of one of the doors. The small white circle of his torch played on tightly closed curtains, a cheap lacquered sideboard, a wireless set, a table, uncomfortable leather arm-chairs with big, garish, mauve and orange cushions in satin; there were no pictures on the papered walls. A living-room, certainly. But there was something more, which caused him to breathe an audible sigh of relief and relax a little. The musty smell and the dust which lay thick on everything, showed that the flat had not been occupied for some time. He stepped forward, tripped on something, and shone his torch down on it. Then he whistled softly and said 'Well, well,' several times.

For what lay on the floor was the body of an elderly woman, and there was no doubt that she was very dead indeed.

He was curiously unsurprised: the spectre had been laid, the mysterious attraction of the deserted toyshop exorcized and explained. Then he checked himself; the appearance of the body which lay there was no occasion for random analyses. Becoming conscious that the torch was an encumbrance, he stepped back and tried the light switch by the door, but no light resulted, for the bulb was not in place under its cheap frilly shade. Hadn't he seen a candle on the table in the passage? Yes, it was still there, and it was the work of a moment to light it. He left his torch on the table and returned to the living-room, setting the candle down by the woman's body.

It lay on the right side, with the left arm flung backwards beneath the table, and the legs stretched out. A woman of near sixty, he judged, for the hair was almost wholly grey and the skin of the hands wrinkled and brown. She was dressed in a tweed coat and skirt and a white blouse, which emphasized her plumpness, with rough wool stockings and

19

brown shoes. There was no ring on her left hand, and the flatness of her breasts had already suggested that she was unmarried. Near her, in the shadow of the table, lay something white. Cadogan picked it up, and found it was a scrap of paper with a number pencilled on it in a sloping feminine hand. This paper, after a brief glance, he slipped in his pocket. Then he looked back at the woman's face.

It was not a pleasant sight, since it was discoloured a blackish purple, as were her finger-nails. There was froth at the corner of her mouth, which hung open, showing a gold stopping which winked in the candlelight. In her neck was embedded a thin cord, tied fast behind. It had sunk so deep that the flesh which closed over it made it almost invisible. There was a pool of dried blood on the floor by the head, and Cadogan found the reason for it in a sharp contusion just below the crown. He felt the bone of the skull, but as far as he could tell it was not fractured.

Up to now he had experienced only the passionless curiosity of a child, but the action of touching her brought a sudden revulsion of feeling. He wiped the blood quickly from his fingers and stood up. He must get to the police as quickly as possible. Anything else to be observed? Ah, yes, a gold pince-nez, broken, on the floor nearby . . . And then, abruptly, he stiffened, his nerves tingling like charged electric wires.

There had been a sound in the passage outside.

It was a small sound, an indefinite sound, but it made his heart beat violently and his hand tremble. Oddly enough, it had not previously occurred to him that the person who had killed this woman might be still in the house. Turning his head, he looked steadily out of the half-open door into the darkness beyond, and waited, absolutely motionless. The sound did not recur. In that dead stillness the watch on his wrist sounded as loud as a kitchen alarm-clock. He realized that if anyone were there it was going to be a matter of endurance and nerves: whichever moved first would give the other the advantage. The minutes passed – three, five, seven, nine – like aeons of cosmic time. And reason began officiously to interfere. A sound? Well, what of it? The house, like Prospero's isle, was full of noises. And in any case, what purpose was being served by standing in an unnatural attitude like a waxwork? The aching muscles added their cry, and at last he moved, taking the candle from the table and peering, with infinite precautions, into the passage.

It was empty. The other doors were still shut. His torch stood on the table where he had left it. In any case, the thing to do was to get out of this detestable house as quickly as possible, and so on to the police station. He picked up his torch, blew out the candle, and put it down. A flick of the button, and . . .

No light came.

Savagely, uselessly, Cadogan wrestled for perhaps half a minute with the switch, until at last he realized what was the matter: the thing weighed too light in his hand. With a sick premonition he unscrewed the end and felt for the battery. It had gone.

Trapped in the pitch blackness of that musty-smelling passage, his self-control suddenly failed. He knew there was a soft, padding step coming towards him. He knew that he threw the empty torch blindly, and heard it strike the wall. And he sensed, rather than saw, the blazing beam of light which shone out from behind. Then there was a dull, enormous concussion, his head seemed to explode in a flare of blinding scarlet, and there was nothing but a high screaming like the wind in wires and a bright green globe that fell twisting and diminishing, to annihilation in inky darkness.

He awoke with his head aching and a dry, foul mouth, and after a moment staggered to his feet. There was a rush of nausea and he clung to the wall, muttering stupidly to himself. In a little while his head cleared and he was able to look about him. The room was small, scarcely more than a closet, and contained a miscellaneous collection of cleaning things – a pail, a rag mop, brushes, and a tin of polish. A faint light glowing through the small window made him look at his watch. Half past five: unconscious four hours, and now it was nearly dawn. Feeling a little better, he cautiously tried the door. It was locked. But the window – he stared – the window was not only unlocked, but open. With difficulty he climbed on to a packing-case and looked out. He was on the ground floor, and beyond him was a deserted and neglected strip of garden, with creosoted wooden fences running down on either side and a gate, standing ajar, at the bottom. Even in his weakened condition it was easy to climb out. Once outside the gate the nausea seized him again, the saliva flowed into his mouth, and he was violently sick. But he felt better for it.

A turn to the left, and he was at an alley-way which brought him back into the road down which he had walked four hours before – yes, unmistakably it was the same road, and he was three shops away from the toyshop – he had counted – on the side nearest Magdalen Bridge. Pausing only to notice landmarks and fix the position in his mind, he hurried off towards the town and the police station. The growing light showed him a plate which bore the words IFFLEY ROAD, as he came out at a road-junction where there was a stone horse-trough. So that was it. Then Magdalen Bridge, grey and broad, and safety. He looked back and saw that he was not being followed.

Oxford rises late, except on May morning, and the only person at large was a milkman. He stared very blankly indeed at the bloodied and dishevelled figure of Richard Cadogan, staggering up the long curve of the High Street; and then, presumably, dismissed him as a belated reveller. The grey freshness of the new day washed the walls of the Queen's and University College. Last night's moon was a lustreless coin pasted on the morning sky. The air was cool and grateful to the skin.

Cadogan's head, if still aching abominably, now at least permitted him to think. The police station, he seemed to remember, was in St Aldate's, somewhere near the post office and the town hall, and it was in that direction that he was heading now. One thing puzzled him. He had found in his pocket his torch, complete with battery, and what was more, his wallet, with Mr Spode's cheque, still perfectly safe. A considerate assailant, evidently . . . Then he remembered the old woman with the cord tight round her neck, and was not so pleased.

The police were courteous and kind. They listened to his rather incoherent story without interruption, and asked a few supplementary questions about himself. Then the sergeant in charge of the night shift, a substantial red-faced man with a wide black moustache, said:

'Well, sir, the best thing we can do now is to get that crack on the head dressed and give you a cup of hot tea and some aspirin. You must be pretty much under the weather.'

Cadogan was slightly annoyed at his failure to grasp the urgency of the situation. 'Oughtn't I to take you back there at once?'

'Well, now. If you were out four hours, as you say, I don't expect they'll have left the body lying there conveniently for us, as you might say. The rooms above aren't occupied, then?'

'I don't think so.'

'No. Well, that means we can easily get there before they open the shop, and have a look round. Curtis, clean up the gentleman's head and put a bandage on it. Here's your tea, sir, and your aspirin. You'll feel better for the rest.'

He was right. Cadogan felt better not only for the rest and the tea and the ointment on his bruised skull, but also for the cheerful solidity of his companions. He thought a little wryly of the craving for excitement upon which, the evening before, he had discoursed to Mr Spode in the garden at St John's Wood. There had been quite enough of it, he decided: quite enough. It is perhaps fortunate that he did not know what was still in store.

It was full daylight, and the multitudinous clocks of Oxford were chiming 6.30, when they got into the police car and drove back down the High Street. The milkman, still on his rounds, shook his head with mournful resignation on seeing Richard Cadogan, turbaned like an oriental potentate with his bandages, sitting in the middle of a police escort. But Cadogan did not observe him. He was taking a moment off from consideration of the lethal toyshop to enjoy being in Oxford. He had scarcely had time to look around him previously, but now rushing smoothly amid noble prospects down to the high tower of Magdalen, he drew a deep breath of sheer pleasure at the place. Why – why in heaven's name did he not live here? And it was going to be another fine day.

They crossed the bridge, reached the road-junction where the horse-trough stood, and plunged into the Iffley Road. Staring along it:

'Hello,' said Cadogan, 'they've put the awning up.'

'You're sure of the place, sir?'

'Yes, of course. It's opposite a red-brick church of some kind – Nonconformist, I think.'

'Ah yes, sir. That'll be the Baptist Church.'

'All right, driver. You can pull up now,' said Cadogan excitedly. 'There's the church on our right, there's the alley-way I came out of and there –'

The police car drew into the kerb. Half rising in his seat, Cadogan stopped and stared. In front of him, its window loaded with tins, flour, bowls of rice and lentils, bacon, and other groceries in noble array, was a shop bearing the legend:

WINKWORTH
FAMILY GROCER AND PROVISION MERCHANT

He gazed wildly to right and left. A chemist's and a draper's. Farther on to the right, a butcher, a baker, a stationery shop; and to the left, a corn merchant, a hat shop, and another chemist . . .

The toyshop had gone.

2. The Episode of the Dubious Don

Out of the grey light came a gold morning. The leaves were beginning to fall from the trees in the Parks and in St Giles', but they still made a brave show of bronze and yellow and malt-brown. The grey maze of Oxford – from the air, it resembles nothing so much as a maze – began to stir itself. The women undergraduates were the first abroad – cycling along the streets in droves, absurdly gowned and clutching complicated files, or hovering about libraries until the doors should be open and admit them once again to study the divine mysteries which hang about the Christian element in *Beowulf*, the date of the *Urtristan* (if any), the complexities of hydrodynamics, the kinetic theory of gases, the law of tort, or the situation and purposes of the para-thyroid gland. The men rose more circumspectly, putting a pair of trousers, a coat, and a scarf over their pyjamas, shambling across quadrangles to sign lists, and shambling back to bed again. Art students emerged, subduing the flesh in their endeavour to find a good light, elusive and nearly as unattainable as the Grail itself. Commercial Oxford, too, awoke; shops opened and buses ran; the streets were thronged with traffic. All over the city, in colleges and belfries, the mechanism of clocks whirred, clanged, and struck nine o'clock, in a maddening, jagged syncopation of conflicting tempo and timbre.

A red object shot down the Woodstock Road.

It was an extremely small, vociferous, and battered sports car. Across its bonnet were scrawled in large white letters the words LILY CHRISTINE III. A steatopygic nude in chromium leaned forward at a dangerous angle from the radiator cap. It reached the junction of Woodstock

25

and Banbury roads, turned sharply to the left, and entered the private road which runs up beside the college of St Christopher, patron saint of travellers (for the benefit of the uninitiated, it should here be said that St Christopher's stands next door to St John's). It then turned in at a wrought-iron gate and proceeded at about forty miles an hour down a short gravel drive which was bordered with lawns and rhododendron bushes and which terminated in a sort of half-hearted loop where it was just impossible conveniently to turn a car. It was evident that the driver had his vehicle under only imperfect control. He was wrestling desperately with the levers. The car made directly for the window where the President of the college, a thin, demure man of mildly epicurean tastes, was sunning himself. Perceiving his peril, he retreated in panic haste. But the car missed the wall of his lodging and fled on up to the end of the drive, where the driver, with a tremendous swerve of the wheel and some damage to the grass borders, succeeded in turning it completely round. At this point there seemed to be nothing to stop his rushing back the way he had come, but unhappily, in righting the wheel, he pulled it over too far, and the car thundered across a strip of lawn, buried its nose in a large rhododendron bush, choked, stalled, and stopped.

Its driver got out and gazed at it with some severity. While he was doing this it backfired suddenly – a tremendous report, a backfire to end all backfires. He frowned, took a hammer from the back seat, opened the bonnet and hit something inside. Then he closed the bonnet again and resumed his seat. The engine started and the car went into reverse with a colossal jolt and began racing backwards towards the President's Lodging. The President, who had returned to the window and was gazing at this scene with a horrid fascination, retired again, with scarcely less haste than before. The driver looked over his shoulder, and saw the President's Lodging towering above him, like a liner above a motor-boat. Without hesitation, he changed into forward gear. The car uttered a terrible shriek, shuddered like a man smitten with the ague, and stopped; after a moment it emitted its inexplicable valedictory backfire. With dignity the driver put on the brake, climbed out, and took a brief-case from the back seat.

At the cessation of noise the President had approached his window again. He now flung it open.

'My dear Fen,' he expostulated. 'I'm glad you have left us a little of the college to carry on with. I feared you were about to demolish it utterly.'

'Oh? Did you? Did you?' said the driver. His voice was cheerful and slightly nasal. 'You needn't have worried, Mr President. I had it under perfect control. There's something the matter with the engine, that's all. I can't think why it makes that noise after it's stopped. I've tried everything for it.'

'And I see no real necessity,' said the President peevishly, 'for you to bring your car into the grounds at all.' He slammed the window shut, but without any real annoyance. The eccentricities of Gervase Fen, Professor of English Language and Literature and Fellow of St Christopher's, were not on the traditional donnish pattern. But they were suffered more or less gladly by his colleagues, who knew that any treatment of Fen at his face value resulted generally in their own discomfiture.

Fen strode with great energy across the lawn, passed through a gate in a mellow brick wall against which, in their season, the peaches bloomed, and entered the main garden of the college. He was a tall, lanky man, about forty years of age, with a cheerful, lean, ruddy, clean-shaven face. His dark hair, sedulously plastered down with water, stuck up in spikes at the crown. He had on an enormous raincoat and carried an extraordinary hat.

'Ah, Mr Hoskins,' he said to an undergraduate who was perambulating the lawn with his arm round the waist of an attractive girl. 'Hard at it already, I see.'

Mr Hoskins, large, raw-boned and melancholy, a little like a Thurber dog, blinked mildly. 'Good morning, sir,' he said. Fen passed on. 'Don't be alarmed, Janice,' said Mr

Hoskins to his companion. 'Look what I've got for you.' He felt in the pocket of his coat and produced a big box of chocolates.

Meanwhile Fen proceeded into an open passage-way, stone-paved, which led from the gardens into the south quadrangle of the college, turned into a doorway on the right, passed the organ scholar's room, ran up a flight of carpeted stairs to the first floor, and entered his study. It was a long, light room which looked out on the Inigo Jones quadrangle on one side and the gardens on the other. The walls were cream, the curtains and carpet dark green. There were rows of books on the low shelves, Chinese miniatures on the walls, and a few rather dilapidated plaques and busts of English writers on the mantelpiece. A large, untidy flat-topped desk, with two telephones, stood against the windows of the north wall.

And in one of the luxurious armchairs sat Richard Cadogan, his face wearing the look of a hunted man.

'Well, Gervase,' he said in a colourless voice, 'it's a long time since we were undergraduates together.'

'Good God,' said Fen, shocked. 'You're Richard Cadogan.'

'Yes.'

'Well, of course you're very welcome, but you've arrived at rather an awkward time . . . '

'You're as unmannerly as ever.'

Fen perched on the edge of the desk, his face eloquent of pained surprise. 'What an extraordinary thing to say. Have I ever said an unkind word – '

'It was you who wrote about the first poems I ever published: "This is a book everyone can afford to be without." '

'Ha!' said Fen, pleased. 'Very pithy I was in those days. Well, how are you, my dear fellow?'

'Terrible. Of course you weren't a professor when I saw you last. The University had more sense.'

'I became a professor,' Fen answered firmly, 'because of my tremendous scholarly abilities and my acute and powerful mind.'

'You wrote to me at the time that it was only a matter of pulling a few moth-eaten strings.'

'Oh, did I?' said Fen uneasily. 'Well, never mind all that now. Have you had breakfast?'

'Yes, I had it in hall.'

'Well, have a cigarette, then.'

'Thanks . . . Gervase, I've lost a toyshop.'

Gervase Fen stared. As he offered his lighter, his face assumed an expression of the greatest caution. 'Would you mind explaining that curious utterance?' he asked.

Cadogan explained. He explained at great length. He explained with a sense of righteous indignation and frustration of spirit.

'We combed the neighbourhood,' he said bitterly. 'And do you know, there isn't a toyshop *anywhere* there. We asked people who had lived there all their lives and they'd never heard of such a thing. And yet I'm certain I got the place right. A grocer, I ask you! We went inside, and it certainly was a grocer, and the door didn't squeak either; but then there is such a thing as oil.' He referred to this mineral without much confidence. 'And on the other hand, there was that door at the back exactly as I'd seen it. Still, I found out that all the shops in that row are built on exactly the same plan.

'But it was the police that were so awful,' he moaned in conclusion. 'It wasn't that they were nasty or anything like that. They were just horribly kind, the way you are to people who haven't long to live. When they thought I wasn't listening they talked about concussion. The trouble was, you see, that everything looked so different in daylight, and I suppose I hesitated and expressed doubts and made mistakes and contradicted myself. Anyway, they drove me back to St Aldate's and advised me to see a doctor, so I left them and came and had breakfast here. And here I am.'

'I suppose,' said Fen dubiously, 'that you didn't go upstairs at this grocery place?'

'Oh, yes, I forgot to mention that. We did. There was no body, of course, and it was all quite different. That is, the stairs and passage were carpeted, and it was all clean and airy, and the furniture was covered with dust sheets, and the sitting-room was quite different from the room I'd been in. I think it was at that point that the police really became convinced I was crazy.' Cadogan brooded over a sense of insufferable wrong.

'Well,' said Fen carefully, 'assuming that this tale isn't the product of a deranged mind –'

'*I am perfectly sane.*'

'Don't bawl at me, my dear fellow.' Fen was pained.

'Of course, I don't *blame* the police for thinking I was mad,' said Cadogan in tones of the most vicious reprehension.

'And assuming,' Fen proceeded with aggravating calm, 'that toyshops in the Iffley Road do not just take wing into the ether, leaving no gap behind: what could inspire anyone to substitute a grocery shop for a toyshop at dead of night?'

Cadogan snorted. 'Perfectly obvious. They knew I'd seen the body, and they wanted people to think I was mad when I told them about it – which they've succeeded in doing. The crack on the head could be produced as the reason for my delusions. And the window of the closet was left open deliberately, so that I could get out.'

Fen gazed at him kindly. 'Very nice, as far as it goes,' he said. 'But it doesn't explain the fundamental mystery of the business – why the grocery shop was turned into a toyshop in the first place.'

Cadogan had not thought of this.

'You see,' Fen continued, 'they couldn't have known you were going to blunder in. You're the fly in the ointment. The groceries were removed, and the toys substituted, for some entirely different purpose. Then they had to be switched back again, in any case.'

Something like relief was coming back to Cadogan's mind. For a while he almost wondered if he were, in fact, suffering from delusions. Belying all outward appearance, there was something extremely reliable about Fen. Cadogan assembled his sharp-cut, supercilious features into a frown.

'But why?' he asked.

'I can think of several good reasons,' said Fen gloomily. 'But they're probably all wrong.'

Cadogan stubbed out his cigarette and groped for a fresh one. As he did so his fingers came in contact with the scrap of paper he had picked up near the body. He was astonished to realize that he had forgotten all about it until this moment.

'Here!' he cried excitedly, pulling it out of his pocket. 'Look! Tangible proof. I picked this up by the body. I didn't remember I had it. I'd better go back to the police.' He half rose, in some agitation, from his chair.

'My dear fellow, calm yourself,' said Fen, taking the scrap of paper from him. 'Anyway, what is this thing tangible proof of?' He read out the pencilled figures. '07691. A telephone number, apparently.'

'Probably the number of the woman who was killed.'

'Dear good Richard, what an extraordinary lack of perceptivity . . . One doesn't carry one's own telephone number about with one.'

'She may have written it down for someone. Or it may not have been hers.'

'No.' Fen ruminated over the scrap of paper. 'Since you seem to be forgetting rather a lot of things, I suppose you didn't come across her handbag and look inside it?'

'I'm certain it wasn't there. Obviously, it's the first thing I should have done.'

'One never knows with poets.' Fen sighed deeply and returned to the desk. 'Well, there's only one thing to be done with this number, and that is to ring it.' He took off the receiver, dialled 07691, and waited. After a while there was an answer.

'Hello.' A rather tremulous woman's voice.

'Hello, Miss Scott,' said Fen cheerfully. 'How are you? Have you been long back from Baluchistan?'

Cadogan gazed at him blankly.

'I'm sorry,' said the voice. 'But I'm not Miss Scott.'

'Oh.' Fen gazed at the instrument in great dismay, as though he were expecting it to fall apart at any instant. 'Who is that speaking, please?'

'This is Mrs Wheatley. I'm afraid you have the wrong number.'

'Why, so I have. Very stupid of me. I'm sorry to have bothered you. Good-bye.' Fen seized the telephone directory and flipped over the pages.

'Wheatley,' he murmured. 'Wheatley . . . Ah, here it is. Wheatley, Mrs J. H., 229 New Inn Hall Street, Oxford 07691. The lady seemed to be in very good health. And I suppose you realize, my dear Cadogan, that it might be any one of a thousand exchanges besides this?'

Cadogan nodded wearily. 'Yes, I know,' he said. 'It's hopeless, really.'

'Look here, did you go round to the back of the shop with the police? The way you got out?'

'Actually, no.'

'Well, we'll do that now. I want to have a look at the place, anyway.' Fen considered. 'I've got a tutorial at ten, but that can be put off.' He scribbled a message on the back of an envelope and propped it up on the mantelpiece. 'Come on,' he said. 'We'll drive.'

They drove. Driving with Fen was no pleasure to a man in Cadogan's condition. It was all right in St Giles' because St Giles' is an immensely broad street where it is quite difficult to hit anything, except for the pedestrians who constantly scuttle across its expanses like startled hens, in a frantic and perilous gauntlet race. But they nearly smashed into a tradesman's van in Broad Street, despite its width, they tore across the traffic lights by the King's Arms just as they were changing, and they traversed Holywell Street and Long Wall Street in rather under a minute. Their eventual emergence into the thronged High Street Richard Cadogan describes as being by far the most horrifying episode of his entire adventure, for Fen was not the man to wait for anyone or anything. Cadogan stopped his eyes and ears and tried to meditate on the eternal verities. Yet somehow they did it, and were across Magdalen Bridge, and for the third time that morning he found himself in the Iffley Road.

Fen brought Lily Christine III to a shuddering standstill some way away from the location of the phantom toyshop.

'You've been here before,' he pointed out. 'Someone might recognize you.' The car backfired. 'I wish it wouldn't do that . . . I'm going to spy out the land. Wait till I come back.' He climbed out.

'All right,' said Cadogan. 'You'll find it quite easily. Just opposite that church.'

'When I get back, we'll go round behind the shop.' Fen strode off with his customary vigour.

The morning shopping rush had not yet begun, and the establishment of Winkworth, Family Grocer and Provisioner, was empty except for the grocer himself, a fat man swathed in priestly white, with a rotund and jolly face. Fen entered with a good deal of noise, observing, however, that the door did not squeak.

'Good morning, sir,' said the grocer amiably, 'and what can I do for you?'

'Oh,' said Fen, who was looking curiously about him, 'I want a pound of' – he cast about in his mind for something suitable – 'of sardines.'

Manifestly the grocer was somewhat taken aback. 'I'm afraid we don't sell them by weight, sir.'

'A tin of rice, then.' Fen frowned accusingly.

'I beg your pardon, sir?'

'Are you Mr Winkworth?' Fen hastily dismissed the subject of purchases.

'Why, no, sir. I'm only the manager here. It's *Miss* Winkworth as *owns* the shop – Miss Alice Winkworth.'

'Oh. May I see her?'

'I'm afraid she's away from Oxford at the moment.'

'Oh. Does she live above here, then?'

'No, sir.' The man looked at him oddly. 'No one lives above here. And now, about your purchases – '

'I think I'll leave them till later,' said Fen blandly. 'Much later,' he added.

'I shall be at your service any time, sir,' the grocer answered magniloquently.

'A pity' – Fen watched the man closely – 'a pity you don't sell toys.'

'Toys!' the grocer ejaculated, and it was obvious that his astonishment was genuine. 'Well, sir, it's hardly likely you'd find toys in a grocer's shop, is it?'

'No, it isn't, is it?' said Fen cheerfully. 'Nor dead bodies either. Good morning to you.' He went out.

'It's no good,' he told Cadogan, who was sitting in Lily Christine III, trying to adjust his bandage and staring in front of him. 'I'm convinced that man knows nothing about it. Though he did behave rather queerly when I asked about the owner of the shop. A Miss Alice Winkworth, apparently.'

Cadogan grunted ambiguously at this information. 'Well, let's go round to the back, if you think it will do any good.' His tone indicated little confidence in this prospect.

'And by the way,' Fen added as they walked down the narrow, sloping alley-way which led to the back of the shops, 'was there anyone about when you came with the police this morning?'

'In the shop, you mean? No, no one. The police let themselves in with skeleton keys, or something. The door was locked by then.'

They counted the creosoted wooden fences which marked off the little garden.

'This is it,' said Cadogan.

'And someone's been sick here,' said Fen with distaste.

'Yes, that was me.' Cadogan peered in at the gate. The neglected overgrown enclosure, which had seemed so sinister in the half-light, looked quite ordinary now.

'You see that small window?' he said. 'To the right of the front door? That's the sort of closet place I got out of.'

'Is it, now?' Fen answered thoughtfully. 'Let's go and have a look at it.'

The small window was still open, but it was higher from the ground than Cadogan had remembered, and even Fen, tall as he was, could not see inside. Somewhat disappointed they went on to the back door.

'This is open, anyway,' said Fen. Cadogan banged against a dustbin which stood beside it. 'For goodness' sake try to avoid making that terrible noise.'

He moved inside with some caution, and Cadogan followed him. He was not very clear what they were supposed to be doing. There was a short corridor, with a kind of kitchen, untenanted, on the left, and the door of the closet, half open, on the right. From the shop in front came the murmur of voices and the bell of the cash register.

But the closet contained cleaning things no longer. There were, instead, piles of groceries and provisions. And Cadogan was seized by a sudden doubt. Was the whole thing, after all, a delusion? Surely it was all too fantastic to be real? After all, it wasn't impossible that he should have fallen on his way into Oxford, struck his head, and dreamed the entire business – its quality was nightmarish enough. He blinked about him. He listened. And then, in some alarm, he tugged Fen by the sleeve.

There was no doubt about it. Footsteps were approaching the closet.

Fen did not hesitate a moment. 'Every man for himself,' he said, leaped on to a pile of boxes and projected himself feet first out of the window. Unfortunately in so doing he knocked over the boxes with a great clatter, and thus cut off Cadogan's line of retreat. There was no time to pile them up again, and the back door was out of the question – the handle of the closet was already turning. Cadogan seized a tin of baked beans in his right hand, and one of kidney pudding in his left, and waited, adopting a forbidding aspect.

Fatly expectant, the grocer entered his closet. His eyes bulged and his mouth gaped in stupefaction when he saw the intruder, but to Cadogan's surprise he made no aggressive movements. Instead, he raised both hands above his head, like an Imam invoking Allah, called out 'Thieves! Thieves! Thieves!' in a loud theatrical voice, and fled away as fast as his bulk would allow. Evidently he was much more afraid of Cadogan than Cadogan was of him.

But Cadogan did not stop to think of these things. The back door, the neglected garden, the gate, and the alley-way marked the stages of his frantic retreat. Fen was sitting in Lily Christine III, reading *The Times* with elaborate concentration, and a small, vaguely interested crowd had gathered round the front of the shop to listen to the grocer's continued cries. Cadogan scuttled across the pavement and into the back of the car, where he lay down on the floor. With a jerk they started.

Once over Magdalen Bridge, he sat up and said *'Well?'* with some bitterness.

'Sauve qui peut,' said Fen airily – or as airily as was possible above the outrageous din of the engine. 'And remember, I have a reputation to keep up. Was it the grocer?'

'Yes.'

'Did you cosh him one?'

'No, he ran away in a fright . . . Well, I'm damned,' said Cadogan, staring. 'I've brought a couple of tins away with me.'

'Well, we'll have them for lunch. That is, if you're not arrested for petty larceny before then. Did he get a look at you?'

'Yes . . . I say, Gervase.'

'Well?'

'I want to get to the bottom of this business. My blood's up. Let's go and see this Wheatley woman.'

So they drove to New Inn Hall Street.

3. The Episode of the Candid Solicitor

Two hundred and twenty-nine, New Inn Hall Street proved to be a modest and attractive lodging-house almost next door to a girls' school; and its proprietress, Mrs Wheatley, a small, timid, bustling, elderly woman who twisted her apron nervously in her hands while she talked.

'I'll deal with this,' Cadogan had said to Fen when they arrived. 'I have a plan.' In point of fact, he had no plan of any kind. Fen had agreed to this, rather grudgingly. He had then settled down to do *The Times* crossword puzzle, filling in the literary clues without difficulty. But the rest eluded him, so he sat looking crossly at the passers-by.

When Mrs Wheatley opened the door to him, Cadogan was still trying to think what to say.

'I expect,' she said anxiously, 'that you're the gentleman about the Rooms.'

'Exactly.' He was greatly relieved. 'The Rooms.'

She showed him inside.

'Very nice weather we're having,' she said, as though personally responsible for this phenomenon. 'This would be the sitting-room.'

'Mrs Wheatley, I'm afraid I've deceived you.' Now he was inside the house, Cadogan decided to abandon his stratagem. 'I'm not about the Rooms at all. The fact is' – he cleared his throat – 'have you a friend or relation, an elderly lady, unmarried, with grey hair and – er – given to wearing tweeds and blouses . . . ?'

Mrs Wheatley's pinched, anxious face lit up. 'You don't mean Miss Tardy, sir?'

'Er – what was the name again?'

'Miss Tardy, sir. Emilia Tardy. "Better Late than Never"

we used to call her. On account of the name, you see. Why, Emilia's my oldest friend.' Her face clouded. 'Nothing's wrong, is it, sir? Nothing's happened to her?'

'No, no,' Cadogan said hastily. 'Only I met your – ah – friend some time ago, and she said that if ever I was in Oxford I was to be sure to look you up. Unfortunately, I never quite caught her name, though I remembered yours.'

'Why, that's right sir.' Mrs Wheatley beamed. 'And I'm very glad you've come – very glad indeed. Any friend of Emilia's is welcome here. If you'd like to just come down to my sitting-room and take a cup of tea, I could show you a photograph of her to refresh your memory.'

This was luck, Cadogan reflected as he followed Mrs Wheatley to the basement; for he had little doubt that Emilia Tardy and the woman he had seen in the toyshop were one and the same. The sitting-room turned out to be cluttered up with wicker chairs, budgerigars, flowed calendars, reproductions of Landseer, and unattractive plates depicting unstable Chinese bridges. There was an enormous stove along one side, with a kettle simmering on it.

The confusions attendant upon the brewing of tea over, Mrs Wheatley hastened to a drawer and reverently brought forth a rather faded brown photograph.

'Here she is, sir. Now, was that the lady you met?'

Unquestionably it was, though the photograph must have been ten years old, and the face he had seen had been swollen and discoloured. Miss Tardy smiled kindly and vaguely at the photographer, her pince-nez balanced on her nose, her straight hair a little deranged. But it was not the face of an ineffectual spinster; there was a certain self-reliance in it, despite the vague smile.

He nodded. 'Yes, this is she.'

'Might I ask if it was in England you met her, sir?' Looking over his shoulder, Mrs Wheatley timidly twisted her blue apron in her hands.

'No, abroad.' (From the form of the question, a safe bet.) 'And quite a long time ago now – six months at least, I should think.'

'Ah, yes. That would be when she was last in France. A great traveller, Emilia is, and how she has the courage to live among all those foreigners is beyond me. You'll pardon my curiosity, sir, but it's four weeks since I heard from her, and that's rather strange, as she's always been a most faithful writer. I'm afraid something may have happened to her.'

'Well, I'm sorry to say I can't help you there.' As he sipped his tea and smoked his cigarette in that cheerful, ugly room, under the anxious eyes of little Mrs Wheatley, Cadogan felt a slight dislike for his presence. But no purpose would be served by brutally telling his hostess of the facts of the case, even if he had really known what they were.

'She travelled – travels – a lot, then?' he asked in the tautologous fashion of modern conversation.

'Oh, yes, sir. Small places mostly, in France and Belgium and Germany. Sometimes she only stops a day or so, sometimes months on end, according to how she likes it. Why, it must be three years if it's a day since she was last in England.'

'A rather unsettled sort of existence, I should have thought. Has she no relatives? She did strike me as being rather a lonely sort of person, I must say.'

'I think there was only an aunt, sir . . . Let me give you another drop of tea in your cup. There . . . And she died some time ago. A Miss Snaith she was, very rich and eccentric, and lived on Boar's Hill, and had a liking for comic poems. But as to Emilia, she enjoys travelling, you know; it suits her. She's got a little bit of money of her own, and what she doesn't spend on the children, she spends on seeing new places and people.'

'The children?'

'Devoted to children, she is. Gives money to hospitals and homes for them. And a very nice thing to do, I say. But if I may ask, sir, how was she looking when you saw her?'

'Not too well, I thought. I didn't really see much of her. We were thrown together for a couple of days in a hotel – the only English people there, you know, so naturally we chatted a bit.' (Cadogan was appalled at his fluency. But didn't Mencken say somewhere that poetry is only accomplished lying?)

'Ah,' said Mrs Wheatley. 'I expect you found her deafness a trouble.'

'Eh? Oh yes, it was rather. I'd almost forgotten.' Cadogan wondered about the mentality of the person who would go up behind an old, deaf woman, strike her on the head, and choke her with a thin cord. 'But I'm sorry to hear you've had no word from her.'

'Well, sir, it may mean she's on her way home from somewhere. She's a great one for surprising you – just turning up on your doorstep without a word of warning. And she always stays with me when she's in England, though goodness knows she'd be quite lost in Oxford, as I only moved here two years ago, and I know for a fact she's never been here – ' Mrs Wheatley paused for breath. 'But I got that worried I went and asked Mr Rosseter – '

'Mr Rosseter?'

'That's Miss Snaith's solicitor. I thought Emilia being a near relative he might have heard something from her when the old lady died. But he didn't know anything.' Mrs Wheatley sighed. 'Still, we mustn't cross bridges before we come to them, must we, sir? I've no doubt everything's all right really. Another drop of tea?'

'No, really, thank you, Mrs Wheatley.' Cadogan rose, to an accompaniment of loud creaking, from his wicker chair. 'I should be going now. You've been most hospitable and kind.'

'Not at all, sir. If Emilia should arrive, who should I say called?'

Fen was in an atrabilious mood.

'You've been the devil of a time,' he grumbled as Lily Christine III got under way again.

'But it was worth it,' Cadogan answered. He gave a résumé of what he had learned, which lasted almost until they were back at St Christopher's.

'Um,' said Fen thoughtfully. 'That is something, I agree. At the same time, I don't quite see what we're going to do about it. It's very difficult trying to deal with a murder at second hand, and no *corpus delicti*. There must have been quite a substantial van knocking about when you were unconscious. I wonder if anyone in the neighbourhood saw or heard anything of it?'

'Yes, I see what you mean: to cart toys and furniture and groceries about. But you're quite right, you know: the problem is – why change the place into a toyshop at all?'

'I'm not sure that that isn't a bit clearer now,' said Fen. 'Your Mrs Wheatley told you Miss Tardy would be lost in Oxford. So if you wanted to get her to a place she'd never be able to find again – '

'But what's the point? If you're going to kill her it doesn't matter what she sees.'

'Oh,' said Fen blankly. 'No, it doesn't, does it? Oh, my dear paws.' He brought the car to a halt at the main gate of St Christopher's and made a feeble attempt to smooth down his hair. 'The question is – who is her heir? You said she'd got an income of her own, didn't you?'

'Yes, but not very much, I fancy. I think she must have been a sort of Osbert Sitwell spinster, living cheaply in *pensions*, drifting along the Riviera . . . But, anyway, not well enough off to be worth murdering for her money.' A violent detonation came from the exhaust pipe. 'You really ought to take this thing to a garage.'

Fen shook his head. 'People will kill for extraordinarily small sums. But I must confess I don't quite see the point of spiriting the body away when you've done it. Admittedly the murderer might be willing to wait until death was presumed, but it still seems odd. This Mrs Wheatley had no idea she was in England?'

'None,' said Cadogan. 'And I gathered that if anyone on this eart' knew about it, she would.'

'Yes. A lonely woman whose disappearance wouldn't cause very much surprise. Do you know' – Fen's voice was pensive – 'I think this is rather a nasty business.'

41

They got out of the car and entered the college by a small door set in the big oaken gate. Inside a few undergraduates lingered, carrying gowns and staring at the cluttered notice-boards, which gave evidence of much disordered cultural activity. On the right was the porter's lodge, with a sort of open window where the porter leaned, like a princess enchanted within some medieval fortalice. In all, that is, except appearance, for Parsons was a large formidable man with horn-rimmed glasses, a marked propensity for bullying, and the unshakable conviction that in the college hierarchy he stood above the law, the prophets, the dons, and the President himself.

'Anything for me?' Fen called out to him as they passed.

'Er – no, sir,' said Parsons, gazing at a row of pigeon-holes within. 'But – ah – Mr Cadogan – '

'Yes?'

The porter seemed disturbed. 'I wonder' – he glanced round at the loitering undergraduates – 'I wonder if you'd just come inside a moment, sir?'

Puzzled, Cadogan went, and Fen followed him. The lodge was stifling with the heat of a large electric fire, half-heartedly designed to represent glowing coals. There were racks of keys, odd notices, a gas-ring, a university calendar, a college list, appliances for the prevention of fire, and two uncomfortable chairs.

Parsons was frankly conspiratorial. Cadogan felt as if he were about to be initiated into some satanic rite.

'They've come for you, sir,' said Parsons, breathing heavily. 'From the police station.'

'Oh, God.'

'Two constables and a sergeant it was. They left about five or ten minutes ago, when they found you weren't here.'

'It's those bloody tins I took,' said Cadogan. The porter gazed at him with interest. 'Gervase, what am I going to do?'

'Make a full confession,' said Fen heartlessly, 'and get in touch with your lawyer. No, wait a minute,' he added. 'I'll ring up the Chief Constable. I know him.'

'I don't want to be arrested.'

'You should have thought of that before. All right, Parsons, thank you. Come on, Richard. We'll go across to my room.'

'What shall I say, sir,' said Parsons, 'if they come again?'

'Give them a drink of beer and pack them off with specious, high-sounding promises.'

'Very good sir.'

They crossed the north and south quadrangles, meeting only a belated undergraduate trailing out in a bright orange dressing-gown to his bath, and climbed once more the staircase to Fen's study. Here Fen applied himself to the telephone, while Cadogan smoked lugubriously and inspected his nails. In the house of Sir Richard Freeman on Boar's Hill the bell jangled. He reached peevishly for the instrument.

'Hello!' he said. 'What? What! Who is it . . . ? Oh, it's you.'

'Listen, Dick,' said Fen, 'your damned myrmidons are chasing a friend of mine.'

'Do you mean Cadogan? Yes, I heard about that cock-and-bull story of his.'

'It's not cock-and-bull. There was a body. But, anyway, it's not that. They're after him for something he did in a grocery store.'

'Good heavens, the fellow must be cracked. First toyshops and now grocers. Well, I can't meddle in the affairs of the City Constabulary.'

'Really, Dick . . . '

'No, no, Gervase, it can't be done. The processes of the law, such as they are, can't be held up by telephone calls from you.'

'But it's *Richard* Cadogan. The poet.'

'I couldn't care less if it was the Pope . . . Anyway, if he's innocent it'll be all right.'

'But he isn't innocent.'

'Oh, well, in that case only the Home Secretary can save him . . . Gervase, has it ever occurred to you that *Measure for Measure* is about the problem of Power?'

'Don't bother me with trivialities now,' said Fen, annoyed, and rang off.

'Well, that was a lot of use,' said Cadogan bitterly. 'I may as well go to the police-station and give myself up.'

'No, wait a minute.' Fen stared out into the quadrangle. 'What was the name of that solicitor – the one Mrs Wheatley saw?'

'Rosseter. What about it?'

Fen tapped his fingers impatiently on the window-sill. 'You know, I've seen that name somewhere recently, but I can't remember where. Rosseter, Rosseter . . . It was – Oh, my ears and whiskers!' He strode to a pile of papers and began rummaging through them. 'I've got it. It was something in the agony column of the *Oxford Mail* – yesterday, was it, or the day before?' He became inextricably involved in news-sheets. 'Here we are. Day before yesterday. I noticed it because it was so queer. Look.' He handed Cadogan the page, pointing to a place in the personal column.

'Well,' said Cadogan, 'I don't see how this helps.' He read the advertisement aloud:

' "Ryde, Leeds, West, Mold, Berlin. Aaron Rosseter, Solicitor, 193 A Cornmarket." Well, and what are we to conclude from that?'

'I don't exactly know,' said Fen. 'And yet I feel somehow I ought to. Holmes would have made mincemeat of it – he was good on agony columns. Mold, Mold. What is Mold, anyway?' He went to the encyclopedia and took out a volume. After a moment's search: ' "Mold," ' he read. ' "Urban district and market town of Flintshire. Thirteen miles from Chester . . . centre of important lead and coal mines . . . bricks, tiles, nails, beer, etc. . . . " Does that convey anything to you?'

'Nothing at all. It's my opinion they're all proper names.'

'Well, they may be.' Fen restored the book to its place. 'But if so, it's a remarkable collection. Mold, Mold,' he added into tones of faint reproof.

'And in any case,' Cadogan went on, 'it'll be the wildest coincidence if it's got anything to do with this Tardy woman.'

'Don't spurn coincidence in that casual way,' said Fen severely. 'I know your sort. You say the most innocent encounter in a detective novel is unfair, and yet you're always screaming out about having met someone abroad who lives in the next parish, and what a small world it is. My firm conviction,' he said grandiosely, 'is that this advertisement has something to do with the death of Emilia Tardy. I haven't the least idea what, as yet. But I suggest we go and see this Rosseter fellow.'

'All right,' Cadogan replied. 'Provided we don't go in that infernal red thing of yours. Where on earth did you get it, anyway?'

Fen looked pained. 'I bought it from an undergraduate who was sent down. What's the matter with it? It goes very fast,' he added in a cajoling tone.

'I know.'

'Oh, all right then, we'll walk. It's not far.'

Cadogan grunted. He was engaged in tearing out Rosseter's advertisement and putting it in his pocket-book. 'And if nothing comes of it,' he said, 'I shall go straight to the police, and tell them what I know.'

'Yes. By the way, what did you do with those tins you stole? I'm feeling rather peckish.'

'They're in the car, and you leave them alone.'

'Oughtn't you to adopt a disguise?'

'Oh, don't be so stupid, Gervase ... It's not the being arrested I mind. They're not likely to do more than just fine me. It's all the bother of explaining and arranging bail and coming up before magistrates ... Well, come on, let's go, if you think it will do any good.'

The Cornmarket is one of the busiest streets in Oxford, though scarcely the most attractive. It has its compensations – the shapely, faded façade of the old Clarendon Hotel, the quiet gabled coaching yard of the Golden Cross, and a good prospect of the elongated pumpkin which is Tom Tower – but primarily it is a street of big shops. Above one of these was 193A, the office of Mr Aaron Rosseter, solicitor, as dingy, severe, and uncomfortable as most solicitor's offices.

What was it, Cadogan wondered, which made solicitors so curiously insensible to the graces of this life?

A faintly Dickensian clerk, with steel-rimmed spectacles and leather pads sewn to the elbows of his coat, showed them into the presence. The appearance of Mr Rosseter, though Asiatic, did not justify the Semitic promise of his baptismal name. He was a small, sallow man, with a tremendous prognathous jaw, a tall forehead, a bald crown, horn-rimmed spectacles, and trousers which were a little too short for him. His manner was abrupt, and he had a disconcerting trick of suddenly whipping off his glasses, polishing them very rapidly on a handkerchief which he pulled from his sleeve, and restoring them with equal suddenness to his nose. He looked a trifle seedy, and one suspected that his professional abilities were mediocre.

'Well, gentlemen,' he said, 'and may I know your business?' He examined the rather overwhelming presence of Gervase Fen with faint signs of trepidation.

Fen beamed at him. 'This person,' he said, pointing to Cadogan, 'is a second cousin to Miss Snaith, for whom I believe you acted during her lifetime.'

Mr Rosseter was almost as startled at this dramatic revelation as Cadogan. 'Indeed,' he said, tapping his fingers very rapidly on the desk. 'Indeed. I'm very pleased to know you, sir. Do me the honour of sitting down.'

Blinking reproachfully at Fen, Cadogan obeyed, though as to what honour he could be doing Mr Rosseter in lowering his behind on to a leather chair he was not entirely clear. 'I had rather lost touch with my cousin,' he announced, 'during the last years of her life. Actually she was not, properly speaking, a second cousin at all.' Here Fen glared at him malevolently. 'My mother, one of the Shropshire Cadogans, married my father – no, I don't mean that exactly, or rather, I do – anyway, my father was one of seven children, and his third sister Marion was divorced from a Mr Childs, who afterwards remarried and had three children – Paul, Arthur, and Letitia – one of whom (I forget which) married, late in life, a nephew (or possibly a niece), of a Miss Bosanquet. It's all rather complex, I'm afraid, like a Galsworthy novel.'

Mr Rosseter frowned, took off his glasses, and polished them very rapidly. Evidently he did not find this funny. 'Perhaps you would state your business, sir?' he barked.

To Cadogan's alarm, Fen burst at this point into a noisy peal of laughter. 'Ha! ha!' he shouted, apparently overcome with merriment. 'You must forgive my friend, Mr Rosseter. Such a droll fellow, but no business sense, none at all. Ha! ha! ha! A Galsworthy novel, eh? That's very, very funny, old man. Ha! ha!' He mastered himself with apparent difficulty. 'But we mustn't waste Mr Rosseter's valuable time like this – *must we?*' he concluded savagely.

Repressing the imp of mischief within him, Cadogan nodded. 'I do apologize, Mr Rosseter. The fact is that I sometimes write things for the B.B.C., and I like to try them out on people beforehand.' Mr Rosseter made no reply; his dark eyes were wary. '*Yes,*' said Cadogan heavily. 'Well, now, Mr Rosseter: I heard only the bare facts of my cousin's death. Her end was peaceful, I hope?'

'In fact,' said Mr Rosseter, 'no.' His small form, behind the old-fashioned roll-top desk, was silhouetted against a window overlooking the Cornmarket. 'She was, unhappily, run over by a bus.'

'Like Savonarola Brown,' put in Fen, interested.

'Really?' said Mr Rosseter sharply, as though he suspected he was being trapped into some damaging admission.

'I am sorry to hear that,' said Cadogan, trying to inject something like sorrow into his voice. 'Though, mind you,' he added, sensing failure in this endeavour, 'I only met her once or twice, so I wasn't exactly bowled over by her death. *"No longer, mourn for me when I am dead then you shall hear the surly sullen bell"* – you understand.'

'Of course, of course,' Fen sighed unnecessarily.

'No, I'll be frank with you, Mr Rosseter,' said Cadogan. 'My cousin was a rich woman and had few – ah – relatives. As regards the will . . . ' He paused delicately.

'I see.' Mr Rosseter seemed a little relieved. 'Well, I'm

afraid I must disappoint you there, Mr – er – Cadogan. Miss Snaith left the whole of her fairly considerable fortune to her nearest relative – a Miss Emilia Tardy.'

Cadogan looked up sharply. 'I know the name, of course.'

'Quite a considerable fortune,' Mr Rosseter enunciated with relish. 'In the region of a million pounds.' He looked at his visitors, pleased with the effect he had created. 'Large sums, naturally, were swallowed up in estate and death duties, but well over half of the original amount is left. Unfortunately, Miss Emilia Tardy is no longer in a position to claim it.'

Cadogan stared. 'No longer in a position – '

'The terms of the will are peculiar, to say the very least of it.' Again Mr Rosseter polished his glasses. 'I have no objection to telling you gentlemen of them, since the will has been proved, and you may discover the details yourself from Somerset House. Miss Snaith was an eccentric old lady – I might say very eccentric. She had a strong sense of – ah – family ties, and had, moreover, promised to leave her estate to her nearest surviving relative, Miss Tardy. But at the same time she was a woman of – ah – old-fashioned views, and disapproved of the kind of life her niece was leading, travelling and living, as she did, almost wholly on the Continent. In consequence, she added a curious proviso in her will: I was to advertise for Miss Tardy in the English newspapers, with a certain specified regularity, but not in the Continental ones; and if within six months of the date of Miss Snaith's death Miss Tardy had not appeared to lay claim to her inheritance, then automatically she forfeited all right to it. In this way Miss Snaith proposed to revenge herself for Miss Tardy's way of life and for her neglect of her aunt, with whom, I believe, she had not communicated for many years, without on the other hand transgressing the letter of her promise.

'Gentlemen, the period of six months came to an end at midnight last night, and I have had no communication from Miss Tardy of any kind.'

There was a long silence. Then Fen said:

'And the estate?'

'It goes entirely to charity.'

'To charity!' Cadogan exclaimed.

'I should say to various charities.' Mr Rosseter, who had been standing all this time, relapsed into the swivel chair behind his desk. 'In point of fact, I was occupied with the details of the administration when you came in; Miss Snaith appointed me as her executor.'

Cadogan felt blank. Unless Rosseter was lying, a superb motive had been whisked away from under their noses. Charities did not murder elderly maiden ladies for the purpose of obtaining benefactions.

'That, then, is the position, gentlemen,' said Mr Rosseter briskly. 'And now if you'll forgive me' – he gestured – 'a great deal of work – '

'One more thing, if you'll be so kind,' Fen interrupted. 'Or, now I come to think of it, two. Did you ever meet Miss Tardy?'

It seemed to Cadogan that the solicitor avoided looking Fen in the eye. 'Once. A very strong-willed and moral person.'

'I see. And you put an advertisement in the *Oxford Mail* the day before yesterday – '

Mr Rosseter laughed. 'Ah, that. Nothing to do with Miss Snaith or Miss Tardy, I assure you. I'm not so unpopular' – he grinned with unconvincing roguishness – 'as to have only *one* client, you know.'

'A curious advertisement – '

'It was, wasn't it? But I'm afraid I should be violating a confidence if I were to explain. And now, gentlemen, if ever I can deal with any business for you . . . '

The Dickensian clerk ushered them out. As he departed, Cadogan said wryly:

'My only second cousin. A millionairess. And she leaves me nothing – not even a book of comic verse,' he added, remembering Mrs Wheatley's comment on this preposession of Miss Snaith. 'Well, it's a hard world.'

It was a pity he did not look round as he spoke. For Mr

Rosseter was gazing after him with an odd expression on his face.

The mild sun gleamed on the thronged street outside. Cycling undergraduates pushed between the jams of cars and buses, and the housewives of Oxford shopped.

'Well,' said Cadogan, 'was he telling the truth?'

'We might know,' said Fen aggrievedly, as they pushed along the crowded pavement, 'if you hadn't started off by behaving like something out of a mental home.'

'Well, you shouldn't suddenly foist these impostures on me. There's one thing, the centre of interest seems to have shifted from Miss Tardy to Miss Snaith and her millions.'

'As far as I'm concerned, it's shifted to Mr Rosseter.'

'How do you mean?'

'You see' – Fen cannoned into a woman who had suddenly stopped in front of him to look at a shop window – 'you see, any ordinary solicitor, if two total strangers rushed into his office and demanded details of his clients' private affairs, would quite certainly just kick them out. Why was Mr Rosseter so candid, so open and informative? Because he was telling a pack of lies? But as he quite rightly remarked, we can check what he said from Somerset House. All the same, I don't trust Mr Rosseter.'

'Well, I'm going to the police,' said Cadogan. 'If there's anything I hate, it's the sort of book in which characters don't go to the police when they've no earthly reason for not doing so.'

'You've got an earthly reason for not doing so immediately.'

'What's that?'

'The pubs are open,' said Fen, as one who after a long night sees dawn on the hills. 'Let's go and have a drink before we do anything rash.'

4. The Episode of the Indignant Janeite

'Which in effect,' said Cadogan, 'leaves us exactly where we were before.'

They were sitting in the bar of the 'Mace and Sceptre', Fen drinking whisky, Cadogan beer. The 'Mace and Sceptre' is a large and quite hideous hotel which stands in the very centre of Oxford and which embodies, without apparent shame, almost every architectural style devised since the times of primitive man. Against this initial disadvantage it struggles nobly to create an atmosphere of homeliness and comfort. The bar is a fine example of Strawberry Hill Gothic.

It was only a quarter past eleven in the morning, so few people were drinking as yet. A young man with a hooked nose and a broad mouth was talking to the barman about horses. Another young man with horn-rimmed glasses and a long neck was engrossed in *Nightmare Abbey*. And a pale, rather grubby undergraduate with untidy red hair was talking politics to an earnest-looking girl in a dark green jersey.

'So you see,' he was saying, 'it's by such means that the moneyed classes, gambling on the Stock Exchange, ruin millions of poor investors.'

'But surely the poor investors were gambling on the Stock Exchange too.'

'Oh, no, that's quite different . . .'

Mr Hoskins, more like a vast, lugubrious blood-hound than ever, was sitting at a table with a dark and beautiful girl called Miriam. He was drinking a small glass of pale sherry.

'But, darling,' said Miriam, 'it will be simply *awful* if the proctors catch me in here. You know they send women down if they catch them in bars.'

'The proctors never come in in the mornings,' said Mr Hoskins. 'And in any case, you don't look a bit like an undergraduate. Now, just don't you worry. Look, I've got some chocolates for you.' He pulled a box from his pocket.

'Oh, you *darling* . . . '

The only other occupant of the bar was a thin, rabbit-faced man of about fifty, greatly muffled up in coats and scarves, who was sitting by himself drinking rather more than was good for him.

Fen and Cadogan had been running over the facts of the case as far as they knew them, and it was the result of this investigation which had prompted Cadogan's remark. Those facts boiled down to dispiritingly little:

(1) A grocery shop in Iffley Road had been turned into a toyshop during the night, and then back into a grocery shop.

(2) A Miss Emilia Tardy had been found dead there, and her body had subsequently vanished.

(3) A rich aunt of Emilia Tardy, Miss Snaith, had been run over by a bus six months previously, and had left her fortune to Miss Tardy under certain conditions which made it as likely as not that Miss Tardy would never even become aware of her inheritance (if Rosseter was telling the truth).

'And I suppose,' said Fen, 'that he wasn't allowed to communicate directly with any known address of Miss Tardy. By the way, I was meaning to ask you: did you feel the body at all?'

'Yes, I did, in a sort of way.'

'What was it like?'

'*Like?*'

'Yes, yes,' said Fen impatiently. 'Cold? Stiff?'

Cadogan considered. 'Well, it was certainly cold, but I don't think it was stiff. In fact I'm sure it wasn't, because the arm flopped back when I moved it to look at the head.' He shivered slightly.

'It doesn't help *much*' – Fen was pensive – 'but it's reasonable to suppose, in view of what we know, that she was killed before the witching and important hour of midnight. And that in turn suggests that she did in fact see the advertisement and, presumably, applied to Mr Rosseter. *Hence*, again presumably, Mr Rosseter was lying. And that makes it all very odd indeed, because in that case it's quite likely that Mr Rosseter didn't kill her.'

'Why?'

'You agree that the person who knocked you on the head was probably the murderer?'

'Yes, Socrates.'

Fen glared malignantly and drank some whisky. 'And in that case he got a good look at you?'

'All right, all right.'

'Well now, suppose Mr Rosseter is the murderer. He recognizes you when you come into his office, he knows you've seen the body, and he's horrified to hear you inquiring about an aunt of the murdered woman and about the murdered woman herself. So what does he do? He gives a detailed account of the provisions of the will, which we can check, and then – then, mark you – says he's had no communication from Miss Tardy, *knowing* that after what you've seen you simply won't believe him. *Ergo*, he didn't recognize you. *Ergo*, he didn't knock you on the head. *Ergo*, he wasn't the murderer.'

'That's rather clever,' said Cadogan grudgingly.

'It isn't clever at all,' Fen groaned. 'It leaks at every joint, like an Emmett railway engine. In the first place, we don't know that the person who hit you was the murderer; and in the second, all that stuff about the will may be mere hooey. There are other staring gaps, too. It's possible Miss Tardy wasn't killed in the toyshop at all. But in that case, why take her body there, *and then take it away again*? The whole thing's quite topsy-turvy, and we simply don't know enough to form an opinion.'

Cadogan's admiration waned somewhat. He regarded gloomily a group of newcomers to the bar as he emptied his pint glass. 'What can we do now, anyway?'

Possible courses of action, when discussed, resolved themselves into four:

(1) Attempt to trace the body (impossible).

(2) Interview Mr Rosseter again (dubious).

(3) Get some further information about Miss Alice Winkworth, proprietress of Winkworth, Family Grocer and Provisioner (possible).

(4) Ring up a friend of Fen's at Somerset House and check on the details of Miss Snaith's will (practicable and necessary).

'But as far as I'm concerned,' Cadogan added, 'I'm going off to the police. I'm sick of rushing about, and my head still aches like a thousand devils.'

'Well, you can wait a minute till I've finished my whisky,' said Fen. 'I'm not going to make myself sick just because of your miserable, nagging conscience.'

They had been talking in low tones, and he was relieved at being able to raise his voice. Also he had consumed a comfortable amount of whisky. His ruddy, cheerful face grew ruddier and more cheerful; his hair stood up with unquenchable vitality; he fidgeted his long, lanky form about in his chair, shuffled his feet, and beamed on the dark, supercilious features, now particularly dejected, of Richard Cadogan.

' . . . and then the public schools,' the young man with red hair was piping. The peruser of *Nightmare Abbey* looked up wearily at the mention of this hoary topic; the hook-nosed person at the bar continued to talk uninterruptedly about horses. 'The public schools produce a brutal, privileged, ruling-class mentality.'

'But didn't you go to one yourself?'

'Yes. But, you see, I shook it off.'

'Don't the others, then?'

'Oh, no, they have it for life. It's only the exceptional people who shake it off.'

'I see.'

'The fact is, the whole economic life of the nation has got to be reorganized . . . '

'Now, don't you worry about the proctors,' Mr Hoskins

was soothing his companion. 'There's nothing to fear. Let's both have another chocolate.'

'We might as well play a game while we're waiting,' said Fen, who still had a good deal of whisky left in his glass. 'Detestable Characters in Fiction. Both players must agree, and each player has five seconds in which to think of a character. If he can't, he misses his turn. The first player to miss his turn three times loses. They must be characters the author intended to be sympathetic.'

Cadogan grunted, and at this point a University proctor entered the bar. The proctors are appointed from the dons in rotation, and go about accompanied by small, thickset men in blue suits and bowler hats, who are known as bullers. Members of the University *in statu pupillari* are not allowed on licensed premises, and so their main occupation is to process dismally from bar to bar, asking people if they are members of the University, taking the names of those who are, and subsequently fining them. Not much obloquy or enthusiasm is attached to this procedure.

'Gosh!' said dark-haired Miriam in a small voice.

The self-elected reorganizer of the nation's finances blenched horribly.

Mr Hoskins blinked.

The young man with glasses retired deeper into *Nightmare Abbey*.

The hook-nosed person, on being nudged by the barman, stopped talking about horses.

Only Fen was unmoved. 'Are you a member of this University?' he shouted cheerfully to the proctor. 'Hey, Whiskers! Are you a member of this University?'

The proctor started. He was (as dons go) a youngish man who had grown a pair of large cavalry moustaches during the Great War, and had never had the heart to cut them off. He gazed glassily about the room, carefully avoiding Fen's eye, and then went out.

'Oooh!' said Miriam, expelling a long sigh of relief.

'He didn't recognize you, did he?' said Mr Hoskins. 'Here, have another chocolate.'

'You see?' said the red-haired youth indignantly. 'Even

the capitalist universities are run on a terror basis.' With a trembling hand, he lifted his half-pint of ale.

'Well, let's get on with the game,' said Fen. 'Ready, steady, go.'

'Those awful gabblers, Beatrice and Benedick.'

'Yes. Lady Chatterley and that gamekeeper fellow.'

'Yes. Britomart in *The Faerie Queene*.'

'Yes. Almost everyone in Dostoevsky.'

'Yes. Er – er – '

'Got you!' said Fen triumphantly. 'You miss your turn. Those vulgar little man-hunting minxes in *Pride and Prejudice*.'

At this exultant shout the muffled, rabbity man at the nearby table frowned, got unsteadily to his feet, and came over to them.

'Sir,' he said, interrupting Cadogan's offering of Richard Feverel, 'surely I did not hear you speaking disrespectfully of the immortal Jane?'

'The Leech-Gatherer,' said Fen, making a feeble attempt to carry on. Then he abandoned it and addressed the newcomer. 'Look here, my dear fellow, you're a bit under the weather, aren't you?'

'I am perfectly sober, thank you. Thank you very much.' The rabbity man fetched his drink, drew up his chair, and settled down beside them. He raised one hand and closed his eyes as though in pain. 'Do not, I beg of you, speak disrespectfully of Miss Austen. I have read all of her novels many, many times. Their gentleness, their breath of a superior and beautiful culture, their acute psychological insight – ' He paused, speechless, and emptied his glass at a gulp.

He had a weak, thin face, with rodent teeth, red-rimmed eyes, pale, straggling eyebrows, and a low forehead. Despite the warmth of the morning, he was dressed in the most extraordinary fashion, with fur gloves, two scarves, and (apparently) several overcoats.

Sensing Cadogan's startled inventory: 'I am very sensitive to cold, sir,' said the rabbity man with an attempt at dignity,

'And the autumn chill – ' He paused, groped for a handker-chief and blew his nose with a trumpeting noise. 'I hope – I *hope* that you do not object, gentlemen, to my joining you?'

'Yes, we do,' said Fen, irritated.

'Don't be unkind, I beg of you,' said the rabbity man beseechingly. 'This morning I am so very, very happy. Allow me to give you a drink. I have plenty of money . . . Waiter?' The waiter appeared at their table. 'Two large whiskies and a pint of bitter.'

'Look here, Gervase, I really ought to be going,' Cadogan put in uneasily.

'Don't go, sir. Stay and rejoice with me.' There was no doubt that the rabbity man was very drunk indeed. He leaned forward conspiratorially and lowered his voice. 'This morning I got rid of my boys.'

'Ah,' said Fen without amusement. 'And what did you do with the little bodies?'

The rabbity man giggled. 'Ah! You're trying to catch me out. My schooldays, I mean. I am – I *was* a schoolmaster. A poor birchman. The specific gravity of mercury is 13.6,' he chanted. '*Caesar Galliam in tres partes divisit.* The past participle of *mourir* is *mort*.'

Fen gazed at him with distaste. The waiter brought their drinks and the rabbity man paid for them out of a rather grubby wallet, adding a huge tip.

'Your health, gentlemen,' he said, raising his glass. Then he paused. 'But I haven't introduced myself. George Shar-man, at your service.' He bowed low from the waist, and nearly sent his drink flying; Cadogan saved it just in time.

'At this moment,' said Mr Sharman meditatively, 'I should be teaching the Lower Fourth the elements of Latin Prose Composition. And shall I tell you why I'm not?' Again he leaned forward. 'Last night, gentlemen, I came into a large sum of money.'

Cadogan jumped and Fen's eyes hardened. Legacies seemed to be in the air that morning.

'A ver' large sum of money,' Mr Sharman pursued indistinctly. 'So what do I do? I go to the headmaster and I say, "Spavin," I say, "you're a domineering old sot, and I'm not going to work for you *any* more. I'm a gentleman of independent means now," I said, "and I'm going to get some of the chalk out of my veins." ' He beamed complacently about him.

'Congratulations,' said Fen with dangerous amiability. 'Congratulations.'

'An' thass not all.' Mr Sharman's utterance was becoming progressively more clouded. 'I'm not the on'y lucky one. Oh, no. There're others.' He gestured broadly. 'Lots 'n lots of others, all as rich as Croesus. An' one of them's a beautiful girl, with the bluest azure eyes. My luve is like a blue, blue rose,' he sang in a cracked voice. 'I sh'll ask her to marry me, though she is only a shop-girl. Only a shop-girl's daughter.' He turned earnestly to Cadogan. 'You mus' meet her.'

'I should like to very much.'

'That's the way,' said Mr Sharman with approval. He trumpeted again into his handkerchief.

'Have another drink with me, old man,' said Fen, adopting an attitude of bibulous comradeship and slapping Mr Sharman on the back. Mr Sharman hiccupped. ''S on me,' he said. 'Waiter . . . !'

They all had another drink.

'Ah,' said Fen, sighing deeply. 'You're a lucky man, Mr Sharman. I wish a relative would die and leave me a lot of money.'

But Mr Sharman waggled his finger. 'Don' try to pump me. I'm not telling anything, see? I'm keeping my mouth shut.' He shut his mouth, illustratively, and then opened it again to admit more whisky. 'I'm surprised,' he added in a tearful voice. 'After all I've done for you. Tryin' to pump me.'

'No, no . . . '

A change came over Mr Sharman's face. His voice grew weaker, and he clutched at his stomach. ''Scuse me, gen'lmen,' he said. 'Back in a moment.' He got to his feet, stood swaying like a grass in the wind, and then tottered unsteadily in the direction of the lavatories.

'We shan't get much out of him,' said Fen gloomily. 'When a man doesn't want to tell something, drunkenness only makes him more obstinate and suspicious. But it's a queer coincidence.'

' *"The owl,"* ' Cadogan quoted, looking after Mr Sharman's weedy, muffled form, ' *"for all his feathers was a cold."* '

'Yes,' Fen said. 'Like the old person of – *Oh my fur and whiskers.*'

'What in God's name is the matter?' Cadogan asked in alarm.

Fen got hastily to his feet. 'Keep that man here,' he said with emphasis, 'until I get back. Ply him with whisky. Talk to him about Jane Austen. But don't let him go.'

'But look here, I was going to the police . . . '

'Don't be so spiritless, Richard. This is a clue. I haven't the least idea where it will lead, but so help me, it's a clue. Don't go away. I shan't be long.' And Fen strode out of the bar.

Mr Sharman returned to his seat both more sober and more wary than he had been.

'Your friend gone?' he asked.

'Only for a short while.'

'Ah.' Mr Sharman stretched himself luxuriously. 'Glorious freedom. You've no idea what it is to be a schoolmaster. I've watched strong men go to pieces under it. It's a perpetual war. You can keep the boys off for maybe thirty years, but they get you in the end.'

'It sounds terrible.'

'It is terrible. You get older, but they're always the same age. Like the emperor and the crowd in the Forum.'

Then they talked about Jane Austen, a subject made difficult for Cadogan by his imperfect knowledge of that author. Mr Sharman, however, made up for this deficiency in both knowledge and enthusiasm. Cadogan felt his dislike for the man increasing – dislike for his bleary little eyes, his projecting front teeth, his pedagogue's assumption of culture; unquestionably Mr Sharman was an unpleasant illustration of the effects of a powerful greed suddenly satisfied. He did not refer again to his inheritance, or to the 'others' who shared it with him, but perorated resolutely on *Mansfield Park*. Cadogan made monosyllabic replies, and considered with a certain impatience the curious behaviour of Gervase Fen. As it grew nearer lunchtime the bar filled up with hotel visitors, actors, undergraduates. The noise of chatter rose in volume, and the sunlight pouring through the Gothic windows cut the haze of cigarette smoke into pale-blue triangles. 'The only solution, I think,' said someone suddenly and with conviction, 'is liquid soap.' Solution to what? Cadogan vaguely wondered.

'And then look at the character of Mr Collins,' Mr Sharman was remarking. With reluctance Cadogan focused his attention on this personage.

At five minutes to midday there was a loud roar outside, accompanied by a clattering like saucepans at war. A moment later Fen pushed through the swing doors of the hotel to the sound of a sharp detonation. He was greatly exuberant, and carried a brightly jacketed book which he regarded with affection. Ignoring the bar on his left, he went on into the hotel proper, down a blue-carpeted corridor towards the porter's box. Ridley, the porter, resplendent in blue and braid, greeted him with a certain apprehension, but he only entered one of the nearby telephone boxes. There he put through a call to Somerset House.

'Hello, Evans,' he said. 'Fen here . . . Yes, very well, thanks, my dear fellow, and how are you . . . ? I wonder if you'd look something up for me?'

An indistinct crackle.

'I can't hear a word you're saying . . . What I want is the details of the will of a Miss Snaith, Boar's Hill, Oxford, who died about six months ago. It can't have been proved until quite recently . . . What? Oh, well ring me back, will you? Yes . . . At the "Mace and Sceptre". Yes. All right . . . Good-bye.'

'My soul cleaveth to the dust,' he sang without much humility as he jogged the receiver-rest, inserted two more pennies, and dialled a local number. Once again the telephone shrilled in the study of the Chief Constable of Oxford on Boar's Hill.

'Well?' said that dignitary. 'Oh, my God, is it you again? Not more about this Cadogan man?'

'No,' said Fen, hurt. 'As a matter of fact, no. Though I must say I think you're being most unhelpful.'

'It's no use. The grocer's kicking up a stink about it. You'd better keep out of the way. You know what happens when you start interfering in things.'

'Never mind that now. Have you any recollection of a Miss Snaith who lived near you?'

'Snaith? Snaith? Oh, yes, I know. Eccentric old lady.'

'Eccentric? How?'

'Oh, terrified of being murdered for her money. Lived in a sort of fortified grange, with damned great fierce mastiff dogs all over the shop. Died a short while ago. Why?'

'Did you ever meet her?'

'Oh, once or twice. Never really knew her. But what – '

'What sort of things was she interested in?'

'*Interested* in? Well – education, I believe. Oh, and she was always writing a lot of trashy books about spiritualism. Don't know if she ever published them. Hope not. But she was terrified of dying – particularly of getting herself murdered – and I suppose it consoled her to think there was an after-life. Though I must say, if I'm going to come back after I'm dead and spell out idiotic messages on ouija boards, I'd rather not know about it beforehand.'

'Anything else?'

'Well, she was really quite a nice old thing, and very sensitive to kindness. But as I say, she was terrified people wanted to kill her. The only person she really trusted was some solicitor fellow – '

'Rosseter?'

'Come to think of it, that was the name. But look here, why – '

'I suppose there's no doubt her death was an accident?'

'Lord, no. Run over by a bus. She just walked into it – there was no one else anywhere near her. You can imagine that, in view of the circumstances, we investigated pretty carefully.'

'Did she travel about much?'

'No, never – that was another odd thing. Stuck in Oxford all her life. Strange bird. By the way, Gervase about *Measure for Measure* –'

Fen rang off. He was not prepared to discuss *Measure for Measure* at the moment. While he was considering what he had learned the bell rang in the call-box, and he lifted the receiver.

'Hello,' he said. 'Yes, this is Fen. Oh, it's you, Evans. You've been quick.'

'Traced it easily,' said the disembodied spokesman of Somerset House. 'Elizabeth Ann Snaith, "Valhalla", Boar's Hill, Oxford. Will dated August 13th, 1937, and witnessed by R. A. Starkey and Jane Lee. Estate £937,642 – tidy packet. Personalty, £740,760. A few small bequests – to servants, I imagine – but the bulk of it goes to "my niece, Emilia Tardy", with a lot of queer provisions about advertising for her only in English papers, not communicating direct, and Lord knows what gallimaufry of rubbish. Oh, and a time limit of six months after the Snaith's death to claim the bequest. Looks as if she was doing everything she could to prevent the miserable Tardy woman getting her paws on the money.'

'And what happens if she doesn't claim it?'

At the other end there was a pause. 'Half a tick, it's over the page. Ah, yes. In that case, it all goes to a Mr Aaron Rosseter, of 193A Cornmarket, Oxford. Lucky devil. That's all, I think.'

'Ah.' Fen was thoughtful. 'Thanks, Evans. Thanks very much.'

'Any time,' said that official. 'Give my love to Oxford.' He rang off.

Outside the call-box, Fen stood for a minute, and considered. The guests of the hotel drifted past him, stopping to ask the porter for timetables, taxis, newspapers. Ridley dealt with them with practised competence. In the dining-room the tables were being laid for lunch, and the head waiter was checking off reservations from a list pencilled on the back of a menu.

Unquestionably, Mr Rosseter had a very good motive for murdering Miss Emilia Tardy. If he was only one of the executors of the will, he would have had no chance of cheating Miss Tardy out of her inheritance by failing to advertise for her. So when, in fact, she appeared . . . Fen shook his head. It didn't really fit. For one thing, it was scarcely conceivable that Miss Snaith should have put such extraordinary powers into Mr Rosseter's hands, however much she trusted him; for another, if Mr Rosseter had murdered Miss Tardy and knocked Cadogan on the head, why had he not recognized him, or, if he had, why had he been so extremely informative? Of course it was not necessarily the murderer who had knocked Cadogan on the head; possibly an accomplice . . . But, then, why the toyshop?

Fen sighed deeply and patted the book he was carrying. His spirits were extremely volatile, and at the moment he felt a trifle depressed. He waved to Ridley and went back to the bar. Cadogan and Mr Sharman had reached a conversational *impasse*; Mr Sharman had by now voided the whole of his views on Jane Austen, and Cadogan could not think of any fresh topic. At present, however, Fen was intent on avoiding them; he addressed himself, instead, to the melancholy, raw-boned Mr Hoskins.

Mr Hoskins was not in any way a troublesome undergraduate: he did his work with efficiency if not zeal, refrained from drunkenness and comported himself in a gentlemanly manner. His only remarkable characteristic was the unfailing spell which he appeared to cast upon young women. At the moment he was sitting before his second small glass of pale sherry and urging black-haired Miriam to the further consumption of chocolates.

Excusing himself to the girl, who gazed up at him with a kind of holy awe, Fen got Mr Hoskins outside.

'Mr Hoskins,' said Fen with mild severity. 'I shall not inquire why you are devoting the golden hours of your youth to the illegal consumption of sherry in that imitation of Chartres Cathedral – '

'I'm much obliged to you, sir,' said Mr Hoskins without any special perturbation of spirit.

'I only wish to ask,' Fen proceeded, 'if you will do me a service.'

Mr Hoskins blinked and silently bowed.

'Are you interested in the novels of Jane Austen, Mr Hoskins?'

'It has always appeared to me, sir,' said Mr Hoskins, 'that the women characters are poorly drawn.'

'Well, you should know,' said Fen, grinning. 'Anyway, there's a dreary, sordid fellow in there who has a passion for Jane Austen. Could you keep him here for an hour or so?'

'Nothing easier,' said Mr Hoskins with benign self-assurance. 'Though I think perhaps I had better go and pack my young woman off first.'

'Of course, of course,' said Fen hastily.

Mr Hoskins bowed again, returned to the bar, and shortly reappeared, shepherding Miriam with soothing explanations to the door. There he pressed her hand warmly, waved after her, and returned to Fen.

'Tell me, Mr Hoskins,' said Fen, seized by a sudden disinterested curiosity, 'how do you explain your extraordinary attraction for women? Don't answer if you think I'm being impertinent.'

'Not at all.' Mr Hoskins conveyed the impression that he found this query most gratifying. 'It's really very simple: I quieten their fears and give them sweet things to eat. It seems never to fail.'

'Oh,' said Fen, a little taken aback. 'Oh. Well, thank you very much, Mr Hoskins. And now, if you'll come back to the bar . . . ' He began to give instructions.

Cadogan was only too delighted to be released by Mr Hoskins from his vigil. When he and Fen left the bar Mr Hoskins and Mr Sharman were already conversing most amicably.

'Well, what's going on?' he inquired when they got outside. He was a trifle hazy after five pints of beer, but his head was aching much less.

Fen drew him down the passage and they sat down by the reception desk, in two hard wooden chairs of vaguely Assyrian design. Fen explained about the telephone calls.

'No, no,' he said peevishly, cutting short Cadogan's startled outcry on the subject of Mr Rosseter. 'I really don't think he can have done it.' He gave his reasons.

'That's mere quibbling,' Cadogan answered. 'It's only because you have these romantic fancies about that advertisement – '

'I was coming to that,' said Fen malevolently. He paused to examine a young and elaborate blonde who was walking by, clad in furs and with very high heels. 'Because in fact there is a connection between that advertisement and Miss Snaith.'

'And what may it be?'

'This.' With something of a flourish, Fen brought forth the book he had been carrying; it was rather with the air of a prosecuting counsel who has some piece of particularly damaging evidence to reveal. Cadogan studied it without much comprehension. It was entitled *The Nonsense Poems of Edward Lear*.

'You may recall,' Fen went on, waving his index finger didactically about in the air, 'that Miss Snaith was interested in comic verse. This' – he tapped the book authoritatively – 'is comic verse.'

'You amaze me.'

'Comic verse of the highest order, moreover.' Fen suddenly abandoned his instructive manner and became aggrieved. 'There are actually people who imagine that Lear was *incapable* of making the last lines of his limericks different from the first; whereas the fact is – '

'Yes, yes,' said Cadogan impatiently, taking the newspaper cutting from his pocket book. 'I see what you mean. "Ryde, Leeds, West, Mold, Berlin". Some fantastic method of designating people by means of limericks.'

'M'm.' Fen scrabbled through the pages. 'And I somehow darkly suspect that our Mr Sharman is one of them. Look here – there was an Old Person of Mold who shrank from sensations of Cold; so he purchased some muffs, some furs, and some fluffs, and wrapped himself up from the cold. In the picture he looks like a sort of globular bear. Doesn't that fit?'

'Yes, but – '

'Moreover, Mr Sharman came into a substantial legacy *last night*. And so did some others, apparently.'

'Ryde, Leeds, West, and Berlin.'

'Exactly. The Old Man of the West, you remember, wore a pale, plum-coloured vest – '

'There was another, wasn't there, who never could get any rest.'

'Yes, but they set him to spin on his nose and chin, and there's nothing distinctive about that, except therapeutically.'

'Ah.' Cadogan paused and reflected that he had drunk too much. 'What about Ryde?'

'There was a Young Lady of Ryde,' Fen read after some further search, 'whose shoe-strings were seldom untied. She purchased some clogs and some small spotted dogs, and frequently walked about Ryde. It really isn't uncommon, you know, for people's shoe-strings to be seldom untied, and clogs are scarcely conceivable. Which leaves the small spotted dogs.'

'I remember Berlin.'

'So do I. He was an Old Man whose form was uncommonly thin . . . ' For the first time Fen hesitated. 'It does all sound a bit wild, doesn't it?'

'Well, what's your idea?'

'I haven't any really.' Fen considered. 'It's just this rather shaky train of correspondences; Miss Snaith – comic verse

– Rosseter – advertisement – Sharman's inheritance. But I confess it had occurred to me that Sharman and the "others" he talked about might be the legatees in case Miss Tardy didn't put in her claim.'

'But they aren't. Rosseter is.'

'On the face of it, yes.' Taking a cigarette from a gold case, Fen put it slowly into his mouth. 'There are such things as secret trusts, you know. You leave your money to one person and direct him to pass it on to another – with certain safeguards to make sure he does. In that way the general public can't find out who's getting it.'

'But why on earth should Miss Snaith go in for such a rigmarole?'

'I don't know.' Fen lit his cigarette and tried to blow a smoke-ring. 'I dare say Rosseter could tell us, but he won't. A heel,' he added, being somewhat prone to out-of-date americanisms.

'Nor will Sharman,' Cadogan said gloomily. His face lightened as he observed a popular woman novelist stumble on getting into the lift. 'I tried.'

'Oh, you've been blundering about, have you,' said Fen with interest, 'like a bull in a china shop? Well, I was pretty sure he wouldn't let anything out, anyway.'

'By the way, why did you foist him on that under-graduate?'

'Chiefly to keep him under surveillance while I was talk-ing to you.'

'I see. Well, we've only got to find a man with a plum-coloured vest, a man who's uncommonly thin, a girl with some small spotted dogs, a – by the way, what about Leeds?'

'Her head was infested with beads.'

'My dear Gervase,' said Cadogan, 'it's all quite fantastic and hopeless.'

But Fen shook his head. 'Not entirely,' he said. 'If we can discover a beautiful shop-girl with blue eyes and a small spotted dog . . . Let's start now.'

'Start? Now?'

They started.

5. The Episode of the Immaterial Witness

Considering the matter afterwards, tediously rehearsing it to bored or frankly incredulous audiences, Cadogan became eventually convinced that this was by far the most extraordinary and improbable episode of the entire business. It is true that his sense of the fitness of things was somewhat impaired by beer; it is also true that the improbable has less weight in the City of Oxford than in any other habitable quarter of the globe. But still, even at the time, he felt that a poet and a professor who insisted on combing the shops of the town for a blue-eyed, beautiful girl with a small spotted dog, in the hope that her discovery might throw some light on the disappearance of a toyshop from the Iffley Road, were hardly likely to remain long at large in a sane and self-respecting society. However, it was evident that Gervase Fen felt no such qualms; he was confident that Mr Hoskins would cling on to Mr Sharman for as long as he was left to his vigil; he was confident that Mr Rosseter's advertisement had something to do with the death of Miss Tardy, and that he had interpreted it rightly; he was confident that a beautiful, blue-eyed shop-girl with a small spotted dog could not long elude them in a town the size of Oxford (Cadogan, on the contrary, was of opinion that she could elude them indefinitely); and he appeared, in any case, to have nothing else in the world to do but look for her.

His plan was that each of them should walk down one side of George Street, entering every shop on the way, investigating for beautiful, blue-eyed girls, and, where these proved to exist, making such inquiries about their pets as seemed possible in the circumstances; this procedure to be continued throughout the shopping centre. Standing on the crowded pavement, and listening to the clocks strike fifteen minutes after midday, Cadogan assented to this gloomily enough; in any case, he reflected, he would almost certainly be arrested before he got far.

'Ryde is the only Young Lady in those five limericks,' Fen remarked, gazing a trifle despondently down the length of George Street, 'so it must mean the girl Sharman was talking about. We'll meet and compare notes at the end of the street.'

They set forth. The first shop on Cadogan's beat was a tobacconist's, presided over by a plump, peroxided woman of uncertain age. It occurred to Cadogan that the difficulties of the undertaking were greatly increased by the consideration that (*a*) there could be no certainty regarding Mr Sharman's standards of female pulchritude, and (*b*) one can seldom make out the colour of a person's eyes without peering very closely at them. Affecting short-sightedness, he thrust his face close to that of the peroxided woman. She recoiled hastily and simpered at him. Her eyes, he decided, must be either blue or green.

'What can I do for you, sir?' she asked.

'Have you a small, spotted dog?'

To his surprise and annoyance, she gave a little shriek and called out: 'Mr Riggs! Mr Riggs!' An agitated, pimply young man in brilliantine and a creased morning suit appeared from the back of the shop.

'What is it, Miss Blount?' he said. 'What is it?'

Miss Blount pointed a wavering finger at Cadogan and said faintly: 'He asked me if I had a small, spotted dog.'

'Really, sir . . . '

'Well, and what's the matter with that?'

'Well, sir, don't you think . . . perhaps a little . . . that is to say somewhat – ah – '

'Unless the vocabulary of bawdry has undergone accretions since my young days,' said Cadogan, 'no.' He stalked out.

In the shops which he subsequently visited he had no more success. Either there were no beautiful girls with blue eyes or else they did not possess small, spotted dogs. He was received alternately with fury, amusement, mystification, and frigid politeness. Periodically he saw Fen emerge on the opposite side of the road, wave a negative across the surge of traffic, and disappear again. He became disheartened and began to buy things at the shops he entered – a tube of toothpaste, some bootlaces, a dog-collar. When he finally met Fen at the traffic lights where George Street joins the Cornmarket, he was burdened about like a Christmas tree.

'What in God's name are you doing with all those things?' said Fen, and then, without waiting for an answer: 'This really is rather a job, you know. Nothing on my side of the road. One woman seemed to think I was proposing marriage.'

Cadogan miserably shifted a wicker basket, the most substantial of his purchases, from one arm to the other. He grunted. In fact, his mind was occupied with the virtual conviction that they were being watched. Two heavily-built men in dark suits had been following their progress and were now standing near them on the opposite corner, mutually engaged in a prolonged effort to light a cigarette. They could not conceivably be the police; consequently, they must have something to do with the death of Emilia Tardy. But as he was about to point them out to Fen, he was gripped suddenly by the arm.

'Look!' Fen exclaimed.

Cadogan looked. A girl had just emerged from an alley-way which ran behind one of the shops in the Cornmarket. She was about twenty-three, tall, with a finely-proportioned, loose-limbed body, naturally golden hair, big candid blue eyes, high cheek bones, and a firmly moulded chin. Her scarlet mouth broke into an impish smile as she called back to someone in the alley-way. She wore a shirt and tie, a dark brown coat and skirt, and brogue shoes, and walked with the insouciant swinging grace of perfect health.

And beside her trotted a Dalmatian dog.

'It isn't very small,' Fen said, as she walked towards them.

'Well, it may have grown,' said Cadogan. Relief at not

having to enter any more shops made him unwisely raise his voice. 'That must be the girl.'

She heard, saw them, and stopped. The lingering smile faded from her red lips. With something like panic in her eyes, she changed direction and cut across the road, walking so fast down Broad Street that she almost ran, and glancing back over her shoulder.

After a moment's initial stupefaction Fen grabbed Cadogan's sleeve and urged him across the road after her, regardless of changing lights and an ominous grinding of gears among the cars waiting to proceed. They reached the opposite pavement much as Orestes, hounded by the Furies, must have staggered into Iphigenia's grove in Tauris. Out of the corner of his eyes Cadogan saw that the two men in dark suits were moving after them. For a moment the girl was lost from view behind the windows of a large china-shop, but they soon caught sight of her again, pushing hastily through the ambling crowds on the pavement. By mutual consent, they began to run after her.

Broad Street lives up to its name; it is also quite short and straight. In the centre of it there is a taxi-rank, and at the end you can see Hertford College, Mr Blackwell's Bookshop, the Sheldonian Concert Hall (fronted by a row of the stone heads of Roman emperors, severe and admonitory as the totems of some primitive tribe), and the Bodleian Library. The midday sun, pleasant and warm, struck splinters of blue and gold from the ashen stone walls. Indefatigably the women undergraduates pedalled to their last assignments of the morning. And Fen and Cadogan ran, Cadogan shouting 'Hi!' in a penetrating voice.

The girl, too, began to run as they drew nearer to her, the dog cantering beside her. But both Fen and Cadogan were vigorous, active men, and they would have caught up with her in a minute or less had their way not been suddenly blocked by a substantial form in the uniform of the Oxford Constabulary.

'Now then,' said the form conventionally. 'What's all this?'

Cadogan panicked, but he realized after a second that the

constable had not recognized him, and was merely taking exception to their satyr-like pursuit.

'That girl,' Fen fumed, pointing his finger after her. 'That girl.'

The constable scratched his nose. 'Well, now,' he said. 'We're all for love in the Force, but fair's fair, you know. One of you at a time, and no stampeding. You'd better go and get some lunch,' he added kindly. Evidently he suspected that this would constitute some sort of anaphrodisiac.

'Oh, God,' Fen exclaimed disgustedly. 'Come on, Richard. It's no use trying to follow her now.' Watched by the benevolent eye of the law, he led the way across the road to Balliol College and entered its Gothic portals with some dignity. Once inside, however, they hastened through the grounds and into the precincts of Trinity, which stands next door. A hasty reconnoitring at the wrought-iron gates showed the constable, his mind at ease after their display of resignation, strolling away towards the Cornmarket with his back to them; and the girl hesitating outside the Sheldonian Theatre. It also showed the two men in dark suits prowling about the window of a tailor's opposite. Cadogan pointed them out to Fen and explained his suspicions.

'H'm,' said Fen thoughtfully. 'I rather think it might be as well to lose them if we can. On the other hand, we can't risk losing the girl at the same time. We'd better go after her as fast as possible, and hope for the best. Obviously whoever knocked you on the head last night wants to keep an eye on you, but they don't seem keen on doing more than just follow.' He was plainly exhilarated by the entire proceedings. 'All right, let's go.'

As they came out again into Broad Street, the girl saw them, and after a moment's indecision turned and went into the Sheldonian, leaving the dog outside. It sat down patiently to wait. Fen and Cadogan hastened their steps. The two men in dark suits, whose acquaintance with the topography of Oxford was plainly uncertain, did not observe and begin to follow them until they were practically at the gates of the Sheldonian.

This building, designed by Sir Christopher Wren, consists (apart from some mysterious, warren-like passages about its circumference) of a tall, circular hall, with galleries, an organ, and a painted roof. In it, concerts are given; in it, University degrees are conferred and ceremonial confabulations held; in it, the larger choirs and orchestras rehearse. Such a rehearsal – of the Handel Society – was in progress now, under the impassioned conducting of the preternaturally thin and energetic Dr Artemus Rains. As Fen and Cadogan mounted the stone steps and crossed the paving to the door, a blast of Hölderlin's fatalism, as interpreted by Brahms and translated by the Rev. J. Troutbeck, met their ears. *'Blindly,'* sang the choir, *'blindly at last do we pass away.'* The orchestra accompanied them with racing arpeggios, and acid, fiery chords on the brass.

Fen and Cadogan peered in. The orchestra occupied the well of the hall. Round it, ranged in tiers, stood a choir of three hundred or more, copies raised, eyes straying uneasily between the printed music and the frenetic gesticulations of Dr Rains, mouths opening and shutting in unanimous pantomime. *'But man may not linger,'* they chanted, *'for nowhere finds he repose.'* Among the altos, hooting morosely like ships in a Channel fog – which is the way of altos the world over – Cadogan caught sight of the girl they were seeking. He nudged Fen and pointed. Fen nodded, and they entered the hall.

Or rather, they attempted to do so. Unhappily, at this crucial moment their way was barred by a plain but determined woman undergraduate, with spectacles and a slight squint.

'Your membership cards, please!' she hissed in a stage whisper.

'We're only coming in to listen,' said Fen impatiently.

'Shhh!' The girl put a finger to her lips. The uproar beyond them increased in volume. 'No one is allowed in, Professor Fen, except members of the choir and orchestra.'

'Oh. Oh, aren't they,' said Fen. He indicated Cadogan. 'But this is Dr Paul Hindemith, the eminent German composer.'

'Pleased to meet you,' Cadogan whispered in a foreign accent. *'Sehr vergnugt. Wie geht's Ihnen?'*

'Never mind all that now,' Fen put in. 'I know Dr Rains will be delighted to see us.' And without waiting for any further protest, they pushed their way inside.

The girl with the blue eyes and the golden hair was embedded in the very middle of the altos, and there was no way to get near her except through the basses, who stood nearby, behind the orchestra. Accordingly, they hacked out a path between the instrumentalists, under the envenomed gaze of Dr Artemus Rains. The second horn, a sandy, undersized man, went quite out of tune with indignation. Brahms thundered and trumpeted about their ears. *'Blindly,'* the chorus roared, *'blindly from one dread hour to another.'* They knocked over the music-stand of the tympanist, sweating with the effort of counting bars, so that he failed to come in at his last entry.

The haven of the basses achieved at last, a number of further difficulties presented themselves. The Sheldonian is not particularly spacious, and the members of a large choir have to be herded together in conditions not unreminiscent of the Black Hole of Calcutta. When Fen and Cadogan, pushing, perspiring, and creating a great deal of localized pother, had penetrated the basses to a certain distance (Cadogan shedding wicker basket, bootlaces, and dog-collar broadcast as he went) they could literally get no farther; they were wedged, and even the avenue by which they had come was now irrevocably closed and sealed. Everyone was staring at them. Moreover, an old man who had sung in the Handel Society choir for fifty years thrust a copy of the Brahms at them. This was unfortunate, as Fen, seeing no chance of moving for some time and being content to stop where he was and keep an eye on the girl they were pursuing, took it into his head to improve the shining hour by joining in the singing; and Fen's voice, though penetrating, was neither tuneful nor accurate.

'*We STAAAAY not,*' he came in suddenly, '*but WAAAANDER.*' Several of the basses in front turned round as if someone had struck them in the back. '*We grief-laden,*' Fen pursued unconcernedly, '*grieee-EEEF-laden mortals!*'

This was too much for Dr Artemus Rains. He banged with his baton on the rostrum, and the choir and orchestra faded into silence. There was a general murmur of interested comment and everyone stared.

'Professor Fen,' said Dr Rains with painful restraint. A hush fell. 'You are not, I believe, a member of this choir. That being the case, would you kindly oblige me by going away?'

Fen, however, was not easily abashed, even by the presence of four hundred vaguely hostile musicians. 'I think that's a most illiberal sentiment. Rains,' he countered across the gaping tiers of choristers. 'Most illiberal and discourteous. Just because I happen to make one small error in singing an extremely difficult passage – '

Dr Rains leaned his spidery form forwards across the rostrum. 'Professor Fen – ' he began in a silky voice.

But he was not allowed to finish. The girl with the blue eyes, profiting by this sudden focusing of attention, had pushed her way through the altos and was now heading at a brisk pace towards the door. Unnerved by this fresh interruption, Dr Rains swung round tc glare at her. Fen and Cadogan got on the move again with alacrity, clawing their way back through the basses and the orchestra without ceremony or restraint. But this process delayed them, and the girl had been out of the hall at least half a minute by the time they reached open ground. Dr Rains watched them go with a theatrical expression of sardonic interest.

'Now that the English Faculty has left us,' Cadogan heard him say, 'we will go back to letter L.' The rehearsal started afresh.

It was nearly one o'clock, so when they emerged again, somewhat hastily, into the sunlight, Broad Street was comparatively empty. For a moment Cadogan could not see the girl; then he caught sight of the Dalmatian loping up the street the way they had come, with the girl a few paces ahead. On the opposite pavement the two men in dark suits were examining the contents of Mr Blackwell's window.

Pointing at them: 'Scylla and Charybdis are still after us, I see,' Fen remarked with some pleasure. 'But we haven't time for them now. That girl must have something pretty weighty on her mind to run away from two complete strangers in a crowded street. Of course, if you hadn't bawled out: "That must be the girl" – '

'She may have recognized me,' said Cadogan. 'It may have been her that knocked me on the head.'

'We must put the heat on that broad.'

'Eh?'

'Oh, never mind.'

So the pursuit began again, though more circumspectly this time. Fen and Cadogan followed the girl, and Scylla and Charybdis followed Fen and Cadogan. They turned right into tree-lined St Giles', passed the car-park and the entrance to Beaumont Street, passed the gate of St John's.

And then, to Cadogan's astonishment, the girl turned into St Christopher's.

It is an inconvenient and longstanding tradition of the college of St Christopher that lunch is eaten at 1.30 and that week-day Mattins precedes it at one o'clock. The service had consequently just began when Fen and Cadogan arrived. The porter, Parsons, in addition to the information that the police had once again been and departed, was able to tell them that the girl had gone into the chapel a few moments before, and pointed to the Dalmatian which lingered outside as proof; and to the chapel Fen and Cadogan followed her.

This part of the college was well restored at the end of last century. Death-watch beetles would be out of place in it, but at the same time it does not look objectionably new. The glass is pleasant if undistinguished, the organ pipes, painted gold, are arranged in a simple and attractive geometrical pattern, and the pew-ends – as in most collegiate chapels, the pews face each other like the seats in a railway compartment – are neither objectionably florid nor plain and dull. The only unusual feature is a separate enclosure for women, locally known as the Witches' Kitchen, which possesses an entrance of its own.

On this particular morning the President of the college, isolated like a germ in his private pew, was feeling disgruntled. For one thing, Fen's erratic manoeuvres earlier on with Lily Christine III had shaken him more than he would have liked to admit; for another, the *Sunday Times* had refused to print a poem he had offered them; for a third, accustomed since boyhood to lunching at one o'clock, he had never since his appointment become used to its postponement to 1.30. When the one o'clock service began, his stomach was crying out for food; by the second lesson, his gastronomic misery had reached its apex; and for the rest of the time he settled down to a dull, aching misery, extremely prejudicial to his devotions. As a consequence, he frowned when a young woman with golden hair and blue eyes entered the Witches' Kitchen during the first hymn; he frowned still more when, a few moments later, Fen and Cadogan arrived, noisily whispering; and he openly scowled when after a brief interval they were followed by two men in dark blue suits whose knowledge of the Anglican liturgy was plainly sketchy to a degree.

In order to get as near to the girl as possible, Fen and Cadogan made their way up to a public pew by the choir. Scylla and Charybdis settled themselves nearby. The ritual went its way with an effortless grace, and until it was over no one moved. Fen, who disapproved of congregational singing, occupied himself with staring at anyone who opened his mouth. Cadogan, abandoning reflection on the tortured series of events in which he was involved, joined the President in a muted craving for lunch (by an unfortunate chance, the First Lesson was largely concerned with the comestibles in favour with ancient Jewry). The girl worshipped unobtrusively. Scylla and Charybdis rose and fell with evident unease. Only the Lord's Prayer seemed to strike a chord, and then they were unhappily unaware that at one point in the proceedings it is curtailed, and so said 'For Thine is the Kingdom' when everyone else was pronouncing the Amen.

But only at the end did the real problems of the position present themselves. Strict rules of precedence govern the exodus from St Christopher's chapel, and they are rigidly enforced by the ushers, who are chosen from the under-graduate scholars in rotation. The women, already segregated like an Asiatic seraglio, leave by their own door. The choir and chaplain process to the vestry at the East end while all stand. And the body of the congregation go out of the west door in the order of their proximity, beginning with the President and Fellows. Matters are further retarded by the habit of genuflexion. Anyone uncertain of these things will do best to cower in his seat, and pretend to be listening to the organ voluntary, until everyone else has gone.

The trouble in the present instance was this: that whereas the girl with the blue eyes could leave immediately, and without delay, neither Scylla and Charybdis, who were far enough from the door, nor Fen and Cadogan, who were even farther, could hope to be outside within about three minutes; since Fen was not sitting with the other Fellows, he could not push through and join them. Obviously, the girl was aware of this. If she had left during the service they could have feigned illness and followed her at once. But when the service ended nothing short of an apoplectic fit could get them from the building in anything but their proper order.

She went, in fact, immediately the Blessing had been spoken, just as the organist was launching into the so-called Dorian Toccata, and just as Fen and Cadogan were becoming clearly conscious of the problem which faced them. Three minutes would give the girl ample time to lose herself somewhere in the rambling college precincts, and they might for all they knew never see her again. The ushers, very grim and muscular, forbade any exhibition of disorder. There was only one thing to do, and at a whispered instruction from

Fen they did it. They joined themselves on to the end of the choir, and, with an empurpled chaplain bringing up the rear, processed out with it. Out of the corner of his eye, Cadogan saw Scylla and Charybdis, starting from their seats, held back by one of the ushers. The other was taken unawares by this abnormal mode of exit, and made no movement until it was too late. His eyes fixed on the scrawny neck and sur-pliced back of the Cantoris bass in front of him, Cadogan pursued his way at a solemn and deliberate shuffle to the vestry.

Once inside, both he and Fen pushed their way rapidly through the giggling choirboys and out of the door which led into the north quadrangle. The chaplain glowered malevolently. 'Quiet!' he said to the boys, and pronounced the final prayer. At the end of it a thought struck him.

'And send down, we pray,' he added, 'upon the Professors of this ancient and noble University a due sense of the dignity of Thy house and of their own dignity. *Amen.*'

There was no trace of the girl in the quadrangle. Parsons had seen nothing of her, nor had one or two idling under-graduates whom Fen questioned. St Giles' was a blank in either direction.

'Isn't there something,' Cadogan said, 'which lawyers call a material witness? Well, this girl seems to be an – '

Fen interrupted. His lean, ruddy face was perplexed, and his hair stood up more than ever. 'She must be somewhere in the college, but at the same time I don't see how we can search every room in the place ... Let's go through to the south quadrangle.'

They were not in luck's way. The south quadrangle, with its rococo fountain in the centre and its Jacobean colon-nades, was deserted except for a lounging youth, the posses-sor of spots, a floppy red neck-tie, and green corduroy trousers. From his stammering adolescent embarrassment they got no information whatever.

'Well, we seem to have lost her,' said Cadogan. 'What about some lunch?' He hated missing meals.

'Of course, it may be another instance of the most obvious

place,' Fen answered, ignoring this summons to the flesh-pots. 'That is, the chapel. Let's go back there.'

'Some lunch would be very nice.'

'Damn it, she can't have got far. Come on, and stop moaning like an animal about your food. It's disgusting.'

So they returned to the chapel. In it, nothing and nobody. Nor yet in the vestry. From the vestry there runs a passage wholly cut off from the light, which leads into a sort of paved hall where one or two of the Fellows of the college have rooms. There is a switch, but no one can ever find it, and no one ever bothers to put it on. It was rather incautiously that Fen and Cadogan entered this brief black gully. Too late, when he felt an arm clamped about his waist from behind like a steel vice, when he heard a sudden muffled exclamation from Fen, did Cadogan remember Scylla and Charybdis. Those unimportant decorations of their pursuit had suddenly burst through the haze of facetious comment into a dangerous actuality. On the two branches of Cadogan's carotid artery, running beneath the ears, a thumb and forefinger were powerfully and expertly pressed. He tried to cry out, and failed. In the few moments which elapsed before he lost consciousness, he was aware of a faint, a ridiculously faint scuffling beside him. Twisting his head from side to side, in a vain attempt to escape that angry grip, his eyes darkened.

6. The Episode of the Worthy Carman

'Fen steps in,' said Fen. 'The Return of Fen. A Don Dares Death (A Gervase Fen Story).'

Cadogan moaned and opened his eyes. He was surprised to find that this action made no difference to his vision at all, except that a pattern of green and purple stars disappeared and was replaced by one of orange golf-balls. The background was as black as ever. He closed his eyes, so that the golf-balls were banished and the stars reinstated, and moaned again, rather more self-consciously this time. Beside him Fen's voice droned on. He became painfully aware of his physical body, bit by bit; he experimented with moving parts of it, but did not get very far with this, as his hands and feet were tied. Then he shook his head and felt suddenly much better. Moreover, he had not, as he initially suspected, been struck blind; over to his left there showed a thin line of white light.

'Murder Stalks the University,' said Fen. 'The Blood on the Mortarboard. Fen Strikes Back.'

'What's that you're saying?' Cadogan asked in a faint, rather gurgling voice.

'My dear fellow, are you all right? I was making up titles for Crispin.'

'Where are we?'

'I think we're in the cupboard at the end of the passage where they attacked us. I'm an idiot not to have taken more care. Are you tied up?'

'Yes.'

'So am I. But it must have been rather a hurried job, and it ought to be easy enough to get loose.'

'All right, Houdini, get on with it.'

'Very well,' said Fen, pained. 'You think of some way of getting us out of here.'

'Make a noise. Shout.'

'I've made every sort of noise. The trouble is, there's seldom anyone about here, particularly at lunch-time. Wilkes and Burrows have rooms outside, but Wilkes is deaf and Burrows is always gadding about in London. We shall simply have to wait until someone comes. This part of the college is too isolated for any noise to be heard elsewhere.'

'All the same, I think we ought to try.'

'How tiresome you are . . . Well, what shall we do?'

'We ought to shout, "Help", oughtn't we? And batter our feet on the door.'

'Very well, only be careful you don't kick me.'

They banged and shouted for some time, but without result.

'We might as well save our breath, I suppose,' Cadogan said at last. 'What do you think the time is?'

'Only about ten or five to two. I never went under completely, and I was vaguely conscious all along of what was going on. I came round properly almost as soon as they'd got us in here.'

'There's something sticking into my bottom.'

'This is interesting, you know' – in the darkness Fen's voice assumed a faintly pedagogic tinge – 'because it seems to indicate that if we'd caught that girl she could have told us something important; and Scylla and Charybdis were obviously out to stop us hearing it. Also, I have a nasty feeling that at the moment they may be busy silencing her . . . ' His voice faded away.

After a time he resumed: 'Rosseter, or the fellow who knocked you on the head, could have set them on to us. My money is distinctly on the latter.'

'Sharman?'

'No – he never moved from the bar after we'd met him. If he'd recognized you (and made the arrangement beforehand) he wouldn't have talked so freely. Sharman is out.'

There was a long and gloomy silence. In their cramped

position, both men were beginning to get pins and needles. Cadogan's mouth was dry and his head aching and he wished for a cigarette.

'Let's play "Unreadable Books",' he suggested.

'All right. *Ulysses*.'

'Yes. Rabelais.'

'Yes. *Tristram Shandy*.'

'Yes. *The Golden Bowl*.'

'Yes. *Rasselas*.'

'No, I like that.'

'Good God. *Clarissa*, then.'

'Yes. *Titus* – '

'Shut up a minute. I think I can hear someone coming.'

There were, in fact, footsteps approaching on the stone floor outside – light and erratic footsteps.

'Now, all together,' said Fen briskly. 'One ... two ... three ... ' They let out a deafening, horrible noise. ' "*Like a wind*," ' Fen quoted reflectively, ' "*that shrills all night in a waste land where no one comes ...*" '

The footsteps wavered, came near, stopped. The key turned in the lock, the door of the cupboard opened, and a flood of daylight made them blink. A small, deaf, and very aged don, wearing his gown, peered in.

'A rat!' he squeaked dramatically. 'A rat i' the arras!' He made motions of plunging a sword into them, and this exasperated Fen.

'Wilkes!' Fen said. 'For God's sake let us out of here.'

'What do you think you're up to, eh?' Wilkes asked.

'Untie us, you silly old man,' Fen shouted at him in annoyance.

'Some babyish prank, I suppose,' Wilkes proceeded without perturbation. 'Heh. Well, I suppose someone has to save you from the consequence of your follies.' With shaky but determined fingers, he attacked the knot of the handkerchief which was tied round Fen's wrists. 'All this detecting, that's what it is. People who play with fire must expect to be burned, heh.'

'Prosing away . . . ' Fen grumbled. He untied the thick

string from his ankles, and hoisted himself stiffly out of the cupboard. 'What's the time, Wilkes?'

'Half past kissing time,' said Wilkes. 'Time to kiss again.' He freed Cadogan's wrists. The college clock whirred and struck two. Cadogan extricated himself and stood upright, feeling very groggy.

'Now, listen, Wilkes,' said Fen with great earnestness, 'because this is important –'

'Can't hear a word.'

'I said THIS IS IMPORTANT.'

'What's important?'

'I haven't told you yet.'

'I know you haven't; that's why I asked. Heh.' Wilkes rubbed his hands together delightedly and capered about on the stone paving. Fen stared at him malignantly. 'But you needn't think I don't know. It's that girl you've been chasing. I saw you.'

'Yes, yes. Have you seen *her*?'

'Casanova Fen.'

'Oh, my fur and whiskers.'

'I saw her,' said Wilkes, 'when I was coming in here.'

'*Well?*' Fen could not contain his impatience.

'The bogles have got her.'

'No, really, Wilkes. This is desperately urgent – '

'Heh,' said Wilkes. 'Hah. Urgent, eh? I don't believe a word of it. Anyway, she was in the quadrangle when I came over, talking to a couple of thugs. They seemed in a hurry to get her away – '

He got no further, for Fen and Cadogan had gone. As they pounded through stone-flagged corridors and Gothic arches, to emerge into the front quadrangle beneath the decaying stone bust of the founder, Cadogan, puffing and groaning with the effort, envied Fen his unexpected athletic ability. The undergraduates who had lunched in hall were wandering back to their rooms, but no outsider was to be seen. A united rush took them to the gate, and showed them, on the opposite side of St Giles', the girl, the Dalmatian, and the two men in the act of boarding a black Humber sedan which stood there. They ran into the road, shouting and waving, but the only effect of this was to hasten matters. The doors were rapidly closed, the engine started, and the big car moved off up the Banbury road.

'Lily Christine!' said Fen, like one invoking a genie. 'Where is Lily Christine?' he demanded more peremptorily on perceiving no sign of the car.

'You left her outside the "Mace and Sceptre",' Cadogan reminded him.

'Oh, my dear paws,' Fen exclaimed disgustedly. He stared up and down the road. If there had been a car parked he would certainly have stolen it, but there was not. And the only vehicle heading in the Banbury direction was a large eight-wheeled lorry. None the less, he hailed it, and it rather surprisingly stopped.

' 'Ullo,' said the driver to Cadogan. 'You're that mad bloke I picked up last night. *Telegraph poles.*' He laughed a mellow, reminiscent laugh.

'Hello,' said Cadogan. 'We want to chase a black Humber – look, you can still see it.'

The driver looked. 'Godelpus,' he said. 'What do yer think this thing is – a ruddy tornado? Not but what,' he appended modestly, 'she won't do a fair lick if yer don't mind breakin' a few bones over it.'

Cadogan looked desperately up the road, but no other vehicle was in sight. He became aware that Fen was engaged in a muted altercation with old Wilkes, who had just scampered up. 'No, no, Wilkes,' he was saying. 'You'll only be a terrible hindrance. Go back to your rooms.' He flapped his hands at Wilkes, shooing him away.

'For heaven's sake, come on,' said Cadogan impatiently, 'or we might as well not go at all.' With a good deal of bickering, the three of them scrambled up into the cabin, and the lorry started.

It certainly could move. The effect was something like vibro-electric massage between two mill-stones.

'She's empty now,' the driver explained, as the speed-ometer needle wavered on forty. They went over a rut and he bounced into the air and swore. 'That blasted car's out of sight. We'll never catch 'er.'

Fen seemed disposed to agree. Owing to the exigencies of space in the lorry's cabin, he was obliged to have Wilkes on his knee, and he had left no one in doubt as to his feelings about this arrangement. His temper was not improved by Wilkes's evident pleasure at the situation. Cadogan had begun to want his lunch again. The driver was relatively impassive, apparently regarding such invasions of his cabin as all in the day's work. They made an odd spectacle.

'I can't think why you had to come, Wilkes,' Fen grumbled bitterly. 'You're only getting in the way.'

'Pah,' said Wilkes contemptuously. 'What's it all about? Eh? You just tell me that. Heh.' He banged his head on the roof. ' Damn,' he said. 'Damn, damn, damn, *blast*.'

The houses of the Banbury road fled by them. They were getting into more open country now, and the lorry was doing fifty, regardless of the speed limit. But still, as Fen reminded them, it was custom more honoured in the breach than the observance. 'What's the betting that car's turned off somewhere along here?' he added.

'About a hundred to one, I should imagine,' Cadogan replied. 'But it's a nice ride, anyway.'

'What?' said Wilkes.

'I said it was a nice ride.'

'I'm glad you think so,' said Wilkes huffily. 'If you had this man's bony knees sticking into you, you wouldn't be so pleased with yourself.'

They came to a cross-roads where there was an A.A. man, and the driver slowed down.

' 'Ere, mate,' he called. 'You seen a black 'Umber go by 'ere?'

'The cops 'll 'ave yer,' said the A.A. man. 'The cops 'll 'ave yer if yer go on at that speed. Breakin' the lor.'

'Never mind that, cocky,' said the driver. 'What abaht that 'Umber? You see it?'

'Coupla minutes ago,' the A.A. man conceded reluctantly. 'Drivin' like a bloody maniac. 'E turned left.'

Satisfied, the driver swung the wheel round, and they

roared off in the direction which had been indicated. Soon they were away from all houses except for an occasional cottage or farm. The fields stretched flat on either side, with a low range of hills on the northern horizon. Several times they passed over narrow, humped bridges spanning little winding streams, bordered with willows and alders. The hedges were white and fluffy with clematis, dark with ripe blackberries. The sun of that lovely Indian summer glowed hot overhead, and the sky, a porcelain blue, was cloudless.

'Industrial civilization,' said the driver unexpectedly, 'is the curse of our age.' Cadogan stared at him. 'We've lorst touch with Nachur. We're all pallid.' He gazed with severity at Fen's ruddy countenance. 'We've lorst touch' – he paused threateningly – 'with the *body*.'

'I haven't,' said Fen acrimoniously, jogging Wilkes.

Enlightenment was upon Cadogan. 'Still reading Lawrence?' he asked.

'Ar,' said the driver affirmatively. 'Thass right.' He felt about him and produced a greasy edition of *Sons and Lovers* for general inspection, then he put it away again. 'We've lorst touch,' he continued, 'with *sex* – the grand primeval energy; the dark, mysterious source of life. Not,' he added confidentially, 'that I've ever exactly felt that – beggin' your pardon – when I've been in bed with the old woman. But that's because industrial civilization 'as got me in its clutches.'

'Oh, I shouldn't say that.'

The driver raised one hand in warning. 'But it 'as. A soul-less machine, that's all I am – nothin' but a soul-less machine – ' He broke off. "Ere, wot do we do nah?'

They were approaching a fork in the road, the first turning they had come to since leaving the A.A. man. There was a cottage, set well back from the road, on their left, but no human being from whom they could inquire about the black Humber. It was a hopeless dilemma.

'Let's go left,' Cadogan suggested. 'After all, Gollancz is publishing this book. I wonder – '

What he wondered they never knew. For at that moment,

from the cottage which they were passing, they heard a shot.

'Halt, driver!' Cadogan shouted excitedly. 'Halt, in the name of Lawrence!' The driver pulled up sharply, flinging them back in their seats. Wilkes hurled his arms round Fen's neck.

'Clinging on,' Fen groused, 'like the Old Man of the Sea – '

But he did not continue. Something pushed its way through the thick hedge and out on to the grass verge. It was a Dalmatian, and there was a spreading red stain on its side. It took a few shaky steps towards them, barked once, and then whimpered and lay down on its side and died.

Sally Carstairs was hating life – the more so as up till now life had always treated her so well. Not financially, of course; she and her mother had had little enough to manage on since her father died. (But somehow they had managed, and made a comfortable home, and got on well together, apart from ordinary small squabbles.) Not, for that matter, in the way of riotous enjoyment and halcyon days; working at Lennox's, the drapers, was scarcely an ennobling or creative occupation. But apart from these handicaps, life was almost compelled to treat Sally Carstairs well; she took it easily in her stride, and was not daunted and abashed by the small doubts and anxieties which afflict *hoi polloi*; she had, in fact, a total lack of affectation, an unfeigned interest in the world and in other people, and a superabundance of that natural vitality on which (though she did not know it), a lorry-driver was at this moment lecturing two dons and a major English poet. 'You're a noble filly,' a middle-aged man had once told her. 'Golly, what an insult,' Sally had said, firmly removing his hands from the direction in which they were straying. But there had been an element of truth in it; Sally had that high nervous energy and air of first-rate physical breeding which is rare in any stratum of society, but most often found in what are euphemistically termed the lower classes; and that she had no pretension to intellect was very largely beside the point. Life had been a good and pleasant thing to her – until last night.

She looked round the small parlour of the cottage. It was ugly and badly furnished – the very opposite of her own little parlour at home. The chairs and table and cupboards were of cheap wood, stained a dull, depressing brown; the covers and curtains were a sickly green, and very thread-bare; and the pictures on the walls gave evidence of a cheer-less religiosity – St Sebastian transfixed by arrows, hapless Jonah being tumbled overboard, and (more surprisingly) a voluptuous Susannah disporting herself before the eyes of two bored-looking Elders. Sally shuddered elaborately, and then, becoming conscious that she really was shivering, sat down with her bag on her knee and tried to pull herself together by gazing through the grimy, leaded window at the neglected garden outside. In the next room, she could hear the two men conferring together in low tones. If only she weren't so helpless and alone . . . But she hadn't dared say anything to her mother.

Her mind went back over the events of the day. She had not intended to go to that rehearsal of the Handel Society, though she knew she ought to: she had been far, far too worried to want to sing. But that man with the cold eyes had shouted out something about her, and she had pan-icked. After all, they *might* have been the police. And then when the taller of the two, whom she vaguely remembered having seen about the town, turned out to be Professor Fen, she had been more alarmed than ever, though she remem-bered being vaguely surprised at the same time, that a man whose exploits as a detective were so well known should wear such an amiable aspect; adding to herself afterwards: 'Idiot! Whatever did you expect?' The chase had been a nightmare, even when it became obvious that they weren't the police (they would certainly have stopped the rehearsal if they had been). But she had been to St Christopher's chapel before, and knew that if they followed her in there she would have a chance of eluding them at the end of the service; in any case she was so alarmed that she hadn't been able to think of any other way. She had not, at the time, asked herself what good this headlong flight was supposed to be doing; it had been instinctive, and she was inclined to think now that it had also been absurd. Still . . .

Then there were the other two men, the ones who were with her now. They had caught up with her just after she left the chapel, when she thought she really was free again. But despite their appearance – 'like something out of a bad thriller,' she told herself – she had felt some confidence in them. For one thing, they spoke politely, and Sally instinctively trusted courtesy. The older of the two – the one with the squashed nose, who was obviously the leader – had said:

'Excuse me, miss, but I'm afraid you're being bothered by those two men. Don't let them trouble you – they're not the police, you know, and they haven't any information, not about what went on last night.'

She turned to him sharply. 'Do you know – '

'A little bit, miss. Berlin told us – you remember Berlin?' She nodded. 'And as a matter of fact, miss, it was him that sent us out to find you. Seems he's discovered something about last night which pretty well clears you. He wants us to take you along for a talk with him now.'

She hesitated, torn between a sudden, overwhelming relief and an irrational anxiety. 'I – Where is it? Is it far?'

'No, miss, it's out Banbury way. We've got a car outside, and it won't take ten minutes.' Then, noticing her hesitation: 'Come, come, miss, there's no reason for us to wish you any harm, is there? From what I've heard, you're in such a mess already that nothing could make it worse. And look at the thing this way: even if Berlin was the murderer – which he isn't – the last thing he'd want to do would be to harm the one person that hasn't got a watertight alibi. Isn't that true?'

She winced, but the reasoning seemed sound, so in the end she assented. 'What about those two who were following me?'

The younger man grinned. 'That's all right, miss. We set them off on a false scent. They'll be well away by now.'

So she had gone with them. Someone had shouted at them as they were getting into the car, but they had started off so quickly that she had been unable to see who it was. And now – well, now they had arrived, and it seemed odd that there was no one here to meet them. The men had said that he must have been delayed, and had suggested she wait; they had then excused themselves and gone out to talk. And now she no longer wanted to wait, and was uneasy, and hated the ugly little room she was in.

'Danny!' she called.

The Dalmatian, which had been wandering restlessly about the room, came and put its head in her lap. She stroked and patted it, and then made up her mind that at all costs she must leave this place. Earlier on she had tried the windows and found them barred; so the only way out was through the tiny hall where the two men were talking. Mistrust had grown so large in her that it was with great slowness and hesitation that she opened the door. She caught some such words as 'Always be able to find out who owns this place,' and then they turned to look at her.

They were not the same men, except outwardly. Their whole attitude had changed. The younger of them, she saw, was greedily appraising her body, and there was something in the eyes of the other which was worse.

'I think – I think I must go now,' she said weakly, and knew as she spoke that it was hopeless. 'Will you drive me back to Oxford?'

'No, miss. I don't think you can go yet. In fact, not for a long time yet,' the older man said. 'You're going to be kept here for quite a while.'

She made a dash for the door, but the younger man was quicker. He flung his arm round her and put one hand over her mouth. She bit and kicked and fought furiously, for Sally was not the kind of girl who faints when in physical danger. The dog snarled and barked, biting at the man's heels. 'For Christ's sake,' he shouted at the other, 'get that animal out of the way!' There was a sudden, violent explosion and a scream of pain from the dog. For a moment

Sally got her mouth free. 'You devils!' she half choked. 'Danny . . . go! Go, boy!' Then again the hot, sweaty hand stifled speech. The dog hesitated, and slunk away into the back part of the cottage.

'Stop that animal!' the younger man bawled. 'No – come and help me with this bitch.'

Interlocked, the three swayed together in the little hall. Sally's strength was ebbing, and they had got her left arm twisted agonizingly behind her back. She made one last attempt to break away, and then felt a hand crushing her neck. In a very few moments the world went black.

Sally returned to consciousness feeling less ill than she might well have expected. It is true that her head ached and that her body felt as if it did not belong to her, but both these disabilities seemed to be clearing up rapidly. Her first action was to make sure that her skirt was decorously over her knees; her second was to say 'golly!' in rather a small voice.

She was in the parlour again, and lying on a couch which smelt of moth-balls. Around her, in various stages of inactivity, were four men, two of whom she had seen before. Gervase Fen, the hair sticking up like porcupine quills from the crown of his head, was examining the picture of Susannah and the Elders with attention; Richard Cadogan was watching her anxiously with his bandage askew, so that he looked like a Roman emperor after a prolonged and vehement debauch; Wilkes stood in the background, pouring whisky into a glass and drinking it himself; and the lorry-driver, breathing heavily, was engaged in a general rodomontade.

'. . . the bastards,' he was saying. 'I might 'a' known there'd be a back drive aht of 'ere. No use trying to stop 'em, o' course; any'ow one of 'em 'ad a gun.' He was about to spit with disgust, but, seeing that Sally's eyes were open, desisted. 'Well, miss,' he said, ' 'ow are yer nah?'

'Gosh,' said Sally, and sat up. As there were no ill results of this, she gained confidence. 'Did you rescue me?'

'Hardly that,' said Cadogan. 'Our two friends vanished in their car as soon as they saw us coming. We found you lying in the hall. Are you all right?'

'I – yes, I think I'm all right, thanks.'

Fen concluded his inspection of Susannah, and turned round. 'I think they did the same tr – ' He broke off. 'Here, Wilkes, stop drinking that whisky.'

'There isn't very much,' said Wilkes reproachfully.

'Well, isn't that all the more reason why you shouldn't drink it all, you greedy, alcoholic old man?'

'It's all right, honestly,' said Sally. 'And I hate whisky, anyway.'

'Give me some, then,' said Fen.

'Danny.' Sally's eyes were anxious. 'What happened to him? My dog, I mean.'

'I'm afraid he's dead,' said Cadogan. 'Shot.'

She nodded, and for a moment there was a hint of tears in her eyes. 'I know.'

'If it hadn't been for him we shouldn't have known you were here.' Which wasn't true, Cadogan reflected – the shot would have brought them in in any case. But there was no point in labouring this; the dog had done its job.

'And now,' said Fen kindly, 'will you tell us what it's all about?'

But here, unexpectedly, they came up against a brick wall. Sally was a very frightened girl. She had trusted one set of people today, and she was not going to trust another, however much they seemed to wish her well. And besides, what she had to say she had sworn to keep secret for ever – for her own good. Not Fen, nor Cadogan, nor Wilkes (who admittedly was not much use), nor the lorry-driver, nor any of them in combination, could get a word from her. Warnings, reassurances, and cajolery were alike useless. She was grateful, she said, very grateful, but she couldn't tell them anything; and that was all. At last, Fen, muttering to himself, slipped out into the little hall and rang up the 'Mace and Sceptre'.

'Mr Hoskins?' he said when he was connected. 'This is

Fen speaking. I have another job for you, if you can manage it.'

'Yes, sir?' said Mr Hoskins's melancholy voice.

'There's an attractive young woman here we can't persuade to trust us. Can you do anything about it?'

'It is possible.'

'Good. Come at once. Come in Lily Christine III – she's outside the hotel. You carry on up the Banbury Road until you get to a cross-roads with an A.A. man. There you turn left, and keep straight on over three bridges until you get to a fork. There's a cottage on the left just before you reach the fork, and we're in there. You can't mistake it.'

'Very good, sir. And about Mr Sharman – '

'Oh, yes. Well?'

'It's just on closing time, sir, and we shall have to be leaving. However, he seems to have enjoyed my company' – Mr Hoskins scarcely seemed to find this credible – 'and he's given me his address, so that I can visit him.'

'Splendid. Abandon Mr Sharman to his fate, then. Is he very drunk?'

'Very drunk.'

'Well, good-bye.'

'Good-bye.'

Fen was just leaving the phone when a thought struck him, and he turned back again to dial the number of the Chief Constable.

'Hello.'

'Hello. It's me again.'

'Oh, Lord, is there no justice . . . ? What is the matter now? Look here, Gervase, you're not harbouring this fellow Cadogan, are you?'

'How could you imagine such a thing . . . ? I want to know who's the owner of a cottage.'

'What for?'

'Never you mind what for.'

'What's it called, then?'

'What's it called?' Fen bellowed into the parlour.

'What's what called?' Cadogan answered.

'This cottage.'

'Oh . . . "The Elms", I noticed on the way in.'

' "The Elms," ' said Fen into the phone.

'I wish you wouldn't shout like that. It gave me quite a start. What road's it in?'

'B507, just where it joins B309. Somewhere between Tackley and Wootton.'

'All right. I'll ring you back.'

'I thought you had a private line to the police station. Can't you use that?'

'Oh, so I have, I'd forgotten. Wait a minute.' There was a long pause. Finally:

'Here it is. The cottage belongs to a Miss Alice Winkworth. Does that satisfy you?'

'Yes,' said Fen thoughtfully. 'I rather think it does. Thanks.'

'Gervase, it's a common view that *Measure for Measure* is about chastity – '

'Very common indeed,' said Fen. 'Quite reprehensible. Good-bye.' He rang off.

Back in the parlour, he explained discreetly that transport was arriving for them; at which the driver, who had been showing signs of impatience for the last few minutes, said he must go. 'If I dally 'ere much longer,' he explained, 'I'll lose my job. That's what'll 'appen.' They all thanked him. 'It's a pleasure,' he said airily. 'Not but what you're probably all cracked. Any'ow, good luck with it, whatever it is.' He winked at Cadogan. 'Dawgs,' he said, and went out laughing quietly to himself.

Since there was nothing to be said or done, they stood or sat about virtually in silence until a devastating noise, followed by a single loud explosion, heralded the arrival of Mr Hoskins.

He was superb. He offered Sally a chocolate, and settled his large form into a chair with an air which inspired confidence even in Cadogan. They all discreetly retired from the room (the necessity of explaining matters to Wilkes was obviated by the fact that he had finished the whisky and gone out to look for more). And in less than ten minutes Mr Hoskins came to fetch them, and they returned to find Sally's blue eyes sparkling and her mouth curved in a smile.

'Golly, I've been an ass,' she said. 'I did want to tell you – honestly – but it's so awful and I've been so worried . . . An old lady was murdered last night.' She shivered a little and went on quickly: 'I didn't kill her.'

'All right,' said Fen. 'Who did?'

Sally looked up at him. 'That's the awful thing,' she replied. 'I haven't the slightest idea.'

7. The Episode of the Nice Young Lady

Fen remained cheerfully unperturbed by this rather disappointing utterance. 'If you were there when Miss Tardy was killed – '

'You know who it was?' Sally broke in. 'Has the body been found?'

'Found,' said Fen grandiosely, 'and lost again. Yes, we know a little about it, but not much. Anyway, let's have your story – from the beginning.' He turned to Cadogan. 'I suppose there's no chance of its having been accident or suicide? Considering the other circumstances, it's scarcely probable, but we may as well clear as much ground as possible straight off.'

Cadogan, casting his mind back to the dark, airless little sitting-room in the Iffley Road, shook his head. 'Certainly not accident,' he said slowly. 'That cord round her neck had been carefully knotted. As to suicide – well, is it even *possible* to commit suicide like that? Anyway, let's hear what Miss – Miss – '

'Sally Carstairs,' said the girl. 'Call me Sally. Everyone does. And you want to hear what happened. Golly, it's queer, but I honestly want to tell someone now . . . Have you got a cigarette?'

Fen produced his case, and a lighter. Sally sat in silence for a moment, frowning a little and blowing out smoke. The afternoon sun glowed on her fair hair, and threw into relief her determined little chin. She looked perplexed, but no longer afraid. Wilkes returned from his fruitless search for alcohol, and, being adjured to silence by Fen, sat down with surprising meekness. Mr Hoskins blinked his sleepy, melancholy grey eyes. Cadogan was trying to put his bandage straight. And Fen leaned his tall, lanky form against the window-sill, his hands in his pockets, a cigarette in his mouth, and his pale blue eyes interested and watchful.

'You see, it really all started more than a year ago,' Sally said. 'It was July, I think, and very hot, and there were only two days to go to my fortnight's holiday. I know it was a Tuesday, too, because I'm always alone in the shop on Tuesday mornings, and there was only five minutes to go before I locked up for the lunch hour – '

On the big plate-glass window a bluebottle buzzed insistently, like an alarm clock which refuses to be switched off. The volume of traffic in the Cornmarket had abated. The sun blazed on the pink and blue underwear in the window, gradually draining it of colour, but inside the shop it was dark and cavernous and cool. Sally, folding away black silk knickers in a large red cardboard box, paused to push back a lock of hair from her forehead and then went on with her work. How anyone could wear the horrid ugly things was beyond her. Anyway it was nearly lunch-time, and this was her afternoon off; in a minute or two she could lock the shop, leave the key for Janet Gibbs at No 27 and go home to her lunch and her book. Then in the afternoon she would drive up to Wheatley with Philip Page, who was safe if rather pathetic, and in the evening go with Janet to a flick. It would not, she reflected, be exactly riotous fun, but at all events it wouldn't be the shop, and in any case she would soon be on holiday and away from Oxford for a bit. She devoutly hoped that no one would take it into their heads to buy anything at this stage. It would mean closing late and then gobbling her lunch and rushing back to the 'Lamb and Flag' to meet Philip for a drink before they set off, and she'd left herself little enough time as it was...

A big car drew up outside, and she sighed inwardly as she heard the click of the shop-door. Still, she smiled and went forward to help the old lady who came in on the arm of her chauffeur. She was certainly a phenomenally ugly old lady: she was fat, for one thing, and she had a long nose, and her brown face was scored with a thousand deep wrinkles; she looked like a witch, and moreover, had a witch's temperament, for she commented with feeble petulance on the clumsiness of Sally and the chauffeur before they succeeded in getting her settled.

'Now, child,' she commanded. 'Let me see some handkerchiefs.'

She looked at handkerchiefs; she looked at handkerchiefs until Sally could have screamed. Nothing pleased her: the linen of this kind was of too poor a quality, the size of this made them look like sheets, the frills on these were ridiculously over-elaborate, these were so plain that they were fit only for jam-pot covers, the hem of these others was badly sewn and would come undone in no time, and these would be perfect but for the initials in the corner. The clock crept on, to a quarter, to twenty past one. The chauffeur, who was evidently used to this sort of thing, stared at the ceiling. And Sally, mastering her impatience with extreme difficulty, smiled, and was polite, and ran from the shelves to the counter with ever more boxes of handkerchiefs. But she nearly (not quite) lost control of her temper when at last the old lady said:

'No, I don't think there's anything here I want. All this has tired me very much. I have to take great care of myself, because of my heart, you see.' The self-conscious parade of feebleness repelled Sally. 'Jarvis!' The chauffeur moved forward. 'Come and help me out of this place.'

But as she was going she turned again to Sally, who was now faced with the additional delay of getting all the handkerchiefs back to their proper places, and said unexpectedly: 'I suppose I've delayed you terribly, my dear. You'll be wanting your lunch.'

'Not at all, madam,' said Sally, smiling (with something of an effort, it must be confessed). 'I'm sorry there was nothing you liked.'

The old lady regarded her intently for a moment. 'You're a courteous girl,' she said. 'Courteous and considerate. I like people who are courteous and considerate, and there aren't many of them nowadays. I wonder – '

She was interrupted by a scratching on the other side of a door leading out of the shop, behind the counter; and Sally was shocked to see that she started and trembled violently.

'What's that?' she whispered.

Sally stepped back to the door. 'It's only my dog,' she said, herself startled by the violence of the old lady's reaction. 'Danny. I expect he wants his dinner.'

'Oh.' The old lady got a grip on herself with difficulty. 'Let him in, my dear.'

Sally opened the door, and Danny, then a six-months-old puppy, frisked towards them.

'Well, well,' said the old lady. 'A small, spotted dog. Jarvis, pick him up so that I can pat him.' The chauffeur obeyed, and Danny, whose taste in human beings was at this stage unexclusive, licked him heartily on the nose.

'There's my pretty . . . ' The old lady chuckled suddenly. 'And you're the young lady of Ryde,' she said to Sally.

Sally, not knowing what else to do, smiled again.

'Will you be here tomorrow, child, if I come in? It won't be about handkerchiefs this time.'

'Yes. Yes, I shall.'

'I shall see you then. Now, I won't delay you any longer . . . Jarvis, take my arm.' Slowly the old lady hobbled out.

That, for the moment, was that. But on the next day the old lady did come in, as promised, took Sally's name and address, and gave her an envelope.

'Keep this,' she said, 'and don't lose it. Do you see the *Oxford Mail* every day?'

'Yes.'

'Go on seeing it, then. Look in the personal column every day without fail. When you see the name Ryde – not your own name, but Ryde – in an advertisement, take that envelope to Lloyds Bank and give it to the manager; he'll give you another one in exchange. Take that to the address given in the advertisement. Do you understand?'

'Yes, I understand, but –'

'It's a little trinket.' The old lady's manner was curiously emphatic. 'Not worth more than a few shillings, but I want to leave it to you in my will. It has a great sentimental value to me. Now, will you promise to do all this?'

'Yes, I promise. It's very kind of you –'

'On your word of honour?'

'On my word of honour.'

And that was the last Sally ever saw of her.

She put the envelope away in a drawer, unopened, and only remembered it when she looked down the personal column of the *Oxford Mail*. This became a rather meaningless ritual, but she continued to do it just the same, for it took no trouble and very little time; and she was surprised to find that on one occasion when she had forgotten, and thought the paper had been burnt, she was really quite agitated. Which was absurd, of course, the whole thing was too fairy-godmotherish to be real, and, as far as she came to any conclusion at all, she decided that the old lady must have been mad.

And, then, one day more than a year later, the advertisement actually appeared: 'Ryde, Leeds, West, Mold, Berlin. – Aaron Rosseter, Solicitor, 193A Cornmarket.' Sally was so surprised that for a moment she could do nothing but stare at it; then she pulled herself together and glanced at her watch. The shop would be closing soon for lunch, and she would go to the bank straight away. Of course it would look extremely idiotic if the whole thing was a practical joke, but that had to be risked. In any case she was too curious to leave matters where they were.

And the thing happened precisely as the old lady had said: in exchange for her envelope she was given a large, bulky brown one, and emerged into the busy rush of Carfax, feeling dazed, with a dream-like sense of unreality. She went straight to the address given in the advertisement, but the office was closed for lunch, and so she had to return later in the day.

She disliked Mr Rosseter the moment she saw him, and it

was with considerable mistrust that she delivered up the envelope to him. He was very polite, very obsequious; he asked questions about her occupation, her family, her income. And finally said:

'Well, I have a very good piece of news for you, Miss Carstairs: you have been left a large sum of money under the will of Miss Snaith.'

Sally stared at him. 'Do you mean the old lady who – '

Mr Rosseter shook his head. 'I'm afraid I'm not aware of the circumstances in which you made Miss Snaith's acquaintance. There, in any event, is the fact. There will be another six months before the estate is wound up, but you may rely on me to communicate with you again as soon as possible.'

Sally said: 'But there must be some mistake.'

'No mistake at all, Miss Carstairs. These papers prove your claim. Of course, there will be some small delay before you actually receive the money, but I've no doubt the bank will in the meantime advance any sum you may require.'

'Look,' said Sally desperately. 'I only saw this Miss – Miss Snaith twice in my life. She came into the shop as a customer. Golly, you're not telling me she's left me some money just because she looked at some handkerchiefs and didn't buy any?'

Mr Rosseter whipped off his glasses, polished them with his handkerchief, and replaced them on his nose. 'My late client was a very eccentric old lady, Miss Carstairs – very eccentric indeed. Her actions were seldom what other people would consider reasonable.'

'You're telling me,' said Sally. 'But, anyway, why all this business about the envelopes and the advertisement? Why couldn't she just leave it to me in the ordinary way?'

'Ah, there you've touched on another aspect of her eccentricity. You see, Miss Snaith lived in constant terror of being murdered. It was a mania with her. She took the most elaborate precautions, and lived in a state of seige, even against her own servants and relations. What more natural than in leaving money to strangers she should see to it that they knew nothing of the arrangement beforehand and so, should they perhaps be of a murderous disposition, should have no temptation to – shall we say? – hasten matters.'

'That's right,' said Sally, remembering. 'She told me she was only leaving me a cheap trinket. What a queer old thing she must have been – I feel rather sorry for her, really.' She paused. 'Look, Mr Rosseter: I don't want to seem curious, but I *still* don't see – '

'Where the envelopes come into it? That's very simple. Miss Snaith chose to leave her money in the form of a secret trust – that is to say that in the will *I* was nominated as her heir. The real heirs – as yourself – had then to apply to me for their inheritance. The papers you obtained and of which there are duplicates at the bank, are devised to make sure that I do not wrongfully cheat you of your inheritance.' Mr Rosseter permitted himself a discreet chuckle.

'Oh,' said Sally blankly. 'Oh, I see.' She collected her bag and was getting ready to go, when something else occurred to her. 'And how much do I inherit?'

'In the region of a hundred thousand pounds, Miss Carstairs.'

'I – I don't think I heard – '

Mr Rosseter repeated the sum. Sally was simply dumb-founded: she had never dreamed of anything like this. A hundred thousand! It was astronomical, incredible. Sally was not selfish or prone to pamper herself, but what girl, at a moment like that, would not have seen the beatific vision of frocks, of cars and travel and ease and luxury? Anyhow, Sally did. And she had expected a hundred at the most.

She sat down again, rather suddenly, thinking: this *is* a dream.

'Quite a considerable fortune,' Mr Rosseter pursued amiably. 'I congratulate you, Miss Carstairs. Of course, you will need someone to handle your affairs. May I suggest myself?'

'I – yes, I suppose so. This is all quite a shock, you know.'

It certainly was a shock: so much so, that when Sally left Mr Rosseter's office she had to keep reminding herself that, after all, the interview had been real. It was like trying to persuade someone of something which they *would* not believe was true; and at the same time, being that other, incredulous person as well. A curious, irrational feeling of superstition prevented her from saying anything about it, even to her mother, for Sally had had some experience of counting chickens before they were hatched, and of the disenchantment which sometimes followed. So for the moment she went on with her normal life.

Then, next morning, a letter arrived for her. The address at the head of it was 193A Cornmarket, and apart from the signature it was typewritten. It ran:

DEAR MISS CARSTAIRS

I hope you will forgive my presumption in writing to you in this way, but I was wondering if you would do me a small favour. Another of the beneficiaries under Miss Snaith's will, a Miss Emilia Tardy, is arriving in Oxford by train this evening, and it is important that I should see her at once. Miss Tardy does not know Oxford at all, and, moreover, is rather a helpless old lady. Would it be asking too much of you to meet her and bring her down to my flat in the Iffley Road – No. 474? Of course, I would do so myself, but I shall be unavoidably detained on business, and my clerk, whom I would otherwise have sent, is away on holiday.

The train gets in at 10.12, and Miss Tardy is a plump, elderly lady with gold pince-nez. If it is possible for you to do this kindness, do not trouble to reply to this; if not, would you ring me at my office – Oxford 07022?

With many apologies for troubling you,

Yours truly,

AARON ROSSETER.

It was possible; and Sally went to the station that evening as she had been asked.

In the parlour of the cottage, Sally looked up at her listeners. 'I don't know if I'm making it all frightfully obscure,' she said apologetically.

'Not in the least,' said Fen grimly. 'Certain things are becoming quite crystal clear.'

'*Scoundrel*,' said Wilkes in a surprising outbreak of ethical fervour. Cadogan had sketched out the situation to him while Mr Hoskins had been exercising his wiles.

'What did you do with the letter?' Fen asked.

'I'm afraid I burned it,' said Sally helplessly. 'I didn't think it was important, you see.'

'Oh,' said Fen. 'Well, it can't be helped. You know, I want to be a bit more certain about dates. This is October 5th . . . Just a minute.' He disappeared into the hall, where he could be heard talking into the telephone, and after a while returned. 'I thought so,' he said. 'I've been getting the *Oxford Mail* to go back through their files. Miss Snaith departed this miserable planet six months ago yesterday, that is, on April 4th of this year.'

'So Miss Tardy's lease ran out at midnight last night,' Cadogan interposed.

'Yes – midnight last night. But the more interesting point is that Rosseter's advertisement, which ought to have gone in *today*, went in the day before yesterday – isn't that right?' Sally nodded. 'Two days early, in fact. Go on Sally. We haven't really got to the point yet, have we? Have another cigarette.'

'Not another just now, thanks.' Sally wrinkled her brow. 'No, there's worse to come yet. I met the train, you see, and found Miss Tardy all right, and explained that I was from Mr Rosseter, and she seemed quite to expect it, so that was all right. We got a taxi and drove down to Iffley Road – the train was ten minutes late, by the way, and, of course, it was quite dark by then. I liked Miss Tardy: she'd travelled an awful lot, and talked very interestingly about it, and a lot, too, about some children's homes she was interested in. But I didn't say anything to her about the will.

'Well, Mr Rosseter's flat was just above an awful little toyshop place, and we went in at the door of the shop and up the stairs at the back, like he'd told me, and into the sitting-room at the front. It looked awfully dusty and unoccupied, and we were very surprised that there was no one there. But I thought we must have got the wrong room, so I told Miss Tardy to sit down there a minute – she wasn't in very good health, poor dear, and those steep stairs had exhausted her – and I went to the next door along and knocked. Then I got an awful fright, because a man came out with bandages all over his face: I don't know who he was. But he explained he'd had an accident and burned his face, and that Mr Rosseter wasn't back yet. He apologized for the state the flat was in, too – he said a cistern had burst in Mr Rosseter's own house and he'd had to move into the flat temporarily. Then he said Mr Rosseter had asked him to entertain Miss Tardy until he arrived, and gave his name as Mr Scadmore; so I introduced them and after a bit I left. Or rather, I pretended to leave. Actually, I felt there was something queer about it all – a sort of intuition, I suppose – and I wanted to see Miss Tardy safely out of the house. So I banged the shop-door loudly (it squeaked, too) and settled down to wait a bit in the shop. It was hellish creepy and I didn't really know what I was doing, but somehow I was anxious.

'The first thing I realized was that there were other people in the house besides Miss Tardy and the man who called himself Mr Scadmore. There was a lot of talk and walking about, and then a long silence, and then after about twenty minutes there was quite an outburst of excitement. I wanted to see what was happening, so I crept up the stairs. And then before I could get away Mr Rosseter came down the stairs, and with him a man and a woman, both of them with masks on.

'He stopped dead when he saw me, and said in a shaky sort of voice: "Oh, you're still here, are you? You were very foolish to stay. You'd better come up and see what's happened." I was terrified, but I thought I'd better go up for the sake of Miss Tardy. She – she was lying on the floor, all blue and puffy, with a piece of string round her neck. The man with the bandaged face was bending over her. He – Mr Rosseter – said: "She's been murdered, you see, but you're not going to say anything about it – ever. You keep quiet and you'll get your money and no one will bother you. You see, you were only to get the money if she didn't claim it before midnight, and she's been murdered before she could make a proper legal claim." He talked very quickly, in a dull, monotonous sort of voice, and he was sweating horribly The others all kept their eyes on me all the time, and no one moved. I was cramped and dirty from the shop below, and I felt all itchy, as though there were insects crawling over me.' Sally shivered. 'He said: "Perhaps you killed her. I don't know. It's very convenient for you, and the police will want to know all about it, especially as you brought her here." I said: "But you told me to." He said: "I shall deny it, and no one will believe you. I shall say I didn't send you that letter, and you can't prove I did. These others will all swear you knew perfectly well you were bringing her to her death. I don't get any advantage out of it: you do. They'll believe me rather than you. So you'd better keep quiet. We'll look after things here. All you've got to do is to go home and forget about her and us." So – I – I –'

'So you went home,' Fen put in quietly. 'And jolly sensible too.'

'I've been an awful coward,' Sally said.

'Nonsense. In your position, I should have fled the country. Was there anything else?'

'No, that was really all. I've told it very badly. Oh, I think the man with the bandages round his face was a doctor: and one of the others called him "Berlin". It's one of the names in the advertisement, you know. Those men you chased away told me he'd found something that would clear me. I had to go with them. I remember he was very thin.'

Fen nodded. 'What about the other two?'

'I was really too frightened to notice them much. The woman was plump and oldish, and the man was a weedy, undersized creature. Of course I couldn't see their faces.'

'Sharman?' Cadogan suggested.

'Probably,' said Fen. 'That covers Berlin, and Mold, and

Leeds – presumably the woman, and Ryde – yourself, Sally – and leaves only West out of account. Can you tell us anything about times?'

Sally shook her head. 'I'm sorry. It was all some time between eleven and twelve – I heard midnight striking as I walked home.'

There was a long silence. Then Cadogan said to Fen: 'What do you think happened?'

Fen shrugged. 'Fairly obviously a plot on the part of certain of the residuary legatees, Rosseter abetting, to kill Miss Tardy and prevent her claiming the inheritance. Once she was dead the body would be disposed of, and presumably has been, and everything would go according to plan. You, Sally, were to take Miss Tardy to the toyshop, to avoid any of the actual conspirators being even thus remotely implicated should anything ever be suspected; and afterwards' – he smiled grimly – 'well, you wouldn't think anything more of it, would you? If you did, Rosseter would deny he wrote you that letter, deny everything. In those circumstances, and with no *corpus delicti* and no toyshop, what sort of a case could be made out against anyone, and for what crime? Unfortunately it all went wrong: *(a)* you stayed in the shop instead of going away; *(b)* Cadogan here blundered in and found the body; and *(c)* Cadogan was afterwards seen chasing after you with obvious intent to get information. That being the case, you couldn't be left at large; you had to disappear, too. And you very nearly did. The only thing that mystifies me is why Rosseter should have been so shaken, and why he should have thought you might have killed the woman. It rather suggests . . . No, I don't know what it suggests. Anyway, I'm going back to Oxford to have another talk with Rosseter – and I shall stop at the college on the way to collect a gun.'

8. The Episode of the Eccentric Millionairess

There was one interruption, however, before he was able to carry out this plan. The five of them squeezed into Lily Christine III with great difficulty. Sally sat on Cadogan's knee, which Cadogan rather liked, and they set off, with Fen driving, on a hurried, nerve-tearing passage of the narrow road, bouncing over bridges like a scenic railway, and missing stray livestock and pedestrians by inches. How they failed to mutilate or kill the A.A. man at the junction with the Banbury road Cadogan was never able to imagine; they left him staring after them, too horrified even to call out. Cadogan, in telegrammatic, broken sentences, acquainted Sally and Mr Hoskins with what they knew of the case so far.

'Golly,' said Sally when he had finished; and added a little shyly: 'You do believe what I told you, don't you? I know it sounds fantastic, but –'

'My dear Sally, this is such a wild business I'd believe you if you said you were the Lady of Shalott.'

'You do talk funnily, don't you?' But the words were swept away in the rush of wind and the din of the engine.

'What?' said Cadogan.

Wilkes turned round in the front seat. He could hear better when there was a noise going on. 'She says you talk funnily.'

'Do I?' It had not previously occurred to Cadogan that he talked funnily: the thought disturbed him.

'I didn't mean to be rude,' Sally said. 'What do you do? What's your job, I mean?'

'I'm a poet.'

'Golly.' Sally was impressed. 'I've never met a poet before. You don't look like one.'

'I don't feel like one.'

'I used to read poetry at school,' Sally continued reminiscently. 'There was one bit I liked. It went:

> Annihilating all that's made
> To a green thought in a green shade.

I haven't the foggiest what it means, but it sounds nice, anyway. It was in a book called *Poetry for the Middle Forms* . . . I'm not sitting too hard on you, am I?'

'No, I like it.'

'It must be jolly good fun being a poet,' Sally mused. 'No one to boss you about, and no one to make you work when you don't want to.'

'It'd be all right if one earned any money at it,' Cadogan replied.

'Go on. How much do you earn?'

'From being a poet? About two pounds a week.'

'Golly, that isn't much. Perhaps you aren't very important yet.'

'I think that's probably it.'

This seemed to satisfy Sally, for she sang happily to herself until Fen's mounting a pavement with two wheels while taking a particularly sharp corner diverted all their minds from the subject.

It was shortly after this that the interruption occurred. As they neared Oxford, shops began to appear, traffic increased, and the signs of undergraduate habitation became more numerous. Just before they arrived at the turning which leads off to Lady Margaret Hall, Cadogan, who had been staring vacantly at the landscape, suddenly shouted to Fen to stop, and Fen did this so suddenly that they were nearly overwhelmed by a following car, which fortunately circumvented them, though not without abuse. Fen twisted round in his seat and said:

'What in God's name is the matter?'

Cadogan pointed, and their eyes followed the direction of his arm. A hundred yards or so behind where they had stopped was a toyshop.

'I *think* it's the same one,' said Cadogan, clambering out of the car. 'In fact, I'm almost sure . . . ' The others followed him, and they clustered round the window.

'Yes,' said Cadogan. 'Because I remember thinking how ugly that doll with the cracked face looked.'

'I remember it, too,' said Sally.

'And there's that box of balloons I knocked over . . . Anyway, it looks like it.' Cadogan searched for the name above the shop. It was 'Helston', in faded white letters, elaborately scrolled.

He and Fen went inside. The shop was inhabited only by a dusty young man with a shock of red hair.

'Good afternoon, sir. Good afternoon, sir,' he said. 'What can I do for you? A doll's house for the little girl?' He had been reading a manual on salesmanship.

'What little girl?' said Fen blankly.

'Or a box of bricks or some toy soldiers?' Cadogan bought a balloon and went outside to present it to Sally.

'Is the owner of the shop in? It's a Miss Alice Winkworth isn't it?' Fen asked.

'Yes, sir, Miss Winkworth. No, sir, I'm afraid she's not in. Anything I can do for you . . . '

'No, I wanted to see her personally. You haven't her address, I suppose?'

'No, sir, I'm afraid I haven't. You see, I've only been here a short while. She doesn't live on the premises. I know that.'

So there was really nothing more to be said. But as he was leaving, Fen asked:

'Did you notice anything unusual about the shop when you opened this morning?'

'Well, sir, it's funny you should say that, because several things seemed out of place, like. I was afraid there'd been a burglary, but then there was no sign of breaking in, and nothing that I could see was missing . . . '

When they were in the car again, and heading for St Christopher's: 'Obviously that's the normal habitat of the toyshop,' Fen said. 'It's interesting, though not unexpected, to find that this Winkworth woman owns it. She seems to have provided the scenery for the whole affair. I suppose she's Leeds.'

'We ought to have buried Danny,' said Sally suddenly. 'We oughtn't to have left him like that.' They drove in silence to the front gate of St Christopher's.

Parsons, the porter, hailed them as they passed through the lodge. 'The police have been a third time for Mr Cadogan,' he said sombrely. 'They're getting rather angry. They went and had a look in your room, Professor Fen. I saw to it they didn't disturb anything.'

'What did you tell them?'

'Said I didn't know anything about it. *Perjury.*' Parsons retired, grumbling, to study the *Daily Mirror.*

They all crossed the two quadrangles to Fen's room. 'What do the police want him for?' Sally whispered to Fen.

'*Pornographic books,*' said Fen impressively.

'No, seriously.'

'He stole some food from the grocer's – when we were looking round this morning.'

'Golly, what a stupid thing to do.'

Fen's room proved to contain an occupant. Mr Erwin Spode, of Spode, Nutling, and Orlick, publishers of high-class literature, rose to his feet in a twitter of nervousness as they came in.

'Hello, Erwin,' said Cadogan in surprise. 'What are you doing here?'

Mr Spode coughed nervously. 'In point of fact, I was looking for you. I was in Oxford, so I thought I'd look you up. About that American lecture tour.'

Cadogan groaned. 'Let me introduce you,' he said. 'Mr Spode, my publisher: Professor Fen, Miss Carstairs, Mr Hoskins, Dr Wilkes.'

'I thought that as this was your college I should perhaps find you here.' Mr Spode addressed himself to Fen. 'I hope you'll forgive the intrusion.' His semicircular profile bore marks of anxiety, and his thin hair was ruffled. He rubbed his face with a handkerchief. 'It's hot,' he complained.

It certainly was hot. The sun was falling lower in the

heavens, but it still blazed with unabated strength. The green and cream of the room were cooling, and all the windows were flung wide, but it was still hot. Cadogan felt he could do with a bathe.

'When did you arrive?' he asked Mr Spode, less because he wanted to know than because he could think of nothing else to say.

'Last night,' said Mr Spode with something very like frank dismay.

'*Oh?*' Cadogan's interest was abruptly aroused. 'But you said when you left me you were going back to Caxton's Folly.'

Mr Spode became more unhappy than ever; he coughed repeatedly. 'I called in at my office on the way back, and found a message asking me to come up here at once. I drove. I would have given you a lift, but when I rang up you'd already left. I'm staying at the "Mace and Sceptre",' he concluded defensively, as if this both explained and excused everything.

Fen, who had been arranging about tea for them all with an elderly, mirthless individual who proved to be his scout, returned to the room, unlocked a drawer in his untidy desk, and took out a small automatic pistol. For a moment conversation was still: something of the implication of that act was borne in on everyone present.

'I'm sorry I shall have to desert you,' he said. 'But this interview really won't wait. Make yourselves at home. Sally, don't budge from here until I get back – remember you're still very dangerous to these people. Mr Hoskins, don't take your eyes off Sally for a moment.'

'I find it practically impossible to do so already, sir,' said Mr Hoskins gallantly. Sally favoured him with an impish grin.

Curiosity, and the desire for tea, were conducting a mimic battle in Cadogan's brain; curiosity emerged triumphant. 'I'm coming too,' he announced.

'I don't want you,' said Fen. 'Remember what happened last time.'

'But if I stay here,' Cadogan argued, 'the police will find me.' ('And about time too,' Fen muttered.) 'Besides that, I'm curious.'

'Oh, my dear paws,' was Fen's comment. 'I suppose it's useless to try and stop you.'

'I think I might go to the station first, though, and collect my bag: there's a gun in it.'

'No,' said Fen rudely. 'We don't want you blazing away like a cowboy all over the streets of Oxford. Besides, think what would happen if you were arrested with it on you . . . Stop arguing and come along.' Such was the force of Fen's personality that Cadogan stopped arguing and went along.

'I'm not sorry to have escaped Spode,' he told Fen as they walked towards Mr Rosseter's office.

'Why?'

'He wants me to lecture in America on modern English poetry.'

'No one ever asks me to lecture in America on anything,' said Fen gloomily. 'You ought to be glad. I should be.' His temperament was inclined to be mercurial. 'What do you think of the girl, Sally?'

'Beautiful.'

'No, you old lecher,' said Fen affectionately. 'I mean, is she telling the truth?'

'I'm pretty sure of it. Aren't you?'

'I should think so, but I have a distrustful nature just the same. After all, it's a somewhat unusual business, isn't it?'

'So unusual that no one in his senses would invent it.'

'Yes, you may be right there. You know it occurs to me – somewhat belatedly – that the time-limit hasn't much significance after all. Miss Tardy had to be got rid of before she could start kicking up a fuss about her claim, that's all. And, of course, it was preferable that she should disappear before anyone knew she was in England. I wonder when exactly she arrived, and if she stayed the night anywhere, or visited anyone before she came to Oxford. I should rather guess not – that would leave too many obvious traces; in those circumstances getting rid of her would be a risk.'

'What do you think's happened to the body?'

Fen shrugged. 'A furnace, perhaps – or someone's back garden. It'll probably be impossible to trace at this stage.'

They passed the Church of St Michael, standing almost opposite the shop where Sally worked, crossed the Cornmarket, and made their way past the Clarendon Hotel towards Mr Rosseter's office. The rush of traffic was abating. Cadogan felt extremely hungry, and his head was beginning to ache again; he was also conscious that he had had too much beer at the 'Mace and Sceptre'.

'I feel like Gerontius,' he said gloomily, breaking a long silence.

'Gerontius?'

' "This emptying out of each constituent . . . " Sick, I mean.'

'Never mind. We'll have some tea at Fuller's when we've seen Rosseter . . . Here we are.'

They clattered up the dusty wooden staircase, lined with indifferent sporting prints and with caricatures by du Maurier of forensic luminaries long since extinguished. The outer office, where the Dickensian clerk should have been, was empty, and they went on to the frosted-glass door which led into Mr Rosseter's own room. Cadogan noticed that Fen's hand was in the pocket which contained the pistol, and that he pushed open the door without immediately stepping inside. The long room with its low ceiling was also untenanted, and the big desk which stood in front of the windows looking out over the Cornmarket was bare. Some of the heavy volumes of law reports had been dragged out of their shelves to reveal a small wall safe, with the door standing open. The sunlight which slanted transversely through the windows lit up a room denuded and abandoned.

'He must have done a bunk,' said Cadogan without surprise.

'I wonder,' said Fen. He went on into the room.

'Both of you put up your hands,' said a voice behind them. 'Immediately, please, or I shall shoot.'

Cadogan wheeled round, and in that split second he saw the hammer of a revolver jerk back as the trigger tightened, and resigned himself – without much enthusiasm – to eternity. But no shot followed.

'That was a very stupid thing to do, Mr Cadogan,' said Mr Rosseter, his voice shaking a little. 'You should remember that I cannot afford to take the slightest risk.'

The gun he held had something strange about the barrel – a sort of tube pierced with holes like a sieve. The hand which held it glistened with sweat, but was perfectly steady. Mr Rosseter no longer wore the sombre clothes which are the livery of his profession; instead, he was dressed in a light grey pin-stripe suit. The green eyes behind his glasses were narrowed almost to slits in the intent focus of a careful marksman. His bald crown, slightly pointed at the top, shone with the refraction of the light, and Cadogan noticed for the first time that his fat, carefully manicured hands were covered with a reddish down.

'I thought you would be coming here sooner or later, gentlemen,' he continued. 'So I waited for you on the floor above. You'll be glad to hear that I've given my clerk a holiday: we can talk undisturbed. Go into my office please, and don't attempt to lower your hands; I shall be too far behind you for it to be worth while.' He followed them in, and Cadogan heard him turn the key in the lock.

'You must let me relieve you of that pistol, Professor. Throw it on the floor, please . . . Thank you. Mr Cadogan, I shall be compelled to see if you . . . ' He ran his hands over Cadogan's clothes.

'You're tickling,' said Cadogan.

'My apologies,' said Mr Rosseter sarcastically. 'You may lower your hands now, but don't make any sudden movements, please. As you'll appreciate, I'm really in a very nervous condition. Keep at the end of the room, by the door.' Kicking Fen's gun over by the desk, he backed after it, and lowered himself cautiously into the swivel chair. Then he rested the barrel of the gun on the edge of the desk, but without relaxing; they were two to one, and he was not inclined to rely on Providence. 'As an inveterate cinemagoer,' he went on, 'I am aware of the danger of having you too close at hand. From where you are I can shoot one of you without the other having time to rush me before I can move the gun. And I really am quite a sound shot – last year, for example, I won the Swedish International Championship at Stockholm.'

'While these biographical details are unusually interesting,' said Fen mildly, 'that isn't what we came here for.'

'Of course not,' Mr Rosseter purred. 'Most inconsiderate of me. The fact is, gentlemen, that ever since I had reported to me the stupid failure' – his voice rose – 'the stupid failure of those two men, I haven't been at all my normal self. I haven't been well, gentlemen.'

'Very regrettable,' said Fen.

'But I knew you would be coming to see me, so, of course, I had to wait. You have really been a great nuisance indeed. I had to settle with you – that is, I should have wanted to kill you even if it had not been essential to my own safety.'

'I don't really see how you expect to get away with it.'

'Well, now: in the first place, this revolver, as you see, is silenced; in the second, I have facilities for concealing your bodies until such time as I am out of reach of the law – '

'We have friends, you realize, who know where we are. They'll be very curious if we don't return.'

'Of course you have friends,' said Mr Rosseter benignly. He seemed virtually to be complimenting them on the fact. 'I hadn't quite overlooked that. They will receive a message to say you have chased me up to – Edinburgh, shall we say? Anywhere that's suitably remote.'

'And yourself?'

'I shall just have time to catch the evening plane from Croydon. In Paris I shall lose my identity, and midday tomorrow I shall be on a boat belonging to a country with which Britain has no extradition treaty . . . You see, it's all very tiresome, and not at all what I originally intended. Now I shall have no time at all to wind up Miss Snaith's estate.'

Cadogan asked: 'Did you kill Miss Tardy?'

'There is the injustice of it all.' With his left hand, Mr Rosseter gestured broadly, evoking the phantoms of an intolerable persecution. 'I did not. I had fully intended to, but someone was before me.'

Fen looked up sharply. 'You know who?'

Mr Rosseter chuckled suddenly – a homely cachinnation of genuine pleasure, without a trace of sinister overtones. 'As it happens, I do – and how surprised you'll be when I tell you! It all looked so difficult – so implausible. Almost a locked-room mystery; certainly an "impossible murder". But I solved it. I solved it.' He chuckled again. 'And the murderer – who, of course, is one of the residuary legatees – is going to pay me for that knowledge. Blackmail – an amiable art. My flight, you see, will make no effectual difference to the disposal of Miss Snaith's money; the executorship will be vested elsewhere, and in due time the residuary legatees will receive their inheritance. One of them, however, will not enjoy very much of it, because it will mostly be conveyed to me in another country. If it is not, a disinterested friend of mine will hand over a lot of very interesting information to the police.' He nodded towards a brief-case which was leaning against the side of the desk. 'I shall post that information to him as soon as I am clear of Oxford.'

'It doesn't occur to you,' Fen suggested, 'that your residuary legatees will come in for a good deal of attention from the police after you've left?'

'Of course they will,' Mr Rosseter's manner was bland. 'But what are they to be charged with? Your murder? But I shall be the obvious culprit. The murder of Miss Tardy? But how is it to be established? Solely on the evidence of the Carstairs child? My dear sir, the police would not be so idiotic as even to issue a warrant. I should say that I was careful to ascertain from Miss Tardy that there is absolutely no evidence that she came into this country at all. She caught the Dieppe boat which arrived at midday yesterday, and came straight to Oxford without stopping anywhere or seeing anyone. As to the evidence of ticket-collectors and such people, even if they remembered her (which is exceedingly unlikely), a clever counsel could tie them in knots with the greatest of ease. Finally, the body has now been disposed of beyond all hope of recovery. No, no: the residuary legatees may undergo some unpleasantness, but they have absolutely nothing to fear.'

For the first time, Cadogan properly realized that Mr Rosseter genuinely did mean to kill them: now he had told them all this there was nothing else he could do. Cadogan felt a sudden sickening in his belly; every word Mr Rosseter said, every new fact he gave them, hammered down their coffins with one more nail. Yet he looked out of the window at the street he knew so well, and found he was hardly able to believe his own imminent destruction. Two logics struggled inside him: the logic of 'I am certainly awake, and, that being so, the thing is bound to happen'; and the logic of 'These things simply do *not* happen.' He glanced at Fen. There was no longer any trace of the habitual fantastic naïvety in those hard blue eyes; but it was impossible to tell what he was thinking.

'And now,' Mr Rosseter was saying, 'you will want to know all about it – from the beginning. I have half an hour to spare before I need go, and you deserve to hear the details. The earliest stages I need not go over again. You know of Miss Snaith's feelings about her niece, Miss Tardy; you know of her eccentricities; and you have discovered, no doubt, that I am named in the will as the residuary legatee. You must be aware by now, however, that in this respect I am merely the instrument of a secret trust. The reason for this arrangement you shall hear: it is simply the prosaic fact that Miss Snaith altered the residuary legatees in her will so frequently that the making of new wills became a nuisance to everybody. Under a secret trust she could make these changes with much greater convenience. Naturally, as her legal adviser I deplored so unconventional a scheme, but there was nothing I could do about it. And the final arrangement was that I made out for her certain sureties which could be donated to anyone whom she chose to select as her heir. Their names she declined to give me, since, as you know, she went in exaggerated fear of violent death; and so imagined, no doubt, that I should seek out the objects of her beneficent intentions and incite them to murder her. Such childishness seems scarcely conceivable, but there, in any event, is the fact. On her death I was to receive a paper containing the names of these legatees, and when the six months which were allowed to Miss Tardy were out, I was to advertise for them in the *Oxford Mail*. They would then take their sureties to the bank, and there obtain the papers which both proved their claim and insured the inheritance against possible depredations by myself. I should add that Miss Snaith, who was devoted to the works of Edward Lear, chose to identify the residuary legatees by names taken from his limericks. They appeared in the advertisement which you saw – Ryde, Leeds, West, Mold, and Berlin.'

(*The Premature Burial*, Cadogan thought: didn't the hero of that story listen to his own coffin being hammered down?)

'I advertised for Miss Tardy in the way the will required,' Mr Rosseter went on. The gun was still held steady on the edge of the desk. 'You understand that at the time I had no criminal intentions; I merely thought it a pity that so much money should be wasted on nonentities to whom Miss Snaith imagined she was indebted for some trivial kindness. And I confess I was annoyed that she had seen fit to leave nothing to me. I am afraid that some of my past career, gentlemen, would perhaps not bear a very close investigation; I would not mention this were it not that the fact has an important bearing on what follows.'

Another nail.

'Three days before the six months was up, I received a letter from Miss Tardy formally claiming her inheritance, and announcing that she was on her way to England. She wrote from Dinkelsbühl, in Germany. And about an hour afterwards the event occurred which initiated this entire business.

'A man came to see me here – let us for the moment call

120

him Berlin. He had discovered that I was Miss Snaith's lawyer, and had received from her one of the sureties which I mentioned; and, putting two and two together, had come to ask me if he were a beneficiary under the will. I said, of course, that I could tell him nothing. And it was then that my past career rose up to confront me.

'He had been in America at the time when I was there, and was acquainted with certain facts about me – enough, at all events, to make my career extremely difficult if they were ever revealed. I was compelled, gentlemen, to tell him about the will and about Miss Tardy, and the idea that so much money was slipping from his grasp was evidently intolerable to him. At first he demanded that I should suppress Miss Tardy's claim, but I told him, of course, that such a scheme was ludicrous and impossible. Then he suggested that Miss Tardy should be intimidated into signing the money away. Now, the likelihood of such a course having any ultimate effect was exceedingly small; any such document which Miss Tardy might sign would have to be produced in court by the residuary legatees, and the circumstances of its signing would be thoroughly investigated. But while he talked I had been considering a plan of my own, so I did not choose to acquaint him with these difficulties. In fact, I pretended to agree.

'We made arrangements for a further discussion of the matter later on, and he left. I then went ahead with my own idea. I wired Miss Tardy, inventing some specious legal technicality to induce her to come straight to me when she arrived in England; and I advertised, two days prematurely, for the other legatees. In due course, all of them, but one visited me here. I need not go into more detail than to say that two of them were people of uncertain reputation, and that greed induced them to become accomplices in this absurd intimidation plot, and offered me a part of their inheritance as payment for my own services. One of them offered to provide the scene of action, a shop in the Iffley Road which was to be temporarily "disguised" as a toyshop so that Miss Tardy should never be able to locate it again

121

after she left. All this business was merely a comedy as far as I was concerned. The conspirators were to be masked, too, to prevent their recognizing one another subsequently. I deferred to this nonsense, inwardly wondering at the idiocy which provoked it; because all the time I knew that the only effective thing to do with Miss Tardy was to kill her.'

There was a moment's silence. Outside, Cadogan could hear the hum of traffic, and see the sunlight winking on the windows of a deserted flat opposite. A sparrow settled on the sill, ruffled its feathers, and flew off again.

'It was a pity everything went so badly,' Mr Rosseter continued reflectively. He had not at any time taken his finger from the trigger. 'A great pity, in the first place, someone killed the woman before I was able to proceed with my own scheme; in the second, the Carstairs girl returned to the shop and saw us; and in the third, you, Mr Cadogan, blundered in and saw the body. Those were all quite unforseeable accidents. The plan itself was, I think, nicely contrived. Miss Tardy had telegraphed the time she would arrive, and the Carstairs girl was to act, unsuspecting, as a decoy. She would not see me when she arrived at the toyshop, but only our friend Berlin, who would give a false name; so she could not connect me with the affair, if anything went wrong, except by the letter, which I should swear I had not written. I need not trouble you with the whole business, except to say that if anything went wrong and Miss Tardy's disappearance were noticed, then the maximum suspicion would fall on the residuary legatees and little or none on myself. Of course, I hoped that all would go smoothly and that Miss Tardy would simply disappear. I should kill her – naturally without letting it appear that I had done so – and remind them of the unpleasantness of their position. I am not unexperienced in violent death, or in what the Americans call a frame-up. They would be only too grateful (in the financial way) for having things hushed up, and all thereafter would be well.

'As you know, the plan miscarried.' Mr Rosseter rose and

122

strolled to the side of the desk. 'But let me tell you what actually happened. And let me give you the names of the people concerned – it is ridiculous to continue with these childish pseudonyms.' He stood silhouetted blackly against the window. 'In the first place there was – '

Something like a backfire sounded in the street outside. Mr Rosseter stopped in the middle of the sentence. His eyes blurred, like lamps swept suddenly with a gust of rain, and his mouth dropped open, showing a trickle of blood in one corner. He fell forward on to his desk, and from there slipped down to the floor. Cadogan found himself staring dazedly at a neat round hole in the window-pane.

9. The Episode of the Malevolent Medium

'He's dead all right,' said Fen, who was bending over the body. 'Bullet in the neck – something like an express rifle, I should think. Blackmailers do occasionally end up this way. Better him than us anyway.'

Cadogan was not even relieved at their miraculous deliverance; he interpreted this, rightly, as being due to the fact that he had never really believed he was going to be killed. But Fen gave him little opportunity to meditate on these matters.

'The shot entered horizontally,' he said, 'which means it must have come from the upper windows of the house opposite. In fact, our friend will just be leaving there. Let's go across.' He picked up his gun and took the key of the office door from Mr Rosseter's pocket.

'Oughtn't we to phone the police?'

'Later. Later,' said Fen, dragging Cadogan from the room. 'It'll be a fat lot of good phoning the police if the murderer gets away.'

'But of course he'll get away.' Cadogan tripped on a stair-rod and nearly fell. 'You don't think he's standing over there waiting for us, do you?' But to this question he got no reply.

The lights at Carfax were holding up the traffic in one direction, so they crossed the Cornmarket without delay. They wasted some minutes, however, in searching for the entrance to the flat opposite, and when found in an alley behind the shops, it proved to be locked.

'If *this* belongs to Miss Alice Winkworth too,' said Fen, 'I shall scream.' He really looked as if he might.

A constable standing on the opposite pavement was

watching their antics with some curiosity, but Fen was so oblivious of this important fact that he had opened a window and was climbing in before Cadogan could stop him. The constable hastened across to them and addressed himself to Fen's disappearing form with some indignation.

'Here! Here!' he called. 'What do you think you're doing?'

Having succeeded in getting in at the window, Fen now turned round and leaned out of it again. He spoke rather like a cleric addressing his congregation from the pulpit.

'A man has just been shot dead in the flat opposite,' he answered. 'And he was shot from here. Is that sufficient reason for you?'

The constable stared at Fen in much the same way as Balaam must have stared at his ass. ' 'Ere, are you joking?' he said.

'Certainly I am not joking,' said Fen implacably. 'Go and see for yourself, if you don't believe me.'

'Holy God,' said the constable, and hastened back across the Cornmarket.

'He's a simple fellow,' Cadogan commented. 'You might be robbing this flat, for all he knows.'

'It's empty, you fool,' Fen rejoined; and disappeared. In a very short time he was back at the window.

'There's no one about,' he said. 'But there's a fire-escape leading down to a little green place round the corner, and the window beside it has been forced. Heaven knows where the rifle is – anyway, I haven't time to search for it now.'

'Why not?'

Fen climbed through the window and dropped on to the pavement beside Cadogan. 'Because, you old malt-worm, I don't want to get delayed giving evidence to that constable. We should have to go down to the station, and that would mean an hour at least.'

'But look here, isn't it about time the police took over this business altogether?'

'Yes,' said Fen frankly. 'It is. And if I were a public-spirited citizen that's what I should let them do. But I'm not a public-spirited citizen, and anyway I consider this business is our party. The police wouldn't believe us when we put the thing to them in the first place; *we've* done all the investigation and *we've* run all the risks. I consider we've a perfect right to go on and finish the business in our own way. In fact, my blood's up. There's something romantic about me,' he added reflectively. 'I'm an adventurer *manqué*: born out of my time.'

'What nonsense.'

'Well, you keep out of it if you like. Go on, run and talk to the police. They'll put you in the can, anyway, for stealing those groceries.'

'You seem to forget that I'm ill.'

'All right,' said Fen, with elaborate unconcern. 'Do what you like. It doesn't matter to me. I can manage without you.'

'It's ridiculous to take this attitude – '

'My dear fellow, I quite understand. Say no more about it. You're a poet, after all, and it's to be expected.'

'What is to be expected?' said Cadogan furiously.

'Nothing. I didn't mean anything. Well, I must go before that policeman comes back.'

'Of course if you insist on behaving like a child of two, I shall feel compelled to go with you.'

'Oh? Will you? I dare say you'd only be a hindrance.'

'Not at all.'

'You've only been a hindrance so far.'

'That's quite unjust ... Look out, there's that policeman again.'

The alley curved round behind the building and debouched at its farther end in Market Street, which joined the Cornmarket more or less opposite Mr Rosseter's office. It was here that Fen and Cadogan cautiously emerged; the constable was for the moment out of sight.

'The Market,' said Fen tersely. And hurrying along the street, they turned in at an entrance on the right.

The Oxford Market is a large one, standing in the right angle formed by the High Street and the Cornmarket. Here they could hope to evade the attentions of the constable, should he choose to follow them, though as Fen remarked, he could scarcely do so until someone else arrived to keep an eye on Mr Rosseter's office. There were two main passages, lined with stalls selling meat, fruit, flowers, vegetables, and down one of these they strolled, buffeted by beetle-like housewives intent upon bargains. The air smelt delightfully of raw things and, after the sunlight outside, the great barn-like building was cool and dim.

'All I say,' Fen pursued, 'is that this is our pigeon and no one else's. It may be the glory of a law-abiding age that one doesn't, literally, have to fight one's own battles, but it makes life tame. As a matter of fact, we're perfectly within our rights. We've detected a felony and are searching for the criminal, and if the police choose to get in the way it's their bad luck.' He tired abruptly of these sophistries. 'Not that I care a twopenny damn whether I'm within my rights or not. Here's a café. Let's go in and get some tea.'

The café was small and primitive, but clean. Cadogan drank his tea avidly and began to take a proper interest in things again. Fen meanwhile had departed to find a telephone and was talking to Mr Hoskins in his own room.

'Mr Spode left,' Mr Hoskins was saying, 'shortly after Cadogan and yourself – I don't know where he was going, but he seemed a trifle uncomfortable, in the social sense, I mean. Sally and Dr Wilkes are still here.'

'Good. You'll be pleased to know that Rosseter has just been bumped off under our very noses. But he said he didn't kill Miss Tardy.'

'Good Lord.' Mr Hoskins was manifestly startled at this information. 'Was he telling the truth, do you suppose?'

'I should think so. He was proposing to kill us at the end of it, so he hadn't much reason for lying. Someone shot him with a rifle from the flat opposite – someone he was bl – Oh, my fur and whiskers.'

'Are you all right?' Mr Hoskins asked.

'Physically, but not in the head. I've just realized something, and it's too late now. Never mind, you shall hear all about it later. In the meantime, I wonder if you can possibly discover the identity of a suspect for me – Berlin? He's a doctor, and uncommonly thin. It sounds easy, but in practice it may be rather awkward.'

'I'll see what I can do. But I shall have to leave Sally. She says she ought to have gone back to the shop hours ago.'

'She *must stay in my room*. Wilkes will look after her. It's a pity he's so hale and susceptible in his dotage, but that's a risk she'll have to take.'

'Are you coming back now? Where can I get hold of you if I find the man?'

'I shall be at the "Mace and Sceptre" about a quarter past six. Ring me there.' Fen lowered his voice and began to give instructions.

When he returned to the table Cadogan had finished the buttered scones and was eating a piece of angel-cake. 'The Episode of the Guzzling Bard,' said Fen as he lit a cigarette. 'You may kick me if you like ... No,' he went on crossly. 'Don't fool about, it's only a figure of speech. I suppose senescence is clouding my brain.'

'What's up?' said Cadogan with his mouth full.

'It's surely not necessary for you to take such big bites at a time ... It's a question of where our homicidal friend went after he left the flat.'

'Well, where did he go?'

'Obviously to Rosseter's office. Don't you remember the information which would hang him was in Rosseter's brief-case? There was no point in killing him unless the murderer got that. And I was so childishly excited that I left it there.'

'Lor',' said Cadogan, impressed. 'And we might have cleared the whole business up there and then.'

'Yes. Anyway it's too late now. Either the murderer's got it, or the police. A subsidiary point which interests me is how the murderer took his rifle away. I think it was only a small one – might even have been a ·22 – but he'd have to have had something innocent-looking, like a golf-bag, to carry it away in.' Fen sighed profoundly.

'What do we do now?'

'I think we seek out Miss Alice Winkworth.'

A woman sitting at a nearby table got up and came over to them. 'You mentioned my name?' she said.

Cadogan jumped, and even Fen lost hold momentarily on his equanimity. The interruption went beyond logic; and yet, when all things were considered, there was no great reason why Miss Alice Winkworth should not be eating tea in the same café as themselves. To them it appeared odd; to her, no doubt, it appeared odd also; but an outsider would have been wholly unmoved by the coincidence.

She gazed down on them with manifest disapprobation. Her face was fat, yellow-complexioned, and moonlike, with a rudimentary black moustache, a pudgy nose, and small, suilline eyes – the face of a woman accustomed to exercising an egotistical authority. It was surmounted by greying hair coiled into buns over the ears, and a black hat sewn with a multitude of tiny red and purple beads. On the fourth finger of her right hand was an ostentatious diamond ring, and she wore an expensive but ill-fitting black coat and skirt.

'You were talking about me?' she repeated.

'Sit down,' said Fen amiably, 'and let us have a chat.'

'I have no intention of sitting with you,' Miss Winkworth replied. 'You, I suppose, are Mr Cadogan and Mr Fen. I hear from my employees that you have pestered them with questions about me, and that you, Mr Cadogan, took it upon yourself to steal part of my property. Now that I have found you, I shall go straight to the police and inform them that you are here.'

Fen stood up. 'Sit down,' he said again, and his tone was no longer amiable.

'How dare you threaten – '

'As you well know, a woman was murdered last night. We need some information which you can give us.'

'What nonsense: I deny – '

'She was murdered on your property and with your connivance,' Fen went on remorselessly, 'and you benefit from her death.'

'You can prove nothing – '

'On the contrary I can prove a great deal. Rosseter has talked. He is also – as perhaps you know – dead. You're in a very unfortunate position indeed. You'd do better to tell us what you know.'

'I shall see my lawyer. How dare you insult me in this way? I'll have the pair of you in gaol for libel.'

'Let's have no more of this foolery,' said Fen abruptly. 'Go to the police if you like. You'll be immediately arrested for conspiracy to murder, if not for the murder itself.'

Hesitation and fear were in the woman's greedy little eyes.

'Whereas,' Fen continued, 'if you tell us what you know it may be possible to keep you out of it altogether. I say it *may*: I don't know. Now, will you take your choice?'

Suddenly, heavily, Miss Winkworth slumped down into a chair, pulling out a lavender-scented lace handkerchief with which she wiped the perspiration from her hands. 'I didn't kill her,' she said in a low voice. 'I didn't kill her. We never meant to kill her.' She looked round suddenly. 'We can't talk here.'

'I see no reason why not,' said Fen. And indeed, the café was almost empty. A single waitress leaned against a pillar by the door, her pale face vacant, a dish-cloth in her hand. The proprietor tampered inexpertly with his shining tea-urn.

'Now,' said Fen curtly. 'Answer my questions.'

They had great difficulty in getting any connected story out of Miss Winkworth, but eventually the general outlines emerged with sufficient clarity. She confirmed Mr Rosseter's account of the intimidation plan, adding to it some unimportant detail; but asked if she knew the identities of the other two men involved, she shook her head.

'They were masked,' she said. 'I was, too. We used the names the old woman gave us.'

'How did you come to meet Miss Snaith in the first place?'

'I'm a medium. A psychic medium. I have Powers. The old woman wanted to get in touch with the Beyond; she was afraid of dying.' A trace of slyness crept into the eyes and the corners of the mouth. 'Of course, you can't always get in touch when you want to, so I sometimes had to arrange things so that she wouldn't be disappointed. Very comforting messages we got then – just the sort of thing she liked.'

'So the poor misguided creature left you money for faking ectoplasm. Go on. You own the shop in Iffley Road and the one in the Banbury Road, don't you?'

'Yes.'

'Were you responsible for changing the stock?'

'Yes. I took the toys down from the Banbury Road to the Iffley Road in my car. It wasn't very difficult. We put all the groceries into the back of the other shop and left the toys in their place. The blinds were down over both shops, so an outsider wouldn't notice the change.'

'You know,' Fen said to Cadogan, 'there's something richly comic in the thought of these criminal lunatics lugging toys and groceries about at dead of night. I agree with Rosseter – one can scarcely imagine a more childish scheme.'

'It worked, didn't it?' said the woman venomously. 'The police wouldn't believe your friend here when he talked about his precious toyshop.'

'It didn't work for long. A toyshop that stays where it is is an unsuspicious object enough, but one that moves ... Good heavens! The thing cries out for investigation. By the way, how did you hear about Cadogan and the police?'

'Mr Rosseter found out. He rang up and told me.'

'I see. Who was responsible for getting the toys back to the other shop afterwards?'

'Whoever got rid of the body.'

'And that was – ?'

'I don't know,' said the woman surprisingly. 'They drew lots for it.'

'*What?*'

'I've told you: they drew lots. It was a dangerous job, and no one would volunteer. They drew lots.'

'This goes from comedy to farce,' said Fen drily. 'Not that there isn't a grain of sense in it. And who got the fatal card?'

'They weren't to say. I don't know. Whoever did it was to take back the toys as well. I left my car, and the keys of both shops. The car was to be left in a certain place – I found it this morning – and the keys returned to me by registered post. Then I went away. I don't know who stayed behind.'

'What time was this?'

'I suppose I left about half past midnight.'

'Ah,' said Fen. He turned to Cadogan. 'And you blundered *in medias res* shortly after one. You must have given the body-snatcher a nasty shock.'

'He gave me one,' Cadogan grumbled.

They stopped talking as the waitress came over to clear away the tea things and give them their bill. When she had departed again:

'And who precisely was involved in this thing?' Fen asked.

'Me and Mr Rosseter and the two men called Mold and Berlin.'

'What were they like?'

'One of them was – well, undersized; the other was very thin. That one – the one we called Berlin – was a doctor.'

'All right.' Fen tapped the ash from his cigarette into a convenient saucer. 'Now let's hear precisely what happened.'

Miss Winkworth was sullen. 'I'm not going to tell any more. You can't make me.'

'No? In that case, we'll go along to the police. They'll make you, all right.'

'I've got my rights – '

'A criminal has no rights in any sane society.' Cadogan had never known Fen so harsh before; it was a new and unfamiliar aspect of his character. Or was it merely an expedient pose? 'Do you think that after your filthy little conspiracy to murder a deaf, helpless woman anyone is going to trouble himself about your rights? You'll do better to keep out of the way – and not put them to the test.'

Miss Winkworth put her handkerchief to her pudgy nose and blew. 'We didn't mean to murder her,' she said.

'One of you did.'

'It wasn't me, I tell you!' The woman raised her voice, so that the proprietor of the café stared.

'I'll be the judge of that,' said Fen. 'Talk more quietly if you don't want the whole world to know about it.'

'I – I – You won't let me get into trouble, will you? I didn't mean any harm. We weren't going to hurt her.' The voice was a small, poisoned whine. 'I – I think it was about a quarter past ten when we finished arranging the shop. Then we all went upstairs. Mr Rosseter and Mold and me went into one of the back rooms, and the man called Berlin stayed out to meet the old woman. He'd got bandages round his face, so he wouldn't be recognized again. Mr Rosseter was in charge of everything – he said he'd tell us what to do and how to do it. We were paying him money to help us.'

In memory, Cadogan was back in that dark, ugly little place; the linoleum-floored passage with the rickety table where he had left his torch, the two bedrooms at the back, the two sitting-rooms at the front; steep, narrow, uncarpeted stairs; the smell of dust and the gritty feel of it on the fingertips; the curtained windows, the cheap sideboard and leather armchairs; the sticky warmth and the faint smell of blood and the blue, puffy face of the body on the floor . . .

'Then the girl brought in the woman and went away again – or so we thought. We heard the man called Berlin talking to the woman for a bit, and then he came back to us. Then Mr Rosseter said he'd need to talk to the woman, and we must wait. I thought that was funny, because he wasn't wearing a mask, but I didn't say anything at the time. Before he went out he told us we'd better separate and wait in different rooms. The man called Mold asked why – he'd been drinking and he was aggressive – but the other one told him to be quiet and do what he was told; he said he'd discussed the whole thing with Mr Rosseter,

Front (Iffley Road)

and it was essential to the plan. I thought Mr Rosseter looked a bit surprised at that, but he nodded. Berlin went into the other room at the front, and I stayed where I was, and Mold went into the second bedroom. Then after a while Berlin came in and joined me, and a bit later Mr Rosseter – '

'Just a moment,' Fen interposed. 'Where was Rosseter all this time?'

'He was with the woman. I saw him go in.'

'Was she alive when he came out?'

'Yes. I heard her voice, saying something to him as he closed the door.'

'Did anyone else go in while he was there?'

'No. I had the door open and I could see.'

'And when he left he came straight back to your room?'

'That's right. He told Berlin and me it was going to be a job to frighten her, and he and Berlin argued for a bit about something, and I said if they didn't shut the door she'd hear them. So they shut it.'

'Then Sharman must have murdered her,' Cadogan interposed.

134

'Hold on a moment,' Fen said. 'What were they arguing about?'

'It was something legal, about witnessing and so on. I didn't understand it. Then about five minutes after, the other man – Mold – came in and said he thought there was someone prowling round the shop, and we'd better keep quiet for a bit, and we did. I wondered if the woman wouldn't get away in the meantime, but Mr Rosseter whispered it was all right, because she wasn't frightened yet and that he'd told her he had some papers to prepare which might take a certain time. Well, we stayed quiet for quite a time, and I remembered towards the end of it hearing one of the town clocks strike a quarter to twelve. Finally, Mr Rosseter and Berlin began arguing again, and said it was all a false alarm, and Mr Rosseter gave the man Mold a gun and a legal paper and told him to go and get on with it.'

'Just a minute. You'd all been together in that room from the time Mold came in and told you someone was prowling around?'

'Yes.'

'No one left it for even a moment?'

'No.'

'How long would you say you all waited there?'

'About twenty minutes.'

'All right. Go on.'

'This man Mold seemed to be the one they'd chosen to do the job. He said he'd call us in when we were needed, and then he went away. But after about a minute he came back and said there was no light in the room where the woman was. Someone had taken the bulb out. He thought the woman had gone, and he was groping about looking for a candle he knew was there when he fell over her, lying on the floor. We went back there with a torch and she was dead, all puffy with a string tied round her neck. The man called Berlin said he was a doctor, and bent down to look at her. Mr Rosseter seemed all yellow and frightened. He said someone from outside must have done it, and we'd better look in the shop downstairs. Just as we were going down, we saw a girl who was hiding there. Mr Rosseter showed her the body, and said something to her which frightened her, and sent her away. We didn't like that, but he said we were masked, so she wouldn't recognize us again, and she'd keep quiet for her own good. Berlin got up from the body and looked at us queerly and said suddenly: "No one here did this." Mr Rosseter said: "Don't be a damned fool. Who else could have done it? You'll all be suspected if it ever comes out." Then Mold said: "We've got to keep it quiet," and I agreed. It was then they decided to draw lots about who should get rid of the body.'

Abruptly, the woman stopped. The recital had been, physically, a strain, but Cadogan saw no sign of any moral appreciation of the acts she had been recounting. She talked about murder as she might have talked about the weather – being far too selfish, thick-skinned, and unimaginative to see the implications either of that final, irrevocable act or of her own position.

'We get nearer the heart of things,' said Fen dreamily. 'Personnel: Mold (equals our Mr Sharman), Berlin (the doctor, unidentified), Leeds (this creature here), Ryde (Sally), and West – where does the enigmatical West come into it, I wonder? Did he claim his inheritance? Rosseter said nothing about him. The impression one gets is that there was a great deal of fumbling and failure all round – except in one instance, of course. God knows what nonsense Rosseter told Sharman and the doctor, or what their precious plan was; it's of no importance now, anyway. I suppose it doesn't really matter, either, how Rosseter proposed to contrive his murder and frame-up; that went astray, too. The real point is not who *intended* to kill the woman, but who *did*. I confess I shall be interested to discover what the doctor meant when he said no one there could have done it – it links up with Rosseter's talk about an impossible murder.' He turned again to the woman, who was sniffing at a small yellow bottle of sal volatile; Cadogan noticed that her finger-nails were ringed with dirt. 'Would it have been possible for anyone to
136

have been hiding in the flat or the shop before you arrived?'

'No. It was locked, and, anyway, we had a good look round.'

'Could anyone have got through the window of the room Miss Tardy was in?'

'No, it was nailed up. They all were. I haven't used the flat for a year.'

'Which lets West out,' said Fen. 'If anyone had come through the shop Sally would have said, and there's no other way up to the flat except by the staircase from the shop, is there?'

'No.'

'No fire-escape, for instance?'

'No. It's my belief,' said the woman suddenly, 'that that girl did it.'

'As far as we've got at present, it's quite possible,' Fen admitted. 'Except,' he added to Cadogan, 'that I don't think she'd have been so ready to tell us things if she had. A bluff like that would have needed colossal nerve, and in any case it wasn't necessary for her to say anything at all. We shall see.' He glanced at his watch. 'Five-twenty – we must go. I want to make sure Sally's all right, and then go on to the "Mace and Sceptre" to wait for a message from Mr Hoskins. We shall have to return by devious routes; if that constable's done his job, half the police of Oxford will be running about looking for us by now.' He stood up.

'Listen,' said the woman urgently. 'You'll keep my name out of it, won't you? Won't you?'

'Good heavens, no,' said Fen, whose habitual cheerfulness seemed to be restored. 'Your evidence is far too important. You never really thought I should, did you?'

'You bastard,' she said. 'You bloody bastard.'

'Language,' said Fen benevolently. 'Language. Don't try to leave Oxford, by the way; you'll only be caught. Good afternoon.'

'Listen to me – '

'Good afternoon to you.'

10. The Episode of the Interrupted Seminar

The sun's rays no longer shone directly into the room at New College; it was cool and pleasant. The Uccello Martyrdom which hung over the fireplace was almost in shadow. First editions were disposed without ostentation on the shelves. The armchairs were deep and comfortable, each attended by an immense brass ashtray, and on the mahogany sideboard decanters and glasses winked. The owner of the room, Mr Adrian Barnaby, reclined at his ease, holding a glass of madeira, eating iced cake, and listening with distaste to the conversation of the other undergraduates who infested his room. These Restoration tea-and-madeira parties, he reflected, would be all very well if they did not involve people coming in only imperfectly washed and dressed after their exertions on the river; and now he came to examine the matter, there were a number of people who, he was sure, he had not invited; and for the matter of that, never even seen before. A faint movement of indignation stirred within him. His eyes lighting on a hairy youth who stood nearby, wolfing buttered scones, he leaned forward with the air of one about to impart a confidence and said:

'Who are you?'

'Oh, that's all right, you know,' said the youth. 'I came with Rabbit, you know. He said you wouldn't mind.'

'Rabbit?' Mr Barnaby was unenlightened.

'Yes. Look. That chap over there, with the tousled hair.'

'Ah,' said Mr Barnaby, who could summon up no recollection of Rabbit in any context.

'I say, I hope it's all right, you know,' said the hairy youth. 'Barging in, and all that.'

'Of course,' Mr Barnaby replied. 'You're most welcome.'

'Delicious sherry this is.' The youth indicated his glass of madeira. Mr Barnaby smiled beneficently at him as he moved off.

Another young man, almost as elegant as Mr Barnaby himself, approached his host. 'Adrian,' he said, 'who are all these *awful people*? They're talking about rowing.'

'My dear Charles, I know: *bumps* and things. Like a *phrenologist* ... I shall really have to sport my oak, or we shall have the whole rowing tribe in here. Look!' Mr Barnaby squeaked, sitting up suddenly. 'There's another of them coming in now.'

But a moment after he relapsed into smiles, for the new-comer was, in fact, Mr Hoskins, who had never been known to indulge in any sport save the most ancient of them all. He elbowed his unwieldy form apologetically through the chattering groups and confronted Mr Barnaby with a tran-scient smile on his melancholy face.

'My dear Anthony, how delightful to see you,' said Mr Barnaby with pleasure. 'I'm sorry there are all these frightful gymnasts about, but they simply invited themselves. What will you have to drink?'

'What is that that Charles is drinking?'

'Oh ether and milk, or some terrible chemical affair of that sort. But you know Charles. The poor dear cannot be made to realize that the romantic decadence is over. He still writes verses about *affreuses juives* and things. How about some madeira?'

When Mr Hoskins's madeira had been brought: 'Adrian,' he said. 'Do you know anything about the local doctors?'

'Good heavens, no – you're not *ill*, are you, Anthony?'

'No, perfectly fit. I'm trying to identify a man for Fen.'

'For Fen ... ? I know: someone has committed some *ghastly crime*.' Mr Barnaby enunciated the words with relish. 'But I go to a doctor in London when I'm unwell. Now, I wonder who ... Of course. Gower.'

'Gower?'

'A hypochondriac Welshman, my dear Anthony, in *Jesus*. But he has lodgings in Holywell only a few yards away from here. He's seen every doctor within *miles*. We might go to him now if you liked. I shall be *only too glad to escape from this party*.'

'It's very good of you.'

'Nonsense. I'm being quite *selfish* and egotistical. Come along, now. Finish your madeira first.'

They made their way out, Mr Barnaby uttering unnecessary apologies and excuses as they went. The second gate of the college brought them into Holywell, and after a very short walk, during which Mr Barnaby chattered incessantly, they came to Mr Gower's lodging. The bedroom in which Mr Gower was found reclining gave evidence of hypochondria on a scale hardly conceivable since the days of Molière. It was thronged with bottles, close-stools, medicine glasses, and throat sprays; the tightly-closed windows made it insufferably hot, and the curtains were drawn so as to admit only the minimum of light. It was, however, possible to see that Mr Gower's appearance was almost abnormally healthy.

'Look you, I am ill, now,' Mr Gower remarked as they entered the room. 'I am not needing visitors when I am trying to preak a fever.'

'My dear, you look too wasted,' said Mr Barnaby. A phantom expression of pleasure appeared on Mr Gower's face. 'I'm sure you might Pass Beyond *at any moment*. This is Mr Hoskins, whom I've brought to see you.'

'We oughtn't to be disturbing you, in your condition,' said Mr Hoskins funereally. Mr Gower extended a limp hand from the bedclothes for him to shake.

'My dear Teithryn, I bought you some fruit,' said Mr Barnaby, whose capacity for improvisation was considerable, 'but in a moment's absent-mindedness, I *ate it myself*.'

'Fruit is forbidden me, look you,' said Mr Gower. 'But I thank you for your kind thought. How can a poor invalid help you, now?'

'Do you know of an Oxford doctor,' Mr Hoskins asked, 'who is abnormally thin?'

'Oh, it is doctors, is it? They are all charlatans, look you.

140

I know them all. Their accounts are pigger than their success, I assure you. I haf no illusions about these doctors. The man you speak of is one of the worst – purgation is his remedy for everything. I do not advise you to go to him.'

'What is he called?'

'His name is Havering – Dr Havering, and he is a heart specialist. But do not take yourself to him, now. He is no good. I am tiring myself with talking, look you.'

'Of course,' said Mr Hoskins soothingly. 'We'll leave you. Havering, was it?'

'You poor, poor thing,' said Mr Barnaby. 'You must try to sleep. I'll tell your landlady that *no one* is to disturb you.'

'Please replace the wedges in the door when you leave,' said Mr Gower. 'When it rattles, it goes through and through my head.' He turned over in bed to indicate that the interview was now at an end and Mr Hoskins and Mr Barnaby departed.

'Dear Gower,' said the latter when they were in the street again. 'He seems absolutely to thrive on these awful potions and philtres. But you got what you wanted, didn't you, Anthony?'

'Yes,' said Mr Hoskins, standing irresolute. 'I think I'd better go and see this Havering man. But I want some people with me. He may turn nasty.'

'Oh, dear, how frightening,' Mr Barnaby responded dutifully, but without much evidence of alarm. 'You are *brave*, Anthony. Let me come with you.'

'All right. And we might collect some of that gang in your room.'

'Oh, must we?' Mr Barnaby seemed disappointed. 'Still, I suppose it's *brawn* that counts in these murderous affairs. We'll look up the man's address in the telephone book, and then collect some others. They'll think it's a kind of rag, my dear. What fun. I know some quite *formidable* men.'

For once Mr Barnaby did not prove to be exaggerating; he did know some formidable men. They were assembled by a means peculiar to Oxford – vague promises of excitement accompanied by more definite promises of drink. Mr

Barnaby proved an excellent impresario – 'like a *recruit-officer*, my dear Anthony, too Farquhar' – full of lurid, unlikely detail, invented at high speed. When about twelve more or less interested and intoxicated people had been got together, Mr Hoskins addressed them collectively with dark allusions to murder and young women in distress, and they all cheered. Dr Havering was discovered to live near the Radcliffe Infirmary in the Woodstock Road, and thither, somewhat heartened by Mr Barnaby's madeira, the rout proceeded to make its way. Unaware of the crisis that was approaching, Dr Havering sat alone in his consulting-room and stared out of the window.

Fen and Cadogan made their way back to St Christopher's without let or hindrance. It seemed likely that the search for Cadogan had been temporarily abandoned, and it was possible that the constable whom they had informed of Mr Rosseter's murder had not succeeded in identifying them yet. In any case, the porter, when they reached the College, had no further intrusions to report.

'Wilkes and Sally are probably playing strip rummy by now,' said Fen, as they mounted the stairs to his room; then, more seriously: 'I hope they're all right.'

They were, though Sally showed a marked inclination to worry about her afternoon's absence from the shop. Wilkes had found Fen's whisky, and was more or less asleep; he was awakened, however, by the violent ringing of the telephone. Fen answered it; the voice of the Chief Constable, charged with indignation, came over the wire.

'So there you are,' it said. 'What the hell do you think you're up to? As far as I can make out, you and this madman Cadogan have witnessed a murder and just run away.'

'Ha, ha,' said Fen unsympathetically. 'You should have listened to me in the first place.'

'Do you know who did it?'

'No. I should be finding out now if you weren't wasting my time with idiotic telephone calls. Was a brief-case found near the body?'

'What do you want to know for? No, it wasn't.'

'I thought it wouldn't be,' said Fen placidly. 'Has the news of Rosseter's murder got about yet?'

'No.'

'Certain?'

'Of course I'm certain. They're not releasing it till to-morrow. No one but you and this Cadogan maniac and the police know anything about it. Now, listen to me. I'm coming into town and I want to see you. Stay where you are, do you hear? You ought to be locked up – and your precious friend. I've had about enough. I wouldn't put it past you to have killed this solicitor creature yourself.'

'I've been thinking over what you were saying about *Measure for Measure* – '

'Pah,' said the Chief Constable, and rang off.

'Fire in the windlass,' Fen sang cheerfully as he replaced the receiver. 'Fire down below. So fetch a bucket of water, boys, there's f – By the way, Sally, I suppose no one came through the shop while you were hiding there?'

'Golly, no.'

'You're absolutely sure?'

'Absolutely. I should have been scared out of my wits if anyone had.'

'Well, tell us what's been going on,' said Wilkes testily. 'Not going to keep it to yourself, are you? Heh, *Detective*?'

'Mr Rosseter,' said Fen, regarding Wilkes with a jaundiced eye, 'has received the due reward of his deeds. We know something of what went on in that shop, but not enough to tell yet who killed Miss Tardy. Rosseter intended to, but didn't. The others had some plan of intimidating her into signing away the money. We've met the owner of the toyshop – as nasty a creature as you could hope to find.'

'Mr Hoskins has gone off to look for the doctor,' said Sally.

'Yes. Why did Spode leave?'

'Dunno. I expect he had an engagement or something. He just gulped down a cup of tea and went.'

'Nothing else happened – no visitors or phone calls?'

'An undergrad left an essay for you. I've been reading it. It's called' – Sally puckered up her attractive forehead – ' "The Influence of *Sir Gawain* on Arnold's *Empedocles on Etna".'*

'Good heavens,' Fen groaned. 'That must be Larkin: the most indefatigable searcher-out of pointless correspondences the world has ever known. Still, we can't bother about that now. I've got a seminar on *Hamlet* at a quarter to six and it's nearly that now. I shall have to cancel it if the police aren't to catch up with me. Wait a minute.' He snapped his fingers. 'I have an idea.'

'God help us all,' said Wilkes with feeling.

'Lily Christine's still outside, isn't she?' Fen asked Cadogan, who nodded bewilderedly.

'Good,' said Fen. 'Now we'll all go down to this seminar – except you, Wilkes,' he added hastily.

'I'm coming too,' said Wilkes with determination.

'Why are you always so tiresome?' said Fen irritably. 'One's never rid of you.'

'Do let him come, Professor Fen,' Sally pleaded. 'He's been so sweet.'

'*Sweet,*' said Fen meaningly, but seeing no alternative, gave in with an ill grace. He got his hat and a raincoat from a cupboard and they all trooped out, Cadogan wondering what on earth Fen was proposing to do. He soon knew.

The lecture-hall in which Fen's seminar was to be held was a small one. That it pertained normally to the classical faculty was indicated by a dun-coloured photographic reproduction of the Hermes of Praxiteles at one end, and a companion picture of an Aphrodite Kallipygos at the other. Upon this, in moments of tedium, the male students were accustomed wistfully to gaze. An incredibly ruinous edition of Liddell and Scott lay on a table raised on a slight dais at the front. On the wooden benches about twenty undergraduates sat, the women, gowned, chattering feverishly, and the men, ungowned, staring absently about them. Their texts and notebooks lay scattered on the desks.

When Fen came in, followed by the others, there was an

expectant hush. He climbed the dais and regarded them for a moment before speaking. Then he said:

'It is my troublesome duty to discuss with you this evening *Hamlet*, by the well-known English playwright, William Shakespeare. Perhaps I had better say it *should be* my troublesome duty, since I have, as things are, no intention of doing anything of the sort. You may recall that the name character in that play makes at one point a remark to the effect that the native hue of resolution is too often sicklied o'er with the pale cast of thought, and that moreover *enterprises of great pitch and moment* with this regard their currents turn awry and lose the name of action. More briefly though less accurately (and remember, please, that poetry is nothing if not accurate), this means "Cut the cackle and get down to the horses." That, with the assistance of two gentlemen here present, I propose to do now.'

Poetry nothing if not accurate, the women wrote in their books.

'Ladies and gentlemen,' Fen proceeded dramatically, 'I am being pursued by the police.' Everyone looked interested. 'Not for any crime I have committed, but simply because, in their innocence, they do not know that I am tracking down the perpetrator of a particularly cold-blooded and brutal murder.' Here there was some tentative applause from the back. Fen bowed.

'Thank you. Perhaps the first thing I'd better do is to introduce these other people to you.' He looked round with distaste. 'This bedraggled-looking object here is Mr Richard Cadogan, the eminent poet.'

Loud, embarrassing cheers.

'This is Dr Wilkes, who was dug up when the foundations of the New Bodleian were laid.'

More cheers, rather louder. ('New Bodleian,' Wilkes commented benevolently. 'Horrid erection.')

'And this is an attractive woman called Sally.'

Very loud cheers from the male undergraduates, and some shouts of 'Telephone number?' Sally grinned, rather shyly.

'They are my companions,' Fen continued sententiously. 'I might almost say my allies.'

'Get on with it,' Wilkes put in suddenly. 'We can't hang about here all night while you perorate. What are you going to do?'

'Be quiet, Wilkes,' said Fen irritably. 'I'm coming to that ... Mr Scott,' he called to a tall, lanky young man sitting at the back of the room.

'Yes, sir?' said Mr Scott, standing up.

'Do you drive a car, Mr Scott?'

'Yes, sir.'

'Mr Scott, are you prepared to risk losing your dinner by impersonating me?'

'Certainly, sir.'

'You'll require a great deal of resource, Mr Scott.'

'I have boundless resource, sir.'

'Good – admirable. If you understand me, you'll have to look like me trying to disguise myself.' Fen produced a pair of dark glasses from his pocket. 'If you'll put these on – and my hat and coat – '

Mr Scott did so. He strode experimentally up and down the lecture-room. At a short distance, the resemblance proved to be quite deceptive. Fen nodded his approval.

'We now need someone to impersonate Mr Cadogan,' he announced. 'Mr Beavis, you're about the right height. But you ought to have a hat and coat and dark glasses, too.' He considered. 'Sally dear, would you go up to my room? You'll find the hat and coat in my wardrobe – any ones will do – and the dark glasses in the left-hand top drawer of my desk. I wonder if a false beard . . . No, perhaps not.'

Sally ran off.

'Now, gentlemen, what I want you to do is this. In a few minutes the police will be here, searching for me and Mr Cadogan. You know my car?'

'Couldn't mistake it, sir.'

'No. I see what you mean. It's standing near the main gate – not locked, or anything. As the police arrive, I want you gentlemen to get into it and drive off as fast as you can go.

It will need rather careful timing if you're to induce them to follow you and at the same time get a sufficient start.'

'You want us to decoy them away, sir?' said Mr Scott.

'That's it. And lead them any sort of dance you like, all over the country. I leave that to your ingenuity. There's plenty of petrol in the tank, and Lily Christine will go very fast. Obviously, they musn't catch up with you and discover you're not us.'

'I don't think this is going to work,' Mr Beavis remarked with some apprehension.

'It will work,' Fen responded confidently, 'because no one *expects* this sort of trick outside a book. I should add that I'll pay your fines for breaking the speed limit and get you out of any other variety of trouble you may land in. By a bit later this evening I hope to have everything cleared up, but in the meantime I must have the police out of my way. Well, are you game?'

Mr Scott and Mr Beavis looked at one another. Then they nodded. Sally returned with hat, coat, and glasses, and helped Mr Beavis on with them.

'He doesn't look like me,' said Cadogan.

'He looks very like you indeed,' said Fen. 'That same shuffling, furtive gait . . . Thank you all for your attention, ladies and gentlemen. This seminar is now concluded. Next time,' he added, suddenly mindful of his duties, 'we will return to *Hamlet* and discuss it in relation to sources, particularly the no-longer-extant earlier version. You will find that a splendid field for wild surmise . . . Now. If everything is ready – '

The undergraduates, now that the spell was broken, took their departure, chattering excitedly the while. Mr Scott and Mr Beavis, conferring in low tones, went to take up their station.

'I don't think much of *her* figure,' said Sally, who was examining the Aphrodite.

'Let's all go up to the tower,' said Fen. 'There's a window there, and we can see what happens.'

They had not long to wait. A black police car drove up, and from it emerged the Chief Constable, with iron-grey hair and moustache, a sergeant, and a constable. They looked very purposeful and grim. Mr Scott and Mr Beavis waited until they were about to enter at the main gate, and then darted from a nearby doorway and flung themselves into Lily Christine III. There was a horrifying moment when Cadogan thought the car was not going to start, and then they were off with a roar and a rush down the Woodstock Road, where, had they only known it, Dr Reginald Havering was at that moment confronting his destiny. The noise attracted the Chief Constable's attention just as he was stepping inside.

'There they go!' he shouted in a paroxysm of annoyance. 'Get after them, you fools!' All three men precipitated themselves back into the police car, and in another moment it was moving off.

Fen sighed with relief. 'My poor friend,' he commented. 'Now perhaps we can have some peace for a little while. Come along, everyone. We're going to the "Mace and Sceptre". I'm expecting a message from Mr Hoskins there.'

In those halcyon times, when the rivers ran with strong ale and the supply of spirits was inexhaustible, the bar of the 'Mace and Sceptre' opened at 5.30 in the afternoon. It was just on six when Fen, Sally, Cadogan, and Wilkes arrived. The young man with the glasses and the long neck was sitting in his corner finishing *Nightmare Abbey*, but the only other inhabitant of those Gothic splendours was Mr Sharman, now familiar to them under the name of Mold, rabbit-toothed and muffled as ever, and looking as though he had not moved since they left him to search among the shop-girls of Oxford. He waved to them as they came in, and then shrank back in his chair as he saw Sally, his face suddenly pinched, mean, and frightened.

'Just the man I wanted to see,' Fen said amiably, striding towards him. 'Richard, get us all something to drink, will you?' He towered over puny Mr Sharman. 'Well, Mr Sharman, I expect you remember Miss Carstairs, your co-heir, whom you saw last night in the Iffley Road?'

Mr Sharman licked dry lips. 'I don't know what you're talking about.'

'Come, come.' Fen pulled up a chair for Sally, and then sat down himself. Wilkes was at the bar, helping Cadogan with drinks. 'We've discovered a great deal about things since we saw you last. Far too much for you to keep up the pretence any longer. Rosseter has talked. Miss Winkworth has talked.' Fen assumed a sinister expression. 'And now you're going to talk.'

'I tell you I don't know what you mean. I've never seen this girl in my life. Now, get away from me.'

'In fact, Miss Winkworth – whom you know as Leeds – told us she saw you kill Miss Tardy.'

Mr Sharman panicked. 'That's a lie!' he shouted.

'Still, you do know she was killed, don't you,' Fen pointed out mildly. 'Which means you must have been there.'

'I –'

'Let's have your account of exactly what happened. It had better be a true account, because we have means of checking it.'

'You're not going to get a word out of me.'

'Oh, yes, we are,' said Fen placidly. 'A great many words, in fact.' He paused as Wilkes and Cadogan appeared with beer, whisky, and a cider for Sally. 'Go on, Mr Sharman.'

But Mr Sharman was gaining confidence. His long teeth were revealed in what was almost a smile. 'You're not the police,' he said. 'You've no right to ask me questions.'

'In that case we'll take you along to the police-station, and they'll ask you questions.'

'You've no right to take me anywhere.'

'In point of fact, we have. Every citizen has a right – and a duty – to arrest a criminal found committing a felony. Conspiracy to murder is a felony, you know.' Fen beamed engagingly.

'Prove it,' said Mr Sharman tersely.

Fen regarded him thoughtfully. 'Where murder's concerned, one's bound to put humanitarian feelings on one side, isn't one? Hence the third degree in America. In a case like this one does somehow feel it's justified.'

Fear was in Mr Sharman's red-rimmed eyes. 'What do you mean?'

'I mean we might take you away somewhere and hurt you rather a lot.'

Mr Sharman started to get up from his chair. Cadogan, who had been following the exchange with interest, kicked him hard on the shin. He gave a little yelp and subsided again. 'F – you,' Mr Sharman said viciously.

'Are you going to tell us what you know?' Fen said.

Mr Sharman was thinking. 'A confession made under threats isn't any good in a court of law,' he said. 'And not a soul can testify I was involved in any conspiracy. Yes, I'll tell you, and you can make what you like of it.'

'That's more sensible.'

Some newcomers entered the bar, and Mr Sharman lowered his voice. 'I went to the shop and helped shift those bloody toys about – since you're so clever, you'll know why. Then we waited for the woman to turn up. After she did, Rosseter put us all in different rooms and talked to her for a bit. Then the other three got together – Rosseter and Berlin and the woman – and after a bit I heard someone walking softly round the shop, so I went to warn them. We stayed quiet for a while. Then I went in to see the woman and found the light out and her dead. That's all. Make what you like of it. If it ever comes to the point, I shall deny the lot.'

'*Parturiunt montes,*' said Fen, '*nascetur ridiculus mus.* Well, well, that's quite enlightening, all the same. Did you dispose of the body and knock out Cadogan here?'

'No, I didn't. Rosseter or Berlin must have done. Now go away and leave me in peace.' Mr Sharman wiped a dirty hand across his straggling eyebrows.

A page-boy came into the bar. 'Telephone call for Mr T. S. Eliot!' he piped. 'Mr T. S. Eliot?'

To everyone's surprise, Fen said 'That's me,' got up, and went out, pursued by the interested gaze of the other persons in the bar. In the telephone-box he talked to Mr Hoskins, who was sadly out of breath, and with his normal equanimity gravely deranged.

'The fox is away, sir,' he panted into the instrument. 'In the open, and making for cover.'

'View halloo,' said Fen. 'What direction is he going?'

'If you can get round to St Christopher's you may head him off. He's on a bicycle. Some of my friends are after him. I'm talking from his house. You'll have to be quick.' Mr Hoskins rang off.

Fen reappeared apocalyptically at the door of the bar and beckoned furiously to the others. 'Come on!' he shouted. 'Quick!' Cadogan, who had a mouthful of beer, choked terribly. They rushed to join Fen, leaving Mr Sharman to his own sordid reflections.

'They've got the doctor,' Fen explained excitedly. 'He's out and away. We must run. Oh for Lily Christine!'

They rushed through the revolving doors. Wilkes, whose athletic days were over, seized the only bicycle within sight (needless to say, it was not his) and wobbled unsteadily away on it, while Fen, Cadogan, and Sally ran – like dervishes: down George Street, round the corner by Taphouse's music shop, over the entrance to Beaumont Street (a bus nearly got them here), past the Taylorian, past the Bird and Baby . . . And there they stopped, gasping for breath, to contemplate the amazing spectacle which confronted them.

Down the Woodstock Road towards them an elderly, abnormally thin man was pedalling, his thin white hair streaming in the wind and sheer desperation in his eyes. Immediately behind him, running for their lives, came Scylla and Charybdis; behind them, a milling, shouting rout of undergraduates, with Mr Adrian Barnaby (on a bicycle) well in the van; behind them, the junior proctor, the University Marshal, and two bullers, packed into a small Austin car and looking very elect, severe, and ineffectual; and last of all, faint but pursuing, lumbered the ungainly form of Mr Hoskins.

It was a sight Cadogan was never to forget as long as he lived.

11. The Episode of the Neurotic Physician

At the time, however, events were moving so fast that he had no opportunity to examine the scene in detail. Down into St Giles' came Dr Havering, and along St Giles', travelling in the opposite direction and on the wrong side of the road, came Wilkes. Just in time the doctor perceived his peril. He turned half-right to evade Wilkes and found himself face to face with Fen and Cadogan, who were running towards him. The undergraduate mob was moving up behind. He hesitated, and then with sudden decision twisted away to the left. Wilkes braked violently, nearly falling off in the process. And the doctor cycled furiously into the alleyway which runs between the 'Lamb and Flag' and St John's. Without a moment's hesitation, everyone followed – everyone, that is, except the proctorial authority, which stopped, baffled; for the alley-way is too small to admit a car. After some hesitation they set off to drive round to Parks Road, where the alley debouches, and it was the merest bad luck that they ran over a nail on the way and were delayed so long that they lost all track of the chase.

Some ingenious person has contrived, half-way down the alley, an arrangement of posts and chains, which can only be negotiated on foot, and the pack nearly caught up with Dr Havering here. But he just eluded them, and was to be seen cycling furiously down the short residential road which leads out into the Parks Road near the various science laboratories. The odds, of course, were unequal, and neither Mr Barnaby nor Wilkes, the only two who had bicycles, seemed capable of tackling the doctor singly, or even in combination. Cadogan's heart was pounding fiercely. But there was a sprinkling of determined Blues in Mr Barnaby's army; Fen was still running with an easy, loping stride; and Sally, in perfect training and fortunately wearing flat shoes and a split skirt, seemed to have no difficulty in keeping up. Scylla and Charybdis, defeated, dropped out of the race, but for the time being no one paid any attention to them, and they followed at a clumsy jog-trot.

From Parks Road Dr Havering turned left into South Parks Road, tree-lined and pleasant, with the rout still indefatigably pursuing. Two classical dons, engaged in discussing Virgil, were submerged in it and left looking surprised but unbowed. 'My dear fellow,' said one of them, 'can this be the University steeplechase?' But as no enlightenment was forthcoming, he abandoned the topic. 'Now, as I was saying about the *Eclogues* – '

It was at the end of South Parks Road that Dr Havering made his great mistake – a mistake which can only be ascribed to the workings of blind panic. Doubtless he had hoped to throw off his pursuers long before, and was in the grip of nightmare. In any event, just as Fen was wasting his breath in chanting (rather inappropriately) ' *"But with unhurrying chase, and unperturbed pace, deliberate speed, majestic instancy . . . "* ' he ran down the lane which leads to Parson's Pleasure, abandoned his bicycle, flung sixpence at the gate-keeper, and disappeared inside. And from the hounds a howl of victory went up.

Here a word of explanation is required. Since Oxford is one of the few civilized cities in the world, it gives facilities to its inhabitants for bathing in the only way proper to that activity: which is to say, naked; though as even civilized persons are prone to the original errors of the flesh, some segregation is involved. Parson's Pleasure is set aside for men. It consists of a broad strip of green turf, fenced in and with some stable-like bathing-huts, which runs down to a loop in the river where it by-passes an island. Young women in punts must go round the other way or else, blushing and ashamed, run the gauntlet of much bawdy comment. There is another part of the river, called Dame's Delight, which is available for them, though it is not known

154

that they take advantage of it to any great extent; and with that, at all events, we are not here concerned. The chief point to be observed is that there is no way out of Parson's Pleasure except by the gate or by the river itself, which sufficiently explains the delight of Dr Havering's pursuers.

Mr Barnaby was actually the first to arrive. Dismounting his bicycle, he pressed a pound-note confidentially into the gate-keeper's hand, with the remark: 'These are *all* my friends. Admit *everyone*, please.' In this request, however, he was over-sanguine. Worlds would not have induced the gate-keeper to admit Sally, and she was forced to remain outside, looking rather lorn and dejected. Cadogan, pressing in after the rest, promised to return and give her news as soon as possible.

The evening was warm, and a few people were splashing about or standing on the bank when Dr Havering broke on their tranquillity; one old man, indeed, was so alarmed by the crescent uproar that he fled incontinently back into his bathing-hut. The doctor, after standing irresolute for a moment, looking desperately about him, ran to the opposite side of the enclosure and began trying to climb the fence. He was in the midst of this endeavour when Mr Barnaby appeared. Looking helplessly round, he dropped again on to the springy green turf and made for a punt which was moored just by the springboard. A brief struggle with the punter, and he was in it and pushing away from the shore. But by this time the vanguard had reached him, and it was too late. Shouting incoherently and struggling like a damned soul in conveyance to hell, he was dragged ashore again before the amazed eyes of the bathers.

And here they suddenly heard Sally shouting for help in the lane outside. Scylla and Charybdis, hapless and forgotten in the rear, had caught up with her. Leaving Dr Havering well guarded, Cadogan headed a troop to the rescue. The fight which followed was brief, violent, and decisive, the only casualties being Scylla and Charybdis and Cadogan himself, who received a blow on the jaw from one of his own side which nearly laid him out. Finally, the two men were half-hoisted, half dragged back into Parson's Pleasure (the gate-keeper receiving another pound and a conspiratorial leer from Mr Barnaby) and there triumphantly thrown into the river, while they bawled and cursed dreadfully. Once immersed, their attitude became conciliatory, largely owing to the fact that they were unable to swim. A science don, who was standing slapping his belly on the bank, regarded them helpfully. 'Now is the time to learn,' he said. 'Bring your body up to a horizontal position and relax the muscles. The surface tension will support you.' But they only cried 'Help!' more violently, their hats floating desolately in the water beside them. Eventually the river bore them downstream to a shallower place where they were able to struggle to land. It is probable that after this fiasco they left Oxford, for they were never seen or heard of again.

In the interim, more important matters were afoot. They consisted, in the first place, of Fen's borrowing the punt, by cajolery, from its reluctant possessor; and in the second, in getting Dr Havering into it. In case it should be thought that the doctor acquiesced at all in these proceedings, it must here be stated that he did not – that he pleaded piteously with the astonished sprinkling of nude bathers to rescue him. But even had they not been in their unprotected condition they would have known better than to try to stem an undergraduate rag in mid-career; and this one appeared to be supported – no, engineered – by a celebrated poet and the Oxford Professor of English Language and Literature. Some of them, weakening, even lent their support to the business, which is another testimony to the well-known power of majority opinion. Dr Havering entered the punt with Fen, Cadogan, Wilkes, and Mr Hoskins. Sally promised to go back to Fen's room and wait there. And Mr Barnaby stood with his army on the bank to wave them good-bye.

'Too Watteau, my dear Charles,' he remarked. '*Embarquement pour Cythère*. Or is it *Arthur's soul*, do you suppose, being conveyed to *Avalon*?'

Charles having opined that it was more like the Flying

Dutchman, and the punt being by now in mid-stream, they returned to Mr Barnaby's rooms to drink. And none too soon; as they passed out of Parson's Pleasure, they could distinctly hear the gate-keeper phoning the proctor's office in the Clarendon Building. His tale of woe, floating through an open window, pursued them for a little while, like a wraith, and then receded beyond earshot.

For some while the five men in the punt were silent. Havering's anger had subsided into fear, and Cadogan studied him curiously as, aided by Mr Hoskins, he paddled in a direction vaguely indicated by Fen. Of his thinness there was certainly no question. The skull-bones seemed bursting through the taut, shiny skin of the face, and the body was lean as a rake. Thin cobwebs of white hair straggled over the dome of the head. The nose was sharp and slightly hooked at the end, the eyes large and green, with long lashes, beneath a convex brow; indefinably glassy in appearance. A network of veins was prominently etched on the forehead, the movements were curiously jerky, and the hands trembled persistently, as though with the beginnings of some neural disease. Cadogan was reminded of a starved, vicious, half-wild cur he had once seen crouching in an East End gutter. Like Rosseter, Havering conveyed obscurely an impression of seediness and of professional ill-success.

'Where are you taking me?' Havering's voice, soft and lacking in inflection, broke the silence. 'You'll pay for this – all of you.'

'A nice backwater,' said Fen dreamily. 'Quite close to here. When we arrive you're going to tell us everything that happened last night.'

'You're quite mistaken, sir. I am going to do nothing of the kind.'

Fen made no answer; his pale blue eyes were reflective and far away, scanning the banks, the willows with their branches panoplied over the water, the clumps of rushes with dead branches caught in them, the dull, evening reflection of light in the river. Clouds were coming up in the west to cover the declining sun – rain-clouds. The air was growing colder. A kingfisher, shining with green and blue, rose from an overhanging branch as they passed underneath. Wilkes, in the bow looked very near to sleep. Mr Hoskins, large and melancholy, paddled with steady persistence; Cadogan, still a trifle groggy from his blow on the jaw, with less certainty. If the truth be told, he was becoming a little tired of the adventurous life; in his discourse to Mr Spode the previous night he had not quite contemplated anything like this, or if he had, it had been veiled in the curtains of romance, suitably disguised, bowdlerized, and expurgated. He only hoped that the end was in sight; that Havering was the murderer; and that he was not going to be knocked about any more. He fell to wondering how Mr Scott and Mr Beavis were faring, and then, finding this occupation a trifle barren, said to Mr Hoskins:

'How did you get on to this man?'

Mr Hoskins gave his account in slow and cheerless tones, watched in angry silence by Havering. 'A Welshman from Jesus,' he said, 'put us on to him in the first place. He seemed to think from the description that there could be no mistake, and in fact' – a faint expression of gratification lit up Mr Hoskins' face – 'there was not. I made my way into his consulting-room,' he pursued obliquely, 'by a strategy connected with the perils of parturition, and the necessity in such circumstances of immediate gynaecological aid. Some individuals were fortunately assembled in various positions round the house lest he should attempt to escape. On my first seeing him, I came directly to the point by asking him how he had succeeded in disposing of the body. He was very much alarmed, though now I imagine he will deny it.'

'You young blackguard,' the doctor interposed. 'Certainly I deny it.'

'I pressed my inquiries farther,' Mr Hoskins went on, unperturbed, 'with questions concerning his movements during last night, his inheritance, Mr Rosseter, and some other matters. At every moment I could see his alarm grow ing, though he tried to conceal it. Eventually, I said that in view of the unsatisfactory nature of his replies I must take him with me to the police-station. He said that this was absurd, that I had mistaken his identity, that he had not the least idea what I was talking about, and so forth; adding, however, that he was prepared to accompany me to the police-station in order to prove his own innocence and make me pay for what he mysteriously called a "libellous intrusion". He took leave of me to get his hat and coat and, as I expected, did not return. In a very few minutes, as a matter of fact, he was leading his bicycle, with a small case strapped to the carrier, surreptitiously out of the back gate.'

Here Mr Hoskins paused and frowned. 'I can only explain the fact that our ambush did not there and then capture him by saying that Adrian Barnaby was in charge of that particular section of it, and that he is not a person capable of concentrating for very long on any one thing. What happened, in any case, was that the doctor was mounted and away before the alarm was raised. I stayed for a moment in the consulting-room to phone you at the "Mace and Sceptre", and the rest you know.'

'Ah,' said Fen. 'Why didn't you leave in your car, Havering?'

Havering snarled: 'I was going about my business in the normal way – '

'Oh, my dear paws,' Fen interrupted disgustedly. 'I suppose you thought Mr Hoskins would hear a car. Or was it just that you didn't happen to have it there?' He glanced round. 'Here we are, anyway. Hard a-port . . . No, *port*, Richard – *left* . . . '

The punt swung through a clump of reeds into the back-water he had indicated. It was a stagnant, unhealthy place. A green scum lay on the shallow water, and there were too many mosquitoes for comfort. Cadogan could not think why Fen had brought them here, but by now he was beyond questioning anything that happened; he was as passive as an ox.

'*Now*,' said Fen, standing up.

The punt rocked violently and Wilkes awoke. Cadogan and Mr Hoskins shipped their paddles and looked expectantly at Fen. Alarm was intensified in Havering's large green eyes, but they still had something of the glassy, lifeless look about them; it was like the face of a frightened man, only obscurely seen through a grimy window-pane.

'There has been too much shilly-shallying in this case,' Fen said deliberately, 'and I haven't time to linger, Havering, while you treat us to a lot of childish evasions and outbursts of false indignation. We know quite enough about the murder of Miss Tardy to have you indicted for conspiracy, but we don't yet know who killed her. That's the only reason we're bothering about you.'

'If you think that threats – '

Fen raised a hand. 'No, no. Actions, my good medico – actions. I've no time for threats. Answer my questions.'

'I shall not. How dare you hold me here? How – ?'

'I warned you against chatter of that sort,' said Fen brutally. 'Mr Hoskins, kindly help me to put his head in that filthy-looking water and hold it there.'

A punt is the safest variety of boat for a struggle; virtually nothing will capsize it. Havering never had a chance. Six times his head was plunged into the green scum, Wilkes carrying on a sort of running commentary of obscure encouragement and applause. 'Duck him!' he squealed with medieval ferocity. 'Duck the murderous devil!' Cadogan contented himself with looking on and advising Havering to fill his lungs well before each immersion. When they had held him under for the sixth time: 'That's enough,' Fen said. 'Pluck up drowned honour by the locks.'

Havering fell back, choking and gasping, into the punt. He was certainly a dismal sight. His thin hair clung, damp and disordered, to his skull. The green stuck to him in flecks and patches. He exuded a disagreeable smell, and it was obvious that he would not hold out much longer.

'Damn you,' he whispered. 'Damn you. No more! I'll tell you – I'll tell you whatever you like.' Cadogan suddenly felt a twinge of pity. He produced a handkerchief for Havering

to dry his face and head, and the older man took it grate-
fully.

'Now,' Fen said briskly, 'in the first place, what was it
you knew about Rosseter that induced him to take part in
this plan to get the money?'

'He – he was a lawyer in Philadelphia when I was in practice there as a young man. He was involved in some very
shady business – manipulation of the stock market and
eventually embezzlement of a trustee fund. He – give me a
cigarette, will you?' Havering took one from Fen's case,
puffed nervously at it, and held it between trembling fingers.
'I needn't go into all the details, but the end of it was that
Rosseter – that wasn't his name then – had to get out of the
country and come over here. I never knew him personally,
you understand – only by reputation. A few months later
I wrecked my career in America by performing an abortion.
People weren't so tolerant then. I'd put by some money,
so I came to England and set up in practice. Ten years ago
I settled here – in Oxford. I recognized Rosseter, though
he didn't know me, of course. But I didn't want to take
things up again, so I said nothing and did nothing.' He
looked quickly round, to see how they were taking it. 'I'd
got newspaper clippings about Rosseter, you see, with
photographs. He couldn't afford to have those published.'

A bull-frog was croaking in the rushes, and the mosquitoes
were becoming more insistent. Cadogan lit a cigarette and
blew out thick clouds of smoke in a futile endeavour to keep
them away. It was growing dark and an occasional colourless star showed between the ragged edges of the clouds.
Colder, too: Cadogan shivered a little and drew his coat
more closely round him.

'I built up a fair practice,' Havering went on. 'Particularly
as a heart doctor. From the money point of view, it wasn't
anything spectacular, but it was enough to live on. Then
one day I was called in to attend the old woman.'

'You mean Miss Snaith?'

'Yes.' Havering sucked listlessly at his cigarette. 'She
thought she had a weak heart. There was nothing more

wrong with it than there normally is at that age. But she paid well, and if she wanted to fancy herself on the point of death, I wasn't the one to discourage her. I gave her coloured water to drink and examined her regularly. Then one day, about a month before that bus knocked her down, she said: "Havering, you're a sycophantic fool, but you've made some endeavour to keep me alive. Take this," and gave me an envelope, telling me at the same time to look in the personal column of the *Oxford Mail* – '

'Yes, yes,' said Fen impatiently. 'We know about all that. And you guessed she was leaving you something in her will?'

'She called me Berlin,' Havering said, 'because of some fool rhyme or other. Yes.' He hesitated, seeming for the moment at a loss as to how to proceed. 'I found out Rosseter was her solicitor, and some time after she died I went to see him. I left it for a while, because I didn't want to reopen the past. But she had money, that old woman. She might leave me a lot, and I wanted to *know*.' He stared at them, and Cadogan could see the twilight reflected from the water into his eyes. 'It's funny when you come to think of it – that I should have wanted the money so much. I wasn't badly off, and I wasn't in debt, and I wasn't being blackmailed. I just wanted money – a lot of it. I saw men with a lot of money in America – not the sort of money you get by just working.' He laughed shakily. 'You'd think when you got to my age you wouldn't be worrying about buying women and luxury, wouldn't you? But that was what I wanted.'

He stared at them again. It was a kind of feeble bid for understanding and sympathy, but it made Cadogan's blood run cold. On the bank, a colony of crickets had begun their incessant, metallic cry.

'That's what lots of men have wanted,' Fen commented drily. 'The prison cemeteries are crowded with them.'

Havering almost shouted: 'I didn't kill her! They can't hang me!' Then, quietening a little: 'Hanging's a filthy business. When I was a police doctor I saw an execution at

162

Pentonville. A woman. She screamed and struggled and they took five minutes just putting the rope round her neck. Her nerve had gone, you see. I wondered what it would be like, waiting for the boards to give way under you . . . ' He put his face in his hands.

'Go on with what you were telling us,' Fen said immediately. There was not a trace of emotion of any kind in his voice.

Havering pulled himself together. 'I – saw Rosseter, and told him I knew who he was. He wouldn't admit it at first, but he couldn't hold out long. He told me the provisions of the will – do you know about that?'

'Yes. We know. Go on.'

'We planned to get the Tardy woman to sign away the money. Rosseter said she'd easily be frightened.'

'Not exactly what he told us,' Cadogan interposed.

'No,' said Fen. 'But in the circumstances that was to be expected.'

'I wish I'd had nothing to do with it,' Havering said bitterly. 'Much use I shall have for the legacy. That damned old woman's to blame, with her idiotic schemes.' He paused. 'Rosseter brought in two of the other legatees. I didn't want that, but he said we'd arrange things so that if anything ever came out they'd get the blame. That wasn't so bad. Then the night came, and we got everything ready at that place in the Iffley Road. Rosseter didn't want the woman to see him, because, although she didn't know us, she did know him, and might recognize him. So we arranged that I should put bandages round my face; that would disguise me, but not obviously, because I could say I'd had an accident. Then after I'd sent the girl away the other man – we called him Mold – was to get on with the real business.'

Again Havering paused, glancing round at his auditors. 'I was nervous. I must have been nervous, or I should have seen at once what it meant when Rosseter said he was going in to see the woman. He said, too, that he wanted us to separate to different rooms. I thought that was part of the plan to incriminate the others, so I backed him up. And then when I was alone I suddenly realized that he must be intending to kill her if he was letting himself be seen, and that this separating was to incriminate one of us.' He relit his cigarette, which had gone out. 'It sounds fantastic, doesn't it? And it was fantastic. I think we all knew there was something odd and wrong about it, but the trouble was, we'd left things too much in Rosseter's hands, and now I knew he was double-crossing us. I went to the woman in the other room – to give myself an alibi. Then after a while Rosseter came back. I expected him to have killed her, but he hadn't, because I heard her say something to him as he left the room, about troublesome legal formalities.'

'Just a minute. What time was this? Do you know?'

'Yes, I happened to look at my watch. It was twenty-five past eleven.'

'So she was still alive then. Have you any idea what Rosseter was talking to her about, and why?'

'I don't know. I think perhaps he was setting his stage somehow. You could ask him.'

Cadogan glanced quickly at his companions. The same thought was in all their minds. Was this a neatly contrived bluff, a pretended ignorance of Rosseter's death, or was it the real thing? For the life of him Cadogan could not tell. The remark had been made before it was possible to attend to the facial expression or the inflection of Havering's toneless voice. Wilkes sat placidly in the bow, a small, old figure lighting a battered pipe.

'Rosseter said the woman wasn't going to be as easy to frighten as he'd thought, and that perhaps we ought to abandon the whole scheme as being too dangerous. I argued with him about that for a while, but it was more for form's sake than anything else; I knew he was going to kill her, but I didn't want him to know I knew yet. Then the other man – Mold – came in from his room and said there was someone walking about the shop. We put out the light and stayed quiet for a while – quite a long while. Finally we decided it must be a false alarm, and Rosseter gave the other man a gun and told him to go and get on with the job.'

'What time was this?'

'About a quarter or ten to midnight. After a short while he came back and said the woman was dead.'

There was a tiny pause. Euthanasia, Cadogan thought: they all regard it as that, and not as wilful slaughter, not as the violent cutting-off of an irreplaceable compact of passion and desire and affection and will; not as a thrust into unimagined and illimitable darkness. He tried to see Havering's face, but it was only a lean silhouette in the fading light. Something took root in him that in a week, a month, a year perhaps, would become poetry. He was suddenly excited and oddly content. The words of his predecessors in the great Art came to his mind. *'They are all gone into the world of light.' 'I that in heill was and in gladnesse.' 'Dust hath closed Helen's eye . . . '* The vast and terrifying significance of death closed round him for a moment like the petals of a dark flower.

'I went and examined her,' Havering was saying. 'There was a thin cord round her neck, with the usual bruising. Death, of course, due to asphyxia. It was while I was doing that that the girl appeared. She had been all the time in the shop below. Rosseter sent her away and promised she would keep quiet about what she had seen. He was unnerved, and that surprised me, because I thought he'd killed the woman. We were all unnerved, and wanted to get out, but someone had to get rid of the body and get the toys back to the other shop. We arranged how it was to be done, and then we three men drew lots for it, and it came out that I had to do it. I stayed there for a while, thinking. I was frightened, and afraid I should be caught with the body.

'Then someone came into the shop below.' He looked at Cadogan. 'It was you. What happened you know. I knocked you out and put you in that closet place downstairs. I locked the door so that you wouldn't be able to get into the shop again, and see that it had been changed, but I left the window open so that you could get away. I knew that you'd go to the police, but I thought that if they came back and found the body gone, there would be nothing they could do. I – I didn't want to injure you, you understand – '

'Never mind the apologies,' Fen said. 'What happened to the body?'

'I got it out into the car the woman had left. It was heavy, and I'm not a strong man, so it took a long time. It was beginning to get stiff by then, and I had to push the head and arms about to move it through the car door. That was horrible. I took it to the river and put stones inside the clothes and pushed it in. I thought it was deep there, but it wasn't, and the thing just lay wallowing on the edge, lying in the mud and stones. I had to pick it out again, and carry it somewhere else. It was dark, and once it slipped and the wet arms fell round my neck . . . Then I had to take the stones out again because it was too heavy . . . ' A second time Havering put his face in his hands.

'Where did you put it in the end? Fen asked.

'A little way up the river from here. There are three willows close together at the edge.'

In the twilight a bat was flying; the piercing, strident chatter of the crickets never ceased; and far away in the town the clocks were striking half past seven. The river water was black now, and the small fishes would be clinging to the woman's eyes. In the punt they were no more than silhouettes, the obscurity pierced only by the glowing ends of their cigarettes.

Fen said: 'After her handsbag – what happened to that?'

'Rosseter took it away with him. I don't know what he did with it.'

'Go on.'

'I was wet and filthy, but I had to go back and get those toys away and replace the groceries and change the flat round. By the time I'd finished it was nearly light. I heard you go' – this to Cadogan – 'and I pushed some stores into the closet and went away myself. I don't think anyone saw me.' The toneless voice degenerated to a whine. 'No one can prove anything.'

'How do you mean "changed the flat round"?' Cadogan demanded.

'I cleaned it up and moved the furniture and oiled the door. I knew you'd only seen one room. I thought you'd imagine you'd mistaken the place.'

'You were quite right,' Cadogan conceded. 'For a time I did. But why was the shop-door left open?'

Havering's face darkened. 'It was those other fools – when they left. I didn't know it was open. If it hadn't been, none of this would have happened.'

Fen stretched out his long legs and smoothed his hair. 'While we're on the subject of your going home, would anyone have known you were away last night?'

'No one,' Havering replied sulkily. 'My servant sleeps out. She leaves at nine o'clock at night and doesn't return till 7.30 in the morning.'

'By which time, no doubt, you were in bed and asleep. What were you doing between 4.30 and 5 this afternoon?'

'What?' Havering stared. 'What do you mean?'

'Never mind that. Answer the question.'

'I was – I was returning home from my afternoon round of visits.'

'What time did you get in?'

'A little after five. I don't know exactly.'

'Did anyone see you come in?'

'The maid. But why – '

'What time did you leave your last patient?'

'Damn it, I can't remember,' Havering exclaimed. 'What does it matter, anyway? It's got nothing to do with last night. Listen: I didn't kill that woman, and you can't prove I did. I'm not going to hang. I'm a sick man, and I can't stand much more of this.'

'Be quiet,' Fen said. 'Was it you who set those two men to follow Cadogan and myself?'

'Yes.'

'Where did they come from?'

'I got a man I knew in London to send them down. They were prepared to do anything, and ask no questions, if they were only paid well enough.'

'What happened exactly?'

Havering spoke to Cadogan. 'Rosseter rang me up and said you'd been to see him. He described you, and asked if I knew how you'd come to be meddling in the business. I recognized you as the man in the shop. I was alarmed. I sent Weaver and Faulkes to follow you and prevent you talking to anyone who might give the game away – especially the girl.'

'So when we seemed likely to catch up with her, they disposed of us and took her away to stop her mouth once and for all.'

'I gave no orders to kill – '

'Don't quibble, please. The cottage they took her to belonged to Miss Winkworth. How did they know to take her there?'

'I knew her. I recognized her last night in spite of the mask, and she recognized me. I rang up to tell her the girl was dangerous and would have to be shut up for a few hours. She suggested the cottage near Wootton.'

'Knowing, no doubt, what the euphemism "shut up for a few hours" meant.'

'That's a lie.'

'The girl would have traced the owner afterwards, wouldn't she?'

'We arranged for Weaver and Faulkes to break in. Then no responsibility could fall on her.'

'Let it pass. It's as good an evasion as any. And now' – Fen leaned forward – 'we arrive at the most important point of the lot. Precisely what did you see when you examined the body which made you say no one who was present could have killed Miss Tardy?'

Havering drew a deep breath. 'Ah, you heard that, did you? Well, it's true. I've been a police doctor, as I told you. You can't ever tell exactly how long a person's been dead, but the quicker you get to the body the more accurate you can be. I examined it at about nine minutes to midnight. And I'm willing to swear that that woman died not later than 11.45 and not earlier than 11.35. Do you see what that means?'

'Certainly,' Fen answered placidly. 'As a matter of interest, did you inform any of the others of this fact?'

'I told Rosseter.'

'Ah, yes.' In the darkness Fen smiled. 'Between 11.35 and 11.45 you were all together in a different room. No one could have got in from the outside, either.'

Havering was shivering and half hysterical. 'So unless the girl killed her,' he said, 'no one did, because the thing's impossible.'

12. The Episode of the Missing Link

'Damn!' said Sally. 'It's beginning to rain.'

Unfortunately, it was. Dark rain-clouds made the night sky darker, and there were no longer any stars visible. The drops hissed and spattered in the leaves.

'There used to be a summer-house at the end of the garden,' Cadogan answered. 'Come on. Let's run for it.'

It was still there, and in another moment they were stumbling breathlessly up the steps to shelter. Cadogan struck a match, and the light showed a dusty, comfortless interior, with deck-chairs stacked against the walls, a few garden tools, and a large square box which contained a set of bowling woods. An oak seat faced the doorway, and they sat down on it. Cadogan peered about him in the gloom.

'This gives me the creeps,' he observed; adding without much relevance: 'When I was an undergraduate I made love to a girl in here.'

'Pretty?'

'No, not particularly. She had rather fat legs and her name was – was – Damn, I've quite forgotten. *Tout lasse, tout casse, tout passe.* I remember I wasn't feeling well and didn't put much zest into the business. I don't suppose she enjoyed it especially, poor thing.'

It was an hour since Havering had made his confession on the river, and he was now, apathetic and as though drugged, temporarily immured in a room adjoining Fen's. Fen himself had driven them out because, as he said, he wanted to think. From where they had been strolling on the lawn they could see the lights of his room, and all the lights of the garden front of St Christopher's. Mr Hoskins had gone off with Wilkes to the latter's rooms for a drink, since Fen's whisky proved to be exhausted. So for the moment all – apart from the strains of jazz which issued from an undergraduate chamber – was peace.

'One does extraordinary things,' said Cadogan reflectively. 'But on the whole, not as extraordinary as the things other people do. Look at Miss Snaith. Look at Rosseter. Look at' – he became rather gloomy – 'Fen.'

'D'you spend all your time chasing about after murderers with him?'

'I?' Cadogan chuckled suddenly. 'No – God be praised. But it really is comic.'

'What's comic?'

'Last night – only last night – I was craving for adventure, for excitement: anything to stave off middle age. Goethe said that you ought to be very careful what you wish for, because you'll probably get it. How right he was. I wanted to be delivered from dullness, and the gods have taken me at my word.'

'I shouldn't have thought you'd have led a dull life.'

'I do, though. Seeing the same people, doing the same things. Trying to make what I like doing and what people will pay me for overlap a bit more.'

'But you're famous,' Sally objected. 'Professor Fen said you were, and I've just remembered where I've seen your face before. It was in the *Radio Times*.'

'Ah,' said Cadogan without much enthusiasm. 'I wish they wouldn't publish these things without asking one first. It looked like a mystic trying to communicate with the Infinite and tackle a severe bout of indigestion at the same time.'

'What did you do?'

'Do? Oh, I see what you mean. I read poetry.'

'What poetry?'

'Some of my own.'

Sally grinned in the half-darkness. 'I still can't imagine you writing poetry. For one thing, you're too easy to get on with.'

Cadogan sat up. 'You know, that cheers me. I was afraid I was degenerating into a mere word-spinner, one Wormius hight.'

'Of course, your saying things like that rather ruins it.'

'Sorry. It was a quotation from Pope.'

'I don't care who it was a quotation from. It's really rather rude to quote when you know I shan't understand. Like talking about someone in a language they don't know.'

'Oh dear.' Cadogan was penitent. 'Honestly, it's just habit. And anyway, it'd be far ruder if I were to talk down to you, as if you were a child.'

Sally was still considering the improbability of Cadogan's pretensions to poetry. She felt put out by his saturnine but unremarkable appearance. 'You ought to look different, too.'

'Why?' said Cadogan. He lit a cigarette and gave her one too. 'There's no reason why poets should look like anything in particular. Wordsworth resembled a horse with powerful convictions; Chesterton was wholly Falstaffian; Whitman was as strong and hairy as a goldrush prospector. The fact is, there's no such thing as a poetic type. Chaucer was a Government official, Sidney a soldier, Villon a thief, Marvell an M.P., Burns a ploughboy, Housman a don. You can be any sort of man and still be a poet. You can be as conceited as Wordsworth or as modest as Hardy; as rich as Byron or as poor as Francis Thompson; as religious as Cowper or as pagan as Carew. It doesn't matter what you believe; Shelley believed every lunatic idea under the sun. Keats was certain of nothing but the holiness of the heart's affections. And I'm willing to bet, my dear Sally, that you could pass Shakespeare on the way to work every morning for twenty years without noticing him once ... Good Lord, this is developing into a lecture.'

'Still, poets must be alike in *some* way.'

'Certainly they are. They all write poetry.'

'Well, then, that would make them all alike, at least partly.'

'Would it?' Cadogan exhaled a cloud of smoke and

watched it drift, spectral and gauzy, across the pale oblong of the door. 'If all the poets are collected together in some ante-room of paradise, there'll be a good deal of social discomfort by this time. Marlowe will not be speaking to Dowson, and Emily Brontë will flee at the approach of Chaucer . . . ' He grinned, but went on more seriously: 'I think the only thing poets have in common is a kind of imaginative generosity of heart towards their fellows – and even then one can't be too sure, with people like Baudelaire and Pope and unpleasant little neurotics like Swinburne. No, there isn't such a thing as a poet type. And for a very good reason.'

'Why?'

Cadogan groaned mildly. 'It's very nice of you to be so polite, but I do know when I'm being a bore.'

Sally pinched him. 'Ass,' she said. 'I'm interested. Tell me why a poet doesn't have to be a man who needs a haircut.'

'Because,' said Cadogan, uneasily attempting to gauge the the length of his own hair with his left hand, 'poetry isn't the outcome of personality. I mean by that that it exists independently of your mind, your habits, your feelings, and everything that goes to make up your personality. The poetic emotion's impersonal: the Greeks were quite right when they called it inspiration. Therefore, what you're like personally doesn't matter a twopenny damn: all that matters is whether you've a good receiving-set for the poetic waves. Poetry's a visitation, coming and going at its own sweet will.'

'Well, then, what's it like?'

'As a matter of fact, I can't explain it properly because I don't understand it properly, and I hope I never shall. But it certainly isn't a question of oh-look-at-the-pretty-roses or oh-how-miserable-I-feel-today. If it were, there'd be forty million poets in England at present. It's a curious passive sensation. Some people say it's as if you've noticed something for the first time, but I think it's more as if the thing in question had noticed *you* for the first time. You feel as if the rose or whatever it is were shining at you. Invariably after the first moment the phrase occurs to you to describe it; and when that's happened, you snap out of it: all your personality comes rushing back, and you write the *Canterbury Tales* or *Paradise Lost* or *King Lear* according to the kind of person you happen to be. That's up to you.'

'And does it happen often?'

In the darkness, Cadogan shrugged. 'Every day. Every year. There's no telling if each time, whenever it is, mayn't be the last. . . . In the meantime, of course, one gets dull and middle-aged.'

The rain drummed steadily on the roof of the summer-house.

'I think you ought to be married,' said Sally after a pause. 'You aren't, are you?'

'No. But what an odd diagnosis. Why should I get married?'

'You need someone to look after you, and cheer you up when you get miserable.'

'You may be right,' said Cadogan, 'though I doubt it. I've only been in love seriously once in my life, and that was ages ago.'

'Who was she? No,' said Sally quickly. 'I shouldn't be so inquisitive. I don't expect you want to talk about it.'

'As a matter of fact, I don't in the least mind talking about it,' said Cadogan more cheerfully 'It's all over and done with now. Her name was Phyllis Hume, and she was an actress – dark, with large eyes, and a superb figure. But we should have had the hell of a time if we'd got married; we were both furious egoists, and we could only endure each other in the smallest quantities. If we were together for even a week we fought like Jacob and the Angel.'

'The trouble is,' said Sally, 'you don't know much about women.'

'No, I don't,' Cadogan agreed. 'But then as I don't intend to marry it doesn't much worry me. You, on the other hand – '

'Oh – '

'A lot of people are going to want to marry you.'

'Thanks for the compliment, but why – '

'Because, Sally Carstairs, you're immensely rich.'

She sat up. 'Do you mean I shall still get the money?'

'I don't see why not.'

'But I didn't think – anyway, Miss Tardy claimed it. It'll be hers.'

'I don't know.' Cadogan reflected. 'In the absence of any contesting relatives – and Mrs Wheatley said there *weren't* any – I should think it would be yours. But what I know about the law could be typed on a penny stamp.'

'Oh,' said Sally, quite overwhelmed, 'I *shall* have to be careful.'

'Don't be too careful.'

'How do you mean?'

Cadogan dropped his cigarette on to the floor and trod it out. 'There's a German story about a very rich and very beautiful young woman who was surrounded by suitors. But whenever she made up her mind to marry one of them, she was suddenly afraid that he only wanted her for her money, and the fear was so strong that it drove her to break the engagement. Then one day when she was in Italy she met a young merchant, and the two fell in love with one another. Yet even real love wasn't strong enough to drive out the old obsession, and she decided to test him. She said that she had a fiancé in Germany, that all her own money had gone, and that her fiancé needed ten thousand guilders to set him up in business (ten thousand guilders, she knew, was all the fortune the young merchant possessed). Well, he gave her the money for love of her, and she made him promise to come to Germany on a certain day to see her married. Then she went happily home, because, without knowing it, he'd emerged triumphantly from her test, and she gave orders for the house to be splendidly decorated for his coming. He never came, because she'd tried him too far. He went instead to the wars, and was killed.'

'And her?'

'She died an old maid.'

'She was stupid,' said Sally, 'but I see her point of view. Of course I shall never really be able to believe I own all that money. What would you do with it if it was yours?'

'Go to Italy to escape the English winter,' Cadogan answered promptly, 'and lay down a wine-cellar. What will you do?'

'Get a cottage and a servant for Mummy. Buy a lot of clothes. Buy a car. And go to London and Paris and all over the place . . . ' She ran out of ideas, adding with a laugh: 'But I shall carry on at Lennox's until it comes true.'

Cadogan sighed. 'Well, today's undignified scamper has brought you a fortune. What's it brought me?'

'Adventure,' Sally pointed out with a touch of malice. 'Excitement. Wasn't that what you wanted?'

Cadogan, who was feeling rather stiff, got up and began to wander about. 'Yes,' he said. 'Yes, it was what I wanted. But I don't want any more of it. For excitement, give me a country walk any day; and I'm inclined to think there's a good deal more adventure to be had by just opening the curtains in the morning. I dare say that sounds gutless and middle-aged, but after all, I *am* middle-aged, and there's no escaping the fact; as a matter of fact, after today I welcome it. Being middle-aged means that you know what matters to you. All this business has been strictly meaningless to me, and from now on I shall conserve my energies, such as they are, for significant things. If ever I'm tempted by posters advertising cruises, I shall whisper "Sharman"; whenever I see headlines about international crooks, I shall murmur "Rosseter". I eschew Poictesme and Logres now and for ever. In fact, in a couple of days I shall go back to London and start work again – though I've a nightmare feeling that this business isn't over yet.'

'Oh, golly, I'd almost forgotten about all that.' As she inhaled, the tip of Sally's cigarette grew fiery in the darkness. 'And you haven't told me what you got out of that doctor.'

'He said you were the only person who could have killed Miss Tardy.'

176

There was a sudden paralysing silence, and Cadogan cursed himself savagely. But it was too late to recall the words now.

'What did he mean?' Sally said in a small voice. 'He must've had some reason for saying that.'

Cadogan explained about the problem of the time of death. 'But he may have been lying,' he concluded.

'Do you think he was?'

He hesitated; then: 'Frankly, no,' he said. 'But that doesn't mean you've got anything to worry about. There must be some way round it, if one only knew. Or he may just have been mistaken.' (But he didn't believe it.)

There was another pause. 'You see, it checks with what Rosseter and the Winkworth woman said,' he resumed at last. 'About it having been an impossible murder, and Havering having said at the time that no one there could have done it.'

'Still, he might have been lying to *them*.'

'Why?'

'Because . . . Well, perhaps because he did it himself, and knew the real time of death would give him away.'

'But in that case, why make it impossible for *anyone* to have done it? After all, he didn't know at the time that you were downstairs.'

'He might have been protecting someone.'

Cadogan drew a deep breath. 'I suppose it isn't wholly impossible – but in heaven's name, *who*? Rosseter? Sharman?'

'What about the woman? You said he knew her.'

'Yes, but if you'd *seen* her . . . And, anyway, the only time she was ever alone was while Rosseter was in with Miss Tardy. How could she have done it?'

'They may all have been lying about that.'

'But again, why? The point is that if you're going to cover up a murder, your own or someone else's, you don't deliberately make the thing look impossible – '

'But don't you see – they may have arranged that story after they knew I was there?'

'Oh.' Cadogan was momentarily pulled up short. It certainly appeared possible. But then the salient objection occurred to him. 'In that case, they wouldn't have tried to get rid of you.'

'Yes, because it was safer that you should never hear anything about it at all than that they should have to fall back on this story of me having done it.'

'I see that, but I still think Havering was telling the truth – '

He had been so carried away by dialectic that he had not realized that he was methodically destroying her defence. Now a tearful voice from the darkness brought him to a sense of what he was doing.

'Golly,' said Sally. 'I *am* in a mess.'

'Nonsense,' said Cadogan, quite wild with apology. 'You're not in any kind of mess. We know you didn't do it, and it's only a matter of time till we find out who did.' He put his hand comfortingly on her leg, and then, recollecting himself, hastily withdrew it.

'It's all right, you ass,' Sally gasped, half laughing and half crying. 'You're old enough to be my father.'

'I am *not*.' They both laughed. 'That's better,' he said.

'Oh, I'm behaving like a baby. Don't take any notice. I hate women who cry, anyway.'

'Well, you're not going to improve matters by powdering your nose in the dark.'

'Can't help that. If I look as though I've been through a flour-bin when I get outside, you will tell me, won't you.'

Cadogan promised.

'I ought to be going home, you know,' she said. 'Mummy will be wondering what on earth's become of me.'

'No, don't go yet. Ring her up and stay the evening with us. Anyway, by the time we get inside, Gervase will have found out who the murderer is.'

'Golly, I wish I thought so. He's a strange man, isn't he?'

'I suppose he is if you're prepared for the ordinary kind of don. But underneath – well, I shouldn't like to have him as an enemy. There's something one can only describe as formidable about him – not on the surface, of course. There he's engagingly naïve. But if anyone can get to the bottom of this business, he can.'

'But he doesn't know any more about it than you do.'

'He can put it together better. These problems aren't for my weak intellect.'

'Still, who do *you* think did it?'

He considered, recalling faces rather than facts. Rosseter, yellow and Asiatic, with his prominent jaw and professional ease; Sharman, rabbity, muffled, drunk, and contemptible; Miss Winkworth, with her moustache and pig-like eyes; Havering, neurotic, thin, rigid, frightened. A lawyer a schoolmaster, a fake medium, and a doctor. It was into their hands that a foolish old woman had put her affairs, and with them, the life of her niece. But, of course, there was another – the enigmatic West. Had he ever claimed his inheritance? Was he, perhaps, the controlling force behind the whole affair? Cadogan shook his head.

'A lot of it's clear,' he said aloud. 'There are three threads to it: the plan to intimidate Miss Tardy; Rosseter's plan to kill her; and someone else's plan to do the same thing. The first two came to nothing, and there's nothing you can get a grip on the third. Honestly, I haven't the faintest idea. It seems to lie between Havering, Sharman, and the woman, as there was no possibility of anyone else getting into the shop. But beyond that, I simply don't know. And as you say, it's always possible they're all lying, in which case it looks quite hopeless and we might as well give up.'

In the silence which followed, they became aware that the rain had stopped.

'Well,' Sally said, 'let's go back and see if anything's happened.'

Without speaking again, they walked across the wet lawn to the college and the lighted window of Fen's room.

However, they were not destined to arrive there without interruption. In the passage which leads from the gardens to the back quadrangle, and which is lit by a single electric light sunk in the groined roof, they encountered Mr Spode's plump little form, moving in the same direction as themselves. His face cleared when he saw Cadogan.

'Oh, there you are, my dear fellow,' he greeted them. 'This is luck.'

'Now, look here, Erwin,' said Cadogan severely. 'I don't know what devilry you're up to in Oxford, but I consider it very hard that when I come away for a holiday you should follow me about like some ghastly spectre plaguing me to go and lecture the Americans on a subject in which obviously they have no interest.'

The spectre blinked and coughed. 'It would be a very good tour,' it murmured. 'Yale, Harvard, Bryn Mawr ... Did you know America was full of beautiful women?'

'What in heaven's name has that got to do with it? *I will not go and lecture in America* ... For the Lord's sake, either go up those stairs or get out of the way and allow us to pass.'

'Are you going to see Professor Fen?'

'Where did you think I was going – the Regent's Park Zoo?'

'I have the proofs of your new book on me.'

'And about time, too. Full of misprints, I don't doubt. Come along up, Erwin. Come and have a drink. We're on the point of solving an important criminal case.'

Mr Spode, protesting faintly at the social implications of such an intrusion, was hustled up the stairs. They found Fen on the telephone (he made motions requiring silence as they came in), and Wilkes and Mr Hoskins, markedly the better for whisky, lounging in two of the armchairs. A tall standard lamp, glowing softly near the fireplace, was the only illumination. Fen's pistol lay on the desk, the light falling like a streak of mercury along its short barrel. The atmosphere was subtly different, with a sort of combined tension and satiety, and Cadogan noticed with a shock of astonishment that everyone looked quickly and curiously at Mr Spode as he came in.

'Yes,' Fen was saying to the telephone. 'Yes, Mr Barnaby, as many as you can get. Drunk, are they? Well, provided they haven't lost the use of their legs, that's all right. Have you got the address? Yes; all correct. And for the love of God don't allow them to kick up a great rumpus about it. It's not likely to be a game. Yes, we'll be along, and I promise it's the last time. All right. Good-bye.'

He turned to greet the newcomers. 'Well,' he said amiably. 'It's very pleasant to see you all again. You're just in time for the last act.'

'I want my dinner,' Cadogan said.

'He which hath no stomach to this fight,' Fen chanted, 'let him depart. That includes you.'

'I suppose,' said Cadogan ungraciously, 'that you think you know who the murderer is.'

'It's very simple,' said Fen. *Sancta simplicitas.* Your Mr Spode – '

But this was too much for Cadogan. 'Erwin!' he exclaimed. 'Erwin the murderer! Don't talk nonsense.' He turned to Mr Spode and saw that he was goggling.

'If you only let me finish,' said Fen waspishly, 'you might learn something. I was going to say that your Mr Spode is quite evidently the fifth legatee. The Old Man of the West, you will recall, wore a pale, plum-coloured vest.' He indicated Mr Spode's petunia waistcoat.

'The Missing Link!' Cadogan shouted excitedly. 'Erwin is the Missing Link!'

Mr Spode coughed. 'Hardly very funny, is that, Cadogan?' he said with dignity. 'I haven't the least idea what you people are doing, but when it comes to personal insults – '

'Mr Spode,' Fen interrupted him. 'You are in intellectual darkness. Your firm was situated in Oxford, wasn't it, until about a year ago?'

'Yes,' Mr Spode replied blankly. 'That's so.'

'Did you at any time have dealings with a Miss Snaith, of "Valhalla", Boar's Hill?'

'Oh.' Mr Spode went pale. 'Yes – yes, I did.'

'Professional dealings?'

'Yes. She wanted us to publish a book she'd written. About spiritualism. It was a very bad book.'

'*Did* you publish it?'

'Yes,' said Mr Spode helplessly. 'We did. We never meant to. As a matter of fact, I lost it almost as soon as it arrived.'

'Publishers' offices,' Cadogan muttered explanatorily to the others. 'Always losing things. Continual shambles.'

'We couldn't find it anywhere,' Mr Spode went on. 'You see, we hadn't even *read* it at the time, and no one dared to write and tell her what had happened. She kept ringing up to ask how we liked it, and we had to put her off with all manner of excuses. Then eventually someone found it mixed up with a lot of American correspondence which was never looked at, and we felt we'd simply *got* to do it after keeping it a year.'

'Moral courage in the publishing trade,' Cadogan observed benevolently.

'And she was very grateful,' Fen said. 'And sent you an envelope and asked you to look in the personal column of the *Oxford Mail* – '

Mr Spode gaped at him absurdly. 'How did you know?'

'He saw it in a crystal, Erwin,' said Cadogan. 'Or it was communicated to him by spirits. Anyway, did you do what the old woman told you?'

'No,' said Mr Spode, distracted. 'I didn't. I put the envelope away, meaning to look at it later, and then forgot about it for a time, and when I remembered it – it had got lost,' he concluded feebly.

'Well, you'd better find it again,' said Cadogan, 'because it's worth about a hundred thousand pounds to you.'

'W – what?' Mr Spode looked as if he were ready to faint. As briefly as possible, they explained the whole situation to him. To their annoyance, he kept saying 'Don't be silly; don't be silly' all the time; but in the end they managed to convince him. For Cadogan, the tale gained nothing in the telling, and how Fen was able to deduce from it the name of the murderer he could not think. Sharman, of course, had behaved suspiciously.

'As a matter of interest,' Fen asked in conclusion, 'what did induce you to come to Oxford last night?'

'It was business,' said Mr Spode. 'Nutling is living here, and he wanted me to run over the proofs of Staveling's new novel with him. It's libellous,' Mr Spode complained.

'What time did you get here?'

'About one in the morning, I think. I had a breakdown near Thame, and it took hours to fix. You can check that,' Mr Spode added anxiously.

'And why did you leave the tea-party so suddenly this afternoon? When Rosseter was killed, I was exceedingly suspicious of you.'

'Oh . . . oh . . . Well, the fact is, I'm shy,' said Mr Spode with pathos. They all gazed at him, and he went red. 'Shy,' he repeated aggressively. 'I didn't know anyone, and I felt I wasn't wanted.'

'Of course you were wanted,' said Sally, touched.

'So Erwin isn't the murderer after all.' There was a hint of disappointment in Cadogan's voice.

'No,' said Fen; and added gnomically: 'Though if everyone had their rights he would be.' He regarded Mr Spode judicially, like a cannibal considering the culinary merits of a Christian mission.

'Only a Red Herring,' said Cadogan offensively. 'A Red Herring and the Missing Link, and a wicked niggardly exploiter of divine-genius-as-represented-by-me. And now he's got more money than he'll ever know what to do with, just because he lost a manuscript and hadn't the courage to say so. I could do with some of that money.'

'So could I,' said Fen aggrievedly, momentarily distracted from his high purpose by the injustice and enormity of the economic situation. 'No one ever leaves me any money.' Then, glancing hastily at his watch: 'Good heavens, we must go.'

'You haven't told us who the murderer is.'

'Oh? Haven't I?' said Fen. 'Well, who do you think it is? Use what little ingenuity Heaven has provided you with.'

'Well . . . ' Cadogan hesitated. 'Sharman, I should say.'

'Why?'

'Well, for one thing, you remember the Winkworth woman said that when she and Havering and Rosseter were together they shut the door of the room? He could have gone in to Miss Tardy and killed her then.'

Fen beamed at him. 'But you seem to forget that Rosseter joined Havering and the woman at 11.25. At 11.30, according to the woman, Sharman joined them, and Miss Tardy couldn't have died before 11.35.'

'Havering must have invented that story about the time of death.'

'What for? To protect Sharman, when he was in deadly fear for his own neck?'

'Then he was mistaken.'

'Practically impossible, I should say, as he got to the body so soon after death. The signs of the early stages are fairly definite.'

'Couldn't Sharman have done it when he went in to Miss Tardy with the gun? You remember he talked some non-sense about the light bulb being out, to excuse the delay.'

'My dear Richard, Havering would have known if the woman had only just that minute been killed. That would point straight to Sharman; and again, there's no earthly reason why Havering should protect him once the whole business had come out. Every reason why he shouldn't, in fact. And the correspondence of all the stories is so exact, and containing so much that can be checked, that it's pretty certain they're true. Your theory faces this difficulty, you see: that although Sharman could have strangled the woman between 11.25 and 11.30, or at 11.50, she actually died between 11.35 and 11.45.'

'Oh, very well,' said Cadogan, disgusted. 'Sharman didn't kill her, then. Who did?'

'Sharman, of course,' said Fen, striding across to the door of the room in which Havering was incarcerated.

'W – what?' Cadogan stammered, outraged.

Fen had unlocked the door. 'Do you know, Havering's actually asleep,' he said, peering inside. 'Asleep with a towel round his head and the weight of his crimes upon him.' He re-locked the door.

'Listen, Gervase, this is ridiculous. You've just proved he couldn't have – '

'I wish you wouldn't moan so,' said Fen in exasperation. 'Sharman killed Emilia Tardy. *Sharman killed Emilia Tardy.*'

'All right. All right. You've just disproved it yourself. Don't let that worry you.'

'Oh, my dear paws,' said Fen. 'Of course you're too un-intelligent to see how it was done. Anyway, we must go now and meet Barnaby and his army at Sharman's house. Sally, you'd better not come. Remember, the man's killed two people already.'

'I'm coming,' Sally answered promptly.

Fen smiled at her. 'Bring out the irons,' he said. ' *"He that outlives this day, and comes safe home, will stand a tip-toe when this day is named, and rouse him at the name of Crispin . . ."* No, perhaps not exactly. Come along.'

13. The Episode of the Rotating Professor

George Sharman lived in Great King Street, which is a cheap residential road near Oxford Station. The house which he inhabited (along with a daily slut who came to cook his meals and make a pretence of cleaning), stood a little apart from the rest of the row, and boasted something in the way of a garden; if some barren rhododendron bushes, a great deal of rank grass, several cabbages, and two exuberant but unproductive apple-trees can be dignified with that name. It was small, and constructed of grey stone with a white facing at the front; on the wooden porch, green paint flaked and blistered. Its name was 'The Haven'. The slut, after a day occupied mainly with drinking stout and reading a novelette in the sitting-room, returned to her own house at eight o'clock. So when Fen, Wilkes, Sally, and Mr Hoskins encountered Mr Barnaby at the end of the road, Mr Sharman was presumably its only occupant.

Mr Barnaby was full of bizarre strategies. He was holding a large street-map under a lamp and studying it intently but without much evident comprehension.

'They're *all* here, my dear Anthony,' he told Mr Hoskins. 'Quite fiery and aggressive with spirituous liquors. Positively *every* way of escape is guarded by some desperado of a Blue.'

'Of course, there's every possibility that he's gone already,' Fen said. 'But I'm taking no chances. Wilkes, will you stay well in the background with Sally?' Wilkes, brandishing his umbrella, nodded, and Fen was so taken aback at this immediate acquiescence that he forgot for a moment what he was going to say. Then, pulling himself together: 'Mr Barnaby, you've got someone on the back gate?'

'Oh, but of *course*.'

'Good. Mr Hoskins, stay here and help Mr Barnaby. Richard, the front gate's yours. I shall go in and interview the gentleman, if he's there.'

'Too like the *Somme*,' Mr Barnaby murmured. 'The Eve of Battle, by Burne-Jones.'

They all went, feeling a little foolish, to take up their positions. Rain was falling again, and the reflections of the street lamps gained intensity and precision on the wet black road. No one was about. A sound of muffled altercation from some way away suggested that Mr Barnaby's recruits were dissatisfied with some feature of the campaign. Cadogan stood by a telegraph pole, and putting his ear to it, listened to the singing of the wires. Analysing his feelings, he found that he was less excited than curious. After all, they had everything on their side.

Fen walked briskly up the short asphalt path which led to the door. Seeing a notice requiring him to knock and ring, he knocked and rang. He waited; knocked again; rang again; and eventually, receiving no answer, walked out of sight round the side of the house, where he might be presumed to be entering burglariously by a window. The rain increased in volume, and Cadogan turned up his coat collar. Mr Barnaby could be heard discoursing to Mr Hoskins on some subject unconnected with the present business. Two, three minutes went by without incident. And then, abruptly, the reverberation of a shot came from the house – a violent detonation accompanied by a sharp gash of flame in one of the darkened rooms. Immediately Fen's voice was heard shouting, but the words were indistinct, and Cadogan, his muscles tight and his heart pounding, hesitated where to go and what to do. Finally he stumbled over the wet muddy lawn in the direction in which Fen had gone; that left the front gate unguarded, but along the road, in either direction, there were guards. Rounding the corner of the house, he was aware out of the corner of his eye of a dark figure slipping through the bushes on the other side, and gave a shout of warning. Almost simultaneously Fen dropped from a nearby window, cursing in several languages, and waved him back to his post.

'He's out,' he announced rather obviously. 'And he's got a gun. The other side.' They ran back again, slipping and stumbling in the darkness. Someone in the house next door flung open the window and said: 'Anything the matter?' but they ignored him, and by the time he had got on a hat and coat and arrived outside, almost everyone was gone.

Cadogan was never able to sort out the exact details of the fiasco which followed. It is to be remembered that Mr Barnaby's army was not wholly sober; that in the darkness it was not easy to distinguish friend from foe, with the result that Mr Barnaby was set upon until his distinctive wails revealed the mistake; and that everyone, under the erroneous impression that the quarry was in sight, deserted his post at the crucial moment and joined in a fruitless general beating to and fro. It was soon apparent that Sharman had made his way through a gap in the fence at the back of the garden into an alley beyond; and Fen, unbelievably enraged, sent two undergraduates back to the house in case they were mistaken, dispatched Mr Barnaby (now plaintive with physical injury) and the rest in the direction of the station, and himself, with Cadogan, Mr Hoskins, Sally, and Wilkes, set off along the only other possible escape route, the road which leads out to the suburb of Botley.

'He wanted to create a diversion,' said Fen, 'and, by God, he succeeded. Put not your trust in princes, etcetera . . . Keep an eye out on either side, everyone, and for God's sake remember he's *armed* . . . ' He subsided into a sort of dull complaining, very distressing to listen to.

'Unless he's quite mad he won't have gone to the station,' Cadogan ventured.

'No,' said Fen, a little mollified. 'That's why I sent the others there. They're so tight they couldn't corner a tortoise in a rabbit-hutch . . . Sally, I really think you ought to go back.'

'Me? No fear. Anyway, I've got Dr Wilkes to look after me.'

'You see?' said Wilkes complacently.

'The vanity of the old,' said Fen. 'I suppose you realize, Wilkes, that you ought to be ending your life in ripe contemptation, and not gadding about protecting young girls?'

'You unchivalrous hound,' said Wilkes, and this so abashed Fen that for a short while he was quite silent.

This road, unlike Great King Street, was a busy one, and at several points they had difficulty in forcing their way through the ambuscades of damp umbrellas. The brightly-lighted buses, their radiators steaming beneath the rain, lumbered by. The gutters gurgled and streamed with water. A policeman, caped and imperious, stood at a crossroads directing traffic, but of Mr Sharman there was no visible sign.

'Oh, damn,' said Fen. 'We're never going to find him, you know. He may have gone in anywhere. God rot Barnaby and his minions for making a mess of things.'

But Sally was taking matters into her own hands. She ran into the road, narrowly missing a taxi on the way, and approached the policeman.

'Hullo, Bob,' she said.

'Why, 'ullo, Sally,' he answered. 'Gawd, what a night. You oughtn't ter talk ter me when I'm on point duty, yer know.'

'I'm looking for a man, Bob.'

'When weren't yer?' said Bob, winking. He beckoned a lorry across.

'Oh, funny, aren't you?' said Sally. 'No, really, Bob, this is serious. He must have come up here. Weedy, undersized chap, with rabbity teeth; very muffled up.'

'Ah, yes, I saw 'im, not more'n a minute ago. 'E was nearly crushed to a pudding, crossin' against signals.'

'Where did he go? '

'Into the flicks,' said Bob, jerking his head in the appropriate direction. ' 'Ardly your type, though, I should 'ave thought.'

But Sally was by this time returning to the others, flushed and victorious. 'He's gone into the Colossal,' she told them.

'Good for you,' said Fen. 'It's nice to know there's someone in this party besides me who's got a little *nous*.' He glared malevolently at Wilkes. 'Well, come on.'

The Colossal (which lay less than a hundred yards ahead of them) is one of the smallest and most disreputable cinemas ever contrived. It is also, from the mechanical aspect, primitive to the point of seeming the first successful experiment of the cinematograph's inventor. The usherettes are listless and the commissionaire old, confused, and prone to organize small, unnecessary queues of patrons when any number of seats are available. Very ancient films are shown, liable to every ill that celluloid is heir to, from incessant crackling through *paralysis agitans* to total dislocation, and matters are not improved by an operator who, apart from being constantly intoxicated, seems only imperfectly acquainted with the mechanics of his craft. The Colossal is also a great haunt of couples in an advanced condition of amorous delight, and is frequented by the rowdiest section of undergraduates for the sheer joy of seeing things go wrong.

Outside the doors Fen marshalled his forces. 'There's no point in all of us going in,' he said. 'And someone ought to keep an eye on this exit and the one round the corner. I hope he hasn't gone in and come out again already, but we'll have to risk that. Richard, and you, Mr Hoskins, will you stay outside?'

He went in, accompanied by Sally and Wilkes, to buy the tickets. The commissionaire tried to make them queue, but they brushed him aside. Fortunately, the Colossal has no gallery, so there was no chance of their looking for Sharman in the wrong quarter.

Someone tore their tickets in two, and having performed this simple but destructive act, relapsed into apathy as they pushed through the swing-doors into a warm, vibrating darkness. The screen was for the moment occupied by the image of a door, which was slowly opening to admit the muzzle of a revolver, and this was immediately followed by the spectacle of a white-haired man writing at a desk. Invisible violins played a whole-tone chord, *tremolo*, in a high register, while muted trombones grunted in a diseased but foreboding manner underneath. This music rose to a violent *fortissimo* and was terminated abruptly by an explosion, at which the white-haired man fell forward on to his desk, his pen dropping from a nerveless hand. ('Dead,' said Fen sepulchrally.) At this crisis of affairs, however, they were diverted from attending to what subsequently occurred by being ushered to their seats.

The cinema was not very full. Immediately in front of them was a solid block of undergraduates, but the rest of the seats were sparsely occupied. Near them, a young woman who was showing a surprising length of leg lay stickily clutched in the embraces of a young man, apparently insensible to the alarming events being enacted for her benefit. Someone was asleep in the row in front. Even with nothing more than the illumination from the screen and from the small yellow lights at the side to help them, it should not be insuperably difficult to locate Mr Sharman.

'Pa was a nice guy,' said the film. 'Who'd want to kill him?'

Fen got up and meandered down the gangway. An usherette, anxious to be helpful, approached and indicated to him the whereabouts of the gentlemen's lavatory. He ignored her and continued peering about him.

'O.K., boys,' said the film. 'Take him to the morgue. Now, Mrs Hargben, do you know of anyone who had reason to dislike your husband?'

Fen was getting in the way of the people at the side. One man got up and said: ' 'Ere, sit darn, matey.' 'Sit down yourself,' said someone else behind him. Fen ignored them both and returned to Sally and Wilkes. 'I shall have to try the other side,' he told them.

'Right. Now we'll see the Clancy dame,' said the film. 'It's a nasty business, chief. I don't like it.' Two detectives were wiped off the screen and the hero and heroine, glueily kissing, substituted. There followed without pause a rocky prospect across which a number of cowboys were galloping, firing dementedly at some person or persons in front of them.

'Wrong reel!' sang the undergraduate delightfully. 'Osbert's drunk again!'

At this the screen (perhaps in sympathy) suffered a severe attack of delirium tremens, and finally went completely black, leaving the cinema in almost total darkness.

'Damn,' said Fen.

The undergraduates were rising in a body, forcibly expressing their intention of putting Osbert's head in a bucket. Some of them actually rushed out at the back. The manager, a short, pudgy man in evening dress, appeared in front of the screen, bathed in an ill-chosen red spotlight which made him look like a vampire newly engorged with blood, and pleaded without much optimism for patience.

'A slight technical hitch,' he panted at them. 'It will be remedied immediately. Keep your seats, ladies and gentlemen. Keep your seats, please.' But no one took the least notice of him. From the operator's box came a sound of scuffling and yells.

'Keep your seats,' the manager repeated in futile desperation.

Fen, Wilkes, and Sally were all on their feet. 'We're going to lose him in this mess,' said Fen. 'Come on, we'd better get outside. If he saw us come in, he's pretty certain to take this opportunity.' They pushed their way out. As they went, the film was suddenly superimposed on top of the manager, giving him a curiously spectral appearance.

'Listen, honey,' it said. 'If they ask where you were last night, don't say anything. It's a frame, see?'

But outside the main doors there was nothing but the girl in the pay-box, the large and melancholy form of Mr Hoskins, and the commissionaire, fingering his medals for want of better occupation.

'What's happening?' asked Mr Hoskins. 'I heard an awful uproar.' He brushed the rain-water from his hair, which was now soaking.

'He hasn't come out here?'

'No.'

At this moment there was a sound of running footsteps,

and Cadogan, dripping and in despair, pelted round the corner. 'He's out,' he shouted. 'He's got away.'

Fen groaned. 'Oh, my dear paws,' he said. 'Why didn't you stop him?'

'He had a gun,' Cadogan replied. 'And if you think I'm going to rush at a gun like something out of a film, you're quite mistaken.'

Fen groaned again. 'Which way did he go?'

'Down that side road. He stole a bicycle.'

Without hesitation Fen ran to an untenanted blue Hillman which stood by the kerb, got in, and started it. 'Come on,' he beckoned them. '*La propriété, c'est le vol*, and I'm damned if I'm going to lose him again for want of a vehicle.' Somehow or other, they all piled in, and the car started. The owner, who was drinking pale ale in a nearby public-house, was for quite a long time totally unaware that it had gone.

They turned into the narrow street which ran down by the cinema. The off wheels, slithering through a choked gutter, threw up a wave of water against the red-brick wall, plastered with advertisements, and in the headlights the rain glittered like silver needles. In a short time the road broadened, and they caught sight of Sharman, pedalling like a maniac, and every now and then staring back over his shoulder. As they drew nearer, the lights caught for a moment the white of his eyes and the rodent mouth. They came level, and Fen shouted:

'Listen, Sharman: if you don't stop, I'm going to drive you into the pavement.'

As he did so, Sharman abruptly sheered off and vanished. It was so like magic that for the moment they did not realize that he had turned into a narrow, muddy path on the left. Fen pulled up and backed the car in the hasty and unnerving manner peculiar to all his driving (' *"Five miles meandering with a mazy motion,"* ' Cadogan quoted appositely), but the entrance was too narrow for them to penetrate. They got out, abandoned the car, and ran, splashing into puddles and drenched to the skin, towards a glow of light, a smell of petrol, and the harsh sound of music. But only Sally realized that Sharman was in a cul-de-sac. At the end of it was the Botley Fair, and there was no escape route except by the way they had come.

Passing a steam engine which laboured and fumed in the streaming rain, they found Sharman's bicycle on the ground near the entrance of the first huge striped marquee. Fen left Cadogan and Mr Hoskins on the watch outside, and with Wilkes and Sally pushed through the entrance At the first moment the blare of lights and music dazzled and stunned them. Few people were present – the weather was not good for business. On their right was a shooting-range, at which a brilliantined youth was exhibiting his prowess to a girl; in front, octagonal stalls devoted to the rolling of pennies down on to numbered boards, sparsely patronized; on the left, darts booths, skittles, a cheiromancer. At the far end a massive roundabout was gathering speed, with only two people on it. Dodgem cars aimlessly circled, the contacts at the summit of their poles crackling and flashing against wire netting, the loud-speakers, fantastically over-amplified, roaring forth dance music.

'*Baybee*,' a gargantuan voice sang. '*Don't ever say maybee, baybee*.' The machinery of the roundabout ground and battered with increasing speed, with the heavy, explosive force of a train passing over a subway. It bore a notice: 'There is no limit to the speed of this machine.' In one place the roof was leaking, flooding down on to the dry, trodden mud. A group of young girls, with bare, thin, white legs, berets, cheap wool coats, and scarlet lips, stood lifelessly watching the cars, or the prizes – dolls, toby-jugs, canaries and goldfish, cigarette packets – piled high like the gimcrack splendours of a proletarian heaven. The air was hot, smelling of steam and oil and canvas, and impregnated with incessant noise.

Like a scene from a Graham Greene novel, Cadogan thought as he peered in: somewhere there must be somebody saying a 'Hail Mary' . . .

But they had none of them the time either to assimilate

194

these details, or to indulge in much literary reminiscence. From behind one of the booths, Sharman ducked and ran: ran to the tethered canvas at the far end, clawing for an exit. There was none. He turned with a kind of animal snarl as Fen, pushing Sally forcibly out of the line of fire, went forward. Then in sheer panic he ran to the rapidly moving roundabout, and disregarding the shouts of the attendant, who was leaning against a pole on the wooden platform surrounding it, caught at one of the rails as it was flying past and, with a jerk which must nearly have torn his arms from their sockets, levered himself on. With hardly a moment's hesitation Fen followed him. Somewhere a woman screamed, and the attendant, now thoroughly alarmed, tried to hold him off, and failed. Fen, too, fell, stumbled, fought his way on to that circulating switchback, and clung with aching hands to a wooden motor-cycle, with a plush-seat, while he tried to gain equilibrium against the centrifugal and backward pull. Sharman, a short way ahead of him, was braced and feeling for his gun.

'Bloody fools,' said the attendant to Cadogan, who had just arrived with Mr Hoskins to join Sally and Wilkes. 'Do they want ter kill themselves?'

The lights of the roundabout dimmed suddenly as it reached its normal maximum speed. Islanded in calm, the operator at the centre regarded it with indifference, waiting the few revolutions during which strained muscles would hold out before slowing again.

'You've got to stop that thing,' Cadogan said sharply. 'The first man who got on is a murderer. He's armed and dangerous. Stop it, for God's sake.'

The attendant stared at him. 'Wot the hell – '

'That's perfectly true,' said Wilkes with sudden authority. 'Sally, go and phone the police, and then get on to the others at the station and tell them to come here.' Sally, white and silent, nodded and ran off. People were coming towards them, wondering what the trouble was.

'Gawd,' said the attendant, suddenly convinced. And he shouted to the man at the centre: ''Ere, Bert, stop er! Quick!'

The words were carried away in a violent gust of wind and the iron pounding of the roundabout. The man at the centre shook his head interrogatively. Sharman had got the pistol out of his pocket. He took aim and fired. The man at the controls gaped stupidly for a fleeting second, and dropped out of sight.

'The bastard!' said the attendant with sudden savagery. 'The bastard's shot 'im.'

The keepers of the other booths and side-shows were approaching now. And the roundabout was still gaining speed: it shook the whole marquee with its dull tremendous reverberation. Incongruously, the music blared on: *'Honey-love, honey-dove, I'm cryin' for the moon . . .'* Faces were suddenly pinched, frightened. From one of the other two people on the roundabout came a piercing scream of real terror.

'Lie down!' the attendant bawled. 'Lie down against the rail. My Gawd!' he added in a lower voice, 'if anyone comes orf while she's goin' at that lick they won't live to talk abaht it.'

The speed was still increasing. In the cavern of semi-darkness faces, forms, were only dimly seen, plucked out of sight and thrown back again as if by a giant's hand. In the marquee, everything else had stopped, every stall was deserted. On the fringes of the group below the furious circling wind could be felt.

'We can't stop 'er,' the attendant muttered. 'We can't stop 'er now. Not till the steam gives out.'

'What the hell do you mean?' said Cadogan, suddenly terrified.

'The engine an' all's in the middle. There's no way yer can get to it. If you tried to get on 'er at this speed you'd break yer bloody neck.'

'How long will it keep up?'

The attendant shrugged. ''Alf an hour,' he answered grimly. 'If it doesn't bring the 'ole bloody marquee down first.'

'Oh, God,' said Cadogan: and felt very sick. 'Can't we get one of the rifles and shoot him off?'

'You try shootin' at that thing and you'll 'it anything but 'im.'

The roundabout was going faster.

'I've got it,' Cadogan exclaimed suddenly. 'If we sawed away the skirting-board there, couldn't we get to the centre *underneath* it?'

The man stared. 'You *might*,' he answered. 'But there's a bloody lot of machinery there, and as likely as not you'd get yer 'ead torn orf, even crawlin'.'

'We've got to try it,' Cadogan said, 'if only for the sake of those other two people. They're in a blind panic, and it's ten to one they'll go at any moment.'

The attendant hesitated only a moment. 'I'm with yer,' he said. 'Phil, get me tools.'

Have you ever, indifferent reader, clung to the edge of a roundabout which is moving at high speed? If your feet are braced, you can lean over inwards at an angle of sixty degrees and still not lose your balance: it's only then, in fact, that you are balanced at all. Sit upright, and you will want all your strength to avoid being pulled off, like a pin placed on the outside of a revolving turn-table. It is not, in any event, the place to tackle a desperate man, though it is true that the same disadvantages apply to both sides.

There is another thing, and that is that the senses begin to be affected. After a while, only the agonizing outward pull on your body tells you that you are going round. Everything else, vision included, gives you the illusion that you are going – *up* up a dark, precipitous, endless slope, which becomes the steeper as the speed increases. In the end you imagine a non-existent gravitational pull downwards and find yourself fighting against it. It is a curious sensation, this rushing upwards through a dark tunnel of wind with the faces of the onlookers a slanting, recurrent blur – exhilarating at first, then tiring, and at last, with the sinews strained beyond endurance, wholly unbearable, a nightmare of struggle and misery.

Fen's arms were aching from the first wrench, but at first the sensation was not unenjoyable. It occurred to him belatedly that there was little point in this melodramatic, final pursuit: some quite irrational impulse had urged him to it, just as the desire to escape for a little longer had driven Sharman to this futile temporary refuge. Now he was here he must make the best of it. He remembered with a pang of annoyance that his gun was still lying on the desk in his room, where he had left it; and was subsequently comforted by the reflection that even if Sharman fired at him he was almost certain to miss. Nearer the centre of the roundabout one would have more freedom of movement, but one would also constitute a far easier target. Taking it all in all, he decided to stay where he was; decided, moreover, to do nothing about Sharman until the roundabout stopped, when it would be time enough.

Yet these resolutions all went by the board when Sharman fired his first shot. That wanton useless act roused in Fen something which was neither heroism, nor sentimentality, nor righteous indignation, nor even instinctive revulsion; and having stated the negative side, it is difficult to put into words what, actually, it was, since it is not a common emotion in mankind, and since it lies at the basis of Fen's personality. I suppose that as near as anything would be to say that it was a kind of passionless sense of justice and of proportion, a deeply rooted objection to waste. In any case, if left him with the sudden desire to act; and, singing quietly and untunefully to himself the finale of the Enigma Variations, he crouched down beside one of the wooden motor-cycles, the centrifugal drive flattening him against it, and began to push his way forward.

Sharman, gun in hand, turned, saw him, and waited, holding his fire until it could be effective. His red-rimmed eyes were bright with lunacy, and he was shouting something that was lost in the rush of air. The two men, rising and falling on the hinged and undulating boards, were to all intents and purposes alone in their sloping tunnel of black wind. Outside things became even more inconsiderable and irrelevant with the increase of speed.

Fen went on. It was slow, nerve-racking progress, particularly at the gaps between the rows of motor-cycles. A hand or foot would slip, and the nails would clutch and tear agonizingly in the effort to regain hold. Sweat poured off him, and the bucketing din pounded in his ears. He had no idea of what he was going to do; if he attempted to throw anything it would scarcely leave his hand – and, anyway, he had nothing to throw. However he continued to move towards Sharman, and the two men, had they known it, were about six feet apart at the moment when Cadogan and the attendant were pushing their way under the roundabout towards the controls in the middle. At this point, as a matter of historical fact, Fen's enterprise gave out; he could think of nothing to do: to hurl himself at Sharman was not only a physical impossibility, but would almost certainly result in immediate extinction. And so, being of an old-fashioned turn of mind, he invoked the gods.

They answered. It may be that they remembered him as an ardent supporter (against all the world) of the *deus ex machina* in drama, or it may be that they merely considered that the events of the evening had gone on long enough. What in fact happened was that Sharman momentarily lost his foothold, and, in struggling to regain it, dropped the gun. There was an instant of paralysing realization, and then Fen was on him.

In the nature of things, the struggle could not be a long one. And it was a matter of seconds before both men, locked together, were reeling back towards a gap in the railings, with Fen outermost. He knew what he had to do, and did it. As they reached the gap, he tore both arms from Sharman. The left, flung out to catch the railing, bore excruciatingly for a moment the weight of both their bodies; and then the right, swinging like an axe, struck Sharman sideways and backwards off the edge. The air took the man like a leaf. The white-faced crowd below saw him flung against a supporting pole with sickening violence, saw him hurled down the steps to lie still on the ground at their feet. Almost at the same instant Cadogan and the attendant, after an heroic but unharmed passage, reached the controls. The roundabout lost speed. When it stopped, willing hands helped Fen and the two others, who were frightened but not hurt, on to *terra firma* again. They were sweaty, dizzy, and begrimed. The man at the controls was unconscious, but in no danger; the bullet had broken his arm.

Wilkes rose from Sharman's tattered and bleeding body.

'He's not dead,' he said. 'There are a lot of things broken, but he'll live.'

'To be hanged,' said Fen in a shaky voice. 'Which,' he added more cheerfully, 'will be one Janeite the less, anyway.'

This must be the last recorded comment of the day. Almost as Fen spoke, Mr Scott and Mr Beavis drove up in Lily Christine III; they were followed by the Chief Constable and his minions; they were followed by the owner of the blue Hillman; he was followed by the police whom Sally had telephoned; they were followed by the owner of the bicycle which Sharman had taken; he was followed by Mr Barnaby and his army, much inspired by the resources of the station bar; and they were followed by the Junior Proctor, the University Marshal, and two bulldogs, who had been advised by the railway authorities that trouble was afoot, and who looked as severe, authoritative, and ineffectual as ever.

It was quite a reunion.

14. The Episode of the Prescient Satirist

'Explanations,' said Fen gloomily. 'Explanations, explanations, explanations. Explaining to the police; explaining to the proctors; explaining to the newspapers. I've been leading a dog's life this last forty-eight hours. My reputation is gone. No one respects me any more. My students openly titter. People point at Lily Christine as I pass. And I still don't see what I've done to deserve it.' Fatalistically, he drank his whisky. Nobody looked particularly sympathetic; even after two days it was impossible to be anything but elated.

Cadogan, Wilkes, Sally, and Mr Hoskins were sitting with him in the Gothic bar of the 'Mace and Sceptre'. The time was eight o'clock in the evening, so the room was tolerably full. The young man with glasses and a long neck had finished *Nightmare Abbey* and was now reading *Crotchet Castle*; the undergraduate with the broad mouth was still discussing horses with the barman; and the red-headed socialist held forth as before to his consort on the economic iniquities of the earth.

'Rosseter's inquest,' Fen pursued. 'Police inquiries. Why did I steal a car? Why did Dr Wilkes steal a bicycle? Why did Mr Cadogan steal groceries? *Petty minds*. It turns me sour. There's no justice.'

'I gather that Sharman's confession confirmed your deductions,' said Cadogan, 'but I haven't yet succeeded in gathering what your deductions were.'

'Everything confirms everything.' Fen's gloom was intense. 'Miss Tardy's body was found where Havering said it was. Rosseter's brief-case, and the rifle he was shot with, were found in Sharman's house – it was a small one, by the way, and I think he must have hidden it under his clothes. The police caught the Winkworth woman this afternoon, trying to clear out of the country – did you know that? They've got Havering, of course. I expect they'll both be tried for something or other.' He ordered a second round of drinks. 'Sharman won't be fit for six months, the doctors say. Nor shall I, if it comes to that. I had to apologize to the Chaplain for that business in the vestry. Humiliating. One gets no thanks for anything.'

'I thought all those people's stories of what happened in the toyshop were intended to incriminate Sally.'

'They might have been. I had an open mind on the subject. The only thing was that if, as a hypothesis, they were true, there was one obvious way the murder could have been done, and one obvious person – Sharman – who could have done it.'

'I still don't see it. *Did* she die at about 11.40, as Havering said? Because if so, all the others were together in a different room at the time.'

The drinks arrived and Fen paid for them. 'Oh, yes, she died at 11.40 all right,' he said. 'And not of natural causes either. You see, there are no two ways about it; she was suffocated.'

'*Suffocated?*'

'She must have been. The symptoms of strangulation and suffocation are exactly the same – obviously, because they're both means of cutting off air from the lungs, the one at the mouth, the other at the throat. So if it was impossible for her to have been strangled, she must have been suffocated. Strangulation's almost immediate, you see, but suffocation may take quite a time.'

Cadogan gulped his beer. 'What about marks – bruises – on the throat, thought?'

'They can be induced after death.' Fen groped in his pocket and produced a grubby slip of paper. 'I wrote this down for you. It's from a standard authority. "A long line of medical jurisprudents," ' he read, ' "has established that marks of strangulation inflicted on a living person are hardly if at all

202

to be distinguished from those produced on a corpse, especially if death be very recent."* And death *was* very recent.

'The point about the apparent impossibility of the thing was simply this: that if you strangle a person you've got to be there when he dies, but if you suffocate him, you needn't be.

'Of course, the theory of suffocation pointed immediately to Sharman. You remember the situation? Rosseter talked to the woman, and according to two other witnesses besides himself, she was alive *and talking* when he left her – and if she was talking she couldn't very well have been in the first stages of suffocation. He then joined Havering and the Winkworth woman, and the *only* person who was on his own from then until the time of death was Sharman. It was as simple as that.

'What happened was that *he* had come to realize that this intimidation business was going to be no good. So he went in, knocked the woman unconscious, plugged her nostrils and stuffed a handkerchief down her throat, and left her to die. Then when Rosseter sent him back to her with the gun, he removed the evidences of suffocation and tied the string round her neck (using that tale about the light as an excuse).'

'But for heaven's sake,' Cadogan put in, '*why* arrange a business like that? *Why* make it look impossible? Besides, for all he knew, she might not even be dead by the time he got back, which would ruin the whole plan.'

'Obviously, he didn't intend it to look impossible,' Fen answered impatiently. 'What happened was that when he'd arranged the suffocation machinery he came back and found the others together, when he'd expected them to be in different rooms; and that, for reasons we've discussed, would throw the guilt infallibly on him. So he had to fake the thing to look like something else, and strangulation, in view of the symptoms, was the sole possibility.'

'Then what about that story he told of someone prowling round? Sally said there wasn't anyone prowling.'

'Certainly there wasn't.' Fen's tone was disgusted. 'What

* Hans Gross, *Criminal Investigation* (Sweet and Maxwell, 1934).

he heard was *Sally*. Isn't that so, Wilkes?' he added sharply.

'Eh?' said Wilkes, startled at being thus brusquely addressed.

'You see,' Fen proceeded, 'Wilkes' acute and active mind had jumped instantly to the same conclusion.' He glared malevolently at his aged colleague. 'Naturally, all this depended on the witnesses' stories being true. Fortunately, one didn't have to go into all that, because Sharman gave himself away at our second interview. He said: "Not a soul can testify I was involved in any conspiracy." Well, Rosseter could have testified, if he'd been alive. The only people, apart from the murderer, who knew he was dead were ourselves and the police. Argal, Sharman killed Rosseter; Argal, he also killed Miss Tardy.'

'How did he get Miss Snaith to leave him the money? Has anyone found out?'

'Oh, he published some rubbishy book on education, and she was interested in the subject. They corresponded, and eventually met. He played up to her, and she liked it. Miserable little sycophant.'

In the silence that followed: 'To each according to his needs,' the red-headed undergraduate could be heard saying. 'Not absolute equality, because people have *different* needs.'

'Who's to decide what people's needs are?' his companion asked.

'The State of course. Don't ask such silly questions.'

Fen had reverted to his grievances. 'Just because Scott and Beavis led the Chief Constable half the way to London and back,' he said, 'I don't see that he's entitled to swear at me like a railway navvy.'

'How did they come to turn up at the Fair, by the way?'

'Oh, they ran into some of Barnaby's gang at the station. Which reminds me, we're supposed to be going round to New College to have a drink with him in ten minutes. Let's have another for the road.'

'I'll get it,' said Cadogan. He ordered the drinks. 'Spode's gone back to London. I tried to get him to increase my royalties, but he wouldn't. Evasive as a fish.'

'So you're going to write some poetry now?' Sally asked.

'Yes. That's me *métier*. I might even try my hand at a novel.'

'Flogging dead horses in mid-stream . . . ' Fen grumbled. 'What are you going to do, Sally?'

'Oh – I dunno. I shall keep on with my job for a bit. I shouldn't know how to get through the day otherwise. How about you, Anthony?'

Mr Hoskins stirred. 'I shall continue my studies . . . Good evening, Jacqueline,' he saluted a passing blonde.

'Wilkes,' said Fen sharply.

'Eh?'

'What are you going to do with yourself now?'

'Mind your own business,' said Wilkes.

Cadogan hastily interposed with: 'How about you, Gervase?'

'I?' said Fen. 'I shall pursue my orderly and dignified progress towards the grave.'

The crowd in the bar increased, and the smoke was beginning to sting the eyes. Fen drank his whisky gloomily. The young man with the glasses and the long neck finished *Crotchet Castle* and began *Headlong Hall*. Sally and Mr Hoskins were deep in conversation. Wilkes seemed on the point of slumber. And Cadogan's mind was pleasingly blank.

'Let's play "Awful Lines from Shakespeare",' he suggested.

However, they were not destined to begin this immediately, as: 'Women,' said Mr Hoskins suddenly, 'have strange ways.' Everyone listened with respectful attention. 'But for the eccentricities of Miss Snaith, none of this business would have come about. You remember what Pope said about women in *The Rape of the Lock*?' He looked inquiringly about him. 'It goes like this:

> *With varying vanities from every part,*
> *They shift the moving toyshop of their heart . . .*

Dear me . . .'

More about Penguins
and Pelicans

Penguinews, which appears every month, contains details of all the new books issued by Penguins as they are published. From time to time it is supplemented by *Penguins in Print*, which is our complete list of almost 5,000 titles.

A specimen copy of *Penguinews* will be sent to you free on request. Please write to Dept EP, Penguin Books Ltd, Harmondsworth, Middlesex, for your copy.

In the U.S.A.: For a complete list of books available from Penguins in the United States write to Dept CS, Penguin Books, 625 Madison Avenue, New York, New York 10022.

In Canada: For a complete list of books available from Penguins in Canada write to Penguin Books Canada Ltd, 2801 John Street, Markham, Ontario L3R 1B4.

Michael Innes

What Happened at Hazelwood

The end of Sir George Simney was sudden, unaccountable and violent. He himself, moreover, must have found its approach extremely surprising, since the features of the corpse displayed that expression of astounded and incredulous terror only assumed by persons who see they are about to be murdered in the most pronouncedly bizarre way.

In fact this bad baronet died true to the condition of his kind – mysteriously in his library, at midnight, while a great deal of snow was falling outside.

Money from Holme

Holme is dead.
Long live Holme.

Holme was a painter.
A very good painter.
But, as the exhibition catalogue recorded,
he met a tragic death in a foreign revolution.

Now the absurd art dealer Braunkopf made a small fortune from that exhibition.

And unfortunately, Holme himself turned up at the private view . . .

"Are you there God? It's me, Margaret. I'm in my new bedroom but I still have the same bed. It's so quiet here at night—nothing like the city. I see shadows on my wall and hear these funny creaking sounds. It's scary God! Even though my father says all houses make noises and the shadows are only trees. I hope he knows what he's talking about! I met a girl today. Her name's Nancy. She expected me to be very grown up. I think she was disappointed. Don't you think it's time for me to start growing God? If you could arrange it I'd be very glad. Thank you."

JUDY BLUME is the author of several other novels for young people: *Then Again, Maybe I Won't, Blubber,* and *Deenie,* all available in Laurel-Leaf editions. *Tales of a Fourth Grade Nothing, Otherwise Known As Sheila the Great* and *Iggie's House* are available in Yearling editions. Judy Blume divides her time between Santa Fe, New Mexico and New York City.

Are You There God?
It's Me, Margaret.

✳ ✳ ✳ ✳

by Judy Blume

Published by
DELL PUBLISHING CO., INC.
1 Dag Hammarskjold Plaza
New York, New York 10017

ISBN: 0-440-90419-6

RL: 4.1

Reprinted by arrangement with Bradbury Press, Inc.
Printed in the United States of America

March 1974

30   29   28   27   26

WFH

To My Mother

1

Are you there God? It's me, Margaret. We're moving today. I'm so scared God. I've never lived anywhere but here. Suppose I hate my new school? Suppose everybody there hates me? Please help me God. Don't let New Jersey be too horrible. Thank you.

We moved on the Tuesday before Labor Day. I knew what the weather was like the second I got up. I knew because I caught my mother sniffing under her arms. She always does that when it's hot and humid, to make sure her deodorant's working. I don't use deodorant yet. I don't think people start to smell bad until they're at least twelve. So I've still got a few months to go.

I was really surprised when I came home from camp and found out our New York apartment had been rented to another family and that *we* owned a house in Farbrook, New Jersey. First of all I never even heard of Farbrook. And second of all, I'm not usually left out of important family decisions.

But when I groaned, "Why New Jersey?" I was told,

"Long Island is too social—Westchester is too expensive—and Connecticut is too inconvenient."

So Farbrook, New Jersey it was, where my father could commute to his job in Manhattan, where I could go to public school, and where my mother could have all the grass, trees and flowers she ever wanted. Except I never knew she wanted that stuff in the first place.

The new house is on Morningbird Lane. It isn't bad. It's part brick, part wood. The shutters and front door are painted black. Also, there is a very nice brass knocker. Every house on our new street looks a lot the same. They are all seven years old. So are the trees.

I think we left the city because of my grandmother, Sylvia Simon. I can't figure out any other reason for the move. Especially since my mother says Grandma is too much of an influence on me. It's no big secret in our family that Grandma sends me to summer camp in New Hampshire. And that she enjoys paying my private school tuition (which she won't be able to do any more because now I'll be going to public school). She even knits me sweaters that have labels sewed inside saying MADE EXPRESSLY FOR YOU . . . BY GRANDMA.

And she doesn't do all that because we're poor. I know for a fact that we're not. I mean, we aren't rich but we certainly have enough. Especially since I'm an

2

only child. That cuts way down on food and clothes. I know this family that has seven kids and every time they go to the shoe store it costs a bundle. My mother and father didn't plan for me to be an only child, but that's the way it worked out, which is fine with me because this way I don't have anybody around to fight.

Anyhow, I figure this house-in-New-Jersey business is my parents' way of getting me away from Grandma. She doesn't have a car, she hates buses *and* she thinks all trains are dirty. So unless Grandma plans to walk, which is unlikely, I won't be seeing much of her. Now some kids might think, who cares about seeing a grandmother? But Sylvia Simon is a lot of fun, considering her age, which I happen to know is sixty. The only problem is she's always asking me if I have boyfriends and if they're Jewish. Now *that* is ridiculous because number one I don't have boyfriends. And number two what would I care if they're Jewish or not?

2

We hadn't been in the new house more than an hour when the doorbell rang. I answered. It was this girl in a bathing suit.

"Hi," she said. "I'm Nancy Wheeler. The real estate agent sent out a sheet on you. So I know you're Margaret and you're in sixth grade. So am I."

I wondered what else she knew.

"It's plenty hot, isn't it?" Nancy asked.

"Yes," I agreed. She was taller than me and had bouncy hair. The kind I'm hoping to grow. Her nose turned up so much I could look right into her nostrils.

Nancy leaned against the door. "Well, you want to come over and go under the sprinklers?"

"I don't know. I'll have to ask."

"Okay. I'll wait."

I found my mother with her rear end sticking out of a bottom kitchen cabinet. She was arranging her pots and pans.

"Hey Mom. There's a girl here who wants to know if I can go under her sprinklers?"

"If you want to," my mother said.

"I need my bathing suit," I said.

"Gads, Margaret! I don't know where a bathing suit is in this mess."

I walked back to the front door and told Nancy, "I can't find my bathing suit."

"You can borrow one of mine," she said.

"Wait a second," I said, running back to the kitchen. "Hey Mom. She says I can wear one of hers. Okay?"

"Okay," my mother mumbled from inside the cabinet. Then she backed out. She spit her hair out of her face. "What did you say her name was?"

"Umm . . . Wheeler. Nancy Wheeler."

"Okay. Have a good time," my mother said.

Nancy lives six houses away, also on Morningbird Lane. Her house looks like mine but the brick is painted white and the front door and shutters are red.

"Come on in," Nancy said.

I followed her into the foyer, then up the four stairs leading to the bedrooms. The first thing I noticed about Nancy's room was the dressing table with the heartshaped mirror over it. Also, everything was very neat.

When I was little I wanted a dressing table like that. The kind that's wrapped up in a fluffy organdy skirt. I never got one though, because my mother likes tailored things.

Nancy opened her bottom dresser drawer. "When's your birthday?" she asked.

"March," I told her.

"Great! We'll be in the same class. There are three sixth grades and they arrange us by age. I'm April."

"Well, I don't know what class I'm in but I know it's Room Eighteen. They sent me a lot of forms to fill out last week and that was printed on all of them."

"I told you we'd be together. I'm in Room Eighteen too." Nancy handed me a yellow bathing suit. "It's clean," she said. "My mother always washes them after a wearing."

"Thank you," I said, taking the suit. "Where should I change?"

· Nancy looked around the room. "What's wrong with here?"

"Nothing," I said. "I don't mind if you don't mind."

"Why should I mind?"

"I don't know." I worked the suit on from the bottom. I knew it was going to be too big. Nancy gave me the creeps the way she sat on her bed and watched me. I left my polo on until the last possible second. I wasn't about to let her see I wasn't growing yet. That was my business.

· "Oh, you're still flat." Nancy laughed.

"Not exactly," I said, pretending to be very cool. "I'm small boned, is all."

"I'm growing already," Nancy said, sticking her chest way out. "In a few years I'm going to look like one of those girls in *Playboy*."

Well, I didn't think so, but I didn't say anything. My father gets *Playboy* and I've seen those girls in the middle. Nancy looked like she had a long way to go. Almost as far as me.

"Want me to do up your straps?" she asked.

"Okay."

"I figured you'd be real grown up coming from New York. City girls are supposed to grow up a lot faster. Did you ever kiss a boy?"

"You mean really kiss? On the lips?" I asked.

"Yes," Nancy said impatiently. "Did you?"

"Not really," I admitted.

Nancy breathed a sigh of relief. "Neither did I."

I was overjoyed. Before she said that I was beginning to feel like some kind of underdeveloped little kid.

"I practice a lot though," Nancy said.

"Practice what?" I asked.

"Kissing! Isn't that what we were talking about? *Kissing!*"

"How can you practice that?" I asked.

"Watch this." Nancy grabbed her bed pillow and embraced it. She gave it a long kiss. When she was done she threw the pillow back on the bed. "It's important to experiment, so when the time comes you're all ready. I'm going to be a great kisser some day. Want to see something else?"

I just stood there with my mouth half open. Nancy

sat down at her dressing table and opened a drawer. "Look at this," she said.

I looked. There were a million little bottles, jars and tubes. There were more cosmetics in that drawer than my mother had all together. I asked, "What do you do with all that stuff?"

"It's another one of my experiments. To see how I look best. So when the time comes I'll be ready." She opened a lipstick and painted on a bright pink mouth. "Well, what do you think?"

"Umm . . . I don't know. It's kind of bright, isn't it?"

Nancy studied herself in the heartshaped mirror. She rubbed her lips together. "Well, maybe you're right." She wiped off the lipstick with a tissue. "My mother would kill me if I came out like this anyway. I can't wait till eighth grade. That's when I'll be allowed to wear lipstick every day."

Then she whipped out a hairbrush and started to brush her long, brown hair. She parted it in the middle and caught it at the back with a barrette. "Do you always wear your hair like that?" she asked me.

My hand went up to the back of my neck. I felt all the bobby pins I'd used to pin my hair up so my neck wouldn't sweat. I knew it looked terrible. "I'm letting it grow," I said. "It's at that in-between stage now. My mother thinks I should wear it over my ears though. My ears stick out a little."

"I noticed," Nancy said.

I got the feeling that Nancy noticed *everything!*

"Ready to go?" she asked.

"Sure."

She opened a linen closet in the hall and handed me a purple towel. I followed her down the stairs and into the kitchen, where she grabbed two peaches out of the refrigerator and handed one to me. "Want to meet my mom?" she asked.

"Okay," I said, taking a bite of my peach.

"She's thirty-eight, but tells us she's twenty-five. Isn't that a scream!" Nancy snorted.

Mrs. Wheeler was on the porch with her legs tucked under her and a book on her lap. I couldn't tell what book it was. She was suntanned and had the same nose as Nancy.

"Mom, this is Margaret Simon who just moved in down the street."

Mrs. Wheeler took off her glasses and smiled at me.

"Hello," I said.

"Hello, Margaret. I'm very glad to meet you. You're from New York, aren't you?"

"Yes, I am."

"East side or West?"

"We lived on West Sixty-seventh. Near Lincoln Center."

"How nice. Does your father still work in the city?"

"Yes."

"And what does he do?"

"He's in insurance." I sounded like a computer.

"How nice. Please tell your mother I'm looking forward to meeting her. We've got a Morningbird Lane bowling team on Mondays and a bridge game every other Thursday afternoon and a . . ."

"Oh, I don't think my mother knows how to bowl and she wouldn't be interested in bridge. She paints most of the day," I explained.

"She paints?" Mrs. Wheeler asked.

"Yes."

"How interesting. What does she paint?"

"Mostly pictures of fruits and vegetables. Sometimes flowers too."

Mrs. Wheeler laughed. "Oh, you mean *pictures!* I thought you meant walls! Tell your mother we're making our car pools early this year. We'd be happy to help her arrange hers . . . especially Sunday school. That's always the biggest problem."

"I don't go to Sunday school."

"You don't?"

"No."

"*Lucky!*" Nancy shouted.

"Nancy, *please!*" Mrs. Wheeler said.

"Hey Mom . . . Margaret came to go under the sprinkler with me, not to go through the third degree."

"All right. If you see Evan tell him I want to talk to him."

Nancy grabbed me by the hand and pulled me outside. "I'm sorry my mother's so nosey."

"I didn't mind," I said. "Who's Evan?"

"He's my brother. He's disgusting!"

"Disgusting how?" I asked.

"Because he's fourteen. All boys of fourteen are disgusting. They're only interested in two things—pictures of naked girls and dirty books!"

Nancy really seemed to know a lot. Since I didn't know any boys of fourteen I took her word for it.

Nancy turned on the outside faucet and adjusted it so that the water sprayed lightly from the sprinkler. "Follow the leader!" she called, running through the water. I guessed Nancy was the leader.

She jumped through the spray. I followed. She turned cartwheels. I tried but didn't make it. She did leaps through the air. I did too. She stood straight under the spray. I did the same. That's when the water came on full blast. We both got drenched, including our hair.

"Evan, you stinker!" Nancy shrieked. "I'm telling!" She ran off to the house and left me alone with two boys.

"Who're you?" Evan asked.

"I'm Margaret. We just moved in."

"Oh. This is Moose," he said, pointing to the other boy.

I nodded.

"Hey," Moose said. "If you just moved in, ask your father if he's interested in having me cut his lawn. Five bucks a week and I trim too. What'd you say your last name was?"

"I didn't. But it's Simon." I couldn't help thinking about what Nancy said—that all they were interested in was dirty books and naked girls. I held my towel tight around me in case they were trying to sneak a look down my bathing suit.

"*Evan! Come in here this instant!*" Mrs. Wheeler hollered from the porch.

"I'm coming . . . I'm coming," Evan muttered.

After Evan went inside Moose said, "Don't forget to tell your father. *Moose Freed.* I'm in the phone book."

"I won't forget," I promised.

Moose nibbled a piece of grass. Then the back door slammed and Nancy came out, red-eyed and sniffling.

"Hey, Nancy baby! Can't you take a joke?" Moose asked.

"Shut up, animal!" Nancy yelled. Then she turned to me. "I'm sorry they had to act like that on your first day here. Come on, I'll walk you home."

Nancy had my clothes wrapped up in a little bundle. She was still in her wet suit. She pointed out who lived in each house between mine and hers.

"We're going to the beach for Labor Day weekend," she said. "So call for me on the first day of school and we'll walk together. I'm absolutely dying to know who our teacher's going to be. Miss Phipps, who we were supposed to have, ran off with some guy to California last June. So we're getting somebody new."

When we got to my house I told Nancy if she'd wait a minute I'd give her back her bathing suit.

"I don't need it in a hurry. Tell your mother to wash it and you can give it back next week. It's an old one."

I was sorry she told me that. Even if I'd already guessed it. I mean, probably I wouldn't lend a stranger my best bathing suit either. But I wouldn't come right out and say it.

"Oh, listen, Margaret," Nancy said. "On the first day of school wear loafers, but no socks."

"How come?"

"Otherwise you'll look like a baby."

"Oh."

"Besides, I want you to join my secret club and if you're wearing socks the other kids might not want you."

"What kind of secret club?" I asked.

"I'll tell you about it when school starts."

"Okay," I said.

"And remember—no socks!"

"I'll remember."

We went to a hamburger place for supper. I told my father about Moose Freed. "Only five bucks a cutting and he trims too."

"No, thanks," my father said. "I'm looking forward to cutting it myself. That's one of the reasons we moved out here. Gardening is good for the soul." My mother beamed. They were really driving me crazy with all that good-for-the-soul business. I wondered when they became such nature lovers!

Later, when I was getting ready for bed, I walked into a closet, thinking it was the bathroom. Would I ever get used to living in this house? When I finally made it into bed and turned out the light, I saw shadows on my wall. I tried to shut my eyes and not think about them but I kept checking to see if they were still there. I couldn't fall asleep.

Are you there God? It's me, Margaret. I'm in my new bedroom but I still have the same bed. It's so quiet here at night—nothing like the city. I see shadows on my wall and hear these funny creaking sounds. It's scary God! Even though my father says all houses make noises and the shadows are only trees. I hope he knows what he's talking about! I met a girl today. Her name's Nancy. She expected me to be very grown up. I think she was disappointed. Don't you think it's time for me to start growing God? If you could arrange it I'd be very glad. Thank you.

My parents don't know I actually talk to God. I mean, if I told them they'd think I was some kind of religious fanatic or something. So I keep it very private. I can talk to him without moving my lips if I have to. My mother says God is a nice idea. He belongs to everybody.

3

The next day we went to the hardware store where my father bought a deluxe power lawn mower. That evening, after our first at-home-in-New-Jersey supper (turkey sandwiches from the local delicatessen), my father went out to cut the grass with his new mower. He did fine on the front, but when he got around to the back yard he had to check to see how much grass there was in the bag on the mower. It's a very simple thing to do. The man at the hardware store demonstrated just how to do it. Only you have to turn the mower off before you reach inside and my father forgot that.

I heard him yell, "Barbara—I've had an accident!" He ran to the house. He grabbed a towel and wrapped it around his hand before I had a chance to see anything. Then he sat down on the floor and turned very pale.

"Oh my God!" my mother said when the blood seeped through the towel. "Did you cut it off?"

When I heard that I raced outside to look for the limb. I didn't know if they were talking about the whole hand or what, but I had read about how you're supposed to save limbs if they get cut off because sometimes the doctor can sew them back on. I thought it was a good thing they had me around to think of those things. But I couldn't find a hand or any fingers and by the time I came back into the house the police were there. My mother was on the floor too, with my father's head in her lap.

I rode in the police car with them since there was no one at home to stay with me. I had a silent talk with God on the way to the hospital. I said this inside my head so no one would notice.

Are you there God? It's me, Margaret. My father's had an awful accident. Please help him God. He's really very kind and nice. Even though he doesn't know you the way I do, he's a good father. And he needs his hand God. So please, please let him be all right. I'll do anything you say if you help him. Thank you God.

It turned out that my father hadn't cut off anything but it took eight stitches to sew up his finger. The doctor who sewed him was Dr. Potter. After he was through with my father, he came out to chat. When he saw me he said, "I have a daughter about your age."

I love the way people always think they know somebody your age until you tell them how old you *really* are!

"I'm going on twelve," I said.

"Gretchen is almost twelve too," the doctor said.

Well! He was right about my age.

"She'll be in sixth grade at Delano School."

"So will you, Margaret," my mother reminded me. As if I needed reminding.

"I'll tell Gretchen to look for you," Dr. Potter said.

"Fine," I told him.

As soon as we got home from the hospital my father told my mother to look up Moose Freed in the phone book and arrange for him to cut our lawn once a week.

On Labor Day I got up early. I wanted to fix up my desk in my room before school started. I'd bought a pile of paper, pencils, erasers, reinforcements and paper clips. I'm always real neat until about October. While I was in the middle of this project I heard a noise. It sounded like somebody knocking. I waited to see if my parents would wake up. I tiptoed to their room but the door was still closed and it was quiet so I knew they were asleep.

When I heard the knocking again I went downstairs to investigate. I wasn't scared because I knew I could always scream and my father would rescue me if it turned out to be a burglar or a kidnapper.

The knocking came from the front door. Nancy was away for the weekend so it couldn't be her. And we really didn't know anybody else.

"Who is it?" I asked, pressing my ear to the door.

"It's Grandma, Margaret. Open up."

I unlatched the chain and both locks and flung open the door. "Grandma! I can't believe it. You're really here!"

"Surprise!" Grandma called.

I put a finger over my lips to let her know my parents were still asleep.

Grandma was loaded down with Bloomingdale's shopping bags. But when she stepped into the house she lined them up on the floor and gave me a big hug and kiss.

"My Margaret!" she said, flashing her special smile. When she smiles like that she shows all her top teeth. They aren't her real teeth. It's what Grandma calls a bridge. She can take out a whole section of four top teeth when she wants to. She used to entertain me by doing that when I was little. Naturally I never told my parents. When she smiles without her teeth in place she looks like a witch. But with them in her mouth she's very pretty.

"Come on, Margaret. Let's get these bags into the kitchen."

I picked up one shopping bag. "Grandma, this is so heavy! What's in it?"

"Hotdogs, potato salad, cole slaw, corned beef, rye bread. . . ."

I laughed. "You mean it's food?"

"Of course it's food."

"But they have food in New Jersey, Grandma."

"Not this kind."

"Oh yes," I said. "Even delicatessen."

"No place has delicatessen like New York!"

I didn't argue about that. Grandma has certain ideas of her own.

When we got all the bags into the kitchen Grandma scrubbed her hands at the sink and put everything into the refrigerator.

When she was done I asked, "How did you get here?"

Grandma smiled again but didn't say anything. She was measuring coffee into the pot. You can't make her talk about something until she's ready.

Finally she sat down at the kitchen table, fluffed out her hair and said, "I came in a taxi."

"All the way from New York?"

"No," Grandma said. "From the center of Farbrook."

"But how did you get to the center of Farbrook?"

"On a train."

"Oh, Grandma—you didn't!"

"Yes, I did."

"But you always said trains are so dirty!"

"So what's a little dirt? I'm washable!"

We both laughed while Grandma changed her shoes. She brought a spare pair along with her knitting in one of the shopping bags.

"Now," she said, "take me on a tour of the house."

I led her everywhere except upstairs. I pointed out closets, the downstairs bathroom, my mother's new washer and dryer, and where we sat to watch TV.

When I was finished Grandma shook her head and said, "I just don't understand why they had to move to the country."

"It's not really country, Grandma," I explained. "There aren't any cows around."

"To me it's country!" Grandma said.

I heard the water running upstairs. "I think they're up. Should I go see?"

"You mean should you go *tell!*"

"Well, should I?"

"Of course," Grandma said.

I ran up the stairs and into my parents' bedroom. My father was putting on his socks. My mother was brushing her teeth in their bathroom.

"Guess who's here?" I said to my father.

He didn't say anything. He yawned.

"Well, aren't you going to guess?"

"Guess what?" he asked.

"Guess who's here in this very house at this very minute?"

"Nobody but us, I hope," my father said.

"Wrong!" I danced around the bedroom.

"Margaret," my father said in his disgusted-with-me voice. "What is it you're trying to say?"

"Grandma's here!"

"That's impossible," my father told me.

"I mean it, Daddy. She's right downstairs in the kitchen making your coffee."

"Barbara . . ." My father went into the bathroom and turned off the water. I followed him. My mother had a mouthful of toothpaste.

"I'm not done, Herb," she said, turning on the water again.

My father shut it off. "Guess who's here?" he asked her.

"What do you mean who's here?" my mother said.

"Sylvia! That's who's here!" My father turned the water back on so my mother could finish brushing her teeth.

But my mother turned it off and followed my father into the bedroom. I followed too. This was fun! I guess by then my mother must have swallowed her toothpaste.

"What do you mean, *Sylvia?*" my mother asked my father.

"I mean my *mother!*" my father said.

My mother laughed. "That's impossible, Herb. How would she even get here?"

My father pointed at me. "Ask Margaret. She seems to know everything."

"In a taxi," I said.

They didn't say anything.

"And a train," I said.

Still nothing.

"It wasn't so dirty after all."

Ten minutes later my mother and father joined Grandma in the kitchen where the table was set and the breakfast all ready. It's hard to get mad at Grandma, especially when she flashes her super smile. So my mother and father didn't say anything except what a wonderful surprise! And how clever of Grandma to take a train and a taxi to our new house when she'd never been to Farbrook before.

After breakfast I went upstairs to get dressed. Grandma came up with me to see my room.

"It's a lot bigger than my old one," I said.

"Yes, it's bigger," Grandma agreed. "You could use new bedspreads and curtains. I saw some the other day—pink and red plaid. Then we could get red carpeting to match and a——" Grandma sighed. "But I guess your mother wants to fix it up herself."

"I guess so," I said.

Grandma sat down on my bed. "Margaret darling," she said, "I want to make sure you understand that we'll still be as close as always."

"Of course we will," I said.

"A few miles doesn't mean a thing," Grandma said. "Just because I can't drop in after school doesn't mean I won't think of you every day."

"I know that, Grandma."

"I tell you what—I'll call you every night at seven-thirty. How does that sound?"

"You don't have to call every night," I said.

"I want to! It's my dime," Grandma laughed. "That

way you can tell me what's going on and I'll keep you posted about New York. Okay?"

"Sure Grandma."

"But Margaret . . ."

"What?"

"You answer the phone. Your mother and father might not like me calling so much. This is just between you and me. All right?"

"Sure, Grandma. I love to get phone calls."

We all spent the rest of the day sitting around in our yard. Grandma was knitting me a new sweater, my mother planted some fall flowers, and my father read a book. I sunbathed, thinking it would be nice to start school with a tan.

We ate Grandma's food for supper and every time she bit into a pickle she said, "Mmm . . . nothing like the real thing!"

We drove her back to the Farbrook station while it was still light. Grandma has this thing about walking in New York at night. She's positive she's going to get mugged. Before she got out of the car she kissed me good-by and told my parents, "Now don't worry. I promise I'll only come once a month. Well . . . maybe twice. And it's not to see you, Herb. Or you either, Barbara. I've got to keep an eye on my Margaret—that's all." Grandma winked at me.

With that she grabbed the shopping bag with her shoes and knitting and left, waving good-by until we couldn't see her anymore.

4

On Wednesday night my mother helped me wash my hair. She set it in big rollers for me. I planned to sleep like that all night but after an hour they hurt my head so I took them out. On Thursday morning I got up early but I had trouble eating. My mother said it was natural for me to feel uneasy on the first day of school. She said when she was a girl she felt the same way. My mother's always telling me about when she was a girl. It's supposed to make me feel that she understands everything.

I put on my new blue plaid cotton back-to-school dress. My mother likes me in blue. She says it brings out the color in my eyes. I wore my brown loafers without socks. My mother thought that was dumb.

"Margaret, you have to walk three quarters of a mile."

"So?"

"So, you know you get blisters every time you go without socks."

"Well then, I'll just have to suffer."

"But why suffer? Wear socks!"

Now that's my point about my mother. I mean, if she understands so much about me then why couldn't she understand that I had to wear loafers without socks? I told her, "Nancy says nobody in the sixth grade wears socks on the first day of school!"

"Margaret! I don't know what I'm going to do with you when you're a teenager if you're acting like this now!"

That's another thing. My mother's always talking about when I'm a teenager. Stand up straight, Margaret! Good posture now makes for a good figure later. Wash your face with soap, Margaret! Then you won't get pimples when you're a teenager. If you ask me, being a teenager is pretty rotten—between pimples and worrying about how you smell!

Finally my mother told me to have a good day. She kissed my cheek and gave me a pat on the back. I walked down to Nancy's house.

By the time I got to Room Eighteen of the Delano Elementary School my feet hurt so much I thought I wouldn't make it through the day. Why are mothers always right about those things? As it turned out, half the girls had on knee socks anyway.

The teacher wasn't in the room when we got there. That is, the *real* teacher. There was this girl, who I thought *was* the teacher, but she turned out to be a kid in our class. She was very tall (that's why I thought she was the teacher) with eyes shaped like a cat's. You could see the outline of her bra through her blouse and you could also tell from the front that it wasn't the smallest size. She sat down alone and didn't talk to anyone. I wondered if maybe she was new too, because everybody else was busy talking and laughing about summer vacations and new hair styles and all that.

The class quieted down in a big hurry when a man walked into the room, nodded at us and wrote a name on the blackboard.

MILES J. BENEDICT JR.

When he turned away from the blackboard he cleared his throat. "That's me," he said, pointing to the name on the board. Then he cleared his throat two more times. "I'm your new teacher."

Nancy poked me in the ribs and whispered, "Can you believe it?" The whole class was whispering and grinning.

Mr. Benedict went back to the board. He wrote six phrases. Then he turned to us. He put his hands behind his back and kind of rocked back and forth on his feet. He cleared his throat so I knew he was going to say something.

"Now then . . . uh . . . you know my name. I'll tell you something about myself. Uh . . . I'm twenty-four years old. I'm uh . . . a graduate of Columbia Teachers College and uh . . . this is my first teaching position. Now that you know about me, I want to uh . . . find out about you. So, if you will copy these six phrases off the board and then complete them I'd uh . . . appreciate it. Thank you." He coughed. I thought he was going to wind up with a very sore throat.

Mr. Benedict Jr. handed out the paper himself. I read his phrases.

> MY NAME IS
> PLEASE CALL ME
> I LIKE
> I HATE
> THIS YEAR IN SCHOOL
> I THINK MALE TEACHERS ARE

I nibbled on the edge of my pencil. The first two were easy. I wrote:

My name is Margaret Ann Simon.
Please call me Margaret.

The next two were harder. I liked and hated a million things. And I didn't know what he wanted to know about. Also, he wouldn't answer any questions. He sat at his desk and watched us. He tapped his fingers and crossed his legs. Finally I wrote:

I like long hair, tuna fish, the smell of rain and things that are pink.
I hate pimples, baked potatoes, when my

27

mother's mad and religious holidays.
This year in school I want to have fun.
And also learn enough to go to
seventh grade.
I think male teachers are . . .

That was the worst! How was I supposed to know?
Every teacher is different. But I couldn't think of a
way to fit that in. So I wrote:

I think male teachers are the opposite of
female teachers.

There! That ought to do it. It was a stupid answer
but I thought it was also a pretty stupid question.

At two-thirty Nancy slipped me a note. It said:
*Secret club meets today after school my house—no
socks!*

I went home to change before going to Nancy's. My
mother was waiting for me. "Let's have a snack and
you can tell me all about your first day of school," she
said.

"I can't," I told her. "No time now. I've got to go
to Nancy's house. I'm joining her secret club."

"Oh, that's nice," my mother said. "Just tell me
about your teacher. What's she like?"

"It's a *he*," I said. "His name is Mr. Benedict and
this is his first job."

"Oh gads! A first-year teacher. What could be worse?"

"He's not bad," I told my mother. "I thought he was very nice."

"We'll see how much you learn," my mother said.

I changed into shorts and a polo and walked to Nancy's.

5

The others were already there. Janie Loomis, Gretchen Potter and Nancy. That was it. We sat around on the porch and Nancy brought us cokes and cookies. When Gretchen helped herself to six Oreos at once Nancy asked her how much weight she'd gained over the summer. Gretchen put back four cookies and said, "Not much."

"Did you see Laura Danker come in this morning?" Janie asked.

"Which one is she?" I said.

They all giggled. Nancy spoke to me as if she were my mother. "Margaret dear—you can't possibly miss Laura Danker. The big blonde with the big *you know whats!*"

"Oh, I noticed her right off," I said. "She's very pretty."

"Pretty!" Nancy snorted. "You be smart and stay away from her. She's got a bad reputation."

"What do you mean?" I asked.

"My brother says she goes behind the A&P with him and Moose."

"And," Janie added, "she's been wearing a bra since fourth grade and I'll bet she gets her period."

"Did you get it yet, Margaret?" Nancy asked.

"Get what?"

"Your period," Nancy said, like I should have known.

"Oh—no, not yet. Did you?"

Nancy swallowed some soda and shook her head. "None of us has yet."

I was glad to hear that. I mean, suppose they all got it already and I was the only one who didn't. I'd feel awful.

Gretchen smacked her lips, brushed the cookie crumbs off her lap and said, "Let's get down to business."

• "Agreed," Nancy said. "First of all we need a good club name this year. Everybody think up a name for our club."

It got quiet. Everybody thought. I didn't really think but I pretended to. I didn't even know anything about the club so how could I pick out a name?

Gretchen suggested the SGCT which meant the Sixth Grade Cu-Tees. Janie said that sounded really dumb. So Gretchen told Janie if she was so smart why didn't she suggest a name. Janie suggested the MJB Girls which meant the Miles J. Benedict Girls. Nancy told Janie she'd forgotten the Jr. on the end of his name. Janie got mad and excused herself to go to the bathroom.

"As long as we're on the subject," Nancy said, "what do you think of Miles J.?"

"I think he's cute!" Gretchen giggled.

"He is—but he's too skinny," Nancy said.

Then I finally thought of something to say. "I wonder if he's married!"

Janie joined us again. "My guess is no. He doesn't look married."

"Anyhow, did you see the way he looked at Laura?" Nancy asked.

"No! Did he?" Gretchen opened her eyes wide.

"Naturally! Men can't help looking at her," Nancy said.

"But do you think she looks that way on purpose?" I asked.

The others laughed and Nancy said, "Oh Margaret!" Nancy had a great way of making me feel like a dope.

Then we talked about Mr. Benedict's questions and Gretchen told us that she wrote male teachers are very strict—because if Mr. Benedict thought we were afraid of him he'd bend over backwards to be really easy going and nice. I thought that was pretty clever and wished I had written it myself.

"Well, the whole idea of those questions is just to find out if we're normal," Janie said.

I hadn't thought about that. Now it was too late. "How can he tell if we're normal?" I asked.

"That's easy," Nancy said. "From the way you answered. Like if you said, I hate my mother, my father and my brother, you might be weird. Get it?"

I got it.

Nancy snapped her fingers. "I have the perfect name for our club," she said.

"What is it?" Gretchen asked.

"Tell us," Janie said.

"We'll be the Four PTS's."

"What's it stand for?" Janie asked.

Nancy tossed her hair around and smiled. "The Pre-Teen Sensations!"

"Hey, that's good," Gretchen said.

"I love it," Janie squealed.

We had a secret vote to pass the club name and naturally it passed. Then Nancy decided we should all have secret sensational names such as Alexandra, Veronica, Kimberly and Mavis. Nancy got to be Alexandra. I was Mavis.

Nancy reminded us that nobody in school was to know anything about our secret club and that at secret meetings such as this we were to use our secret names. We all had to solemnly swear. Then we all had to think up a rule.

Nancy's rule was, we all had to wear bras. I felt my cheeks turn red. I wondered if the others wore them already. I didn't think Janie did because she looked down at the floor after Nancy said it.

Gretchen's rule was, the first one to get her period had to tell the others all about it. Especially how it feels. Janie's rule was, we all had to keep a Boy Book, which was a notebook with a list of boys' names in order of how we liked them. Each week we had to change our lists and pass the Boy Books around.

Finally Nancy asked me what my rule was. I couldn't think of one to equal the others so I said, "We meet on a certain day each week."

"Naturally!" Nancy said. "But *what* day?"

"Well, I don't know," I told her.

"Okay, let's think up a good day," Gretchen said. "Tuesday and Thursday are out. I have to go to Hebrew school."

"Oh Gretchen!" Janie said. "You and that Hebrew school business. Can't you get out of it?"

"I'd love to," Gretchen explained. "But I've got to go one more year and then I'm through."

"What about you, Margaret? Do you go?" Janie asked me.

"You mean to Hebrew school?"

"Yes."

"No, I don't go," I said.

"Margaret doesn't even go to Sunday school. Isn't that right?" Nancy asked.

"Yes," I answered.

"How'd you arrange that?" Gretchen asked.

"I'm not any religion," I said.

"You're not!" Gretchen's mouth fell open.

"What are your parents?" Janie asked.

"Nothing," I said.

"How positively neat!" Gretchen said.

Then they all just looked at me and nobody said

anything and I felt pretty silly. So I tried to explain. "See uh . . . my father was Jewish and uh . . . my mother was Christian and . . . "

Nancy's face lit up. "Go on," she said.

This was the first time they were interested in anything I had to say. "Well, my mother's parents, who live in Ohio, told her they didn't want a Jewish son-in-law. If she wanted to ruin her life that was her business. But they would never accept my father for her husband."

"No kidding!" Gretchen said. "How about your father's family?"

"Well, my grandmother wasn't happy about getting a Christian daughter-in-law, but she at least accepted the situation."

"So what happened?" Janie asked.

"They eloped."

"How romantic!" Nancy sighed.

"So that's why they're not anything."

"I don't blame them," Gretchen said. "I wouldn't be either."

"But if you aren't any religion, how are you going to know if you should join the Y or the Jewish Community Center?" Janie asked.

"I don't know," I said. "I never thought about it. Maybe we won't join either one."

"But *everybody* belongs to one or the other," Nancy said.

"Well, I guess that will be up to my parents," I said,

ready to change the subject. I never meant to tell them my story in the first place. "So uh . . . what day should we meet?"

Nancy announced that Friday was no good for a meeting day because she had piano lessons. Janie said she had ballet on Wednesday so I said that only left Mondays and we agreed that Monday would be our meeting day. Next week we had to bring our Boy Books and get checked to make sure we were all wearing bras.

When the meeting was over Nancy raised her arms high above her head. She closed her eyes and whispered, "Here's to the Four PTS's. Hurray!"

"Long live the PTS's," we chanted.

All through supper I thought about how I was going to tell my mother I wanted to wear a bra. I wondered why she hadn't ever asked me if I wanted one, since she knew so much about being a girl.

When she came in to kiss me goodnight I said it. "I want to wear a bra." Just like that—no beating around the bush.

My mother turned the bedroom light back on. "Margaret . . . how come?"

"I just do is all." I hid under the covers so she couldn't see my face.

My mother took a deep breath. "Well, if you really want to we'll have to go shopping on Saturday. Okay?"

"Okay." I smiled. My mother wasn't bad.

She turned out the light and closed my door half-way. Was I glad that was over!

Are you there God? It's me, Margaret. I just told my mother I want a bra. Please help me grow God. You know where. I want to be like everyone else. You know God, my new friends all belong to the Y or the Jewish Community Center. Which way am I supposed to go? I don't know what you want me to do about that.

6

The next day after school Mr. Benedict called me up to his desk. "Margaret," he said. "I'd like to discuss your getting-to-know-you paper. For instance, why do you hate religious holidays?"

Was I sorry I wrote that! How positively stupid of me. If it was true that he was trying to find out if we were normal, I guess he thought I wasn't.

I half laughed. "Oh, I just wrote that," I said. "I really don't hate them at all."

"You must have had a reason. You can tell me. It's confidential."

I raised my right eyebrow at Mr. Benedict. I can do that really good. Raise one without the other. I do it whenever I can't think of anything to say. People notice it right away. Some people actually ask me how I do it. They forget what we were talking about and concentrate on my right eyebrow. I don't know exactly how I do it. What I do is think about it and the eyebrow goes up. I can't do it with my left. Only my right.

Mr. Benedict noticed. But he didn't ask me anything about how I do it. He just said, "I'm sure you have a perfectly good reason for hating religious holidays."

I knew he was waiting for me to say something. He wasn't going to just forget about it. So I decided to get it over with in a hurry. "None of those holidays are special to me. I don't belong to any religion," I said.

Mr. Benedict seemed pleased. Like he had uncovered some deep, dark mystery. "I see. And your parents?"

"They aren't any religion. I'm supposed to choose my own when I grow up. If I want to, that is."

Mr. Benedict folded his hands and looked at me for a while. Then he said, "Okay, Margaret. You can go now."

I hoped he decided I was normal, after all. I lived in New York for eleven and a half years and I don't think anybody ever asked me about my religion. I never even thought about it. Now, all of a sudden, it was the big thing in my life.

That night when Grandma called she told me she'd gotten a subscription to Lincoln Center for the two of us. We'd meet one Saturday a month, have lunch and then go to a concert. Grandma really is clever. She knew my parents would never say no to one Saturday a month at Lincoln Center. That was culture. And they thought culture was very important. And now Grandma and I would have a chance to spend some time alone. But I was glad that Lincoln Center didn't start right away because I didn't want anything to interfere with Bra Day.

First thing on Saturday morning Moose Freed arrived to cut our lawn. My father sulked behind a sports magazine. His finger was a lot better but it was still bandaged.

I sat around outside while Moose cut the grass. I liked the way he sang as he worked. I also liked his teeth. I saw them when he smiled at me. They were very clean and white and one in the front was a little crooked. I pretended to be really busy reading a book but the truth is—I was watching Moose. If he looked toward me I put my nose back in the book in a hurry. Moose would be number one in my Boy Book if only I was brave enough, but what would Nancy think? She hated him.

After lunch my mother told my father we were going shopping. We still had our same car but my mother thought we needed two now, because there weren't any buses in Farbrook and taxis were so expensive. My father said he'd see, but I knew we'd be getting another one soon. My mother can talk my father into anything.

My mother drove to a shopping center where there was a Lord & Taylor. I had on my blue plaid dress and my loafers without socks and three Bandaids on my blisters.

First we went to the ladies' lingerie department where my mother told the saleslady we wanted to see a bra for me. The saleslady took one look and told my mother we'd be better off in the teen department where they had bras in very small sizes. My mother thanked the lady and I almost died! We went down on the escalator and headed for the teen shop. They had a whole display of underwear there. Bras and panties and slips to match. All I ever wore was white underpants and regular undershirts. Sometimes a slip if I was going to a party. My mother went to the counter and told the saleslady we were interested in a bra. I stood back and pretended not to know a thing. I even bent down to scratch a new mosquito bite.

"Come here, dear," the saleslady called.

I hate people who call you dear. I walked over to the counter and raised my right eyebrow at her.

She reached over the top of the counter and said, "Let's measure you, dear." She put the tape measure all the way around me and smiled at my mother. "Twenty-eight," she said. I felt like giving her a pinch.

Then she took out a bunch of bras and put them on the counter in front of us. My mother felt them all.

"Now dear—I suggest the Gro-Bra. It grows *with* you. You're not quite ready for a double A. Suppose you try them on and see which is most comfortable." She led us to a dressing room with a pink door that locked. My mother sat in the dressing room on a chair. I took off my dress. I wasn't wearing anything underneath but pants. I picked up the first bra and stuck my arms into the straps. I couldn't fasten it in back. My mother had to help me. She adjusted the straps and felt the front of me. "How does it feel?" she asked.

"I don't know," I said.

"Is it too tight?"

"No."·

"Too loose?"

"No."

"Do you like it?"

"I guess . . ."

"Try on this one."

She got me out of the first bra and into the next one. I wondered how I'd ever learn to do it by myself. Maybe my mother would have to dress me every day.

The next bra was softer than the first. My mother explained it was made of dacron. I liked the way it felt. My mother nodded. The third one was fancy. It was lace and it made me itch. My mother said it was impractical.

The saleslady knocked on the door as I was getting back into my dress. "How did we do? Did we find something?"

My mother told her *we* did. "We'll take three of these," she said, holding up the soft bra.

When we got back to the counter who should be there but Janie Loomis and her mother.

"Oh, hi, Margaret," she said. "I'm getting some winter pajamas." Her cheeks were bright red and I saw the selection of bras on the counter in front of her.

".Me too," I said. "I'm getting some flannel pajamas for winter."

"Well, see you Monday," Janie said.

"Right—Monday." I was plenty glad that my mother was down at the other end of the counter paying for my bras.

7

When I got home I carried my package straight to my room. I took off my dress and put on the bra. I fastened it first around my waist, then wiggled it up to where it belonged. I threw my shoulders back and stood sideways. I didn't look any different. I took out a pair of socks and stuffed one sock into each side of the bra, to see if it really grew with me. It was too tight that way, but I liked the way it looked. Like Laura Danker. I took the socks out and put them away.

My father congratulated me at dinner. "Well, you're really growing up, Margaret. No more little girl."

"Oh, Daddy!" was all I could think of to say.

On Monday I studied the boys in my class. I had to have some names for my Boy Book before three o'clock. I picked Philip Leroy because he was the best-looking one. Also Jay Hassler because he had nice brown eyes and clean fingernails. I decided to leave it at that and explain I didn't know anybody else.

Right before the bell rang Mr. Benedict told us that he was going to ask us each to do a year-long individual project.

Everybody groaned.

Mr. Benedict held up his hands. "Now it's not as bad as it sounds, class. For one thing, it's personal—between each of you and me. I'm not going to ask what your topic is. I expect you to choose it yourself and work it up in your own way. The only thing I insist on is that it be something . . . uh . . . meaningful."

More groans.

Mr. Benedict looked crushed. "I had hoped you would find this interesting."

Poor Mr. Benedict. He was really disappointed. The way he talked to us I got the feeling we made him nervous. Nobody seemed scared of him at all and you should always be a little scared of your teacher. Sometimes he just sat at his desk and looked out at us like he couldn't believe we were really there. Of course Nancy pointed out that he *never ever* called on Laura Danker. I hadn't noticed.

As we were getting in line to go home he reminded us that on Thursday we'd have a test on the first two chapters in our social studies book. He asked us to please be prepared. Most teachers never say please.

After school we went straight to Nancy's. Before we started our official meeting we talked about Mr. Benedict and his project. We all agreed it was crazy and none of us could think of a single idea.

Then Nancy called the role. "Veronica?"

"I'm here," Gretchen said.

"Kimberly?"

"I'm here," Janie said.

"Mavis?"

"I'm here," I said.

"And so am I . . . Alexandra." Nancy closed the roll book. "Well, let's get to it. We all feel each other's backs to make sure we're wearing our bras."

We all were.

"What size did you get, Janie?" Gretchen asked.

"I got a Gro-Bra," Janie said.

"Me too," I said.

"Me too!" Gretchen laughed.

"Not me," Nancy said, proudly. "Mine's a thirty-two double A."

We were all impressed.

"If you ever want to get out of those baby bras you have to exercise," she told us.

"What kind of exercise?" Gretchen asked.

"Like this," Nancy said. She made fists, bent her arms at the elbow and moved them back and forth, sticking her chest way out. She said, "I must—I must —I must increase my bust." She said it over and over. We copied her movements and chanted with her. "We must—we must—we must increase our bust!"

"Good," Nancy told us. "Do it thirty-five times a day and I promise you'll see the results."

"Now, for our Boy Books," Gretchen said. "Is everybody ready?"

We put our Boy Books on the floor and Nancy picked them up, one at a time. She read each one and passed it around for the rest of us to see. Janie's was first. She had seven names listed. Number one was Philip Leroy. Gretchen had four names. Number one was Philip Leroy. Nancy listed eighteen boys. I didn't even know eighteen boys! And number one was Philip Leroy. When Nancy got to my Boy Book she choked on an ice cube from her glass of coke. When she stopped choking she read, "Number one—Philip Leroy." Everybody giggled. "Number two—Jay Hassler. How come you picked him?"

I was getting mad. I mean, she didn't ask the others why they liked this one or that one, so why should I have to tell? I raised my eyebrow at Nancy, then looked away. She got the message.

When we were through, Nancy opened her bedroom door. There were Evan and Moose, eavesdropping. They followed us down the stairs and outside. When Nancy said, "Get lost, we're busy," Evan and Moose burst out laughing.

They shouted, "We must—we must—we must increase our bust!" Then they fell on the grass and rolled over and over laughing so hard I hoped they would both wet their pants.

On Tuesday, during an arithmetic review, I heard a bird go *peep*. Lots of other kids heard it too and so

·did Mr. Benedict. I know because he looked up. I went back to my problems but pretty soon I heard it again. *Peep.*

After the second *peep*, Mr. Benedict walked to the window and opened it wide. He stuck his head way out looking all around. While he was doing that three more *peeps* came from the room. Mr. Benedict walked to his desk and stood with his hands behind his back. *Peep.* I looked at Nancy. I was sure it came from her. But she didn't look at me or say anything. Mr. Benedict sat down and tapped his fingers on the top of his desk. Pretty soon our room sounded like a pet store full of birds. Every second there was another *peep.* It was hard not to giggle. When Nancy kicked me under the table I knew it was my turn. I looked down and erased my answer to a problem. While I was blowing the eraser dust away I said it—*peep.* By the time Mr. Benedict looked my way another *peep* came from across the room. I think it was Philip Leroy. We kept waiting for Mr. Benedict to say something, but he didn't.

When we came in the next morning our desks had been rearranged. Instead of four tables our desks formed one big U shape across the room. There were name cards taped onto each desk. On one side I was next to Freddy Barnett, who I didn't like at all. I knew for a fact that he was a troublemaker because I saw him stand behind Jay Hassler on the first day of school and just as Jay was about to sit down, Freddy

Barnett pulled his chair away. Jay wound up on the floor. I hate kids who do that! I'd have to be very careful not to fall into the trap of the Lobster. That's what we call him because on the first day of school he was sunburned bright red.

But on the other side of me things were even worse. I was next to Laura Danker! I was afraid to even look her way. Nancy warned me that reputations were catching. Well, I didn't have to worry because Laura didn't look my way either. She looked straight ahead. Naturally, the Four PTS's were all separated. But Nancy (that lucky!) got to sit next to Philip Leroy!

There wasn't any more *peep*ing. Mr. Benedict reminded us of our social studies test the next day. That afternoon we had gym. The boys got to play baseball with Mr. Benedict. The girls were left with the gym teacher, Miss Abbott, who told us to line up in order of size. I was third from the front end. Janie was first. Laura Danker was last. Gretchen and Nancy were in the middle. After we lined up Miss Abbott talked about posture and how important it is to stand up straight. "No matter how tall you are you must never slouch, because height is such a blessing. With that Miss Abbott stood up and took some deep breaths. She must have been at least six feet tall. Janie and I looked at each other and giggled. We were not blessed.

Then Miss Abbott told us since we were in sixth grade and very grown up, there were certain subjects we would cover during the school year. "Certain very private subjects just for girls." That was all she said but I got the idea. Why do they wait until sixth grade when you already know everything!

That night I really worked hard. I read the first two chapters in my social studies book four times. Then I sat on my bedroom floor and did my exercise. "I must—I must—I must increase my bust!" I did it thirty-five times and climbed into bed.

Are you there God? It's me, Margaret. I just did an exercise to help me grow. Have you thought about it God? About my growing, I mean. I've got a bra now. It would be nice if I had something to put in it. Of course, if you don't think I'm ready I'll understand. I'm having a test in school tomorrow. Please let me get a good grade on it God. I want you to be proud of me. Thank you.

The next morning Mr. Benedict passed out the test paper himself. The questions were already on the board. He said to begin as soon as we got our paper. Freddy the Lobster poked me and whispered, "No name."

"What do you mean, no name?" I whispered back.

Freddy whispered, "Nobody signs his name. Benedict won't know whose paper is whose. Get it?"

I got it all right but I didn't like it. Especially since I'd read the chapters four times. But if nobody was going to put a name on the test paper, I wasn't going to either. I felt cheated because Mr. Benedict would never know how hard I'd studied.

I answered all the questions in fifteen minutes. Mr. Benedict asked Janie to collect the papers for him. I couldn't imagine what he would do to us when he found out nobody had put a name on the test. I figured he'd be plenty mad but you can't do much to a whole class except keep them after school. We couldn't all be expelled, could we?

On Friday morning when we walked into our room, there was a test paper on everyone's desk. Every paper was marked and had the proper name on it. I got a ninety-eight. I felt great. Freddy Barnett didn't feel great at all. He got a fifty-three! Mr. Benedict didn't say anything about our names not being on the test papers. He just stood there and smiled. "Good morning, class," he said without clearing his throat. I think he knew he'd won the battle.

Later that day Mr. Benedict reminded us of our individual projects again. He told us not to wait until the last minute and think we could whip something up then. He said by the end of next week we should all know our topic and start in on our notes.

I thought a lot about it, but I didn't know anything meaningful that I was willing to share with Mr. Benedict. I mean, I couldn't very well come up with a year-long study about bras and what goes in them. Or about my feelings toward Moose. Or about God. Or could I? I mean, not about God exactly—I could never tell Mr. Benedict that—but maybe about religion. If I could figure out which religion to be I'd know if I wanted to join the Y or the Jewish Community Center. That was meaningful, wasn't it? I'd have to think about it.

Are you there God? It's me, Margaret. What would you think of me doing a project on religion? You wouldn't mind, would you God? I'd tell you all about it. And I won't make any decisions without asking you first. I think it's time for me to decide what to be. I can't go on being nothing forever, can I?

The following Saturday morning my mother drove me to the highway to get the New York bus. It was my first time going alone and my mother was nervous.

"Listen, Margaret—don't sit next to any men. Either sit alone or pick out a nice lady. And try to sit up front. If the bus isn't air-conditioned open your window. And when you get there ask a *lady* to show you the way downstairs. Grandma will meet you at the information desk."

"I know, I know." We'd been over it three dozen times but when the bus came my mother got out of the car and shouted to the bus driver.

"This little girl is traveling alone. Please keep an eye on her. It's her first trip."

"Don't worry, lady," the bus driver told my mother. Then my mother waved to me. I made a face at her and looked the other way.

I found grandma right where she was supposed to

be. She gave me a big kiss. Grandma smelled delicious. She was wearing a green suit and had on lots of green eyeshadow to match. Her hair was silver blonde. Grandma's hair color changes about once a month.

When we were out of the bus terminal Grandma said, "You look beautiful, Margaret. I love your hair."

Grandma always has something nice to say to me. And my hair did look better. I read that if you brush it good it can grow up to an inch a month.

We went to lunch at a restaurant near Lincoln Center. During my chocolate parfait I whispered, "I'm wearing a bra. Can you tell?"

"Of course I can tell," Grandma said.

"You can?" I was really surprised. I stopped eating. "Well, how do you think it makes me look?"

"Much older," Grandma said, between sips of her coffee. I didn't know whether to believe her or not so I believed her.

Then we went to the concert. I didn't fidget like when I was a little kid. I sat very still and paid attention to the music. During intermission Grandma and I walked around outside. I love that fountain in the middle of Lincoln Center. I love it more than the concerts themselves. And I love to watch the people walk by. Once I saw a model having her picture taken by the fountain. It was freezing cold and she was wearing a summer dress. That's when I decided not to be a model. Even if I did get beautiful some day.

In the cab, on the way back to the bus terminal, I thought about Grandma being Jewish. She was the perfect person to help me start my project. So I asked her, "Can I go to temple with you sometime?"

Grandma absolutely stared at me. I never knew anyone could open her eyes so wide.

"What are you saying? Are you saying you want to be Jewish?" She held her breath.

"No. I'm saying I'd like to go to temple and see what it's all about."

·"My Margaret!" Grandma threw her arms around me. I think the cab driver thought we were crazy. "I knew you were a Jewish girl at heart! I always knew it!" Grandma took out a lace hanky and dabbed her eyes.

"I'm not, Grandma," I insisted. "You know I'm not anything."

"You can say it, but I'll never believe it. Never!" She blew her nose. When she finished blowing she said, "I know what it is. You've made a lot of Jewish friends in Farbrook. Am I right?"

"No, Grandma. My friends have nothing to do with this."

"Then what? I don't understand."

"I just want to see what it's all about. So can I?" I certainly was not going to tell Grandma about Mr. Benedict.

Grandma sat back in her seat and beamed at me. "I'm thrilled! I'm going right home to call the rabbi.

You'll come with me on Rosh Hashanah." Then she stopped smiling and asked. "Does your mother know?"

I shook my head.

"Your father?"

I shook it again.

Grandma slapped her hand against her forehead. "Be sure to tell them it's not my idea! Would I be in trouble!"

"Don't worry, Grandma."

"That's ridiculous!" my mother said when I told her. "You know how Daddy and I feel about religion."

"You said I could choose when I grow up!"

"But you're not ready to choose yet, Margaret!"

"I just want to try it out," I argued. "I'm going to try church too, so don't get hysterical!"

"I am *not* hysterical! I just think it's foolish for a girl of your age to bother herself with religion."

"Can I go?" I asked.

"I'm not going to stop you," my mother said.

"Fine. Then I'll go."

On Rosh Hashanah morning, while I was still in bed, I said,

Are you there God? It's me, Margaret. I'm going to temple today—with Grandma. It's a holiday. I guess you know that. Well, my father thinks it's a mistake and my mother thinks the whole idea is crazy, but I'm going anyway. I'm sure this will help me decide what to be. I've never been inside a temple or a church. I'll look for you God.

9

I had a new suit and a small velvet hat. My mother said everyone wears new clothes for the Jewish holidays. It was hot for October and my father said he remembered it was always hot on the Jewish holidays when he was a kid. I had to wear white gloves. They made my hands sweat. By the time I got to New York the gloves were pretty dirty so I took them off and stuffed them into my pocketbook. Grandma met me at our usual spot in the bus terminal and took me in a taxi to her temple.

We got there at ten-thirty. Grandma had to show a card to an usher and then he led us to our seats which were in the fifth row in the middle. Grandma whispered to the people sitting near her that I was her granddaughter Margaret. The people looked at me and smiled. I smiled back. I was glad when the rabbi stepped out on the stage and held up his hands. While this was going on soft organ music played. I thought it sounded beautiful. The rabbi was dressed in a long white robe. He looked like a priest except he didn't have on the backwards collar that priests wear. Also, he had a little hat on his head that Grandma called a yarmulke.

The rabbi welcomed us and then started a lot of things I didn't understand. We had to stand up and sit down a lot and sometimes we all read together in English from a prayer book. I didn't understand too much of what I was reading. Other times the choir sang and the organ played. That was definitely the best part. Some of the service was in Hebrew and I was surprised to see that Grandma could recite along with the rabbi.

I looked around a lot, to see what was going on. But since I was in the fifth row there wasn't much for me to see, except the four rows in front of me. I knew it wouldn't be polite to actually turn my head and look behind me. There were two big silver bowls filled with white flowers up on the stage. They were very pretty.

At eleven-thirty the rabbi made a speech. A sermon, Grandma called it. At first I tried very hard to understand what he was talking about. But after a while I gave up and started counting different colored hats. I counted eight brown, six black, three red, a yellow and a leopard before the rabbi finished. Then we all stood up again and everyone sang a song in Hebrew that I didn't know. And that was it! I expected something else. I don't know what exactly. A feeling, maybe. But I suppose you have to go more than once to know what it's all about.

As we filed out of the aisles Grandma pulled me to one side, away from the crowd. "How would you like to meet the rabbi, Margaret?"

"I don't know," I said. I really wanted to get outside.

"Well, you're going to!" Grandma smiled at me. "I've told him all about you."

We stood in line waiting to shake hands with the rabbi. After a long time it was our turn. I was face to face with Rabbi Kellerman. He was kind of young and looked a little like Miles J. Benedict Jr. He wasn't skinny though.

Grandma whispered to me, "Shake hands, Margaret."

I held out my hand.

"This is my granddaughter, Rabbi. The one I told you about . . . Margaret Simon."

The rabbi shook my hand. "Yes, of course. Margaret! Good Yom Tov."

"Yes," I said.

The rabbi laughed. "It means Happy New Year. That's what we're celebrating today."

"Oh," I said. "Well, Happy New Year to you Rabbi."

"Did you enjoy our service?" he asked.

"Oh, yes," I said. "I just loved it."

"Good—good." He pumped my hand up and down some more. "Come back any time. Get to know us, Margaret. Get to know us and God."

I had to go through the third degree when I got home.

"Well," my mother said. "How was it?"

"Okay, I guess."

"Did you like it?" she asked.

"It was interesting," I said.

"Did you learn anything?" my father wanted to know.

"Well," I said. "In the first five rows there were eight brown hats and six black ones."

My father laughed. "When I was a kid I used to count feathers on hats." Then we laughed together.

Are you there God? It's me, Margaret. I'm really on my way now. By the end of the school year I'll know all there is to know about religion. And before I start junior high I'll know which one I am. Then I'll be able to join the Y or the Center like everybody else.

10

Three things happened the first week in November. Laura Danker wore a sweater to school for the first time. Mr. Benedict's eyes almost popped out of his head. Actually, I didn't notice Mr. Benedict's eyes, but Nancy told me. Freddy the Lobster noticed too. He asked me, "How come you don't look like that in a sweater, Margaret?" Then he laughed hard and slapped his leg. Very funny, I thought. I wore sweaters every day since I had so many of them. All *made expressly* for me by Grandma. Even if I stuffed my bra with socks I still wouldn't look like Laura Danker. I wondered if it was true that she went behind the A&P with Evan and Moose. Why would she do a stupid thing like that?

What reminded me of Moose was that he cut our grass and cleaned up our leaves and said he'd be back in the spring. So unless I bumped into him at Nancy's house I wouldn't see him all winter. Not that he even knew I existed—I'd had to hide from him ever since that *We must—we must* incident. But I watched him secretly from my bedroom window.

The second thing that happened was that I went to church with Janie Loomis. Janie and I had gotten pretty friendly. We were especially friendly in gym because Ruth, the girl who was second in line, was absent a lot. So Janie and I got to talk and once I came right out and asked her if she went to church.

"When I have to," she said.

So I asked her if I could go with her some time just to see what it was like and she said, "Sure, how about Sunday?"

So I went. The funniest thing was it was just like temple. Except it was all in English. But we read from a prayer book that didn't make sense and the minister gave a sermon I couldn't follow and I counted eight black hats, four red ones, six blue and two fur. At the end of the service everyone sang a hymn. Then we stood on line to shake hands with the minister. By then I was a pro at it.

Janie introduced me. "This is my friend Margaret Simon. She's no religion."

I almost fainted. What did Janie have to go and say that for? The minister looked at me like I was a freak. Then he smiled with an Aha—maybe-I'll-win-her look.

"Welcome to the First Presbyterian Church, Margaret. I hope you'll come back again."

"Thank you," I said.

Are you there God? It's me, Margaret. I've been to church. I didn't feel anything special in there God. Even though I wanted to. I'm sure it has nothing to do with you. Next time I'll try harder.

During this time I talked to Nancy every night. My father wanted to know why we had to phone each other so often when we were together in school all day. "What can you possibly have to discuss after only three hours?" he asked. I didn't even try to explain. Lots of times we did our math homework over the phone. When we were done Nancy called Gretchen to check answers and I called Janie.

The third thing that happened that week was the principal of our school announced over the loudspeaker that the PTA was giving a Thanksgiving square dance for the three sixth-grade classes. Mr. Benedict asked us if we knew how to square dance. Most of us didn't.

Nancy told the Four PTS's the square dance was going to be really super. And she knew all about it because her mother was on the committee. She said we should all write down who we wanted to dance with and she'd see what she could do about it. It turned out that we all wanted Philip Leroy, so Nancy said, "Forget it—I'm no magician."

For the next two weeks our gym period was devoted to square-dancing lessons. Mr. Benedict said if we were being given this party the least we could do to show our appreciation was to learn to do the basic steps. We practiced with records and Mr. Benedict jumped around a lot, clapping his hands. When he had to demonstrate a step he used Laura Danker as his partner. He said it was because she was tall enough to reach his shoulder properly, but Nancy gave me a knowing look. Anyway, none of the boys in our class wanted to be Laura's partner because they were all a lot smaller than her. Even Philip Leroy only came up to her chin, and he was the tallest.

The problem with square-dance lessons was that most of the boys were a lot more interested in stepping on our feet than they were in learning how to dance. And a few of them were so good at it they could step on us in time to the music. Mostly, I concentrated on not getting my feet squashed.

On the morning of the square dance I dressed in my new skirt and blouse.

Are you there God? It's me, Margaret. I can't wait until two o'clock God. That's when our dance starts. Do you think I'll get Philip Leroy for a partner? It's not so much that I like him as a person God, but as a boy he's very handsome. And I'd love to dance with him . . . just once or twice. Thank you God.

The PTA decorated the gym. It was supposed to look like a barn, I think. There were two piles of hay and three scarecrows. And a big sign on the wall in yellow letters saying WELCOME TO THE SIXTH GRADE SQUARE DANCE . . . as if we didn't know.

I was glad my mother wasn't a chaperone. It's bad enough trying to act natural at a dance, but when your mother's there it's impossible. I know because Mrs. Wheeler was a chaperone and Nancy was a wreck. The chaperones were dressed funny, like farmers or something. I mean, Nancy's mother wore dungarees, a plaid shirt and a big straw hat. I didn't blame Nancy for pretending not to know her.

We had a genuine square-dance caller. He was dressed up a lot like Mrs. Wheeler. He stood on the stage and told us what steps to do. He also worked the record player. He stamped his feet and jumped around and now and then I saw him mop his face off with a red handkerchief. Mr. Benedict kept telling us to get into the spirit of the party. "Relax and enjoy yourselves," he said.

The three sixth grades were supposed to mingle but the Four PTS's stuck close together. We had to line up every time there was a new dance. The girls lined up on one side and the boys on the other. That's how you got a partner. The only trouble was there were four more girls than boys, so whoever wound up last on line had to dance with another leftover girl. That only happened to me and Janie once, thank goodness!

What we did was try to figure out who our partner was going to be in advance. Like, I knew when I was fourth in line that Norman Fishbein was going to be my partner because he was fourth in line on the boys' side. So I switched around fast because Norman Fishbein is the biggest drip in my class. Well, at least one of the biggest drips. Also, Freddy Barnett was to be avoided because all he would do was tease me about how come I didn't look like Laura Danker in a sweater. But I noticed that once when he danced with her his face was so red he looked more like a lobster than he did when he was all sunburned.

The girls shuffled around more than the boys because most of us wanted to get Philip Leroy for a partner. And finally I got him. This is how it happened. After everyone had a partner we had to make a square. My partner was Jay Hassler who was very polite and didn't try to step on my foot once. Then the caller told us to switch partners with whoever was on our right side. Well, Philip Leroy was with Nancy on my right side, and Nancy was so mad she almost cried right in front of everyone. Even though I was thrilled to have Philip Leroy all to myself for a whole record, he *was* one of the foot steppers! And dancing with him made my hands sweat so bad I had to wipe them off on my new skirt.

At four o'clock the chaperones served us punch and cookies and at quarter to five the dance was over and my mother picked me up in our new car. (My father gave in around Halloween when my mother explained that she couldn't even get a quart of milk because she had no car. And that *Margaret* couldn't possibly walk to and from school in bad weather and that bad weather would be coming very soon. My mother didn't like my father's suggestion that if she got up early and drove him to the station she could use his car all day long.) Our new car is a Chevy. It's green.

My mother was in a hurry to drive home from the square dance because she was in the middle of a new painting. It was a picture of a lot of different fruits in honor of Thanksgiving. My mother gives away a whole bunch of pictures every Christmas. My father thinks they wind up in other people's attics.

11

By the first week in December we no longer used our secret names at PTS meetings. It was too confusing, Nancy said. Also, we just about gave up on our Boy Books. For one thing the names never changed. Nancy managed to shift hers around. It was easy for her—with eighteen boys. But Janie and Gretchen and I always listed Philip Leroy number one. There was no suspense about the whole thing. And I wondered, did they list Philip Leroy because they really liked him or were they doing what I did—making him number one because he was so good-looking. Maybe they were ashamed to write who they really liked too.

The day that Gretchen finally got up the guts to sneak out her father's anatomy book we met at my house, in my bedroom, with the door closed and a chair shoved in front of it. We sat on the floor in a circle with the book opened to the male body.

"Do you suppose that's what Philip Leroy looks like without his clothes on?" Janie asked.

"Naturally, dope!" Nancy said. "He's male, isn't he?"

"Look at all those veins and stuff," Janie said.

"Well, we *all* have them," Gretchen said.

"I think they're ugly," Janie said.

"You better never be a doctor or a nurse," Gretchen told her. "They have to look at this stuff all the time."

"Turn the page, Gretchen," Nancy said.

The next page was the male reproductive system. None of us said anything. We just looked until Nancy told us, "My brother looks like that."

"How do you know?" I asked.

"He walks around naked," Nancy said.

"My father used to walk around naked," Gretchen said. "But lately he's stopped doing it."

"My aunt went to a nudist colony last summer," Janie said.

"No kidding!" Nancy looked up.

"She stayed a month," Janie told us. "My mother didn't talk to her for three weeks after that. She thought it was a disgrace. My aunt's divorced."

"Because of the nudist colony?" I asked.

"No," Janie said. "She was divorced before she went."

"What do you suppose they do there?" Gretchen asked.

"Just walk around naked is all. My aunt says it's very peaceful. But I'll never walk around naked in front of anybody!"

"What about when you get married?" Gretchen asked.

"Even then," Janie insisted.

"You're a prude!" Nancy said.

"I am not! It has nothing to do with being a prude."

"When you grow you'll change your mind," Nancy told her. "You'll want everybody to see you. Like those girls in *Playboy*."

"What girls in *Playboy*?" Janie asked.

"Didn't you *ever* see a copy of *Playboy*?"

"Where would I see it?" Janie asked.

"My father gets it," I said.

"Do you have it around?" Nancy asked.

"Sure."

"Well, get it!" Nancy told me.

"Now?" I asked.

"Of course."

"Well, I don't know," I said.

"Listen, Margaret—Gretchen went to all the trouble of sneaking out her father's medical book. The least you could do is show us *Playboy*."

So I opened my bedroom door and went downstairs, trying to remember where I had seen the latest issue. I didn't want to ask my mother. Not that it was so wrong to show it to my friends. I mean, if it was so wrong my father shouldn't get it at all, right? Although lately I think he's been hiding it because it's never in the magazine rack where it used to be. Finally, I found it in his night table drawer and I thought if my mother caught me and asked me what I was doing I'd say we were making booklets and I needed some old magazines to cut up. But she didn't catch me.

Nancy opened it right up to the naked girl in the

middle. On the page before there was a story about her. It said Hillary Brite is eighteen years old.

"Eighteen! That's only six more years," Nancy squealed.

"But look at the size of her. They're huge!" Janie said.

"Do you suppose we'll look like that at eighteen?" Gretchen asked.

"If you ask me, I think there's something wrong with her," I said. "She looks out of proportion!"

"Do you suppose that's what Laura Danker looks like?" Janie asked.

"No. Not yet," Nancy said. "But she might at eighteen!"

Our meeting ended with fifty rounds of "*We must —we must—we must increase our bust!*"

12

On December eleventh Grandma sailed on a three-week cruise to the Caribbean. She went every year. She had a bon voyage party in her room on the ship. This year I was allowed to go. My mother gave Grandma a green silk box to keep her jewelry safe. It was very nice—all lined in white velvet. Grandma said thank you and that all her jewelry was for "her Margaret" anyway so she had to take good care of it. Grandma's always reminding me of how nobody lives forever and everything she has is for me and I hate it when she talks like that. She once told me she had her lawyer prepare her funeral instructions so things would go the way she planned. Such as, the kind of box she wants to be buried in and that she doesn't want any speeches at all and that I should only come once or twice a year to see that her grave is looking nice and neat.

We stayed on the ship half an hour and then Grandma kissed me good-by and promised to take me along with her one of these days.

The next week my mother started to address her Christmas cards and for days at a time she was frantically busy with them. She doesn't call them Christmas cards. Holiday greetings, she says. We don't celebrate

Christmas exactly. We give presents but my parents say that's a traditional American custom. My father says my mother and her greeting cards have to do with her childhood. She sends them to people she grew up with and they send cards back to her. So once a year she finds out who married whom and who had what kids and stuff like that. Also, she sends one to her brother, whom I've never met. He lives in California.

This year I discovered something really strange. I discovered that my mother was sending a Christmas card to her parents in Ohio. I found out because I was looking through the pile of cards one day when I had a cold and stayed home from school. There it was—just like that. The envelope said Mr. and Mrs. Paul Hutchins, and that's them. My grandparents! I didn't mention anything about it to my mother. I had the feeling I wasn't supposed to know.

In school, Mr. Benedict was running around trying to find out what happened to the new choir robes. The whole school was putting on a Christmas–Hanukkah pageant for the parents and our sixth-grade class was the choir. We didn't even have to try out. "Mr. Benedict's class will be the choir," the principal announced. We practiced singing every day with the music teacher. I thought by the time Christmas finally rolled around I wouldn't have any voice left. We learned five Christmas carols and three Hanukkah songs—alto and soprano parts. Mostly the boys sang alto and the girls sang soprano. We'd been measured for our new choir robes right after Thanksgiving. The PTA decided the old ones were really worn out. Our new ones would be green instead of black. We all had to carry pencil-sized flashlights instead of candles.

We practiced marching down the halls and into the auditorium singing "*Adeste Fidelis*" in English and Latin. We marched in two lines, boys and girls. And naturally in size places. I walked right behind Janie because Ruth had moved away. My partner turned out to be Norman Fishbein. I never looked at him. I just marched looking straight ahead singing very loud.

A week before the pageant Alan Gordon told Mr. Benedict that he wasn't going to sing the Christmas songs because it was against his religion. Then Lisa Murphy raised her hand and said that she wasn't going to sing the Hanukkah songs because it was against *her* religion.

Mr. Bendict explained that songs were for everyone and had nothing at all to do with religion, but the next day Alan brought in a note from home and from then on he marched but he didn't sing. Lisa sang when we marched but she didn't even move her lips during the Hanukkah songs.

Are you there God? It's me, Margaret. I want you to know I'm giving a lot of thought to Christmas and Hanukkah this year. I'm trying to decide if one might be special for me. I'm really thinking hard God. But so far I haven't come up with any answers.

Our new green choir robes were delivered to school the day before the pageant and were sent home with us to be pressed. The best thing about the pageant, besides wearing the robe and carrying the flashlight, was that I got to sit in the first row of choir seats, facing the audience, which meant that the kindergarten kids were right in front of me. Some of them tried to touch our feet with their feet. One little kid wet his pants during the scene where Mary and Joseph come to the inn. He made a puddle on the floor right in front of Janie. Janie had to keep on singing and pretend she didn't know. It was pretty hard not to laugh.

School closed for vacation right after the pageant. When I got home my mother told me I had a letter.

13

"Margaret—you've got a letter," my mother called from the studio. "It's on the front table."

I just about never get any letters. Probably because I never write anybody back. So I dashed over to the front table and picked it up. *Miss Margaret Simon*, it said. I turned the envelope around but there was no return address. I wondered who sent it. Wondering made it much more fun than ripping it open and knowing right away. It was probably just an advertisement anyway. Finally, when I couldn't stand it any more I opened it—very slowly and *very* carefully so I wouldn't rip up the envelope. It was an invitation! I knew right away because of the picture—a bunch of kids dancing around a record. Also, it said, HAVING A PARTY.

Who's having a party, I thought. Who's having a party and invited me? Naturally I could have found out right away. I could have looked inside. But this was better. I considered the possibilities. It couldn't be a PTS because I would have known. It could be somebody I knew from New York or camp, except I hadn't written to any old friends to tell them my new address.

Anyway, the envelope was postmarked New Jersey. Let's see, I thought. Who could it be? Who? Finally, I opened it.

Come on over on Saturday, Dec. 20
from 5 PM to 9 PM (supper)
1334 Whittingham Terrace
Norman Fishbein

"Norman Fishbein!" I yelled. That drip! I never even talked to him. Why would he invite me to his party? Still, a party is a party. And for supper too!

"Hey Mom!" I yelled, running into the studio. My mother was standing away from her canvas, studying her work. Her paint brush was in her mouth, between her teeth. "Guess what, Mom?"

"What?" she said, not taking the paint brush away.

"I'm invited to a supper party. Here—look—" I showed her my invitation.

She read it. "Who's Norman Fishbein?" She took the paint brush out of her mouth.

"A kid in my class."

"Do you like him?"

"He's okay. Can I go?"

"Well . . . I suppose so." My mother dabbed some red paint on her canvas. Then the phone rang.

"I'll get it." I ran into the kitchen and said a breathless hello.

"It's Nancy. Did you get invited?"

"Yes," I said. "Did you?"

"Mmm. We all did. Janie and Gretchen too."

"Can you go?"

"Sure."

"Me too."

"I've never been to a supper party," Nancy said.

"Me either. Should we dress up?" I asked.

"My mother's going to call Mrs. Fishbein. I'll let you know." She hung up.

Ten minutes later the phone rang again. I answered.

"Margaret. It's me again."

"I know."

"You'll never believe this!" Nancy said.

"What? What won't I believe?"

"We're all invited."

"What do you mean *all*?"

"Our whole class."

"All twenty-eight of us?"

"That's what Mrs. Fishbein told my mother."

"Even Laura?"

"I guess so."

"Do you think she'll come?" I asked, trying to picture Laura at a party.

"Well, her mother and Mrs. Fishbein work on a lot of committees together. So maybe her mother will make her."

"How about Philip Leroy?"

"He's invited. That's all I know. And Mrs. Fishbein said definitely party clothes."

When I hung up I raced back to the studio. "Mom —our whole class is invited!"

"Your *whole* class?" My mother put her paint brush down and looked at me.

"Yes. All twenty-eight of us."

"Mrs. Fishbein must be crazy!" my mother said.

"Should I wear my velvet, do you think?"

"It's your best. You might as well."

On the day of the party I talked to Nancy six times, to Janie three times and to Gretchen twice. Nancy called me back every time she changed her mind about what to wear. And each time she asked me if I was still wearing my velvet. I told her I was. The rest of the time we made our arrangements. We decided that Nancy would sleep over at my house and that Gretchen would sleep over at Janie's. Mr. Wheeler would drive us all to the party and Mr. Loomis would drive us home.

My mother washed my hair at two o'clock. She gave me a cream rinse too, so I wouldn't get tangles. She set it in big rollers all over my head. I sat under her hair dryer. Then she *filed* my nails with an emery board instead of just cutting like usual. My velvet dress was already laid out on my bed along with my new underwear, party shoes and tights. My new underwear was not the ordinary cotton kind. It was nylon, trimmed with lace around the edges. It was supposed to be one of my December tradition gifts. All afternoon I kept thinking that maybe Norman Fishbein wasn't such a drip.

After my bath I was supposed to go to my room and rest so I'd be in good shape for the party. I went to my room and closed the door—only I didn't feel like resting. What I did was move my desk chair in front of my dresser mirror. Then I stood on the chair and took off my robe. I stood naked in front of the mirror. I was starting to get some hairs. I turned around and studied myself sideways. Then I got off the chair and moved it closer to the mirror. I stood back up on it and looked again. My head looked funny with all those rollers. The rest of me looked the same.

Are you there God? It's me, Margaret. I hate to remind you God . . . I mean, I know you're busy. But it's already December and I'm not growing. At least I don't see any real difference. Isn't it time God? Don't you think I've waited patiently? Please help me.

I hopped off the chair and sat down on the edge of my bed, putting on my clean underwear and tights. Then I stood in front of the mirror again. I didn't look at myself for very long this time.

I went into the bathroom and opened the bottom cabinet. There was a whole box of cotton balls. *Sterile until opened*, the package said. I reached in and grabbed a few. My heart was pounding, which seemed stupid because what was I so afraid of anyway? I mean, if my mother saw me grab some cotton balls she wouldn't say anything. I use them all the time—to put calamine on my summer mosquito bites—to clean off cuts and bruises—to put on my face lotion at night. But my heart kept pounding anyway, because I knew what I was going to do with the cotton balls.

I tiptoed back to my room and closed the door. I stepped into my closet and stood in one corner. I shoved three cotton balls into each side of my bra. Well, so what if it was cheating! Probably other girls did it too. I'd look a lot better, wouldn't I? So why not!

I came out of the closet and got back up on my chair. This time when I turned sideways I looked like I'd grown. I liked it!

Are you still there God? See how nice my bra looks now! That's all I need—just a little help. I'll really be good around the house God. I'll clear the table every night for a month at least! Please God . . .

14

Later, my mother brushed my hair. It came out just
right, except for one piece on the left that turned the
wrong way. My mother said that piece made it look
very natural.

My mother and father smiled at me a lot while I
was waiting for Nancy's father to pick me up. I smiled
back. It was like we all knew some special secret. Only
I knew they didn't know *my* special secret! At least
they didn't say anything dumb like doesn't she look
sweet—going to her first supper party! I'd have died!

Mr. Wheeler tooted his horn at quarter to five. My
mother kissed me good-by and my father waved from
his chair. "Have fun," he called.

The Four PTS's squeezed into the back seat of the
Wheeler car (not the station wagon). Nancy's father
told us it was silly to sit like that and besides it made
him feel like a hired chauffeur. But all we did was
giggle. Janie got her hair cut without telling us she was
going to. She said she didn't know it herself until that
afternoon when her mother took her to the beauty
parlor and had a private talk with Mr. Anthony. Then
Mr. Anthony started clipping away and next thing she
knew—she had this new haircut. She looked like an

elf. It did a lot for her. And for a minute I thought about how I would look with the same haircut. But then I remembered how long I'd been suffering to let my hair grow. I decided it would be stupid to cut it all off.

When we got to the party Norman's mother opened the door for us. She was very tall and thin with a face like Norman's. I remembered her from the PTA square dance. Tonight she wasn't dressed like a farmer. She had on black velvet pants and some kind of top that looked like it had diamonds and rubies all over it.

"Good evening, Mrs. Fishbein," Nancy said, in a voice I'd never heard. "Please meet my friend Margaret Simon."

Mrs. Fishbein smiled at me and said, "Glad to meet you, Margaret." Then she took our coats away and handed them to a maid who carried them up the stairs.

"My, you all look so pretty!" Mrs. Fishbein said. "Everyone is downstairs. Nancy, you know the way."

I followed Nancy past the living room. The furniture was all very modern. The chairs looked like carved-out boxes and the tables were all glass. Everything was beige. At Nancy's house the furniture all has lion's paws for feet and there are a million colors. At my house the living room is carpeted but empty. My mother is trying to decide what kind of stuff she wants.

Norman's house was pretty big, because I had to follow Nancy through at least four more rooms before we got to a door leading downstairs.

It looked like most of my class was already there. Including Laura Danker, who I thought looked gorgeous in a soft pink dress with her hair all loose, kind of hanging in her face.

The boys had on sport jackets and some wore ties. Philip Leroy had on a tie the first time I saw him but a few minutes later the tie was gone and his shirt was unbuttoned around the neck. Soon after that, not one boy had his jacket on. They were all in a big heap in the corner.

Mostly, the girls stayed on one side of the room, and the boys on the other. As soon as everyone was there Mrs. Fishbein brought out the food. All kinds of sandwiches and a big dish of cut-up hotdogs in beans. I took some of that and some potato salad and sat down at a table with Janie, Nancy and Gretchen. There were six little tables so practically everyone had a place to sit. As soon as we were all served Mrs. Fishbein and the maid went back upstairs.

I'm not sure who started blowing the mustard through a straw up at the ceiling. I only know that I saw Philip Leroy yell, "Watch this, Freddy!" as he aimed his straw. I saw the mustard fly up and make a yellow splotch on the white ceiling.

Mrs. Fishbein didn't come downstairs again until dessert time. At first she didn't see the ceiling. But she did see the mess on the buffet table. When she looked up she sucked in her breath and the room got very quiet. "What is that on my ceiling?" she asked Norman.

"Mustard," Norman answered.

"I see," Mrs. Fishbein replied.

That was all she said but she looked at every one of us with an I-don't-know-why-your-parents-never-taught-you-any-manners look. Then Mrs. Fishbein stood close to our table and said, "I'm sure these girls aren't responsible for this mess." We smiled at her, but I saw Philip Leroy stick out his tongue at us.

"Now I'm going upstairs to get your dessert," Mrs. Fishbein said, "and I expect you to behave like ladies and gentlemen."

Dessert was tiny cupcakes in all different colors. I ate two chocolate ones before Freddy Barnett came over to our table. "I'm sure these girls didn't do anything naughty!" he mimicked. "These girls are so sweet and good."

"Oh shut up!" Nancy told him, standing up. She was as tall as he was.

"Why don't you shut up, *know it all!*"

"Cut it out, Lobster!" Nancy hollered.

"Who's a lobster?"

"You are!" Nancy gritted her teeth.

Freddy grabbed hold of Nancy and for a minute I thought he was going to hit her.

"Take your lobster claws off me!" Nancy yelled.

"Make me," Freddy told her.

Nancy whirled around but Freddy had hold of her dress by the pocket and next thing we knew Freddy still had the pocket but Nancy was across the room.

"Oh! He ripped off my pocket!" Nancy screamed.

Freddy looked like he couldn't believe it himself. But there he was, holding Nancy's pocket. There wasn't any hole in Nancy's dress—just some loose threads where her pocket used to be. Nancy ran up the stairs and returned a few minutes later with Mrs. Fishbein.

"He tore off my pocket," Nancy said, pointing to Freddy Barnett.

"I didn't mean to," Freddy explained. "It just came off."

"I am shocked at your behavior. *Simply shocked!*" Mrs. Fishbein said. "I don't know what kind of children you are. I'm not going to send you home because your parents expect you to be here until nine and it's only seven now. But I'm telling you this—any more hanky-panky and I'll call each and every one of your mothers and fathers and report this *abominable* behavior to them!"

Mrs. Fishbein marched back up the stairs. We couldn't hold back our giggles. It was all so funny. *Hanky-panky* and *abominable!*

Even Nancy and Freddy had to laugh. Then Norman suggested that we play games to keep out of trouble. "The first game is Guess Who," Norman said.

"Guess Who?" Janie asked. "How do you play that?"

Norman explained. "See, I turn off all the lights and the boys line up on one side and the girls on the other and then when I yell Go the boys run to the girls' side and try to guess who's who by the way they feel."

"No, thank you," Gretchen said. "That's disgusting!"

"Above the neck, Gretchen," Norman said. "Only above the neck."

"Forget it," Gretchen said and we all agreed. Especially me—I kept thinking of those six cotton balls. They weren't so far below my neck.

"Okay," Norman said. "We'll start with Spin the Bottle."

"That's corny!" Philip Leroy shouted.

"Yeah," the other boys agreed.

"We have to start with something," Norman said. He put a green bottle on the floor.

We sat in a big circle, around the green bottle. Norman told us his rules. "You got to kiss whoever's nearest to where the bottle points. No fair boy kissing boy or girl kissing girl."

Norman spun first. He got Janie. He bent down and gave her a kiss on the cheek, near her ear but up higher. He ran back to his place in the circle. Everybody laughed. Then Janie had to spin. She got Jay. She put her face next to his but she kissed the air instead of him.

"No fair!" Norman called out. "You've got to *really* kiss him."

"Okay, okay," Janie said. She tried again. She made it this time, but far away from his mouth.

I felt a lot safer knowing it would all be cheek kissing. I held my breath every time somebody turned the bottle, waiting to see who would get me and wondering who I would get. When Gretchen got Philip Leroy she could hardly stand up. She kept biting her lip and finally she went over to him and gave him the quickest kiss you ever saw. Then I really couldn't breathe because I thought, if he gets me I'll faint. I closed my eyes. When I opened them I saw the bottle pointing straight at Laura Danker. She looked down and when Philip bent to kiss her I think all he got was her forehead and some loose hair.

That's when Jay said, "This is *really* stupid. Let's play Two Minutes in the Closet."

"What's that?" Norman asked.

Jay explained. "We all get a number and then somebody starts by calling like—number six—and those two go in the closet for two minutes and uh . . . well, you know."

"We don't have a closet down here," Norman said. "But we do have a bathroom."

Norman didn't waste any time getting some paper and pencils. He scribbled the numbers on a big sheet of paper—odd ones for the boys, evens for the girls. Then he tore each number off and put first the evens, then the odds in his father's hat. We all picked. I got number twelve.

I was half scared and half excited and I wished I had been experimenting like Nancy. Nancy would know what to do with a boy in the dark, but what did I know? Nothing!

Norman said he'd go first because it was his party. Nobody argued. He stood up and cleared his throat. "Number uh . . . number sixteen," he said.

Gretchen squealed and jumped up.

"Bye bye you two," Nancy said. "Don't be long!"

Long! They were back in three seconds.

"Hey! I thought you said two minutes," Philip Leroy called.

"Two minutes is as long as you can stay," Norman said. "But you don't have to stay that long if you don't want to."

Gretchen called number three which was Freddy Barnett and I hoped I'd remember to never call number three.

Then Freddy called number fourteen and got Laura Danker. We all giggled. I wondered how he would kiss her because I didn't think he could reach her face unless he stood on something. Maybe he'll stand on the toilet seat, I thought. And then I couldn't stop laughing at all.

When they came out of the bathroom Laura's face was as red as Freddy's and I thought that was pretty funny for a girl who goes behind the A&P with boys.

Laura called her number very softly. "Seven," she said.

Philip Leroy stood up and smiled at the boys. He pushed his hair off his face and walked to the bathroom with his hands stuffed in his pockets. I kept thinking that if he really liked her he'd call her number back and the two of them would be in the bathroom together for the rest of the party.

When they came out Philip was still smiling but Laura wasn't. Nancy poked me and gave me her knowing look. I was so busy watching Laura that I didn't hear Philip call number twelve.

"Who's twelve?" Philip asked. "Somebody must be twelve."

"Did you say twelve?" I asked. "That's me."

"Well, come on, Margaret."

I stood up knowing I'd never be able to make it across the recreation room to the bathroom, where Philip Leroy was waiting to kiss me. I saw Janie, Gretchen and Nancy smiling at me. But I couldn't smile back. I don't know how I got to the bathroom. All I know is I stepped in and Philip shut the door. It was hard to see anything.

"Hi, Margaret," he said.

"Hi, Philip," I whispered. Then I started to giggle.

"I can't kiss you if you don't stop laughing," he said.

"Why not?"

"Because your mouth is open when you laugh."

"You're going to kiss me on the mouth?"

"You know a better place?"

I stopped laughing. I wished I could remember what Nancy said that day she showed me how to kiss her pillow.

"Stand still, Margaret," Philip told me.

I stood still.

He put his hands on my shoulders and leaned close. Then he kissed me. A really fast kiss! Not the kind you see in the movies where the boy and girl cling together for a long time. While I was thinking about it, Philip kissed me again. Then he opened the bathroom door and walked back to his place.

"Call a number, Margaret," Norman said. "Hurry up."

I couldn't even think of a number. I wanted to call Philip Leroy's number. But I couldn't remember it. So I called number nine and got Norman Fishbein!

He was really proud. Like I'd picked him on purpose. Ha! He practically ran to the bathroom.

After he closed the door he said, "I really like you, Margaret. How do you want me to kiss you?"

"On the cheek and fast," I said.

He did it just that way and I quickly opened the door and walked away from the bathroom. And that was it!

Later, at my house, Nancy told me she thought I was the luckiest girl in the world and maybe it was fate that brought me and Philip Leroy together.

"Did he kiss good?" she asked.

"Pretty good," I said.

"How many times?" she asked.

"About five. I lost count," I told her.

"Did he *say* anything?"

"Nothing much."

"Do you still like him?"

"Of course!"

"Me too."

"Good night, Nancy."

"Good night, Margaret."

15

I went to Christmas Eve services with the Wheelers, at the United Methodist Church of Farbrook. I asked Nancy if I had to meet the minister.

"Are you kidding!" she said. "The place will be mobbed. He doesn't even know *my* name."

I relaxed after that and enjoyed most of the service, especially since there wasn't any sermon. The choir sang for forty-five minutes instead.

I got home close to midnight. I was so tired my parents didn't question me. I fell into bed without brushing my teeth.

Are you there God? It's me, Margaret. I just came home from church. I loved the choir—the songs were so beautiful. Still, I didn't really feel you God. I'm more confused than ever. I'm trying hard to understand but I wish you'd help me a little. If only you could give me a hint God. Which religion should I be? Sometimes I wish I'd been born one way or the other.

Grandma came back from her cruise in time to pack up and head for Florida. She said New York had nothing to offer since I was gone. She sent me two postcards a week, called every Friday night and promised to be home before Easter.

Our phone conversations were always the same. I talked first: "Hello, Grandma. . . . Yes, I'm fine. . . . They're fine. . . . School's fine. . . . I miss you too."

Then my father talked: "Hello, Mother. . . . Yes, we're fine. . . . How's the weather down there? . . . Well, it's bound to come out sooner or later. That's why they call it the Sunshine State."

Then my mother talked: "Hello, Sylvia. . . . Yes, Margaret's really fine. . . . Of course I'm sure. . . . Okay—and you take care too."

Then I talked a second time: "Bye, Grandma. See you soon."

During the second week in January Mr. Benedict announced that the sixth-grade girls were going to see a movie on Friday afternoon. The sixth-grade boys were not going to see the movie. At that time they would have a discussion with the boy's gym teacher from the junior high.

Nancy passed me a note. It said, *Here we go—the big deal sex movie.*

When I asked her about it she told me the PTA sponsors it and it's called *What Every Girl Should Know.*

When I went home I told my mother. "We're going to see a movie in school on Friday."

"I know," my mother said. "I got a letter in the mail. It's about menstruation."

"I already *know* all about that."

"I know *you* know," my mother said. "But it's important for *all* the girls to see it in case their mothers haven't told them the facts."

"Oh."

On Friday morning there was a lot of giggling. Finally, at two o'clock, the girls lined up and went to the auditorium. We took up the first three rows of seats. There was a lady on the stage, dressed in a gray suit. She had a big behind. Also, she wore a hat.

"Hello, girls," she said. She clutched a hanky which she waved at us sometimes. "I'm here today to tell you about *What Every Girl Should Know*, brought to you as a courtesy of the Private Lady Company. We'll talk some more after the film." Her voice was smooth, like a radio announcer's.

Then the lights went out and we saw the movie. The narrator of the film pronounced it menstroo-ation. "Remember," the voice said, "it's menstroo-ation." Gretchen, who was next to me, gave me a kick and I kicked Nancy on the other side. We held our hands over our mouths so we wouldn't laugh.

The film told us about the ovaries and explained why girls menstroo-ate. But it didn't tell us how it feels, except to say that it is not painful, which we knew anyway. Also, it didn't really show a girl getting it. It just said how wonderful nature was and how we would soon become women and all that. After the film the lady in the gray suit asked if there were any questions.

Nancy raised her hand and when Gray Suit called on her Nancy said, "How about Tampax?"

Gray Suit coughed into her hanky and said, "We don't advise *internal protection* until you are considerably older."

Then Gray Suit came down from the stage and passed out booklets called *What Every Girl Should Know*. The booklet recommended that we use Private Lady sanitary supplies. It was like one big commercial. I made a mental note never to buy Private Lady things *when* and *if* I ever needed them.

For days after that whenever I looked at Gretchen, Janie or Nancy we'd pretend to be saying menstrooation. We laughed a lot. Mr. Benedict told us we'd have to settle down since we had a lot to learn before we'd be ready for seventh grade.

One week later Gretchen got it. We had a special PTS meeting that afternoon.

"I got it last night. Can you tell?" she asked us.

"Oh, Gretchen! You lucky!" Nancy shrieked. "I was sure I'd be first. I've got more than you!"

"Well, that doesn't mean much," Gretchen said, knowingly.

"How did it happen?" I asked.

"Well, I was sitting there eating my supper when I felt like something was dripping from me."

"Go on—go on," Nancy said.

"Well, I ran to the bathroom, and when I saw what it was I called my mother."

"And?" I asked.

"She yelled that she was eating."

"And?" Janie said.

"Well, I yelled back that it was important."

"So—so—" Nancy prompted.

"So . . . uh . . . she came and I showed her," Gretchen said.

"Then what?" Janie asked.

"Well, she didn't have any stuff in the house. She uses Tampax herself—so she had to call the drugstore and order some pads."

"What'd you do in the meantime?" Janie asked.

"Kept a wash cloth in my pants," Gretchen said.

"Oh—you didn't!" Nancy said, laughing.

"Well, I had to," Gretchen said.

"Okay—so then what?" I asked.

"Well . . . in about an hour the stuff came from the drugstore."

"Then what?" Nancy asked.

"My mother showed me how to attach the pad to the belt. Oh . . . you know . . ."

Nancy was mad. "Look Gretchen, did we or did we

not make a deal to tell each other absolutely everything about getting it?"

"I'm telling you, aren't I?" Gretchen asked.

"Not enough," Nancy said. "What's it *feel* like?"

"Mostly I don't feel anything. Sometimes it feels like it's dripping. It doesn't hurt coming out—but I had some cramps last night."

"Bad ones?" Janie asked.

"Not bad. Just different," Gretchen said. "Lower down, and across my back."

"Does it make you feel older?" I asked.

"Naturally," Gretchen answered. "My mother said now I'll really have to watch what I eat because I've gained too much weight this year. And she said to wash my face well from now on—with soap."

"And that's it?" Nancy said. "The whole story?"

"I'm sorry if I've disappointed you, Nancy. But really, that's all there is to tell. Oh, one thing I forgot. My mother said I may not get it every month yet. Sometimes it takes a while to get regular."

"Are you using that Private Lady stuff?" I asked.

"No, the drugstore sent *Teenage Softies*."

"Well, I guess I'll be next," Nancy said.

Janie and I looked at each other. We guessed so too.

When I went home I told my mother. "Gretchen Potter got her period."

"Did she really?" my mother asked.

"Yes," I said.

"I guess you'll begin soon too."

"How old were you Mom—when you got it?"

"Uh . . . I think I was fourteen."

"*Fourteen!* That's crazy. I'm not waiting until I'm fourteen."

"I'm afraid there's not much you can do about it, Margaret. Some girls menstruate earlier than others. I had a cousin who was sixteen before she started."

"Do you suppose that could happen to me? I'll die if it does!"

"If you don't start by the time you're fourteen I'll take you to the doctor. Now stop worrying!"

"How can I stop worrying when I don't know if I'm going to turn out normal?"

"I promise, you'll turn out normal."

Are you there God? It's me, Margaret. Gretchen, my friend, got her period. I'm so jealous God. I hate myself for being so jealous, but I am. I wish you'd help me just a little. Nancy's sure she's going to get it soon, too. And if I'm last I don't know what I'll do. Oh please God. I just want to be normal. ·

Nancy and her family went to Washington over Lincoln's birthday weekend. I got a postcard from her before she got back which means she must have mailed it the second she got there. It only had three words on it.

I . GOT IT!!!

I ripped the card into tiny shreds and ran to my room. There was something wrong with me. I just knew it. And there wasn't a thing I could do about it. I flopped onto my bed and cried. Next week Nancy would want to tell me all about her period and about how grown up she was. Well, I didn't want to hear her good news!

Are you there God? It's me, Margaret. Life is getting worse every day. I'm going to be the only one who doesn't get it. I know it God. Just like I'm the only one without a religion. Why can't you help me? Haven't I always done what you wanted? Please . . . let me be like everybody else.

16

My mother took me to Lincoln Center twice. We used Grandma's subscription tickets. It wasn't as much fun as with Grandma, because number one, I didn't get to ride the bus alone, and number two, my mother thought the concert itself was more important than looking at the people. I wrote Grandma a letter.

Dear Grandma,
I miss you. Florida sure sounds like fun.
School is fine. So are Mom and Dad. I am fine too. I've only had one cold so far and two viruses. One was the throwing up kind.
I forgot to tell you this over the phone, but when we went to Lincoln Center there was slush all over the place so I couldn't sit by the fountain.
I had to wear boots too, and my feet sweated during the concert. Mom wouldn't let me take them off, the way you do. It snowed again yesterday. I'll bet you don't miss that, do you! But snow is more fun in New Jersey than in New York. For one thing, it's cleaner.
Love,
Margaret

Grandma wrote back:

Dear Margaret,
I miss you too. Thank you for your nice letter.
I hope when you were sick your mother
took you to a good doctor. If I had been home
I would have asked Dr. Cohen who he
recommends in New Jersey. There must be one
or two good doctors there. You probably
caught cold because you kept your boots on at
Lincoln Center. Your mother should know better!
From now on, take off your boots the way we
always do—no matter what your mother says!
Only don't tell her I said so.
I met a very nice man at my hotel. His name is
Mr. Binamin. He comes from New York too.
We have dinner together and sometimes see
a show. He is a widower with three children
(all married) . *They* think he should
get married again. *He* thinks he should get
married again. But I'm not saying anything!
I hope your mother and father will let you
come stay with me during spring vacation.
Would you like that? I'm writing a letter
to ask their permission.
Be careful and dress warmly! Write to me again.
All my love,
Grandma

Dear Grandma,
Mom and Dad say I can probably visit you
during spring vacation, but that it's too
soon to make definite plans. I'm so excited
I could die! I'm counting the days already.
I've never been on a plane, as you know. And
Florida sounds like so much fun! Also, I want
to see what's going on with you and that Mr.
Binamin. You never tell us a thing when you call!
I am fine. The snow melted. Mom is painting
a new picture. This one is of apricots, grapes
and ivy leaves. Did I tell you my friends
Nancy and Gretchen got their periods?
See you soon, I hope.
Love and kisses,
Margaret

17

On the first Sunday in March Nancy invited me to spend the day in New York with her family. Evan brought Moose. It was pretty exciting riding all the way to the city with Moose Freed in the same car, except the Wheelers used their station wagon. The boys sat in the back and Nancy and I were in the middle, so if I wanted to see Moose I had to turn around and if I ride looking backwards like that I get car sick.

We went to Radio City Music Hall. Grandma used to take me there when I was little. My parents always say it's strictly for the tourists. I wanted to sit next to Moose but he and Evan found two seats off by themselves.

After the show the Wheelers took us to the Steak Place for dinner. Nancy and I ordered, then excused ourselves to go to the ladies' room. We were the only two in there, which was lucky for us because there were only two toilets and we both had to go pretty bad. Just as I was finishing up I heard Nancy moan.

"Oh no—oh no—"

"What is it, Nancy?" I asked.

"Oh please—oh no—

"Are you okay?" I banged on the wall separating us.

"Get my mother—quick!" she whispered.

I stood in front of her booth then. "What's wrong?" I tried the door but it was locked. "Let me in."

Nancy started to cry. "Please get my mother."

"Okay. I'm going. I'll be right back."

I raced to our table in the dining room, hoping Nancy wouldn't faint or anything like that before I got back with her mother.

I whispered to Mrs. Wheeler, "Nancy's sick. She's in the bathroom crying and she wants you."

Mrs. Wheeler jumped up and followed me back to the ladies' room. I could hear Nancy sobbing.

"Nancy?" Mrs. Wheeler called, trying the door.

"Oh Mom—I'm so scared! Help me—please."

"The door's locked, Nancy. I can't get in," Mrs. Wheeler said. "You've got to unlock it."

"I can't—I can't—" Nancy cried.

"I could crawl under and open it from the other side," I suggested. "Should I?" I asked Mrs. Wheeler. She nodded.

I gathered my skirt around my legs so it wouldn't drag on the floor and crawled under the door. Nancy's face was buried in her hands. I unlocked the door for Mrs. Wheeler, then waited outside by the sinks. I wondered if Nancy would have to go to the hospital or what. I hoped she didn't have anything catching.

In a few minutes Mrs. Wheeler opened the door a crack and handed me some change. "Margaret," she said, "would you get us a sanitary napkin please?" I must have given her a strange look because she said, "From the dispenser on the wall, dear. Nancy's menstruating."

"Does she always act like that?"

"It's her first time," Mrs. Wheeler explained. "She's frightened." Nancy was still crying and there was a lot of whispering going on.

I couldn't believe it! Nancy, who knew everything! She'd lied to me about her period. She'd never had it before!

I put the change into the machine and pulled the lever. The sanitary napkin popped out in a cardboard box. I handed it to Mrs. Wheeler.

"Nancy, calm down," I heard her mother say. "I can't help you if you don't stop crying."

Suppose I hadn't been along that day? I'd never have found out about Nancy. I almost wished I hadn't.

Finally Nancy and her mother came out of the booth and Mrs. Wheeler suggested that Nancy wash up before coming back to the table. "I'm going to tell the others not to worry," she said. "Don't be too long, girls."

I didn't know what to say. I mean, what can you say when you've just found out your friend's a liar!

Nancy washed her hands and face. I handed her two paper towels to dry herself. "Are you okay?" I asked. I felt kind of sorry for Nancy then. I want my period too, but not enough to lie about it.

Nancy faced me. "Margaret, please don't tell."

"Oh Nancy . . ."

"I mean it. I'd die if the others knew. Promise you won't tell about me," she begged.

"I won't."

"I thought I had it that time. You know . . . I didn't just make it all up. It was a mistake."

"Okay," I said.

"You won't tell?"

"I said I wouldn't."

We walked back to the table and joined the others for dinner. Our steaks were just being served. I sat next to Moose. He smelled very nice. I wondered if he shaved because the nice smell reminded me of my father's after-shave lotion. I got to touch his hand a couple of times because he was a lefty and I'm a righty so now and then we'd bump. He said he always has that trouble at round tables. He was definitely number one in my Boy Book, even if nobody knew it but me.

I could only finish half of my steak. The Wheelers took the other half home in a doggie bag. I knew they didn't have a dog but naturally I didn't tell the waitress.

Are you there God? It's me, Margaret. Nancy Wheeler is a big fake. She makes up stories! I'll never be able to trust her again. I will wait to find out from you if I am normal or not. If you would like to give me a sign, fine. If not, I'll try to be patient. All I ask is that I don't get it in school because if I had to tell Mr. Benedict I know I would die. Thank you God.

18

On March eighth I was twelve years old. The first thing I did was sniff under my arms, the way my mother does. Nothing! I didn't smell a thing. Still, now that I was twelve, I decided I'd better use deodorant, just in case. I went into my parents' bathroom and reached for my mother's roll-on. When I got dressed I went down to the kitchen for breakfast.

"Happy Birthday, Margaret!" my mother sang, bending over to kiss me while I was drinking my orange juice.

"Thank you, Mom," I said. "I used your deodorant."

My mother laughed. "You don't have to use mine. I'll get you your own."

"You will?" I asked.

"Sure, if you want to use it regularly."

"Well, I think I'd better. I'm twelve now, you know."

"I know—I know." My mother smiled at me while she cut some banana onto my cereal.

Grandma sent me a hundred-dollar savings bond as she does every year—plus three new sweaters with MADE EXPRESSLY FOR YOU . . . BY GRANDMA labels in them, a new bathing suit and an airline ticket to Florida! Round trip, leaving from Newark Airport at noon on April fourth. Was I excited!

In school Mr. Benedict shook my hand and wished me a lot of good luck in the coming year. He led the class in singing "Happy Birthday" to me. Nancy, Janie and Gretchen chipped in and bought me the new Mice Men record album. They gave it to me at lunch. Nancy mailed me a separate birthday card signed, *A million thanks to the best friend a girl could ever have.* I guess she was still scared I'd give away her secret.

That afternoon Mr. Benedict announced that for the next three weeks a part of each school day would be devoted to committee work. We were going to do projects on different countries. Janie, Nancy, Gretchen and I gave each other looks saying we'd work together, of course.

But that sneaky Miles J. Benedict! He said that since he wanted us to work with people we hadn't worked with before he had made up the committees already. Well, that's a first-year teacher for you! Didn't he know that was a bad idea? Didn't he know he was supposed to let us form our own committees? Teachers never come right out and say they've picked who you should work with. It's bad enough that they fool you a lot by pretending to let you choose a subject when they know all along what you're going to do. But this was ridiculous!

I guess Mr. Benedict didn't think it was ridiculous because he was already reading out names of committees. Each group had four kids in it. Two boys and two girls, with one group left over that had three girls. I really couldn't believe it when he read my group. Norman Fishbein, Philip Leroy, Laura Danker and me! I glanced sideways at Janie. She rolled her eyes at me. I raised my eyebrow back at her.

Mr. Benedict asked us to rearrange our desks into our groups. I was going to have to talk to Laura Danker! There would be no way of getting out of it. I was also going to be spending a lot of time with Philip Leroy, which was pretty exciting to think about.

The first thing Philip did after we moved our desks together was to sing to me.

> "Happy Birthday to you,
> You live in a zoo,
> You look like a monkey,
> And you smell like one too!"

Then he pinched me on the arm—really hard! Enough to make tears come to my eyes. He said, "That's a pinch to grow an inch. And you know where you need that inch!"

I knew it was just a joke. I knew I shouldn't take it seriously. For one thing, I did not smell like a monkey. I was wearing deodorant! And for another thing, it was none of Philip Leroy's business whether or not I needed to grow an inch *anywhere!* As far as I was concerned, Nancy could have him. They deserved each other.

To make matters worse I had to sit facing Laura Danker. I hated her. I hated her for being so big and beautiful and having all the boys stare at her, including Mr. Benedict. Also, I hated her because she knew she was normal and I didn't know a thing about me! I hated Mr. Benedict too—for sticking me with Norman Fishbein. Norman was such a drip!

So all in all my birthday, which started out to be the most perfect day of my life, ended up being pretty rotten. I couldn't wait for spring vacation to come. The only good thing I had to look forward to was my trip to Florida. I was sick of school.

19

At home my mother said she'd never seen me in such a bad mood. The mood lasted the whole three weeks of that dumb committee project. To top off everything else our group voted three to one to report on Belgium. I wanted a more exciting country, like France or Spain. But I lost.

So I ate, breathed and slept Belgium for three weeks. Philip Leroy was a lousy worker. I found that out right away. All he did was fool around. During project time, while Laura, Norman and I were busy looking things up in reference books, Philip was busy drawing funny faces in his notebook. On two days he snuck comic books inside his notebook and read them instead. Norman Fishbein tried hard but he was so slow! And I couldn't stand the way he read with his lips moving. Laura was a good worker. But of course, I never told her that I thought so.

During the third week of Project Belgium Laura and I got permission to stay after school and work in the library. We needed more time with the encyclopedias. My mother was going to pick me up in front of school at four-thirty. Laura was going to walk from school to church because she had to go to Confession.

Now that really started me thinking. For one thing, I never knew she was Catholic. For another, I wondered what she said in Confession. I mean, did she talk about what she did with boys? And if she did, what did the priest say to her? Did she go to Confession every time she did something bad? Or did she save it all up and go once a month?

I was so busy thinking about Laura and the Confessional that I nearly forgot about Belgium. And probably I never would have said anything at all if it hadn't been for Laura. She picked on me first. So she was really to blame for the whole thing.

"You're copying that straight out of the *World Book* word for word," she whispered to me.

"So?"

"Well, you can't do that," she explained. "You're supposed to read it and then write about it in your own words. Mr. Benedict will *know* if you've copied."

Normally I don't copy word for word. I know the rules as well as Laura. But I was busy thinking about . other things and anyway, who did Laura think she was giving orders like that? Big shot!

So I said: "Oh, you think you're so great, don't you!"

And she said: "This has nothing to do with being great."

And I said: "I know all about you anyway!"

And she said: "What's *that* supposed to mean?"

And the librarian said: "Girls—let's be more quiet."

And then Laura went back to work. But I didn't.

"I heard all about you and Moose Freed," I whispered.

Laura put down her pencil and looked at me. "You heard *what* about me and Moose Freed?"

"Oh—about how you and Evan and Moose go behind the A&P," I said.

"What would I do *that* for?" Laura asked.

She was really thick! "I don't know what *you* do it for. But I know why *they* do it . . . they do it so they can *feel* you or something and *you* let them!"

She shut the encyclopedia hard and stood up. Her face was burning red and I saw a blue vein stick out in her neck. "You filthy liar! *You little pig!*" Nobody ever called me such names in my whole life.

Laura scooped up her books and her coat and ran out of the library. I grabbed my things and followed her.

I was really being awful. And I hadn't even planned it. I sounded like Nancy. That's when it hit me that for all I knew Nancy made up that story about Laura. Or maybe Moose and Evan made it up just to brag. Yes, I bet they did! Moose was a big liar too!

"Hey Laura! Wait up," I called.

She walked fast—probably because her legs were so long. I chased her. When I finally caught up to her I could hardly breathe. Laura kept walking and wouldn't look at me. I didn't blame her. I walked alongside her. I took four steps to every two of hers.

"Look," I told her. "I'm not saying it's wrong to do those things."

"I think it's disgusting that you all pick on me because I'm big!" Laura said, sniffling.

I wanted to tell her to blow her nose. "I didn't mean to insult you," I said. "You're the one who started it."

"Me? That's a good one! You think it's such a great game to make fun of me, don't you?"

"No," I said.

"Don't you think I know all about *you* and your friends? Do you think it's any fun to be the biggest kid in the class?"

"I don't know," I said. "I never thought about it."

"Well, try thinking about it. Think about how you'd feel if you had to wear a bra in fourth grade and how everybody laughed and how you always had to cross your arms in front of you. And about how the boys called you dirty names just because of how you looked."

I thought about it. "I'm sorry, Laura," I said.

"I'll bet!"

"I really am. If you want to know the truth . . . well, I wish I looked more like you than like me."

"I'd gladly trade places with you. Now, I'm going to Confession." She walked on mumbling something about how the wrong ones always confessed.

And I thought, maybe she's right. Maybe I was the one who should confess. I followed Laura to her church. It was only two blocks from school. I still had half an hour before my mother was due. I crossed the street and hid behind a bush watching Laura climb the steps and disappear into the church.

Then I crossed back to the other side of the street and ran up the brick steps. I held open the front door and looked inside. I didn't see Laura. I stepped into the church and tiptoed up the aisle.

It was so quiet. I wondered what would happen if I decided to scream; of course I knew I wouldn't, but I couldn't help wondering about how a scream would sound in there.

I was really hot in my heavy coat, but I didn't take it off. After a while I saw Laura come out of a door and I crouched down behind a row of seats so she wouldn't see me. She never even glanced my way. I thought it didn't take her very long to confess.

I felt weird. My legs were getting weak. As soon as Laura left the church I stood up. I meant to leave too. I had to meet my mother back at school. But instead of walking to the front of the church and outside, I headed the other way.

I stood in front of the door that Laura came from. What was inside? I opened it a little. There was nobody there. It looked like a wooden phone booth. I stepped in and closed the door behind me. I waited for something to happen. I didn't know what I was supposed to do, so I just sat there.

Finally I heard a voice. "Yes, my child."

At first I thought it was God. I really and truly

thought it was, and my heart started to pound like crazy and I was all sweaty inside my coat and sort of dizzy too. But then I realized it was only the priest in the booth next to mine. He couldn't see me and I couldn't see him but we could hear each other. Still, I didn't say anything.

"Yes, my child," he said again.

"I . . . I . . . uh . . . uh . . ." I began.

"Yes?" the priest asked me.

"I'm sorry," I whispered.

I flung open the door and ran down the aisle and out of the church. I made my way back to school, crying, feeling horribly sick and scared stiff I would throw up. Then I saw my mother waiting in the car and I got in the back and explained I was feeling terrible. I stretched out on the seat. My mother drove home and I didn't have to tell her any of the awful things I'd done because she thought I was sick for real.

Later that night she brought a bowl of soup to my room and she sat on the edge of my bed while I ate it. She said I must have had a virus or something and she was glad I was feeling better but I didn't have to go to school tomorrow if I didn't feel like it. Then she turned out the light and kissed me goodnight.

Are you there God? It's me, Margaret. I did an awful thing today. Just awful! I'm definitely the most horrible person who ever lived and I really don't deserve anything good to happen to me. I picked on Laura Danker. Just because I felt mean I took it all out on her. I really hurt Laura's feelings. Why did you let me do that? I've been looking for you God. I looked in temple. I looked in church. And today, I looked for you when I wanted to confess. But you weren't there. I didn't feel you at all. Not the way I do when I talk to you at night .Why God? Why do I only feel you when I'm alone?

20

A week before spring vacation the letter came. Only it wasn't from Grandma and it wasn't about my trip to Florida. It was from Mary and Paul Hutchins, my other grandparents. Now that was really strange because since they disowned my mother when she got married naturally they never wrote to her. My father, having no kind thoughts about them, really hit the roof.

"How did they get our address? Answer that one simple question please! Just how did they get our address?"

My mother practically whispered her answer. "I sent them a Christmas card. That's how."

My father hollered. "I can't believe you, Barbara! After fourteen years you sent *them* a Christmas card?"

"I was feeling sentimental. So I sent a card. I didn't write anything on it. Just our names."

My father shook the letter at my mother. "So now, after fourteen years—*fourteen years*, Barbara! Now they change their minds?"

"They want to see us. That's all."

"They want to see *you*, not me! They want to see Margaret! To make sure she doesn't have horns!"

"Herb! Stop it! You're being ridiculous——"

"*I'm being ridiculous!* That's funny, Barbara. That's very funny."

"You know what I think?" I asked them. "I think you're both being ridiculous!" I ran out of the kitchen and stormed up the stairs to my room. I slammed the door. I hated it when they had a fight in front of me. Why didn't they know how much I hated it! Didn't they know how awful they sounded? I could still hear them, shouting and carrying on. I put my hands over my ears while I crossed the room to my record player. Then I took one hand off one ear and turned on my Mice Men record as loud as it would go. There—that was much better.

A few minutes later my bedroom door opened. My father walked straight to my record player and snapped it off. My mother held the letter in her hand. Her eyes were red. I didn't say anything.

My father paced up and down. "Margaret," he finally said. "This concerns you. I think before we do or say anything else you ought to read the letter from your grandparents. Barbara . . ." He held out his hand.

My mother handed the letter to my father and he handed it to me. The handwriting was slanty and perfect, the way it is in third grade when you're learning script. I sat down on my bed.

Dear Barbara,
Your father and I have been thinking about

you a lot. We are growing old. I guess you find
that hard to believe, but we are. Suddenly, more
than anything else we want to see our only
daughter. We wonder if it is possible that we
made a mistake fourteen years ago. We have
discussed this situation with our minister and
dear friend, Reverend Baylor. You remember
him dear, don't you. My goodness, he christened
you when you were a tiny baby. He says it's
never too late to try again. So your father and I
are flying East for a week and hope that you will
let us visit you and get to know our granddaughter, Margaret Ann. Flight details are
enclosed.
Your mother,
Mary Hutchins

What a sickening letter! No wonder my father was
mad. It didn't even mention him.

I handed the letter back to my father, but I didn't
say anything because I didn't know what I was supposed to say.

"They're coming on April fifth," my father said.

"Oh, then I won't see them after all," I said,
brightening. "I leave for Florida on the fourth."

My mother looked at my father.

"Well," I said. "Isn't that right? I leave for Florida
on the fourth!"

They still didn't say anything and after a minute I

knew—I *knew* I wasn't going to Florida! And then I had plenty to say. Plenty!

"I don't want to see them," I shouted. "It isn't fair! I want to go to Florida and stay with Grandma. Daddy—*please!*"

"Don't look at me," my father said quietly. "It's not my fault. I didn't send them a Christmas card."

"Mom!" I cried. "You can't do this to me. You can't! It's not fair—it's not!" I hated my mother. I really did. She was so stupid. What did she have to go and send them a dumb old card for!

"Come on, Margaret. It's not the end of the world," my mother said, putting her arm around me. "You'll go to Florida another time."

I wriggled away from her as my father said, "Somebody better call Sylvia and tell her the change in plans."

"I'll put the call through and Margaret can tell her now," my mother said.

"Oh no!" I shouted. "*You* tell her. It's not my idea!"

"All right," my mother said quietly. "All right, I will."

I followed my parents into their bedroom. My mother picked up the phone and placed a person-to-person call to Grandma at her hotel. After a few minutes she said, "Hello, Sylvia . . . It's Barbara. . . . Nothing's wrong. . . . Everything's fine. . . . Yes, really. . . . Of course I'm sure. . . . It's just that Margaret won't be able to visit you after all. . . . Of course she's here . . . she's standing right next to me. . . . Yes, you can talk to her. . . ."

My mother held the phone out toward me. But I shook my head and refused to take it. So she covered the mouthpiece and whispered, "Grandma thinks you're sick. You've got to tell her you're all right."

I took the phone. "Grandma," I said, "it's Margaret."

I heard Grandma catch her breath.

"Nothing's wrong, Grandma. . . . No, I'm not sick. . . . Nobody's sick. . . . Of course I'm sure. . . . But I do want to come, Grandma. I just can't." I felt the tears in my eyes. My throat hurt when I swallowed. My mother motioned for me to tell Grandma the rest of the story. "I can't come to Florida because we're having company that week." Now my voice sounded very high and squeaky.

Grandma asked me, what company?

"My other grandparents," I said. "You know, Mom's mother and father. . . . Nobody invited them exactly . . . but Mom sent them a Christmas card with our new address and now we got a letter saying they're coming and they want to see me. . . . Well, I know you want to see me too. And I want to see you but Mom won't let me. . . ."

Then I started to cry for real and my mother took the phone.

"We're all sorry, Sylvia. It's just one of those things. Margaret understands. I hope you do too. Thank you, Sylvia. I knew you would. . . . Yes, Herb's fine. I'll put him on. Just a minute." I ran upstairs while my father said, "Hello, mother."

Are you there God? It's me, Margaret. I'm so miserable! Everything is wrong. Absolutely everything! I guess this is my punishment for being a horrible person. I guess you think it's only fair for me to suffer after what I did to Laura. Isn't that right God? But I've always tried to do what you wanted. Really, I have. Please don't let them come God. Make something happen so I can go to Florida anyway. Please . . .

21

That week my mother went crazy cleaning the house, while I waited for something to happen. I thought it would be a telegram saying they weren't able to come after all. I was sure God only wanted to punish me for a little while. Not for the whole spring vacation.

"Cheer up, Margaret," my mother said over dinner. "Things are never as bad as they seem."

"How can you be glad they're coming?" I asked. "After all those stories you've told me about them—how?"

"I want to show them how well I've managed for fourteen years without their help. And I want them to see my wonderful family."

My father said, "You can't expect Margaret to be overjoyed when her plans have been changed at the last minute."

"Look, Herb," my mother said. "I haven't forgiven my parents. You know that. I never will. But they're coming. I can't say no. Try to understand . . . both of you . . . please."

My mother hadn't ever asked me to do that before. Usually it was me asking her to try to understand.

My father kissed her on the cheek as she cleared away the dishes. He promised to make the best of it. I promised too. My mother kissed us both and said she had the best family in the world.

On April fifth my mother and I drove to Newark Airport to meet them. My father didn't come. He thought it would be better if he stayed at home and greeted them there.

All the way to the airport my mother briefed me. "Margaret, I'm not trying to make excuses for my mother and father. But I want you to know that your grandparents have their beliefs too. And fourteen years ago . . . well . . . they did what they thought was right. Even though we know it was cruel. Their beliefs were that important to them. Am I making any sense to you?"

"Some," I said.

When they announced the arrival of flight #894 from Toledo I followed my mother to the gate. I knew it was them right away. I knew it by the way they walked down the airplane stairs, clutching each other. And when they got closer I knew it by my grandmother's shoes—black with laces and fat heels—old lady shoes. My grandfather had white hair around the edges and none on top. He was shorter and fatter than my grandmother.

They looked around a bit before my mother called out, "Here we are—over here."

They walked toward us, growing more excited as they recognized my mother. She gave each of them a short hug. I just stood there feeling dumb until my grandmother said, "And this must be Margaret Ann." When she said it I noticed the cross around her neck. It was the biggest one I ever saw. And it sparkled!

I didn't want them to touch me. And maybe they could tell, because when my grandmother bent over, as if to kiss me, I stiffened. I didn't mean to. It just happened.

I think my mother knew how I felt because she told them we'd better see about the luggage.

When we got home my father met us at our front door and carried in their suitcases. They had two of them. Both brown and both new.

"Hello, Herb," my grandmother said.

"Hello, Mrs. Hutchins," my father answered.

I thought how funny it was for my father to call her "Mrs."

My grandfather shook hands with my father. "You're looking well, Herb," he said.

My father pressed his lips together but finally managed to say, "Thank you."

I thought, this is harder on my father than it is on me!

My mother and I showed my grandparents to their

room. Then my mother went down to see about dinner. I said, "If there's anything you need, just ask me."

"Thank you, Margaret Ann," my grandmother said. She had a funny way of scrunching up her mouth.

"You don't have to call me Margaret Ann," I said. "Nobody does. Just Margaret is fine."

My mother really made a fancy dinner. The kind she has when she's entertaining friends and I'm sent to bed early. We had flowers on the table and a hired lady to wash the dishes.

My mother changed into a new dress and her hair looked nice too. She didn't look like her parents at all. My grandmother changed her dress too, but she still had the cross around her neck.

At dinner we all tried hard to have a conversation. My mother and my grandmother talked about old friends from Ohio and who was doing what these days. My grandfather said mostly, "Please pass the butter . . . please pass the salt."

Naturally I used my best possible manners. In the middle of the roast beef course my grandfather knocked over his water glass and my grandmother gave him a sharp look, but my mother said water couldn't possible hurt anything. The lady from the kitchen wiped it up.

During dessert my mother explained to my grandparents that she had just ordered all new living room furniture and she was sorry they wouldn't be able to see it. I knew she hadn't ordered anything yet, but I didn't tell.

After dinner we sat around in the den and my grandfather asked my father such questions as:

GRANDFATHER: "Are you still in the insurance business?"

FATHER: "Yes."

GRANDFATHER: "Do you invest in the stock market?"

FATHER: "Occasionally."

GRANDFATHER: "This is a pretty nice house."

FATHER: "Thank you. We think so too."

While my grandmother talked to my mother about:

GRANDMOTHER: "We were in California over Thanksgiving."

MOTHER: "Oh?"

GRANDMOTHER: "Yes, your brother has a wonderful wife."

MOTHER: "I'm glad."

GRANDMOTHER: "If only they were blessed with a child. You know, they're thinking of adopting."

MOTHER: "I hope they do. Everyone should have a child to love."

GRANDMOTHER: "Yes, I know. . . . I've always wanted dozens of grandchildren, but Margaret's all I've got."

Then my mother excused herself to pay the lady in the kitchen, who signaled that her taxi was waiting out front. So my grandmother turned to me.

"Do you like school?" she asked.

"Most of the time," I said.

"Do you get good marks?"

"Pretty good," I said.

"How do you do in Sunday school?"

My mother came back into the den then and sat down next to me.

"I don't go to Sunday school," I said.

"You don't?"

"No."

"Father . . . (That's what Grandmother called Grandfather. He called her "Mother.")

"What is it, Mother?" Grandfather said.

"Margaret doesn't go to Sunday school." Grandmother shook her head and played with her cross.

"Look," my mother said, trying a smile. "You know we don't practice any religion."

Here it comes, I thought. I wanted to leave the room then but I felt like I was glued to my seat.

"We hoped by now you'd changed your minds about religion," Grandfather said.

"Especially for Margaret's sake," Grandmother added. "A person's got to have religion."

"Let's not get into a philosophical discussion," my father said, annoyed. He sent my mother a warning look across the room.

Grandfather laughed. "I'm not being a philosopher, Herb."

"Look," my mother explained, "we're letting Margaret choose her own religion when she's grown."

"If she wants to!" my father said, defiantly.

"Nonsense!" Grandmother said. "A person doesn't choose religion."

"A person's born to it!" Grandfather boomed.

Grandmother smiled at last and gave a small laugh. "So Margaret is Christian!" she announced, like we all should have known.

"Please . . ." my mother said. "Margaret could just as easily be Jewish. Don't you see—if you keep this up you're going to spoil everything."

"I don't mean to upset you, dear," Grandmother told my mother. "But a child is always the religion of the mother. And you, Barbara, were born Christian. You were baptized. It's that simple."

"Margaret is nothing!" my father stormed. "And I'll thank you for ending this discussion right now."

I didn't want to listen anymore. How could they talk that way in front of me! Didn't they know I was a real person—with feelings of my own!

"Margaret," Grandmother said, touching my sleeve. "It's not too late for you, dear. You're still God's child. Maybe while I'm visiting I could take you to church and talk to the minister. He might be able to straighten things out."

"Stop it!" I hollered, jumping up. "All of you! Just stop it! I can't stand another minute of listening to you. Who needs religion? Who! Not me . . . I don't need it. I don't even need God!" I ran out of the den and up to my room.

I heard my mother say, "Why did you have to start? Now you've ruined everything!"

I was never going to talk to God again. What did he want from me anyway? I was through with him and his religions! And I was never going to set foot in the Y or the Jewish Community Center—*never.*

22

The next morning I stayed in my room. I wouldn't even go down for breakfast. I caught myself starting to say, *Are you there God*, but then I remembered that I wasn't talking to him anymore. I wondered if he would strike me down. Well, if he wanted to, that was his business!

By afternoon I couldn't stand being in the house, so I asked my mother to drive me downtown to meet Janie for a movie. My mother agreed that I needed to get away for a few hours. Janie and I met at the drugstore on the corner, across the street from the movie theater. We were twenty minutes early so we went into the drugstore to look around. Mostly we liked to inspect the sanitary napkin display.

After a few minutes of looking, I whispered to Janie, "Let's buy a box." It was something I'd thought about for a while, but wasn't ever brave enough to do. Today I was feeling brave. I thought, so what if God's mad at me. Who cares? I even tested him by crossing the street in the middle *and* against the light. Nothing happened.

"Buy it for what?" Janie asked.

"Just in case," I told her.

"You mean to keep at home?"

"Sure. Why not?"

"I don't know. My mother might not like it," Janie said.

"So don't tell her."

"But what if she sees it?"

"It'll be in a bag. You can say it's school supplies," I said. "Do you have enough money?"

"Yes."

"Okay. Now, what kind should we buy?" I asked.

"How about *Teenage Softies*?" Janie said. "That's the kind Gretchen uses."

"Okay." I took a box of *Teenage Softies* off the shelf. "Well, go ahead," I said to Janie. "Take yours."

"Okay, okay." Janie took a box too.

"We need a belt to go with it," I said, getting braver by the minute.

"You're right. Which kind?" Janie asked.

"I like that one. It's pink," I told her, pointing to a small box with a pretty girl's picture on it.

"Okay, I'll take that one too," Janie said, reaching.

We walked to the check-out counter with our stuff and walked away just as fast when we saw that there was a boy behind the cash register.

"I can't go through with it," Janie whispered. She put her boxes back on the shelf. "I'm scared."

"Don't be a dope. What's to be . . ." I was interrupted by a saleslady in a blue doctor's coat.

"Can I help you, girls?" she asked.

Janie shook her head but I said, "We'd like these please." I took Janie's boxes back off the shelf and showed the saleslady what we'd selected.

"Fine, girls. Take them up to the cash register and Max will wrap them for you."

Janie didn't move. She looked like she was cemented to the floor. She had this dumb expression on her face —between crying and smiling. So I grabbed her boxes and headed for Max and the cash register. I plopped everything down in front of him and just stood there not looking at his face and not saying anything either. He added it all up and I motioned to Janie to give me her money. Then I said, "Two bags, please." Max took my money, gave me some change, which I didn't bother to count, and presented me with two brown bags. That was all there was to it! You'd think he sold that kind of stuff every day of the week.

When I got home from the movies my mother asked, "What's that package?"

I said, "School supplies."

I went to my room with my purchases. I sat down on my bed staring at the box of *Teenage Softies*. I hoped God was watching. Let him see I could get along fine without him! I opened the box and took out one pad. I held it for a long time.

Then I took the pink belt out of its box and held that too. Finally I got up and went to my closet. It was dark in there. Especially with the door closed. I wished I had a huge walk-in closet with a light and a lock. But I managed anyway. I got the pink belt around me and attached the pad to it. I wanted to find out how it would feel. Now I knew. I liked it. I thought about sleeping in my belt and pad that night, but decided against it. If there was a fire my secret might be discovered. So I took off the belt and pad, put them back in their boxes and hid them in my bottom desk drawer. My mother never checks there because the mess makes her positively sick!

The next morning my grandparents announced they were moving on to New York.

"You told me a week!" my mother said. "You said you were coming for a week!"

"We did say that," my grandfather told her. "But we've decided to spend the rest of the week in New York, at a hotel."

"I see," my mother said.

My father hid behind his newspaper but I saw the big smile. All I could think of was that they ruined my trip to Florida and now they weren't even staying. It wasn't fair! It was really a cheat!

When my mother got back from driving them to the bus my father said, "How much do you want to bet it was a trip to New York all the time. They just stopped in to see you because it was convenient."

"I don't believe that!" my mother said.

"Well, I believe it," my father said.

"They ruined my vacation," I said.

Nobody answered me.

23

That night the doorbell rang at eight. We were in the den. I said I'd see who was there. I opened the front door.

"Grandma!" I screamed. I threw my arms around her. "What are you doing home?"

"If Mohammed doesn't come to the mountain—the mountain comes to Mohammed."

I laughed, knowing that I was Mohammed and that Grandma was the mountain. There was a man standing next to Grandma. Grandma turned to him. "Morris," she said. "This is my Margaret."

Then Grandma closed the front door and told me, "Margaret darling, this is Mr. Morris Binamin."

"Rhymes with cinnamon," he said to me.

I smiled.

Grandma looked marvelous—very tan and pale blonde. Mr. Binamin had a lot of silver hair, a moustache to match, and black-rimmed eyeglasses. He was tan too. He held Grandma's arm.

"Where are they?" Grandma asked.

"Mom and Dad are in the den," I said.

"With your other grandparents?"

"No . . . they're gone."

"Gone!" Grandma cried. "But I thought they were staying all week."

"We thought so too," I said.

"But Morris and I came especially to see them."

"You did!" I said. "How come?"

Grandma and Mr. Binamin gave each other a secret look. "Well . . . we thought you might need our support."

"Oh Grandma! I can manage just fine by myself."

"I know you can. You're my Margaret, aren't you? Tell me—did they try anything?"

"Like what?" I asked.

"You know," Grandma said. "Church business."

"Well . . . kind of," I admitted.

"I knew it!" Grandma cried. "Didn't I tell you?" she asked Mr. Binamin.

Mr. Binamin shook his head. "You had them pegged right all the time, Sylvia," he said.

"Just remember, Margaret . . . no matter what they said . . . you're a Jewish girl."

"No I'm not!" I argued. "I'm nothing, and you know it! I don't even believe in God!"

"Margaret!" Grandma said, "Don't ever talk like that about God."

"Why not?" I asked. "It's true!" I wanted to ask God did he hear that! But I wasn't speaking to him and I guess he knew it!

By that time my mother and father were in the living room and Grandma was making the introductions.

My parents gave Mr. Binamin the once-over and he was pretty busy sizing them up too.

Then my mother made coffee and served warm Danish. She offered me some milk and ginger snaps but I wasn't hungry. I wanted to get out of there so I yawned very loud without covering my mouth.

"Margaret dear, if you're so tired, why don't you go up to bed," Grandma said.

"I think I will. Goodnight, everybody."

Sometimes Grandma is almost as bad as everybody else. As long as she loves me and I love her, what difference does religion make?

24

Mr. Benedict announced that our individual reports on our year-long project would be due next Friday. They wouldn't be graded so we were to be completely honest and not worry about pleasing him. He hoped we had each learned something of value. On Thursday night I wrote a letter.

May 25

Dear Mr. Benedict,
I have conducted a year-long experiment in
religion. I have not come to any conclusions
about what religion I want to be when
I grow up—if I want to be any special
religion at all.
I have read three books on this subject.
They are: *Modern Judaism, A History of
Christianity,* and *Catholicism—Past and Present.*
I went to church services at the First
Presbyterian Church of Farbrook. I went to
the United Methodist Church of Farbrook on
Christmas Eve. I attended Temple Israel of
New York City on Rosh Hashanah, which is a
Jewish holiday. I went to Confession at

Saint Bartholomew Church, but I had to leave
the Confessional because I didn't know what
to say. I have not tried being a Buddhist or
a Moslem because I don't know any people of
these religions.
I have not really enjoyed my religious experiments
very much and I don't think I'll make up my mind
one way or the other for a long time. I don't
think a person can decide to be a certain religion
just like that. It's like having to choose your
own name. You think about it a long time and
then you keep changing your mind.
If I should ever have children I will tell
them what religion they are so they can start
learning about it at an early age. Twelve is very
late to learn.
Sincerely,
Margaret Ann Simon

On Friday everybody handed in a thick booklet with
a decorated cover. All I had was the letter. I couldn't
put that in with the pile of booklets. I was too embarrassed. It looked like I hadn't done any work at all.

When the bell rang I sat at my desk while everyone
else filed out of the room.

When Mr. Benedict looked up he said, "Yes, Margaret?"

I walked to his desk with my letter.

"I didn't hand in a booklet," I said.

"Oh?"

"I, uh . . . I wrote you a letter instead." I handed it to him, then stood there while he read it.

"I really tried, Mr. Benedict. I'm—I'm sorry. I wanted to do better." I knew I was going to cry. I couldn't say anything else. So I ran out of the classroom.

I got to the Girls' Room before the tears came. I could still hear Mr. Benedict calling, "Margaret— Margaret—" I didn't pay any attention. I splashed cold water on my face. Then I walked home slowly by myself.

What was wrong with me anyway? When I was eleven I hardly ever cried. Now anything and everything could start me bawling. I wanted to talk it over with God. But I wasn't about to let him know that, even though I missed him.

25

On June seventeenth the PTA gave us a farewell party in the gym and none of the sixth-grade girls wore socks. I wore my first pair of sheer stockings and got my first run in them one hour later. All I could think of was I'd be in seventh grade in September and I was growing up. My mind knew it—even if my body didn't.

The party in the gym was a lot like the Thanksgiving square dance. Mrs. Wheeler and Mrs. Fishbein were chaperones but this time they were dressed in regular clothes.

Our class presented Mr. Benedict with a pair of silver cufflinks that Gretchen's mother had gotten wholesale. He seemed very pleased, because he cleared his throat a lot and sounded like he didn't know what to say except thank you—and that although we hadn't started out to be the greatest sixth grade in the world, we'd come a long way. And thanks to us, next year, he'd be an experienced teacher—*very experienced!* Then we all laughed and some of the girls cried but I didn't.

Nancy, Gretchen, Janie and I had lunch downtown by ourselves and talked about how it would feel to go to Junior High. Janie was afraid she wouldn't be able to find her way around and she'd get lost. Gretchen said probably the teachers would all be mean and Nancy said suppose we weren't in any classes together and then we all went home and cried.

Later that day my mother started packing my camp trunk. I watched her put the stacks of shorts and polos into it. Then I heard the lawn mower. Moose was back. First I got excited about seeing him and then I got mad, thinking about Laura and those stories he helped spread around.

I ran downstairs and outside and yelled, "Hey Moose!" He didn't hear me because the mower made too much noise. So I ran over to where he was cutting and I stood right in his way so he'd have to notice me and I shouted again. "Hey Moose!"

He shut off the mower. "You're in my way," he said.

"I want to tell you something," I said.

"Go ahead."

I put my hands on my hips. "You know what Moose! You're a liar! I don't believe you ever took Laura Danker behind the A&P."

"Who said I did?"

"What do you mean who said it!"

"Well, who?"

"Nancy told me that Evan told her that you and Evan——" I stopped. I sounded like an idiot.

Moose shook his head at me. "You always believe everything you hear about other people?" he asked.

I didn't know what to say.

Moose kept talking. "Well, next time, don't believe it unless you see it! Now if you'll move out of my way, I've got things to do!"

I didn't move. "You know what Moose?" I asked.

"What now?"

"I'm sorry I thought you were a liar."

"You know what Margaret?" Moose asked me.

"No, what?"

"You're still in my way!"

I jumped away and Moose turned the mower on again. I heard him singing his favorite song—about the Erie Canal.

I went back into the house. I had to go to the bathroom. I was thinking about Moose and about how I liked to stand close to him. I was thinking that I was glad he wasn't a liar and I was happy that he cut our grass. Then I looked down at my underpants and I couldn't believe it. There was blood on them. Not a lot—but enough. I really hollered, "*Mom—hey Mom—come quick!*"

When my mother got to the bathroom she said, "What is it? What's the matter?"

"I got it," I told her.

"Got what?"

I started to laugh and cry at the same time. "My period. I've got my period!" My nose started running and I reached for a tissue.

"Are you sure, Margaret?" my mother asked.

"Look—look at this," I said, showing her my underpants.

"My God! You've really got it. My little girl!" Then her eyes filled up and she started sniffling too. "Wait a minute—I've got the equipment in the other room. I was going to put it in your camp trunk, just in case."

"You were?"

"Yes. Just in case." She left the bathroom.

When she came back I asked her, "Is it that Private Lady stuff?"

"No, I got you *Teenage Softies*."

"Good," I said.

"Now look, Margaret—here's how you do it. The belt goes around your waist and the pad——"

"Mom," I said. "I've been practicing in my room for two months!"

Then my mother and I laughed together and she said, "In that case, I guess I'll wait in the other room."

I locked the bathroom door and attached a *Teenage Softie* to the little hooks on my pink belt. Then I got dressed and looked at myself in the mirror. Would anyone know my secret? Would it show? Would Moose, for instance, know if I went back outside to talk to him? Would my father know it right away when he came home for dinner? I had to call Nancy and Gretchen and Janie right away. Poor Janie! She'd be the last of the PTS's to get it. And I'd been so sure it would be me! How about that! Now I am growing for sure. Now I am almost a woman!

Are you still there God? It's me, Margaret. I know you're there God. I know you wouldn't have missed this for anything! Thank you God. Thanks an awful lot. . . .